THE
TIME
LABORATORY

The
Time
Laboratory

A maverick machine reaches into the past...

R.V.W. Jackson

This edition ISBN 9798615155536.

This is a work of fiction. Although military, business and academic positions and titles exist, as well as those of government officials and the United Nations, the characters occupying these and other positions in this book are purely in the author's imagination and any resemblance to actual persons is entirely coincidental. Likewise, the descriptions and happenings associated with institutes and other organisations including those with similar names are purely imaginary.

*****

Also available as an Amazon Kindle Edition.

Other books by the same author:
ALGERNON: Radio Ham Extraordinary (May 2017).
THE OBSERVERS: A Collection of Short Stories (March 2017).

Dedication

To Ann, Andy and Rebecca, Mark and Margaret, Pete and Lizzie.

Contents

Acknowledgements

A very big thank you to my wife Elizabeth Ann for her patience and to son Andy who provided help with the cover design; also to son Pete and his wife Lizzie for their valuable comments.

AUTHOR'S NOTE:

As a 'retired' computer scientist, I recall being fascinated by the area of dynamic re-programming, in which the computer is programmed to 'decide' the next step by re-writing its software.

In 2085 two major problems face humankind. Firstly, as we lurch (some might say sleepwalk) into the future, we're ever more reliant on computer systems. Why should this not be an entirely good thing?

Because, secondly, computer systems have taken a leap forward. Dare we trust our reliance on them during their stages of *self-evolution*? Not to mention any possibility of machine consciousness.

Rory MacIntyre is about to find out...

RVWJ (November 2020)

x

"The appearances of things are deceptive..."
Seneca.

1 The Mission

Chadwick Building, University of Liverpool campus, Tuesday 5 June 2085.

Rory MacIntyre felt cautiously optimistic. After three years of hard graft, the results were in. The External Examiner had approved his PhD thesis. Yes, a few minor corrections were needed, but Rory allowed himself a spring in his step as he continued across the campus towards the refurbished Chadwick Building.

He pressed the lift button.

'The lift is out of order,' a robotic voice intoned.

Unusual, he thought. Tall and athletic, Rory climbed with ease the five flights of stairs to the top corridor.

On the wall opposite the stairwell, the familiar brightly coloured poster screen bore the slogan "The TIME is RIPE". The digital screen's continually scrolling images and text extolled RIPE's virtues and achievements. A casual observer couldn't fail to be impressed by the organisation's triumph of interdisciplinary effort between the Department of Physics and the School of Historical Sciences. Next to the poster an office door with a retro-style polished brass plate announced: 'Research Into Past Events (RIPE). Professor B.W.Litchfield.'

The door slightly ajar, Rory knocked and entered the anteroom office occupied by the Professor's personal assistant.

'Hello,' Rory said. 'Where's the boss today?' He looked around. Nobody else about! He kissed her on the cheek.

'Hey!' she protested jokingly. 'You won't be able to do that this afternoon, when our replacement digicams are installed!'

'I know! There's another reason I'm here - to check they haven't replaced you with a robot...' He kissed her other cheek.

'Get off!' she said playfully. 'Bryant is still over at the squash court. You can't expect him to be on demand for a mere PhD student.'

'Postdoctoral, if you don't mind!'

'Oh yes!' she stood up and returned a kiss on his right cheek, stroking the left one with her hand. 'Now that your three years of slave labour are finished, we can see a little more of each other, perhaps?' She embraced him more fully. That is, until they heard sounds of conversation from the stairwell outside. She glanced at the digital readout on her thumbnail. 'It's nearly lunchtime, Rory. So why don't we meet up in the usual place? Say, ten minutes from now. Meanwhile I'll book you an appointment and you can have Prof all to yourself, for half an hour at two thirty. How's that?'

'Thanks, Ros. See you over there. Byeee!' He blew her a departing kiss and made for the research staff common room at at the far end of the corridor. When he arrived he saw just two occupants, in deep conversation. Rory activated a TV wall panel via his wi-fi implant for the latest EBC newscast. As usual, things were depressing at home and abroad and getting worse. A headline screamed, 'Nuclear threat averted!' Other bulletins included: 'Invasion of Antarctica – news blackout upheld!' and 'British Isles crime figures soar!' All accompanied by the turgid throb of monotonous drumbeats.

'Anyone interested?' he called to the two colleagues in the room.

'You're joking!' said one.

'No thanks,' said the other.

With a one second blink of his left eye Rory extinguished the TV and walked back past the Department office, its door now closed. He continued down the stairs and across the campus to the college bar and found Rosalind at a window table. He waved and went to fetch the usual drinks and some sandwiches from the dispenser.

'Hi! Looks good, Rory,' she said.

'It seems prawns are the big deal today, Ros.'

'Yep, thanks. I'll trust your belief in their use-by date. What did you want to see our esteemed Prof about?'

'To make sure he's happy with my PhD thesis corrections – only a couple of minor adjustments.'

'So it's essentially in the bag, then? Well done! What happens now, Rory?'

'I also want Litchfield to hear my idea for a postdoctoral project.'

'More research?'

'Nothing's official yet, Ros. But it should be OK. Listen, it could mean my being tied up for about six months.'

'How tied up? You mean we can't see each other?'

'Afraid not, it would be… kind of, abroad.'

'Lucky you! Where?'

He paused... 'May not be allowed to say,' he continued, between mouthfuls of his sandwich, 'but I may be able to text you. Problem is you couldn't text me – not directly.'

Silence.

'What's wrong, Ros?' Rory asked.

'What's wrong?' Her voice rose and she gripped her plastic knife almost menacingly. 'Rory! You were all over me in the office, but your attention's really on tinkering about in labs and more late nights!'

'Well, it'll soon pass. Then we can…'

Ros got up from her seat, sending it crashing backwards onto the tiled floor. 'It never stops, does it?' she shouted, 'I've had enough of your absences! In fact, I've had enough altogether - this time I'm finishing with you for good!' She strode off, nearly colliding with someone entering via the automatic door.

Rory shrugged resignedly at the stares - and a few smiles - from onlookers. When the surrounding babble of conversation resumed he leaned forward and contemplated the remaining untouched sandwich on her plate. He wrapped it in a napkin. If he gave it to her she'd probably throw it at him. So he devoured it and drained his glass. Outside, in a secluded area, Rory faced the wall of the building and beat it repetitively with both fists. Sometime later, he returned to his bed-sit. Over a cup of black coffee, he began sketching his new research proposal

An hour passed. Time to see Prof. Just as Rory put on his jacket, his mobile phone sprang to life. Ros! Rory's heart bounded.

'Ros? Hi, you OK?'

'No I'm not. This is just to say Professor Litchfield is unavailable today. You're rebooked for 3:00pm on Friday. Bye,' she snapped.

'Ros?'

Click.

Rory shook his head, poured another coffee and resumed editing his work.

Next morning.

Above the flat roof of the offices and laboratories of RIPE, two figures with jet packs had alighted on a maintenance trolley situated on the shadow side of an adjoining tower block.

Preferring silence, they dumped their jet packs and abseiled the rest of the way downwards. After landing on RIPE, they checked their abseil gear and stowed it a few yards from a skylight. One of them brandished electronic listening equipment before they each deftly lowered themselves through the skylight into the building.

'The door's the one to the right of the ad-screen. OK?'

'Check! I see it, Max.'

His colleague produced a small map and whispered: 'The cameras are here… and here.'

'No problem. The ones in this corridor and inside his office aren't operational until tomorrow. Kev's seen to that. And we've forty five minutes before the engineers arrive to repair the lift.'

'You're sure about that?'

'Of course I am! And if all is well we should be out of here in ten minutes.'

'Keep your voice down! And straighten your damn tie, Brad. We've to look the part.'

'Yeah, yeah, OK!' Brad hissed. 'The sniffer says we're all clear.'

They paused at the TV lounge and went inside.

'Where's your phone?' Brad asked.

'Here.' Max checked the time and made a call. A distant telephone rang. It stopped; his mobile responded: 'Professor Litchfield's office…?'

'Hello,' Max said, 'Dr. Graham here, visiting from Glasgow University. I have a folder for Professor Litchfield. It's rather urgent but I have to rush out to catch a flight, so could you be so kind as to collect it for him right away? I'm on the ground floor and I'd like to give it to you personally outside room A12. Sorry about this. Will that be all right?'

'Certainly. I'll see you in a moment, Dr. Graham,' Ros replied.

'You're very kind. Thank you. See you soon, then.'

Brad pressed his ear to the door panel. A remote office door opened and closed.

'Good!' Said Brad. 'Wait, wait, until she gets to the stairs... Now!' He quietly opened the lounge door and stepped outside. The two men calmly walked towards the RIPE office and Max tried the handle. It opened. To one side of Ros's desk he saw Professor Litchfield's inner door ajar. Max knocked.

'Yes? Is that you, Ros?' came a voice from the inner room.

The intruders froze momentarily. Brad broke the silence. 'Er, no. We're from Loughborough University looking for Professor Nandi; we have one of your university maps here. Sorry to interrupt. Could you help us, please?'

'Yes, do come in. Her office is over there, in the History building. You can see it from here, actually.'

Max adjusted his disguise, followed Brad into the inner office and closed the door.

Later, inside the office:

'You'll find Professor Litchfield in his chair. We made him as comfortable as we could,' Ros said.

'That'll be fine. Please leave him to us,' the leading paramedic said.

Within minutes the paramedics and their robotic assistants had Bryant Litchfield, with neck brace, on a stretcher. They took him away via the now working lift. Upwards, to a waiting air-ambulance.

*****

Two days later:

'Professor!' Ros looked in amazement as Bryant Litchfield stood before her, albeit with neck collar and bandaged head.

'Yes indeed. The neck examination went OK. The other's just a scalp wound that the university's health centre can dress every so often. So I'll be wearing this hotel chef's outfit for a while.' He tapped his head bandage cautiously. 'Today I'll be taking another look at Rory's thesis and I'd like to see him this afternoon, say 3:00pm. I think it's already booked. If not then see if you can make it so.'

'It'll be free, Professor. Don't you remember? All your appointments have been cancelled until you say otherwise.'

'Very good. Rory's first bat then.'

At 2:55pm, Rory stood before Ros. She looked up at him as if a fly was about to descend on her favourite meal.

'Oh, it's you,' she said.

'Reporting for duty, ma'am.' Rory saluted, his attempt at humour unappreciated. 'C'mon Ros, don't be so frowzy!' His bantering smile had the opposite effect:

'Listen, Rory! If it wasn't for your appointment with Prof, I'd have you turfed out of here for harassment.'

'Oh dear, d'you think those sandwiches we had were OK?'

'You should know. I heard that you ate mine. Did you?'

'Spies everywhere, eh? Ian Fleming would have drawn inspiration from a network like yours.'

'Ian who?'

'Never mind.' Rory listened at the doorway and glanced at the wall clock. 'I think Prof's here.'

'Thank goodness for that,' said Ros.

'Well, hello there, Doctor MacIntyre!' Professor Bryant Litchfield's greeting boomed from the corridor. Then he entered, still in his overcoat, with his head bandage slightly askew.

Rory shook the outstretched hand. 'Thank you, Prof. How are you feeling?'

'Oh, fine thanks. Let's go in here, shall we?' He motioned Rory into his inner sanctum.

'Be seeing you!' Rory whispered to Ros in passing.

'You won't.' she whispered. And louder: 'But congratulations, anyway.'

She offered him a half-hearted smile and continued with her work. She's playing to the gallery, perhaps? Rory balked at his own cynicism, then bowed to her as he followed Litchfield.

'Thank you, Ros,' Rory said, closing the door behind him.

'What is it between you two?' asked Litchfield, one eyebrow raised, as he settled behind his desk.

'Nothing really, we're just... good friends, occasionally.'

'Hmm, yes. Things like that are notoriously difficult to quantify, aren't they? Let me get you a port, sherry or something! How about Drambuie? Ever tried it?'

Rory laughed. 'In my country we try it most of the time. Many thanks!'

'Might have known I was speaking to an expert.' Litchfield got up stiffly, went to a drinks cabinet, poured, and they raised their glasses.

'To research! Back at Oxford, you know, they had this thing about port and walnuts.'

'Well, there's your chance to impress,' said Rory. 'Why not invite your Oxford friends here and fire them up on walnuts with Drambuie, or a single malt whisky?'

'Well, yes. You're clearly a master of invention. But then they'd probably disown me.' Bryant sat down and gestured Rory to do the same. 'Anyway, I'm impressed by your thesis, Rory.

I'd like to file it on my backup archive, but forgetful as ever, I'll have to look up the password. You see that cupboard up there with the glass doors? Could you please fetch down my green notebook… that one, top shelf, near the left end?'

Rory passed him the book.

'Thanks, Rory. Now let's see… hmm! That's odd. Very odd.'

'A problem, Bryant?'

'There most certainly is, old chap. Several pages torn out! Those raiders pinched my other coat, but fortunately there were no valuables in it. And they took nothing else… except perhaps these very pages. Yes, that's it, Rory. The blighters were after my computer passwords!'

'Then why were they so vicious? They could have just tied you up and blindfolded you,' Rory said.

'Because Rory, believe me, they're very unpleasant people who are obviously used to violence. However, enough about them! You'll gather I was well satisfied with your thesis corrections. Ah, you had another question?'

'I'm working on a draft proposal for some postdoctoral research, but I want to make sure it's of interest to you.'

'Very glad to hear of it, Rory. What's the thrust of the work?'

'Well, we know the state the world's in! Utter chaos. I'd like to explore ways of improving things by using virtual reality to model critical points to see where we went wrong.'

'Presumably you mean Neo-Hyper Reality?' The Professor scratched his chin. 'Hmm… a worthy application area but not very original, Rory. You're familiar with the literature, I trust? Lots of people have tried doing just that as far back as the 2030s. Little success so far, I'm afraid. In fact, I'm beginning to think that line of enquiry is rather fanciful and if persisted in could even give RIPE a dubious name.'

'Do you think I could narrow my choice of scenarios down? Make it more specific. Perhaps by creating a particular kind of disturbance?'

'Aha! That might be in character, I suppose!' Litchfield said with a broad smile. 'Sorry, old man. A bit cheeky of me, but you did let yourself in for it. Go on…'

'Like a meteor strike. Everyone would have to pull together to save the planet. That might throw up some useful strategies that could be adapted for our present predicament.'

'Could be an interesting approach. A version of the disaster movie, eh? Like the work of Al Haroun and Baines, 2064.

Then there's the more recent reference along similar lines – Wang and Li, 2073. You've studied those? I have them on file if you need them. You're getting warmer, but I suggest you think again. Take your time and give me a call when you feel you're ready. '

'OK, Prof. I'll get back to you,' Rory said, getting up to leave. 'And thanks for the discussion.'

A few days later, on a jogging run, Rory pulled out his mobile and rang Litchfield.

'Professor? I think I've got something for you. Can we talk?'

*****

Monday 18 June, 2085. 1:15pm. Staff restaurant.
Rory entered the university's Crown Restaurant. Very nice, he thought, scanning the menu.

'Hello Rory!' Professor Litchfield joined him for the pre-arranged lunch. When it arrived, his Professor continued: 'What did you come up with for your postdoctoral programme?'

'This may sound a bit controversial. Please be frank with me. You know I'm quite thick skinned,' Rory said.

Litchfield inspected a piece of steak on the end of his fork. 'OK, Rory, tell me, then.'

'Please don't get me wrong, Bryant,' Rory said. 'I'm not an ET freak, just interested in the idea of alien encounter as a means of stimulating reactions worldwide.'

The Professor chewed on his morsel.

'Hmm. And…?'

'I'd like to use RIPE's Neo-HR computing facilities to investigate model scenarios involving alien intervention.'

'I see…' Bryant said, 'How many previous studies have you found in this area?'

'Twenty six,' Rory replied.

'Over how many years?'

'About fifteen. All centred around 2065 or thereabouts.'

'And what about the past five years?'

'Apparently none.'

'Well, I can enlighten you on that. Currently, there are four different investigations in progress. Not at RIPE, I may add! You haven't heard of them because they've been unable to have their work published in peer reviewed journals. In fact, I reviewed two of their papers myself.'

Rory looked pensive. 'I suspect they lacked sufficient computing power,' he said, 'in spite of the ongoing breakthroughs in computer systems technologies.'

'You're confident you can do better?'

'Yes. Facilities here are in a league of their own. They seem ideal for the purpose.'

'I'm still not happy about this,' said Litchfield. 'With the ET intervention approach you realise that your scientific reputation and credibility could be at risk?'

Rory met his Prof's level gaze. 'I'm convinced that now's the time to try again. If we wait too long in the present world climate, there'll almost certainly be more government cutbacks and other unpredictable problems.'

'You're certainly determined,' Professor Litchfield said. Tight lipped, he pondered for a moment, then continued: 'Sorry, Rory. I must leave now for another appointment.' He rose from his seat, took a couple of steps and glanced back over his spectacles. 'Let me see your completed proposal by the end of this week.'

*****

Tuesday 26 June, 2085. RIPE conference room.

Rory purposefully approached the room with a door plate: 'RIPE LABORATORY 7/E'. Inside, a long table was laid for coffee with places occupied by Litchfield and four others Rectangular video pads at each position displayed the word 'Welcome'. Rory approached the one vacant chair.

'Hello, Rory. Sit down and let's begin...' Professor Nandi opened a file on her V-pad. Her slender hands hovered above the touch screen.

'You already know each one of us,' she said, 'except perhaps Dr. Neville Ford. He's an invited external adjudicator for RIPE and a sub-contracted software engineer and systems lead-developer. We've all read your proposal and met yesterday to consider it. At this meeting you'll hear the results of our deliberations.'

'Thank you, Professor Nandi,' Rory said.

'First let me check the wording of one of your proposed investigations,' she continued, 'and I quote, "WHAT IF a certain Danish newspaper report on March 12 2003 about an alien encounter was actually true? Investigate the scientific and socio-political impacts and report." Is that its full title?'

'That is correct,' Rory said. 'It's number four on my list of alien encounters.'

'Quite so. We'll come to that in a moment,' she said. And turning to Bryant: 'Professor Litchfield?'

'Thank you. I'm displaying Rory's proposal on our pads and scrolling to page five.' Turning to Rory, his supervisor continued: 'To be frank, Rory, we consider your proposal too ambitious in its present form and wasteful of resources. But I think we all agree it was well researched and interesting. However, with present resources and realistic timescales to consider, more than one alien encounter scenario would be too many. The scenario that appeared least problematic in your proposal was Number Four, the one referred to by Professor Nandi and displayed on our pads just now. You do understand our position on this?'

'Yes,' Rory acknowledged, 'I appreciate the need for a more focussed approach and agree that scenario Number Four would be my best option.'

'For your investigative mission, there would have to be a time limit of six months,' Litchfield said. 'By the way, you'll have noticed that we're joined by Captain Bosworth, from your Territorial Army training team. The reason for that may be made clear shortly, depending on how this meeting goes. For now, I'm going to hand you over to Jeff, in his usual role as Mission Coordinator.'

Jeff, a stocky man in his forties, announced: 'Very well, here's how we see it. At the end, Rory, you may ask us any questions you want. We've looked into the requirements analysis and desired outputs for your project and considered compatibility issues with the RIPE advanced computing system as a means for exploration by one individual, namely yourself.'

Jeff began distributing a single page document to the V-pad of each participant. He continued to address the meeting, saying: 'It wasn't easy, but here's a tentative mission summary I've prepared. For now, let's look at the main points of the mission rationale. The fine print you can read later.'

He started reading aloud:

'One. We require a real-world reference scenario that could be used as an initial setting for an ET encounter.

Two. Rory suggests that a promising one is the March 2003 Læsø Nyheder newspaper report in Denmark about an alien encounter at the Skagen peninsula in the north of the country.

Three. The idea is to assume this report to be 'true' in the computer simulation and to observe the consequences after a reasonable time interval has passed. Rory suggested starting observations from a date in year 2010, which sounds reasonable.

Four. The mission is to be conducted in uninterrupted real-time with a duration of 6 months, or 7 months absolute maximum.

Five. This will require the subject, during his avatar phase, to endure the second longest static hibernation interval known so far in Neo-Hyper-VR, while remaining connected to mission and life support systems.

Six. The subject requests Mode One: Whatever the subject sees or experiences as an avatar will not violate any of the known laws of physics. It involves *total* immersion, with consequential vulnerability.'

'Rory, what do you say to this?' Professor Nandi asked.

'Thank you. I'm aware of the risks,' Rory said. 'And I've mentioned to Captain Bosworth my willingness to accept this mission as an act of military service.'

Jeff fixed his gaze on Rory as he said: 'As you'd be vulnerable to physical harm, accidental or otherwise, there are issues of fitness involving physical and mental training. And remember, you couldn't disclose to the inhabitants of your virtual world that they're part of a simulation. Not that many would believe you. In fact, you'd be so involved that there'd be times when you wouldn't believe it yourself.'

'Rory, you're certain you want to go through with this?' asked Bryant, clearly worried. 'Why not wait until you've accumulated some more experience?'

'I appreciate your concern, but could I please ask a couple of questions?'

'Let Dr. MacIntyre continue,' said Professor Nandi.

'Thank you,' Rory said. 'Jeff, could you give me an idea of what links there'd be between me as an avatar and the real world back here?'

'There'd be a requirement for occasional communications with HQ via secure emails or an approved co-avatar. As backup in the virtual world we would plant a CMI. You're familiar with the term?'

'Yes,' Rory said, 'Cell of Minimal Interaction.'

'Indeed.' Jeff said, 'In fact, you would be given codes to invoke a CMI, including automated rescue and safe return to the present. But only if special circumstances like emergencies demand it.' He went on to clarify the issue for the others present: 'Our military collaborators have liaised with us in improving this technique over the years. It gives the avatar zero interaction with the rest of his or her virtual world while exchanging information with our monitor team. It's well tested and generally reliable, but must be used covertly and when the avatar is alone.'

'On the matter of being alone, who would be the other participants from RIPE in the mission's virtual world?' Rory asked.

'Perhaps Captain Bosworth is best qualified to answer that question,' said Jeff.

'Thank you, Dr. Owen-Williams,' Captain Bosworth said. He sat sphynx-like, his arms resting on the table. 'The answer, Rory, is,' he continued, 'that I would be assigned to be effectively your Commanding Officer. But I wouldn't be holding your hand. The whole idea is that the avatar should be immersed in the new environment and work on their own initiative. When here, I'm contactable via CMI, or I can accept messages. Of course. I might intervene in the virtual world if needed.'

'Thank you, Captain. Would I recognise you?' Rory asked.

'You might recognise me if you saw me.'

'Would there be any other avatars I'd need to know about?'

Captain Bosworth looked away, towards the others in the group, then turned to face Rory.

'Unfortunately, some passwords went missing. We immediately changed them. At worst, there may be difficulties, even rogue avatars, put there by those who don't like us and with interests contrary to what we're trying to achieve. However, I believe any such risks are minimal and could be dealt with. It's my responsibility to provide the necessary on-the-ground security and safety for the mission.'

'In view of the risks to the avatar's well-being and safety,' Dr. Neville Ford asked, 'why are we pursuing the mission at this point?'

'Can I answer that?' Rory asked, leaning forward, looking this way and that, addressing all members of the meeting. He continued: 'We know that our country is presently on a war footing. RIPE may be commandeered by the government at any time, or even closed down through financial cutbacks, before we've had a chance to prove ourselves. And not forgetting our recent intruders, who knows what else may happen? There's no time to waste. If we pull it off, the government will almost certainly allow us to carry on. Besides which, I already have sufficient training and expertise for the task.'

'Almost!' Bosworth said, a grim smile on his swarthy face.

The chairperson broke the silence.

'However, Dr. MacIntyre is right,' said Professor Nandi, 'and we all know it. I propose we complete preparations in the laboratory with a view to commencing his mission seven days from now. Are there any objections?' Her dark eyes flashed around the gathering. 'The motion is carried, then. Thank you, this meeting is concluded.'

On the way out, Litchfield slapped Rory's shoulder. 'Well done! And good luck!'

*****

1:15pm Tuesday 3 July, 2085. RIPE Mission Laboratory.

'Are you comfortable, Rory?' asked Dr. Jeff Owen-Williams as he scrutinised his console. The centre panel of the screen showed a live image of Rory, reclining on what looked like a hybrid between a dentist's chair and an ejector seat of an old-style manned combat aircraft. Not in Jeff's immediate view, another similar chair remained empty. The biometric part of the monitoring and control console had been suitably developed for tracking the health and condition of RIPE's users and explorers.

'I feel fine at the moment,' replied Rory from the nest of tubes, cables and electronic units that surrounded him. And yet it all looked incredibly neat. A tribute to RIPE's systems design team.

'Good. We've completed your life support system and neurological integration checks and all are spot on.' Jeff's commentary continued through Rory's headset display unit. 'Now I'm about to hand you over to computer control. Standing by... Three... two... one... mark!'

Rory felt a slight tremor throughout his body. His head-up screen went blank and then became uniformly blue. Text messages appeared in white, accompanied by the computer's voice-over.

'Good afternoon, Rory,' said the computer. 'I'm Galena, your host computer for this mission. On behalf of RIPE and myself, congratulations on your initiative and dedication to our agreed task. As avatar Keir Wilson you are to embark on a re-run of history, from June 14 to December 3 2010, as influenced by the validated alien encounter event of 2003 specified in your accepted proposal. To confirm your preparedness to proceed, please clench your right hand now...'

Rory clenched a gloved hand as a confirmatory signal.

'Acknowledged. Thank you, Rory.' His visual background changed from blue to pale yellow. Then an official looking document with black edged boxes and text filled the screen. Galena continued: 'Now please give me your parameter confirmations while the technical team prepares for your launch...'

*****

Nine minutes and thirteen seconds later:

'Thank you, Rory, for confirming the starting scenario timeline and physical parameters. Now I need just a few remaining details about the type of alien you require. First, I'll go through these with you and then ask you to confirm your choices by ticking the appropriate box with your cursor.'

The voice continued, accompanied by scrolling screen text:

'Here are the available possibilities:

ONE: Is the alien a specific type of organism similar to those on Earth?

TWO: Is the alien non-hominid or hominid?

THREE: If non-hominid is the alien mammal, reptile, insect or other?

FOUR: If other, please prepare to describe in your own spoken words.

FIVE: Is the alien life cycle simple or in stages, analogous to caterpillar, chrysalis and moth?'

This is unscheduled, Rory noted. The computer itself had obviously decided on introducing the alien-menu presentation.

'For goodness sake,' Rory said to himself, 'Let's keep it simple.'

The computer interrupted: 'By all means, Rory. If you want a default alien type, just say so now.'

Suddenly, his phone-pod vibrated, with an audible alarm signal in his headset.

Then a text message appeared: 'Hi! Neville here, I'm monitoring your choices. As you say, let's keep it simple.'

'Default', Rory complied, with some relief. Then he realised that 'default' may not necessarily mean simple!

'Thank you, Rory,' the computer intoned, 'Your mission specification is complete.'

'Thanks, Galena.'

'The pleasure is all mine, Rory,' the computer said, 'Along with the RIPE team, I hope you have a safe journey.' Galena's blue screen went blank.

'OK Rory, all the best!' Jeff's channel had opened again and he winked from the screen. 'Still comfortable?'

'Yes, just about,' said Rory. 'Cheers everyone and thanks for everything.'

'Thank you for volunteering!' Litchfield appeared on the screen: 'Let me know when you're ready to go, Rory old chap.'

'I've specified a default alien. Not sure how that'll turn out.'

'Well,' Litchfield replied, 'Nev Ford was a major player in configuring the system, so you should be in safe hands. Anyhow, it seems you have everything else you wanted. And it would be rather late to re-adjust any parameters now the project is primed for action.'

'Yeah, let's run with it. Give my love to Ros,' Rory said.

'Your mission's classified, but I'll think of something. Bon voyage, Rory!' His Professor waved.

The screen faded. Then a date counter appeared, along with his avatar name. *A name I'll have to get used to...* 'Thanks, Bryant!' Then Rory realised that by now he would be talking to himself, as the date began to roll backwards in time. After what seemed a long half-minute, the counter stopped: Monday 14 June 2010, 15:43 hours...

Suddenly, Rory - now Keir Wilson - stood on a sunlit hillside out in the open, in a field of tufted grass. In the distance were lakes and trees. A cool breeze chilled his face, but a thick army uniform protected him, his headset replaced by a helmet. He turned to look uphill towards a ridge. Keir blinked and looked again. He discerned the distant silhouette of another soldier, possibly carrying a rifle. Then a pause. Next, the figure began walking towards him.

Keir Wilson murmured: 'This is it. Here goes…'

*****

2 Impact

A few minutes later:

Scattered around the hillside where Keir now stood were a few buildings in various stages of dereliction. He thought he saw movement near one of them. His nostrils twitched. Cordite or similar. Then a loud crack followed by a whine. Something ricochetted off a hard surface somewhere uncomfortably near.

'Blood and sand!' Keir said as he ducked his head.

A futile reaction. The bullet had already kicked a cloud of brick dust at head height from the corner of a gutted building; he estimated about twenty metres ahead.

'Down!' came a shout from his right.

Keir found himself scrabbling at the soft earth, with the feel of cold clay oozing through his fingers. Another shell whined overhead.

'What's going on?' Keir rasped

'Shut it and keep moving… Now, run!'

Keir tried to get up, but felt himself sliding headlong as his boots skidded uselessly in the mire.

'C'mon, move your arse!' the man snarled. His uniform; three stripes. 'Not that way. Over here!' the sergeant shouted.

Keir lurched away from the direction of an enticing doorway and followed him around the left side of the building. They crossed the ridge and were running downhill. The longer grass made the terrain more manageable. Ahead, the grass became reeds.

'Into the ditch!' the sergeant hissed, vanishing from sight. Keir stumbled after him. Suddenly, they were both waist deep in foul water.

'Down!'

Can't go down much further, Keir thought. Surely he doesn't mean… 'Yes, sir!' he said, looking around frantically for something to hold on to.

'Down, you stupid sod!'

Keir felt an iron grip spin him about, forcing his left shoulder below the surface and his face into the bank. Then he felt cold mud slam into his mouth as a deep concussion shook the ground. He waited for the several splashes from flying debris to subside. He tried to look up, when a fragment struck his helmet. To his left the sergeant remained still, his face down in the water.

'Hey!' Keir cried. 'Sarge!' He grabbed at his sergeant's shoulder and lifted him clear.

To Keir's relief, the sergeant coughed water.

'I'll live,' the man spluttered. 'Now perhaps we can sod off out of here.'

'You mean, it's over, Sarge?' Keir asked. A flint-like smell of shattered masonry lingered in a drifting pall of smoke. The building on the ridge had been reduced to a flat layer of rubble. A long blast from a klaxon sounded somewhere behind the hill. They got up, trotted over the ridge and down towards a parked Defender. Another soldier, this one with three pips on his epaulettes, walked towards them.

'Good work, Sergeant, you're dismissed now!' the newcomer said.

The captain turned to face Keir.

'It's you, Captain Bosworth!' Keir said.

'Yes, Corporal Wilson. And well done!' he added. 'Not a bad show for your first live exercise on this terrain.'

'Thanks.' Keir, too numbed to say anything else, tried to concentrate on checking himself for injuries.

'Are you OK?'

'Yes, sir.' Keir nodded assent and stumbled forward, following the captain and yearning to be out of his soaked and reeking uniform. He climbed into the Defender and rested his weary feet in the footwell. If Bosworth could smell anything he didn't show it, as he drove them back to a camp about a mile away. Keir glanced at Bosworth's watch. Four fifteen and a bright summer afternoon; just enough breeze to set the blue United Nations flag gently flapping above the gate-house. They were checked through by the sentry and eventually drew up outside the billeting quarters.

'Keir, go into Shack 113 over there and get changed. There's a sauna for you to use. And a fresh set of clothes and shoes that you should put on. Leave the uniform and any wet towels in the basket next to the shower.'

'Sauna? Quite a luxury!' Keir commented.

'In Finland it's par for the course. Yes, we *are* in Finland, by the way. Near a city called Oulu on the northwest coast facing the Gulf of Bothnia. See you here in ten minutes, precisely. Oh, and there's a green holdall. Remember to bring it with you.'

'Yes, sir!' Keir climbed stiffly out of the vehicle. When he'd bathed and brushed up he returned as instructed to the waiting Defender.

'Feeling better?' asked Bosworth.

'That sauna - marvellous! Ready for anything!'

'Really? No, you relax. You're finished for today. And again, excellent show! Your score's 14/20. Room for improvement, but we look forward to next time. I'm getting out of here. You stay put while I arrange someone to drive you to the hotel at Oulu.'

Keir wondered if the poker-faced Bosworth had other business in the camp, or did he refer to a return to the future?

'Thank you, sir. And for looking after me here.'

'Pleasure's mine, Keir. At least it won't be too long before you're catching a few hours kip. But before that, please read through your personal documents and the itinerary in your bag.'

*****

Afternoon, the following day.

Keir sensed a slight turbulence towards the end of his internal flight from Oulu to the city of Kuopio in Central Finland. Passengers had their seatbelts fastened. Between the clouds and through a window to his right, Keir viewed the panoramic sunset beyond the many lakes below, gleaming like slivers of crystal embedded in the dark, endless stretches of coniferous forest.

'Hey, take a look at that!' said a stocky middle-aged American in the window-seat in front of Keir. He wore a white baseball cap and addressed his female neighbour who had to lean across him for a better view. Keir watched and listened as the man pointed out one of the smaller lakes that had a distinctive shape.

'Yes, I know that one. It's called Kolmisoppi,' the blonde woman said with a Finnish accent.

'Hmm.'

'It means triangle,' she added.

'Looks more like a letter Y to me, ma'am. By the way, the name's Orville Bonnar.' Through the gap between their head-rests, Keir saw him offer a huge fleshy hand. 'I'm visiting your country from Woods Hole, in Massachusetts.'

The man's travelling companion now reclined in her seat, hidden from Keir's direct view.

'My name's Kirsti, Kirsti Kivi.' she replied. 'I work near the University. Down there.'

*****

Kuopio, 8:20pm that evening.

Keir located his designated hotel, the Savonia, on the outskirts of town, not far from Kuopio University campus. After check-in, he threw his bag onto the bed and opened a window. The trees across the road, bordering the forest, sighed gently in reddish light from the setting sun. He took a local map of the district from his table and stretched himself out on the bed.

After what seemed only a few minutes, Keir awoke and noted an hour had gone by. Refreshed and curiosity aroused, he took the elevator. At the ground floor, he found a bar.

'Er, *Kuopion oulut, olkaa hyvä?'* he asked. The novelty of speaking in a foreign language, presumably Finnish, came as a shock. Had he been programmed? He hoped his composure appeared intact.

'Local beer? Certainly, sir. Large or small? Can I get you anything else?' The barmaid's English being impeccable, Keir wondered if she'd detected a British accent. Or had she noticed the English version of the guide map he carried?

'Small, please,' Keir replied. 'Thanks.'

She watched as he perused the map again.

'This path here,' she said. A slender finger entered his field of vision and followed a route up the hill and through the forest to a clearing, where the map showed a tall tower rising above the trees. 'It would be a very pleasant walk,' she added.

Keir couldn't agree more, but resisted the temptation to ask when she would be off duty.

'*Kiitos*. Thanks,' said Keir.

'You're welcome, have a nice evening.'

'Thank you, I will.' He lifted one eyebrow and raised his glass in a casual salute. She smiled but swiftly attended to another guest. A few minutes later, he set off for his walk.

*****

Keir moved under the trees in total silence, apart from his own footsteps. Twigs cracked underfoot on a yielding carpet of pine needles. The upward gradient and the softness of the ground drained his energy. After what seemed like an hour, in fact only twenty minutes, a high concrete pillar arose out of a clearing ahead. Puijo Tower. His guidebook also informed him that its topmost structure comprised a slowly revolving restaurant and viewing gallery. The ground ahead levelled out and he moved closer, stopping at the edge of the clearing. Before him spread an extensive car park in an area containing several low buildings, mainly of timber. These had well-kept fences with gardens, the largest being a hotel and reception hall. Here and there, he noticed traces of brightly coloured confetti that had blown into crevices. With his outstretched arm, Keir leaned against a tree. He gazed upwards, following the profile of the concrete column to where the top of the tower, way above the trees, bathed in the red glare of sunset. He watched the slow red flashes as each of the outward-leaning windows of the rotating restaurant reflected the sunlight. By now he'd totally forgotten the effort of walking. He lowered his gaze and turned slowly around. A roadway into the forest promised an easier return journey. Gaps in the trees allowed him glimpses towards the horizon; a distant shimmer of early sodium streetlights and the crawl of pin-prick headlamps. Still further, he made out dusky reddened profiles of city buildings. Beyond them he saw a distant lake, a tranquil expanse of slate blue.

*****

Keir grabbed his vibrating high security official link-set issued to him by Bosworth, which could also be used as an ordinary mobile phone. The voice sounded clipped and accented.

'Hello Mr. Wilson, Tanskanen here. Welcome to Finland! Are you well?'

Keir reflected that in this world, he is still a postgraduate student. He remembered the name from his briefing papers. It belonged to the head of a private company housed in a low, flat building near the Mineralogy Department of Kuopio University. The staff list confirmed him as Kirsti Kivi's boss.

'Fine thanks, Professor Tanskanen. I'm just admiring your countryside.'

'Quite scenic at Puijo Hill, isn't it?'

'How did you know I'm here?' Keir asked.

'TV cameras. And everyone visits Puijo Tower. You're staying at the Savonia?'

'Yes, I'm just on my way back to the hotel now.'

'Ah, I'm sorry to disturb your walk, Mr. Wilson. But could you please call in at our laboratory for a few minutes?'

'Now?' Keir glanced at his watch, 10:47pm. The long northern sunsets were deceptive.

'It shouldn't take too long, Mr. Wilson.'

Keir then remembered his brief. 'Sorry, I should have contacted you on arrival,' he said, 'but by the time I got here I thought it was rather late. I was going to call you in the morning.'

'We think it's better to deal with this now, if you don't mind. Let's keep to the schedule. See you in about half an hour. Take care and keep to the paths. *Näkemiin*, be seeing you.' Tanskanen rang off.

'OK, have it your way!' Keir murmured resignedly, as he consulted the map and looked around for a possible short cut to the desired path.

The next instant found him on the ground, entangled in a patch of arctic brambles.

Painfully, he retrieved the link-set and map, shoving them both into a pocket. Struggling to his feet, he realised it would take several minutes to remove the thorns from his hands and clothing. Torn trousers revealed an angry gash.

'Blast! Hope Tanskanen's got some plasters,' he growled.

Fortunately, his route down to the laboratory took him past the hotel, where he hastily called in.

'*Anteeksi?* Excuse me?' said a uniformed blond giant who barred his way.

'Wilson's the name. I need to stop by for a moment.'

The night duty concierge looked at him suspiciously and scrutinised his passport and key card before letting him in.

After a wash and change of trousers - he could only find jeans - Keir met him again on the way out.

'Hi! I'm off now. Needed at the Tansys building. Could you please tell me the quickest way from here?' Keir asked, producing his map.

'Follow this path and after two hundred metres it is signposted.'

'Thanks. I'll probably be quite late getting back.'

'Ah! Another party, eh? No problem. But please not to disturb other guests when you return. Have a good evening, *Herra* Wilson.'

*****

Keir found Tanskanen waiting for him at the front entrance of the company building that housed Tansys Oy. The dark suit of his host contrasted markedly with his own less formal appearance with a bloodstain seeping through his jeans. Keir winced as they shook hands. He cautiously shook the gentler hand of Dr. Kirsti Kivi. Her blonde hair swept back to a ponytail, she impaled him with a clear blue eyed smile which more than compensated for his discomfort.

'Sorry to hear about your accident,' she said. 'Let's tidy you up.'

On returning from the men's room, Keir sat nervously while she dressed his thigh with a plaster. Meanwhile, Tanskanen aligned the filled coffee cups on Kirsti's desk and began sorting some papers from his folder.

'There!' said Kirsti when she'd finished. 'Now come and join us.'

'Thanks for the repair job, Dr. Kivi.' Keir said.

'My name is Kirsti, can I call you Keir?'

'Certainly, Kirsti.'

At the door, Tanskanen offered Keir a selection of cheeses and different breads.

'I can especially recommend what we call *musta leipä* – the dark bread,' Tanskanen said.

Glancing around over his coffee and bread, Keir's attention locked on to the array of pictures on the walls.

'The forest ones are prints from the works of our famous Finnish artist, Akseli Gallen-Kallela,' Kirsti explained. 'Some are scenes from our national epic poem, the Kalevala.'

'Incredible,' Keir acknowledged. 'I've never seen the textures of wood and foliage rendered with such feeling.' Other, quite different images, of abstract nature, also caught his attention. Their hard, angular lines and iridescent hues provided stark counterpoint to the forest pictures.

'Those are more technical, of course,' she said. 'You'll recognise them as photographic enlargements of rock sections in polarized light.'

'I've seen plenty of rock sections, but none of them look quite like these.' His attention riveted by one in particular, he said, 'This is like a fantasy landscape. And that other is... just out of this world as well! Who's the artist?'

Tanskanen sipped his coffee indifferently while reading through his papers. Kirsti's eyes fell momentarily to the table.

'Well... actually, they're mine,' she admitted. Then, looking directly at Keir, she said: 'Thank you. I'm glad you like them.'

'Er, Mr. Wilson.' Keir's thoughts were interrupted by the more mechanical tone of the professor's voice. 'We're sorry to have dragged you here so late, but we do need to put you in the picture.' If a pun was intended, he didn't smile. 'Then we can all go and get some sleep, because the expedition assembles at the entrance to this building at seven thirty tomorrow morning. On the dot, as you say in your country.'

'Finc, please go ahead.' Keir said. The pictures had lifted him to a higher plane and he felt totally unfazed.

'We've called you here,' said Kirsti, 'to explain the background behind tomorrow's expedition.'

'Because tomorrow,' Tanskanen added, 'we will introduce you to Mr. Tiihonen. The day before yesterday, he witnessed the meteorite fall first hand while alone at his summer cottage near Lake Kolmisoppi.'

Keir recalled the mention of a meteorite in his briefing papers. And during his flight he'd seen the aerial view of Lake Kolmisoppi.

'Triangle?' he asked.

'Indeed!' said Kirsti. 'That is the lake's name. You speak some Finnish?'

'Not really,' Keir replied. 'Probably just enough to find the bus station.' He chose to withhold mentioning anything about the incoming flight.

'Anyway,' Tanskanen said impatiently, 'if you will permit me to review the events as I understand them...' He picked up a sheet from the desk, adjusted his rimless spectacles and began his account:

'A few kilometres to the west of here, Saturday morning, two days ago, Lauri Tiihonen was near his summer cottage on the eastern shore of Lake Kolmisoppi.' The professor went over to a pen-board to sketch a rough map.

'Here is Kolmisoppi, and here is the jetty where he'd moored his rowing boat after checking his fishing catch.' Tanskanen looked down at his sheet and continued: 'Lauri says: "I glanced up through the trees at the sound of an approaching aircraft, and then I walked to the veranda of my sauna-hut near the edge of the lake." He goes on to tell us that after some fishing, he placed some of his fish at the bottom of a dry well to keep them cool, et cetera, et cetera.'

'Perhaps I should explain to Keir why he was doing this,' Kirsti suggested, 'as he is rather new to Finland and our customs.'

'Just briefly then, please, Dr. Kivi,' Tanskanen conceded, as Keir turned his attention to Kirsti.

'You see, Keir,' she explained, 'Lauri was making preparations for his family barbecue and sauna party. One day next week is doubly significant for him. It is his seventieth birthday, which also coincides with *Juhannus*, the celebration of midsummer in Finland.'

'Thanks, Kirsti,' said Keir, as he recalled some hazy 'memories'. 'I've heard something about your midsummer celebrations.'

Tanskanen looked impatiently at his watch and spoke as he continued drawing:

'Tiihonen lit the stove in the sauna hut, which is here.' He pointed to a square near the eastern shoreline. 'He stood in the doorway, looking out across Kolmisoppi.' An arrow was drawn across part of the lake, pointing north-west. 'Then he heard something behind him strike the roof.' He drew an X on the sauna hut.

'At first, he thought it was just another dead branch from a tree. Then, from the lake, he heard a sound like a lot of distant splashes from... *pikkukivet.* Ah, what do you say in English, gravel, pebbles? Anyway, he saw concentric ripples spreading out from many places.' Tanskanen animatedly drew several overlapping circles in the lake. 'He watched them until the water's surface was calm again.'

The professor put down his board pen and turned over a page in his notes.

'Lauri says: "Meanwhile, an aircraft passed overhead travelling towards Kuopio airport. Then I returned to the boat to continue my work." So, you see, the aircraft is useful. It could give us a time. Tomorrow we go to see what we can find.'

'Thanks Professor,' Keir said. 'I'm looking forward to joining your team.'

'Good. By the way, Kirsti,' Tanskanen said, 'when we arrive, let me deal with Lauri. He isn't very happy at all.' Turning to Keir, he continued, 'The local authorities have allowed the university and us to cordon off the area. We were given five days to conduct our searches. But if we don't complete our work on time, Lauri might have to postpone his planned celebrations at the lakeside.'

Keir nodded thoughtfully. 'What sort of meteorite was it?' he asked.

'We're confident of its classification,' Tanskanen replied. 'But as a visitor from Professor Burton's distinguished group, we would greatly appreciate your independent assessment.' For the first time that evening, the professor allowed himself a thin smile. 'Well, it is time to go, I think. Thank you both for coming. And Kirsti, I understand you will be driving Mr. Wilson back to his hotel?'

Keir realised he had yet to meet his head of department. According to his briefing pack, Professor Burton is head of the Planetary Sciences Department at Oakingwell, a university located somewhere in Lancashire. As they got up to go, Keir brushed past the corner of Kirsti's desk. A few printed sheets, stapled together, fell to the floor. As he picked them up, he recognised it as a scientific paper entitled: 'On Recent Geological Evidence for Extraterrestrial Life in the Universe,' by V.R. Gazetny and I.Y. Karpov. Keir placed it back on the desk and continued towards the door.

Kirsti gathered her belongings while Keir waited in the corridor.

'I will lock up,' said Tanskanen, returning the folder to his leather briefcase. '*Erittäin hyvä yötä*! A very good night!'

As Kirsti's car drew out of the car park, the risen moon sat bright and low on the horizon. Keir felt uncertain... something about it looked different. It cast a subdued glow on her face as they paused at the driveway to the main road.

'Thanks, Kirsti,' Keir said. 'Your hospitality, and your art, prevented that from being a tough time!'

'That is very kind, but you must not worry about Jukka Tanskanen.'

In Kirsti's presence, Keir felt a return of strength and confidence. The moonlight and her faint trace of perfume played on his senses.

'Did you draw and paint before you did photography? Keir asked.

'From childhood. And I still do those things,' she replied. The car accelerated out of the gate and headed east towards the hotel. 'Does your leg feel better?'

'Much better, thanks.'

The memory of her gentle hands on his tortured flesh began to arouse him. Perhaps mercifully, they soon arrived at the hotel.

'Forgive my presumption,' he said, getting out of the car. 'But your partner, husband or whoever is most fortunate.'

'Thank you again, Keir.' Kirsti smiled at him enigmatically. 'I hope you will still think well of me in the future.' Her expression became earnest. 'But I must warn you. There are now other things that overtake us that are perhaps too big to handle.' She passed him something through the car window. 'Please, take this. It is for you to read, but perhaps tomorrow over breakfast, when you have had some sleep.'

Puzzled, Keir took the brown envelope.

'Good night, Keir.' she began closing the window.

'*Hyvä yötä!*' Goodnight. He called after her, as her car slid quietly away.

*****

The hotel concierge recognised him 'Ah, welcome back, *Herra* Wilson!'

On the bed, Keir opened the envelope to reveal a copy of the very paper he'd dropped earlier. He scan-read the leading abstract, then skipped to the final conclusions.

'Evidence of alien life in meteorites? Surely, far too early to say in this 2010 world,' he murmured.

It slid to the floor as sleep overtook him.

*****

The following morning, Keir's alarm rang and he awoke in extreme discomfort. He tried to move but his joints were stiff and the wound in his leg painful. After a struggle, he got out of bed and found his high security mobile link-set.

'Professor Tanskanen? Hi! It's Keir. I have a problem. Leg's pretty bad, I'm afraid. Can hardly move it.'

'I'm sorry to hear that, Keir. How about if I phone a cab for you, to the local hospital, and see how you feel later on?'

Keir's room being some distance from the lift, he began a slow and tortuous expedition to the restaurant. On the way down he saw through a window his taxi had arrived. He grabbed two pieces of dark rye bread from a food table and hobbled to the car.

On examination at the hospital, the nurse who re-dressed his wound assured him: 'It was already well bandaged and should heal nicely.'

'Thanks. Will I be OK by later this afternoon?'

'It would be wise to do as the Doctor suggests and rest. You will be just fine in about three days.'

'Three days!'

*****

After a quick lunch from a nearby university snack bar, Keir arrived that same afternoon at Kirsti's laboratory.

'It's good to see you looking better again,' Kirsti said. 'Sorry you missed this morning's survey and collection phases.'

'I'm sorry, too. But I'm here to help if I can.'

'Very well. If you feel fit enough, you can examine what we've found and then help with sorting and partitioning of the meteorite samples.'

'Sure, Kirsti,' Keir said.

'Excellent! As you know, Keir, sorting and classification of the fragments will be followed by careful division and subdivision of the collected materials ahead of distribution to the many scientific workers at various institutions. Here is your copy of the schedule.'

Keir checked through the wad of documents and found the listed destination for each partition. He felt no doubt that being at the focal point of this process carried its responsibilities.

'I'm quite happy with the arrangements,' he said.

Hopefully, by the end of the day, he would have sufficient notes and information for his report. This could be completed for emailing over the link-set before his flight to the UK the next day. For Keir, the thought of his first entry to the UK in the virtual world filled him with both anticipation and uncertainty.

'This is Elena,' Kirsti introduced her assistant, a tall girl with a shy smile. 'She will help you. I'll be in my office preparing the paperwork on my computer for Professor Tanskanen. You know how it is! If you could please let me have the lab record with your results by about three o'clock.'

'Hi Elena, and thanks, Dr. Kivi,' Keir said. 'Just leave it to us, we'll be fine.'

Keir and Elena worked quickly, completing the classification work within the hour. They were ready to commence partitioning.

'Elena, let's start with Tray Four, please.'

Elena picked up the tray containing the majority of the sample components. They were enclosed in several small plastic bottles with flip lids. To Keir's surprise, she began opening each in turn.

'Elena? I think we should open them just one at a time, to prevent risk of contamination or spillage.'

Perhaps he spoke too quickly, or she didn't understand his slight Scottish accent.

'Elena, could you please hang on a moment?' he said.

But she had already collected the tray. As she rounded the end of the bench, they both heard a buzz beneath her lab-coat.

'Voi!' she cried. 'Sorry, Mr. Wilson. I told Heikki *not* to ring me.'

At that moment, her involuntary arm movement tilted the tray. Keir watched, speechless, as at least half of the containers cascaded sideways into the nearby sink. He dashed to the disaster scene but too late! With horror, Keir gazed helplessly at most of the grey-brown contents; now mixed and splattered over the sink's wet surface.

'Let me deal with this!' Keir heard himself say. 'I'll take the blame. Don't say *anything*, and you'll be OK.'

Head in hands, Elena dashed out and made for the ladies' room. Keir returned to his area of the bench and picked up a spatula. He would attempt a partial recovery - from some containers, at least. But then he heard the faint squeak of a door.

'How's it going?' Kirsti headed towards him from her office. Keir felt the sweat trickling on his brow. But Kirsti swept past him, obviously unaware of any mishap. She still smiled in his direction while pouring the remains of her lukewarm coffee into the sink.

'Fancy a break? I'll make three fresh ones for us,' she offered. Running the tap to rinse her cup, she gazed downwards...

'We had an accident,' Keir said. 'It's entirely my fault.'

Kirsti's face a pallid mask, she said: 'You must please carry on with the remaining samples. And where is Elena? Had she anything to do with this?'

'She's in the toilets. And no, this is my responsibility.'

Later that evening, Tanskanen conceded a terse wave as Keir's taxi set off for the hotel. Back in his room, Keir went online. His report for Oakingwell was shorter than he would have liked. He sent it anyway.

*****

On Keir's 'return' flight to England, he studied the contents of a brown folder from the green hold-all, now his flight bag. He withdrew a brochure of Oakingwell University. While reading through it, he felt many planted memories snapping into place - like network nodes - in his mind. After half an hour he found the process exhausting and dozed off. As he awoke to the clatter of a meal trolley, the dreams he recalled suggested that his subconscious had been primed. Professor Nandi had warned Keir in advance about the likely mental and emotional effects of his pre-programming by Galena, the mission computer. Nandi had been the only person he'd met who had a triple Doctorate; in History, Psychology and Medicine. A founder member of RIPE and probably its most valued asset.

After his airline lunch, Keir began to study the literature on Oakingwell's Planetary Sciences Department and the Meteorites Section in particular. He had scientific papers to read by Professor Brian Burton and his colleagues. He noted the names of co-authors, including Alan Menzies, who would be his PhD supervisor in the virtual world of 2010. Keir's real-world PhD of 2085 had been in physics and computer science, but shortly at Oakingwell he would be back in the third year of a different PhD, researching in earth sciences and specialising in meteorites.

As he read on, more 'memories' and whole swathes of knowledge snapped into place. Then the question arose, 'What was I doing this time last year, or the year before, in the virtual world?' As if on cue, he 'recalled' his interview at Oakingwell, how Professor Burton had oozed charm…

Keir's head lolled sideways again and sleep overtook him for a second time. Now his dreams included people, Burton and Menzies. They were reviewing his progress and giving him tasks. There were days off when he participated in Territorial Army training, assault courses and unarmed combat. He recalled Captain Bosworth, somehow linked to Burton.

Suddenly, he awoke. Seatbelts! Clouds swept past the windows as the aircraft approached Manchester Airport. As he went through passport control and joined the baggage queues to collect his suitcase, he knew he had not brought it with him nor ever seen it before. But he somehow knew it would contain important support items for his mission. Then in his mind he saw an image of its appearance. And soon he saw it drifting into view on the conveyer belt. He hefted the case onto a trolley and went through customs without incident. On his way to the terminal exit, directly ahead, Keir saw a man waiting with a board: 'Kier Wilson for Oakingwell University.'

*****

Keir arrived to find Professor Burton's office door already ajar. He knocked.

'Come!'

Keir entered and took the seat offered by Burton as the latter exchanged glances with Menzies.

'I'll be frank, Keir.' Burton said, adjusting his spectacles with a forefinger. 'Not one of your best performances, was it?' He slowly moved his hands to chest level, thumbs forming the base of a triangle, index fingertips at the apex. And turning to Menzies: 'Wouldn't you agree, Alan?'

This must be Alan Menzies, my supervisor, thought Keir.

Alan nodded in assent.

'Agreed.' Keir replied, addressing both his superiors. 'You know about the spillage of the samples?'

'Aye,' Menzies cocked his head to one side, 'It was in your report, if you remember.'

'I must admit, I found it hard to believe.' Burton interrupted.

'Thank you!' Keir surprised himself with the sound of his own voice.

'But then I contacted Tanskanen,' Burton continued, 'and he told me some story about you covering up for an assistant.'

'Well, yes! Wouldn't you have done the same?' Keir wondered if he'd stepped too far.

'We're asking the questions, Keir,' said Professor Burton, his stare unblinking. His hands now gripped the edge of his desk. 'But the answer is no, I certainly wouldn't! If you want to be Sir Galahad, do it on a stage, not in a laboratory at the scene of a crucial investigation. But I'm more concerned with your management of the operation...' Burton turned with a nod to Menzies.

'It's true, I'm afraid,' Alan said. 'You could see she was inexperienced and should have kept the lids firmly shut on those damn samples until they were in your hands. But I'll give you this; in my view, Dr. Kivi ought to have used a more experienced person, say from Kuopio University, for this job. Huh! Staff shortages, I expect. That Tanskanen's a glorified bean-counter, from what I've heard.'

'He's a first rate scientist and rightly annoyed!' countered Burton. Recovering his composure, he continued: 'Let's forget the should-haves and concentrate on damage limitation. Wilson, let's have your suggestions. Where do we go from here?'

'We concentrate on processing what data we've got, including the digital images,' Keir replied.

'It's true. You've accumulated a lot of those, some in 3D. Quite useful,' Menzies commented.

'That's fine as far as it goes,' said Burton. 'But I wanted more pictures of the site and where stuff was found.'

'We can get those from Dr. Kivi,' Keir suggested.

'Can we really?' Burton said. 'I doubt it, after this debacle. And you were absent during the morning. Instead, you had to go to hospital. Your brief was to be part of the collection team, not to incapacitate yourself by romping around in the woods at twilight!' He thumped the desk, his former frustrations returning. Kier could see the veins standing out on his forehead as he looked at his watch. 'Alan, you've got a class to teach.'

'Sure, I'd better go.' Menzies made for the door, patting Keir's shoulder on the way out. 'Catch up with you later.'

When the door closed, Burton stood up. He leaned across his desk towards Keir. 'Professor Tanskanen drew maps on a pen-board. Do you have any pictures of those?'

'No. I was expecting them to share that information in due course.'

'Ah. Never mind.' Burton sighed. 'I'm going to have to think again about your role in all this, including your future. Please go, I'll be in touch.'

'Thanks, Prof.' Keir said, rising awkwardly from his seat. 'Sorry to have caused you this trouble.'

As Keir stepped out and closed the door, his feelings of guilt turned to anger as the realisation dawned upon him.

'Good grief!' he murmured. 'He expected me to *spy* on them.'

*****

Back at his bed-sit, Keir pondered on what on Earth he had got himself into. He thought of invoking a CMI and requesting his return to the future. *But no, this is my original and unique RIPE mission. And in this virtual world, it's my final year of a PhD.* He wanted to turn his new knowledge, even though largely pre-programmed, into something tangible. The thought crossed his mind as to whether any reference to his Oakingwell PhD existed in the future archive media at Liverpool University. *I'll have to check when I get back*, he thought.

Keir's gaze shifted to the green flight bag on the table. He extracted a yellow folder and a USB memory stick. He laid out his Oakingwell PhD pack and turned on the computer to transfer some files from the memory stick to his Thesis folder on the C-drive. He reviewed its latest contents, including several diagrams. As he did so, he felt more memories clicking into place. They'd probably continue until he became fully integrated, he thought. Burton's implied threat about his future wouldn't prevent completion of his thesis. He felt Alan would see to that. His mobile phone rang. Alan Menzies smiled from the screen.

'Hi Keir, you OK?'

'Yes, yes. Fine.'

'You understand I couldn't say very much just now in the meeting. Politics and diplomacy, right? Anyhow, as far as your PhD work is concerned, don't let him bother you, Keir. I for one wouldn't let that, er, gentleman spike your guns. But he won't anyway. The department needs as many successful PhD completions as it can get. So just crack on and write it up. Have you finished all your diagrams and references yet?'

'Well, not far off. It looks like you can have my draft chapter three by next Monday.'

'Ah, good.'

'Thanks for your support with the meeting, Alan.'

'Pleasure. And if you need job references, ask me and not him. OK?'

'Thanks again. Catch you later.'

'Cheers.'

*****

Keir wheeled around at a knock at his partly open door.

'Hi! Come in and grab a chair!' Keir beckoned to his friend, Frank, whom he recognised from his second nap on the aircraft.

'Hi Keir! Heard you had a run-in with the dreaded Brian.'

'News travels fast, eh?'

'Well, you're not alone, I'm sure. Be thankful he's not *your* supervisor. He's been in a foul mood these past two days and giving me real gyp! Hey! Are you all right, Keir? You look rather knackered!'

Keir felt unsteady on his feet. Something like a gale seemed to be rushing through his head. More memories consolidating. How long must these 'opposite to amnesia' bouts go on for?

'Yeah, probably the flight. I'll be OK in a minute,' Keir said. 'And you're right about supervision, Frank. Alan's one in a million. He's been great from the start.'

'Sounds like he'd give you a good reference.'

Keir wondered how much of his telephone conversation had been overheard. Frank had the reputation of being the departmental news-hound.

'Hope you're right. But no support from a departmental head could cause problems.'

'Hmm. Best of luck with that! Nearly lunch time. Fancy coming for a sandwich?'

Keir glanced at his table of books and papers. 'Not hungry, thanks. Have to get through this job.'

'Fair enough. How about a jar this evening?'

'We'll see. I might catch up with you later.'

*****

Early that evening:

'Come on, now! It really is time you had a night off.' Frank insisted.

Keir regretted he'd left the door of his study-bedroom ajar again. He also regretted his half promise to Frank. His hands paused momentarily at the 2010 vintage computer workstation.

'Sorry, Frank. I really must finish off this chapter tonight!' he said. Avoiding eye contact, he waved an arm in dismissive protest. He saw it getting dark outside, enabling him to monitor his doorway by its reflection in the window. He noticed, with foreboding, Frank being accompanied by Harry. The next instant found Keir Wilson being frog-marched in the rain towards the Gregson College bar, his objections becoming mere token gestures. As Frank leaned forward and opened the heavy swing doors, Keir grimaced at the tide of noise, but there could be no going back.

The three made for a gap in the crowd and at the last second Keir saw why. Holding his breath, he sidestepped a pool of vomit and squeezed past a bearded man with vacant bloodshot eyes. He noticed a corner table, unfortunately not quite far enough away, being hastily vacated. Regrettably, his companions secured it while he fetched a round of drinks.

Avoiding debris on the sticky table, Keir tried to make himself comfortable. Through well established habit, his immediate thoughts switched back to his PhD thesis.

'Wake up, Keir. We have company!' Frank elbowed him into life, indicating a knot of people at the door. Harry rearranged extra seats and Frank tossed Keir a bag of crisps.

'Thanks.' Keir shifted in his chair to make room for someone whom at first he didn't recognise. His 'memories' clicked in and as she sat down he recalled her as Dr. Rowena Smythe. Her retinue included Tom, a biology researcher whom Keir also recognised and another person, whose age and identity were as yet unknown.

'Hi!' Keir forced an amiable greeting. With barely concealed amusement, he surmised that the unknown person might be one of Tom and Rowena's experiments that had gone terribly wrong. The ornate form acknowledged him with a nod. The loose shimmering garment might have been woven from aluminium wire - the hair vermilion and partly covered by a silvery skull-cap. Keir tried not to stare at the heavy make-up to the face, which resembled that of a white-faced clown.

'You all know Tom. And this is Viv. Yes, Viv,' Rowena announced.

The aluminium-clad clown bowed.

'Whose birthday party is it?' Keir asked, curious as to Rowena's reaction. He remained unsure from his background research how much 'political correctness' was an issue at this point in history.

Rowena said nothing. She and Keir remained impassive. Then they exchanged the briefest of icy smiles.

Suddenly, another arrival appeared.

'Ah, glad you could make it,' Rowena said. 'This is Ben.'

The contrast could not have been more striking. The dapper Ben sported an ordinary brown tweed suit. Keir didn't recognise him, either.

'He and Viv are from Graphic Design,' Rowena continued.

'You don't say?' Keir said absently, his thoughts having strayed back to his new research area. Rowena scowled. But the designers nodded in unison and Ben smiled politely as Rowena made a roll call of the rest of the party for their benefit.

'I recognise your symptoms, Keir,' she added. 'Your mind is elsewhere. If it's your thesis, that's good.'

'You're right, of course.' he said. Keir was also aware of his available cash running low. He checked it wasn't his turn for the next round, especially if the number of Rowena's sycophants should increase further.

As her ample frame settled further into her chair, he offered Rowena his packet of crisps.

'A truce, Keir?' she said. Her golden lashes flickered over clear blue eyes. 'Not just now, dearest.' She gave a curt wave of dismissal. 'I'm sure Ben won't say no, though, will you, Ben?'

Viv remained inert, watching, while Ben gladly took the bag.

Keir pretended to check his mobile phone messages and went online. According to his screen, Rowena Smythe had recently accepted the headship of Biological Sciences, and had launched a new Centre for Astrobiology. Out of her fifteen research students, six PhDs were approaching completion. Not a bad score. He snapped the lid shut and pocketed the device. Interesting. Within the year she might become a full Professor.

Just now, Rowena relished being the centre of attention, being as lively and voluble as ever and no doubt intent on having the glass in her hand periodically recharged with her favourite claret. She clearly suffered no fools gladly, so Keir decided to listen rather than say too much. He thought he might stick around for a short while longer. Perhaps he'd learn something new from this tableau in the VR world.

When the next drinks were due, Keir blinked with surprise. From out of the corner of his eye, as Rowena searched for some cash, he thought he saw inside her shoulder bag a mobile phone uncannily like his own. A link-set?

She turned to him, indulging her favourite activity, delivery of advice: 'Look, Keir. In your field you need more contacts and why not try Europe?'

'Or the States?' ventured Frank. But Rowena hadn't finished.

'In fact, it's a pity you haven't got your own paper to give in Paris at the forthcoming conference,' she said, resuming her domination. Everyone listened, while levels in their beer glasses continued to fall at different rates.

'You mean the Organics in Space one?' Keir asked.

'Yes, of course.' Rowena took a sip from her elevated wine glass. She continued: 'And as you know, for someone in your position the right contacts could make all the difference.'

'I've wondered about it, but I'm not yet ready to submit my own paper,' Keir said, 'so it's unlikely Alan or Brian would support me.'

'Pity.' Rowena's moist lips curled into a grin. 'It should be a very good meeting,' she went on, 'quite apart from my own white-hot contribution to the grateful scientific community!' The group laughed in mock derision, neither quite sure nor caring what they were laughing at, as yet another round of drinks appeared on the table.

Rowena gazed at Keir with a look of concern that might have been genuine, but more likely induced by her disappearing drink.

'Actually, I agree with you, dearest,' she said. 'He wouldn't let you go just for the wine, women and song.'

'I can understand Burton's position,' Keir affirmed. 'Alan's already going because he's the lead author on their joint paper.'

'Hmm. As I've suggested, if you *could* go... you'd have me for delightful company, if you could find the time.'

He heard a stifled titter within the gathering, synchronised with someone pouring her another refill of red wine. He remained unfazed.

'You seem to think there's a chance then,' Keir said. 'Do you reckon I could go with Alan, if Burton's in a good frame of mind?'

'Actually,' Rowena's voice became conspiratorial, 'in a day or two you might catch Burton in just the right mood. Next week is a reading week for the students in your department. You know what that means? He'll have zero teaching load and be freed from what he sees as extraneous interruptions to his *real* work.'

'You're right,' Keir said, uncertain as to where that memory had come from.

'Quite so!' she said, 'There are other matters, Kier. But I won't elaborate now.' Rowena drained her glass, but refused a refill.

He'd heard from Frank that the dissent between Rowena and Brian Burton had reached new levels of acrimony.

'Thanks for the advice. Better wander back now.' Keir said, standing unsteadily.

'Don't forget to have a word with Alan.'

'Thanks again, Dr. Smythe. I'll keep you posted, OK?'

'My pleasure, Keir. And it's Rowena, you twit!'

Rowena's incisive gaze followed his movements as he turned to leave the group. She appeared to have something else to say. He took his time lifting the anorak from the back of his chair.

'Keir, how did you get on at Kuopio?'

He tapped his stiff leg. 'I'll be fine,' he said.

'I wasn't referring to your battle scars, dearest. If you choose to prance about the countryside playing soldiers, followed by close encounters with brambles, that's your problem.'

'Good job I'm not looking for sympathy,' he said. *And the 'soldiers' comment. Weren't the Oulu details classified?* he thought. 'Was there something in particular, Rowena?'

Her long eyelashes drooped as she toyed with the stem of her empty glass.

'I know that you're acquainted with that meteorite, the carbonaceous chondrite that fell in Finland recently. Have you looked yet at the Paris conference programme on the web?'

'Like you said, I've been too busy with my thesis.'

'All the more reason. The internet's our life-blood!'

'True enough.' Keir moved his chair back under the table.

'So before you see Alan or Brian about the conference, look up its programme and make sure you do your homework. Impress them.' Smiling sweetly, Rowena added: 'I know you will.'

'No worries, Rowena. And thanks. I'll check it out.' Keir reached for his beer glass, drained it and made for the door. 'Bye, everyone.'

'Bye. Be seeing you, Keir.' She turned to the others, this time allowing Viv to top up her glass.

At the door, Keir glanced back briefly. But Rowena had already resumed her role, leading the discourse in its customary mixture of the profound and trivial, into which Frank and Harry were now completely assimilated. They'd hardly noticed him leave. Keir closed the swing doors, relishing the coolness and silence. So Rowena doesn't know about the lab accident; or being Rowena, she'd certainly have mentioned it. He headed out towards the glistening wetness of the grassed quadrangle, pulling up his collar against the fine rain. Head bowed, he splashed through the puddles on a clockwise negotiation of the perimeter path. Veering left, under a stone archway, he continued across the street, back to his room.

Fumbling at the keyboard, Keir checked his emails. He stored a short official news bulletin about the Kolmisoppi event, then a more extended scientific report. On reading it, he recognised the quoted paragraphs as the good bits of his own report, but with authorship being attributed to Professor Brian Burton.

'Ha! He's one of those, eh?' Keir mumbled. He looked up the Paris conference web site.

An hour later, his last conscious thoughts included the need to get to that conference and meet some key people. Would Burton allow him to go?

*****

3 Valentina

Oakingwell, Tuesday 22 June 2010, 11:15am

Alan knocked once and entered Professor Burton's office. Keir followed and both were waved into chairs, Burton already seated in his swivel chair.

'Hi, Alan. How's things?' he asked.

After the ritual exchange of pleasantries, Alan said, 'I think Keir would like to ask you something.'

Burton's expression suggested he knew what it concerned, but he played along. He moved his papers to one side of his desk. 'Well Keir?' he asked.

'It's about the Paris conference on Organics in Meteorites.' Keir began.

'You'd like to go with Alan, presumably. You have a paper? It's a bit late but I suppose you might just about manage a poster session.'

'I don't have a paper,' Keir said.

'Ah, well. Case dismissed. You both know the policy.'

Brian glanced down at his watch with a furtiveness which could have been theatrical and then looked Keir squarely in the face. Keir recalled his future childhood pet Labrador, when it asked to be let outside. In spite of his disappointment, he couldn't suppress a smile.

Burton raised an eyebrow, turned to Alan and continued: 'If it was so important, then why didn't you both put in for some external funding?'

'Fair comment,' said Alan.

'Anything else?' Burton asked rhetorically, as if the meeting had concluded.

'Yes,' said Alan. 'I'm particularly busy this next few weeks and I could do with some additional time.'

'Really?' Burton asked.

'So I propose,' Alan said, 'that we send Keir to Paris to present our paper.'

Burton thought for a moment, then adjusted his spectacles and peered at his colleagues. 'Keir isn't a co-author. On the other hand, one could argue it might broaden his view of our research while allowing you to catch up on your work here.'

Burton got up, took a folder from his filing cabinet and withdrew several printed sheets.

'Actually,' he continued, 'it would be useful if Wilson here could let us have a similar report of the Paris visit, including his contacts.' Burton conceded a conspiratorial smirk and, addressing Keir, added: 'A second chance, if you will. In Paris, you're unlikely to be recognised and could get on with the job without being interrupted. You might even find useful contacts for your PhD work.' Burton then winked at Alan and keyed himself a note on his laptop.

'Permission granted, then?' Asked Keir.

'Yes. I'll email you both a note, shortly.' Turning again to Keir, he said, 'There'll have to be something for your back pocket. And possibly a late registration fee, about which I'm not too pleased.'

'Thanks, Professor,' Keir said as he and Alan arose to leave.

'There's just one other thing, Alan, before you go.' Burton wasn't finished; the smirk had returned. 'Can you teach maths? Of course you can! Sorry, Alan, no insult intended. Thing is, after the reading week, I'll be extremely busy this semester. Would you mind covering my Monday morning first year astronomy tutorials? Orbital dynamics. Should be a doddle.'

Alan no longer wondered why things had gone quite so smoothly.

'I suppose so, yes.' He realised that it would be futile to protest how rusty he'd become after years of specialising in other fields. Burton would know that already. Such considerations were simply deemed irrelevant.

'Thanks, Alan. That's a great help. Ask John Slater to timetable it, will you?'

'I hope I haven't landed you in it!' Keir said after they left.

'Not really, it was bound to happen sooner or later,' Alan said philosophically. 'Always remember, Burton's favours have their price.'

'And, it seems, ulterior motives,' added Keir.

'Aye, laddie. Considering you've kept yourself mainly in the background with your head down for so long, you're learning well.'

*****

Paris, Tuesday 20 July. The conference, Sorbonne University.
The City of Paris sweltered in a heat haze. Outside the conference building, children spent their parents' money on

copious supplies of ice cream. As the hours passed, the temperature climbed higher and many of the more sensible people took refuge under café parasols or stayed indoors.

Keir glanced down at his link-set which displayed a copy of the conference programme. He scrolled to Day Two and noted the three papers on meteorite research that had already been presented. Now Keir's turn had arrived.

Professor Lucien Fournier, Deputy Head of the Paris Observatory and principal organiser of the conference, occupied the Chair.

'The next paper,' he announced, 'is by Professor Brian Burton and Dr. Alan Menzies from the School of Earth Sciences at Oakingwell University, England. It will be presented by their research student, Mr. Keir Wilson, in the absence of his colleagues, who send their apologies.'

*****

Having already studied Burton's and Menzies' work in depth and drawing on his experience of conferences in the future world, Keir delivered the paper and fielded two of the questions at the end without difficulty.

'Just one more question, please.' Professor Fournier singled out a tall clean shaven man in the third row, who stood up to announce himself.

'Lemaître, Sorbonne. Could Mr. Wilson please show again the set of equations in Figure Four? There's one that seems to be incorrect.'

Keir froze. Delegates in the audience cast each other glances. He hoped that nobody noticed the beads of sweat on his forehead. *Trust him to ask the kind of question I was dreading.* It had been the equation of most difficulty during his study of the paper.

'Indeed,' said Keir, 'let's see what the problem is.'

The questioner grimaced impatiently as Keir clicked through his diagrams on the screen.

'Thank you,' Lemaître said. 'You'll see that the coefficient of the second term is given as alpha squared. Wouldn't it make more sense if you wrote alpha to the power three over two?'

In the electric silence, Keir studied the contentious equation. Should he dismiss it with: Shall we look at that later? Or: Actually, my colleague Dr Menzies could answer that. No. He must fight on his own and hope to win. Suddenly, he noticed his own printed copy of the paper poking out from behind his notes. He grabbed the document and scanned quickly to the paragraph involved.

'I do apologise for the typing error in my presentation,' Keir said. 'You will see that in the actual paper, as reproduced for the Conference Proceedings, the equation is correct.' He switched attention to Lemaître, adding: 'Many thanks for bringing that to our notice.'

The delegate nodded curtly, his face expressionless. Keir felt a wave of relief. Anyone can make a simple typo. Still, he should have checked more carefully.

'Thank you, Mr. Wilson.' Professor Fournier said.

Keir bowed his head courteously and left the rostrum to the sound of spirited applause, interestingly with Lemaître joining in. Soon it would be time for a lunch break.

*****

In the atrium, not far from the dining hall, the clock showed nine minutes to lunch.

Keir looked around. Not unlike some of the conferences he'd attended in the future world, although many of those had been electronic. He recalled that the best times to make contacts would be during interludes such as this. As the shuffling queue continued to leave the lecture theatre, he noticed Lemaître a few paces ahead. Keir drew level.

'Hi! Excuse me,' Keir said. *There is something about the eyes... and the man's set of small but perfect teeth.* 'Have we met before?'

'Yes we've already been introduced, after a fashion, Keir.'

'Forgive me, when was it?'

'The name's Jean-Paul Vivien Lemaître.'

'Hey! You're Viv, aren't you? But didn't Rowena say you were from Graphic Design?'

'Correct. I'm based at the Sorbonne but seconded to Oakingwell for a year. Among other things, I'm helping Rowena with problems in computer graphics. Simulations of planetary accretion in the early solar system. Quite important implications for astrobiolgy.'

'Yes, I agree. Where is Rowena, by the way?'

'Not here. She's got 'flu. I'm giving her paper tomorrow morning. Coming along?'

'I'll be at a meeting with Lucien Fournier.'

'Oh, sorry you can't make it, then. Have you seen our printed paper in the Conference Proceedings?'

'Not yet, but I intend to,' said Keir.

'I might as well tell you now, don't expect miracles. In a few months, our computer work'll be overshadowed by the Edinburgh crowd using Pandora. Anyway, must dash off now. Nice meeting you again. Have fun, Keir.'

'Hope the paper goes well,' Keir shouted after him, adding under his breath, 'It's your turn now, squire. I hope the audience asks you some interesting questions!'

As Viv melted into the crowd, Keir noticed he walked with a slight limp. He looked strikingly different from when they'd met in the Gregson Bar with his shimmering apparel. Here, his true complexion dark and his manner more self-assertive.

'A joker in the pack,' Keir murmured.

*****

Crossing the atrium, Keir looked for delegates from further afield. He turned to a bald headed man of indeterminate age who happened to be standing next to him. The identity tag pinned to the lapel of his tweed jacket read: Academician Ilya Karpov, Moscow Planetary Institute.

In anticipation, the delegate smiled at him affably.

'Good morning,' he said, with a heavy Russian accent.

'Hi. I'm Keir Wilson, from Oakingwell, UK.'

Karpov lowered his gaze to Keir's lapel badge and nodded as they shook hands.

'I'm Ilya Karpov. *Da*! Yes, your university. I've heard of it!' he said.

Keir thought hard, trying to recollect any papers by this researcher. The name sounded familiar but he couldn't place it.

'Did you arrive here with any colleagues?' Keir asked, trying not to sound like an official investigator. He'd never visited Russia, his historical vision of the country being coloured by accounts of the cold war periods and classical spy thrillers. They drifted together in a sea of delegates toward the dining area.

Ilya Karpov said, 'I've come with the lady you see over there. I will introduce you when she has stopped talking.' He gave Keir a knowing wink.

Keir nodded and looked in the direction indicated by Ilya. The woman seemed in her early thirties, trim of figure and wearing a blue and white plaited headband. She looked vivacious and self-assured, with brownish hair and a pale complexion. Her narrow eyes sparkled as she conversed happily with an older, taller woman who had darker hair, flecked with grey.

The headband bobbed distinctively in the crowd, which milled slowly around the buffet tables. He tried not to stare. Too late. Just as he averted his gaze, a flashing eye caught him. Like a snapshot, the glance had gone. But he knew that for an infinitesimal slice of time there had been a communication. He tried not to notice that he had started blushing uncontrollably. This really is stupid, he thought. Back home she's probably married with six kids. Anyway, this is a simulation, isn't it?

Keir made a show of loosening his necktie as he turned to Ilya.

'Glad when this heatwave is over,' he heard himself say.

'*Da*!' Ilya agreed. 'Look, they've opened the windows here. Of course, it is so hot outside that I'm sure it will have the opposite effect!' The Russian laughed and then scratched a fleshy ear, as if he now pondered a different matter.

'You presented your paper very well. How is your research going at your Oakingwall University?' he asked.

'Fine and on track, thank you, Dr. Karpov. Oaking*well*, it is actually,' Keir said. Then he added quickly: 'I'm in the final year of my PhD. It's on mineral luminescence in meteorites.'

'I remember now, that was an excellent review paper you wrote last year.'

'Er, thank you...' More 'memories'.

During his flight to Paris, Keir had read his two papers pre-dating his arrival into the virtual world. Weird! But a useful check on his implanted knowledge.

'So, I think you should definitely talk with my colleague, Valentina Gazetny,' Ilya said.

Keir felt unprepared for his next encounter with the woman wearing the headband, who lithely threaded her way across the room to join them. Ilya made the introductions and the group sat down together.

Valentina Gazetny? Keir recalled seeing her name on the list of delegates in the conference literature pack. Then he remembered the paper that Kirsti had given him in Kuopio.

Academicians Karpov and Gazetny had published a joint paper on what he considered to be tenuous evidence for intelligent life in the universe. The exact title still eluded him, but now he observed her plain gold wedding ring and that she dressed neatly in warm pastel shades, with a white collar.

Ilya stood slightly aside as if to let them talk.

'Ilya has mentioned your PhD research and we know of your group's interests in meteorites,' Dr. Gazetny said. 'Years ago I did some work on luminescence. But now the carbonaceous chondrites are of particular interest to us.' Her accent sounded much less obvious than Ilya's and thankfully this direct meeting had the opposite effect to what Keir had anticipated. He felt attracted but completely at ease in her company. Perhaps her clear sign of being married helped.

He marshalled his thoughts, searching for words to maintain continuity.

'Yes. Forgive me, I'm trying to remember the details of a paper you wrote with Ilya some while ago,' he said.

'Hmm. Which one, I wonder?' Then she smiled and nodded to Ilya. A brief exchange in Russian produced two reprints, which he handed to Keir from his folder. Keir thanked him and noted that neither paper matched the one given to him by Kirsti. He saw that they were both translations in English from different Russian journals; one entitled: 'Complex organic molecules in extra-terrestrial material. A survey.'

'You will see that this publication is a little old now,' Valentina said, 'but in the next survey we hope to cover the Kuopio meteorite fall. After that, we hope to publish a separate paper to include the outcome of any investigations on this meteorite.'

'*Da*,' agreed Ilya, 'we could send you copies, when they are ready.'

'Yes, please!' Keir tried to find a way of repaying them. 'I just hope that what I have here will interest you.' He dug into his folder and extracted a reprint of a recent paper by Burton and his research student, Frank. With difficulty, he concealed his irritation at seeing Burton's name as principal rather than second author.

'I'm surprised these authors are not present at this meeting,' Valentina said, 'We've met them before.'

'Indeed?' Keir said, 'They're probably working on their next paper. Well, I know Frank Higham is anyway.'

'Good! Then they are forgiven.' Valentina's eyes sparkled and Keir began to feel stirred again. She continued: 'Have you thought much about any further implications of their work?'

'Biologically significant material in meteorites?' Keir asked.

He sensed they were both watching him intently. Although Valentina's hair looked plain brownish, something about its texture held his attention.

'More than that,' said Ilya. 'Extraterrestrial life. Intelligent extraterrestrial life, that is.'

Keir turned to face Ilya, not knowing quite what to say. He knew that to evade this controversial issue by claiming it's not really his subject would be lame and possibly insulting in the face of their obvious enthusiasm. His connection with Burton could be their reason for mentioning it, but their insistence puzzled him. He took three plates from a table and passed two of them to his companions. As they began selecting portions to eat, he forced a smile.

'Concrete evidence of higher life forms elsewhere in the universe would be really interesting,' he managed to say. 'But I think it would be more fruitful to search for radio or laser signals than traces in meteorites.'

Back in his future reality, Keir recalled a time when he'd been more enthusiastic about ET life. But now he didn't entertain serious ideas about the subject. Apart, that is, from the 2003 incident that he'd grafted into this virtual world for the RIPE project. This might be a good opportunity to get their take on the situation. Perhaps the substantiated report of an alien encounter could be fuelling their enthusiasm.

'What are your thoughts about the 2003 incident?' he asked.

'Which incident is that?' Valentina asked.

Keir tried not to look confounded. If neither of these specialist companions know anything about it, then who does? He'd assumed at the beginning that everybody in the virtual world, including his Oakingwell colleagues, would have known. As part of the project brief, he'd agreed to wait at least a few days for other people to raise the matter. His strategy of remaining silent while logging the conversations seemed the way forward. But so far, nobody had mentioned it! He felt the pressure unbearable. Even so, he would stick to his brief.

'Sorry, I was thinking of something else,' he said. *Had the encounter incident been dismissed out of hand, or is it being suppressed? Or both.*

All too shortly after their meal, the five minute bell rang to signify the impending start of the afternoon session. Delegates began moving in the directions of the lecture theatres.

Broaching a new subject, Ilya said, 'You've heard that Pandora has recently simulated the reconstruction of simple cellular organisms using DNA sequence data?'

'That's right!' Keir recalled. 'I saw the holographic 3D displays on the web a couple of days ago.'

Ilya and Valentina were attentive but hanging back as they approached the linking corridor where Valentina paused to check a programme list posted on the wall.

'We must leave soon,' she explained. She tilted her head slightly and inflicted upon him another disarming smile. 'We fly back to Moscow tonight. It has been so nice to meet you.'

As she shook his hand, he felt a pang of loss.

'*Da*! Best wishes with your work, Keir. Keep in touch,' Ilya said, grasping Keir's still outstretched hand with a huge warm grip. 'See you perhaps on email!'

'Thank you both. Have a good journey.'

As Keir continued along the short corridor towards the lecture theatre, he glanced over his shoulder. Valentina give him a quick wave from the far end of the buffet lounge.

*****

The conference's afternoon agenda included two parallel sessions. Normally, Keir would have gone to the presentations on Near Earth Objects but instead chose Computation. He took his place in the third row for the first paper of the afternoon. The subject: Pandora.

Professor Rosemary Clarke looked young for her post. Late twenties or early thirties, Keir surmised. She had a remarkable track record of journal publications. *A bit off the beaten track for my brief,* Keir thought. But he admired her work and some of her group's freeware he'd downloaded ran exceptionally well. More 'memories'. *Never mind, let's press on.*

Rosemary began by outlining her computer hardware setup at the Edinburgh Institute for Intelligent Systems. Nothing out of the ordinary, Keir thought. That is, until she described their Pandora network node and its human-computer interface. As he recalled his Galena-propelled foray into this world of 2010, up flashed a screen image of a headset being worn by one of her colleagues. It looked like a much earlier version of the one used at RIPE. Early model or not, surely it's classified? Keir's thoughts were confirmed a moment later.

'I can't divulge much about this,' Rosemary said, 'because it's on loan from the army. But we can assure you of its functionality as a facilitator for the near total immersion experience of the operator. Over here...' she indicated the right hand side of the illustration, 'is an external 3D monitor screen for viewing in the laboratory whatever the operator sees as he or she follows the execution of the software.'

Rosemary paused to take a drink of water. She continued: 'You may have found the title of this talk, "Pandora: An Avatar Amongst the Genes" a little strange,' she continued. 'We thought the idea behind the project a bit strange, too. Even so, we tried it. Essentially, we've harnessed virtual reality to the exploration of genotype-phenotype matching and prediction. Other workers are attempting this, but as you'll find in our Introduction, our unique approach relies upon the excellent previous collaborative work of Tanskanen in Finland and Savage in the UK. Our paper's references nine to seven list their publications. In a nutshell, they've adapted the well proven self-organising neural net schemes of Kohonen to their new computer architecture. And the computer system itself has contributed significantly to raising its architecture to higher levels, through several stages. This is still ongoing, as we speak.'

Rosemary used her remote to show several slides of the hardware from various angles. She continued:

'At Edinburgh, we, including Dr. Mike Savage, have designed and tested the human-computer interface. If you'll forgive the cliché, and with due acknowledgement to Aesop's Fables, we called our system Pandora, because when we started, we didn't know what we were letting ourselves in for. And indeed, as you'll see from the details in Section Two of our paper, which considers what happens when Pandora accepts data which it considers too sparse, the outcomes can sometimes be unpredictable. Hence the need for occasional human intervention.

In Section Three, we've taken DNA and RNA precursors and simulated their assembly into patterns corresponding to chromosome structures for the E. Coli bacillus. By including further models representing the environment of the cell nucleus we've achieved simulated reconstruction of the genome of E.Coli and can show an example phenotype expression here...'

Rosemary clicked the remote. Her next slide showed a roughly tubular object like a bacterium.

Many in the auditorium murmured in approval. Several delegates applauded.

Keir joined in. The idea crossed his mind that one day she might be able to produce an image of Burton in his birthday suit from a fingernail clipping. He must have been the only one laughing. For an instant, Rosemary fixed on him with a brief but quizzical stare. Then she continued:

'Of course, we're a long way from being able to express the human genome, but we felt our technique would be useful for investigating primitive life forms, including those that could possibly be derived from the organic materials in meteorites. So, in Section Four we've explored organic substances found in carbonaceous chondrites. And although many pieces of the jigsaw are missing, we've arrived at a few tentative phenotype images.'

Her remote clicked to invoke the next slide. Keir heard several gasps in the audience.

'You'll find more details in the paper, but here there's only time to summarise our conclusions. Here is the final slide. You'll notice that in Section Five, the main conclusion is that essentially...' Rosemary gathered her papers together on the rostrum as she concluded: '...in our virtual reality technique, the involvement of human observer-operators is vital for this type of computer architecture. We rely on pattern recognition, for which the human brain is particularly effective. In Section Six, Future Prospects, we map out likely future areas for progress, the next step being a paper on Pandora's own assessment of human attributes for interfacing.'

'Thank you, Professor Clarke,' said Fournier, almost drowned out by the applause. 'Unfortunately, we're over-running our schedule,' he remarked, 'There's just time for one question.'

Keir grimaced; beaten to the initiative by a fraction of a second. Not Viv again!

'Lemaître, Sorbonne. Could Professor Clarke please clarify the extent to which the brains of observer-operators, as she calls them, have to become integrated with Pandora's architecture?'

There followed an outline description of the neurological connection between human and machine. Keir noted that, as with Galena, the connections were not invasive but essentially wireless. Important details were classified and the reply necessarily brief. Viv appeared satisfied. He had no option.

Keir pulled out his link-set and used it to update his notes on events so far. He reviewed his last page of text, ending with the question:

'Why no public mention of 2003 incident?'

Under Actions, he wrote: Give it a couple of days then talk to Bosworth. But first, compare Pandora with Galena. Need to visit E. Institute. Then, instinctively, he shielded the little screen with his hand and prepared to leave.

'Oops!' Keir said, at a tall figure standing over him.

'No worries,' the man said, 'I'm just going. Sorry to block your way.'

The delegate smiled but his eyes were expressionless.

Keir rose from his seat, collected his belongings and moved along his row towards the exit. He looked around but the stranger had gone.

*****

4 A Step Too Far

Paris, later that day.

At the afternoon break, as Keir left the dining hall, Professor Fournier met him near the doorway.

'I was impressed by your contribution, Mr. Wilson,' he said, reaching into his folder. 'Here is a message for you from Oakingwell. Perhaps you should open it later, somewhere quiet. See you tomorrow at the observatory.'

Back at his hotel, Keir opened the sealed envelope. Instructions from Burton, hand written and headed: 'For your eyes only. Read and destroy immediately.'

Keir committed the contents to memory, then tore the note into small pieces and consigned them to the en-suite toilet.

'My head of department's paranoid,' Keir murmured. 'That's all I need.'

*****

The next morning, Keir took the Paris Metro and met Professor Lucien Fournier at the Paris Observatory, Meudon.

'Welcome, Keir! I'll show you around - just briefly, then we must leave,' the deputy director said.

After the short tour, they made their way to a restored classic Citroen *Traction Avant*, a 'Light 15', at a garage to the rear of the administration block. Fournier carried a briefcase. In the car, he opened it to reveal several small sealed plastic jars with screw caps. Keir recognised the labelling. Tanskanen's group.

Accompanying documentation included notes on contents description and handling. Each jar of meteorite fractions had a destination address label to one of several assigned Principal Investigators. He noticed that two of the names on the list of nine were Academician Ilya Y. Karpov and Professor Rosemary Clarke.

Fournier handed Keir a jar marked: Kuopio Chondrite Ku-006-05, the delivery address being that of Professor Brian Burton at Oakingwell.

*****

Oakingwell, Tuesday 27 July, 10:00pm.

The door to Frank's room being ajar, Keir stepped inside.

'Hi Keir! To what do we owe this visitation? Grab a chair.' Frank worked at a cluttered table near a window.

'Thanks, Frank. I heard that you worked with Gazetny and Karpov. How long have you known them?'

'About eighteen months. Something I've been doing on the side, hoping to be a co-author of a joint paper with them. Anyway, we'll see. Remind me, do you take sugar?'

'Half please. Did they make any mention of extraterrestrial life?' Keir asked in a casual manner.

'Yes.' Frank looked attentively at his computer screen, his face reflecting the colours of the scrolling pages. 'What's your view, Keir?'

'I don't know.' Keir replied. 'A few scientists seem to be taking it seriously these days. I mean reputable people.'

'True, I suppose,' Frank said. 'My own interest stems from a report on the web.'

'What report was that?' Keir couldn't disguise his keen interest.

'An alien encounter story. Denmark, back in 2003.'

'What did you make of it?' Keir felt the hairs on his neck bristle.

'You've heard about it, then?' Frank asked.

'You're the very first person to tell me,' Keir said.

'All I remember is a current affairs web page quoting short extracts from a newspaper. Don't ask me its name. It reported a school kid playing truant, who reckoned he was confronted by something that looked like a pile of sand on the beach. Then it changed colour and flashed messages at him. That intrigued me, but there was precious little detail and no follow-up.'

'None at all?'

'That's right. I surfed around all that evening but it was the only report I could find. When I looked next day, the original web site had been taken down. Anyway, never mind that. Sounds to me like you've other things on your mind.'

In the pause that followed, Keir decided to put the matter of aliens on hold, unless it arose again.

'What do you think of Karpov and Gazetny, as people I mean?' he asked.

Frank smiled enigmatically at the computer screen: 'Karpov's extremely thorough and I get the feeling he's occupied with things other than science. And she's nice. I take it you've observed?'

'I also noticed she's married. Probably got a tribe of kids. And a husband like…'

'Someone with six-pack and biceps?' Frank interrupted, switching his attention back to the screen.

'You mean she's married to some champion athlete?'

Frank edited more text before responding with a grin: 'She *was* married - to a Russian in the military. But I don't know about any children. Or even if Valentina's her real name.'

'Oh?'

'Yes.' More keyboard tapping, which continued as he spoke: 'The story goes; a few years ago her husband was killed on an assignment in Novaya Zemlya. I wasn't told the details. She never remarried.'

'How did you find that out?' Keir tried to appear detached but felt it hardly worth the effort. Instead, he wiped his brow with his sleeve.

'She has a friend called Irina. I met them both last year at their laboratory in Moscow. A real match maker, that one - I guess she's told Val's life story to every guy who visits the place. But it's no good. As far as I know, Valentina's just not interested, in anyone or anything except her work.'

Frank eased his chair around to face Keir and continued: 'Irina told me that Val got quite shirty with a bloke who tried it on via the sympathy route. And she threatened she wouldn't speak to Irina again if any more was leaked about her private life. Now Irina's a bit more discreet. I say a bit. After a few vodkas she was soon telling me all this.'

'Your Moscow visits,' Keir said. 'Did you find anyone you fancied out there?' He sensed they both knew the identity of 'anyone'.

'Not really. The field is yours, old man. If that's what you want.'

Keir's relief showed.

'I realise she's probably at least five years older than us. And a workaholic.' Keir tried to sound rational, but the memory of that first encounter distracted him.

'I'm sure you're right on both counts. Now it's my turn to be intrigued. In fact, I'm very pleased for you. You've exotic tastes, Keir.'

'So it seems, and thanks for the update. But it's a challenge and a half! Wish I knew how to go about it.'

'Here! Some black coffee.' Frank poured it with a steady hand.

Keir took the mug. If this is a simulation, he thought, it's an extremely convincing one. Hats off to Litchfield, RIPE and Galena! But what are the implications of falling in love with one of the characters in this incredibly detailed and complex virtual world? Keir looked down into the hot, gently swirling coffee. It smelled good. Although it did little to sooth the turbulence in his mind.

Meanwhile, Frank had decided to reach up to a cupboard shelf.

'Keir, have you noticed, the weather's cleared and the moon is up?' He opened a window and handed a pair of 7x50 binoculars to his friend.

Keir 'recalled' their mutual interest in astronomy. But then, the thought struck him. Did he have any memories of the moon seen through binoculars or a telescope? Not in this world. But several in his future world. 'OK, let's have a look,' he said.

Frank passed him the binoculars. Silence.

'Are you all right? Frank asked.

Keir remained speechless. *Where is the crater Aristarchus?* He blinked, but the image remained unchanged in a cloudless sky. While all other features seemed in order, Aristarchus was definitely missing. He knew that in his future world, this crater had been a familiar feature throughout the history of lunar observing. He felt his heart thumping.

'You don't look too well, Keir. 'Frank said. 'Here, have the rest of your coffee and sit down a while.'

*****

11:20am next morning, Brian Burton's office.

After sifting through his emails, Burton noticed that the in-tray on his desk contained a brown envelope and an overdue notice from the library. The latter disclosure elicited an oath, but sandwiched between the library notice and envelope were two faxes. One expected, but the second not addressed to him. He saw that it had been included by mistake. He picked it up and studied the text of the message. Deep in thought, Burton read it again and then reached for his mobile, an official link-set, then paused.

'If I phone them,' he muttered, 'they'll know I've read the fax.' Instead, he walked round to a photocopier in the department office.

'Hello, Brian!' Carole looked up from her secretarial tasks. Burton grunted an acknowledgement and went over to the stack of pigeon holes. He placed the original copy of the fax in Keir's internal post and then returned to his office. He filed the photocopy away and sat at his desk. His thoughtful gaze drifted towards the gleaming facets of a large quartz crystal paperweight. He lifted it a couple of inches from a pile of papers then slammed it down again.

'What on Earth has Wilson been up to?' he asked himself. Yielding to the pressure of events, he pressed his intercom switch.

'Hi, Carole! Would you please get me this Moscow number via the main switchboard, then patch it through to my extension?'

*****

11:30am. Alan Menzies' office.

Alan Menzies put his copy of Keir's report of the Paris conference back in its folder.

'Nice work, Keir, and I heard it was a good presentation.'

'Thanks again for your help, Alan.' Keir said. 'Sorry you had to pick up Burton's orbital dynamics class.'

'Yes. I've a good mind to delegate it to you!' Alan said. 'It's all right. I was just winding you up.'

But Keir's thoughts were elsewhere. He couldn't disclose Burton's instructions, only act on them.

'I want to visit Kuopio in Finland simultaneously with Dr. Gazetny from Moscow Planetary Institute. Following the accident, Tansys plans to recover more samples of the meteorite,' Keir explained. 'Most of the recovered first batch was collected by Tanskanen's group and sent to Paris. The rest, a few grams, went to Kuopio University for their assistance with the search.'

'Look, Keir. Couldn't you just ask Tanskanen and Fournier to send you some?' Alan asked. 'You know that there just isn't the time to apply externally for travel funding and receive it in a realistic timescale. So it'll cost us daft money, not to mention the subsistence and accommodation.'

'It needn't be for long, just a couple of days.' Keir's voice had an edge of desperation. He must have Alan's support while not mentioning Burton's clandestine tactics. His own intervention by email to include Valentina in the plan had been unauthorized. That she'd responded - even positively - by fax worried him. He continued: 'I could try asking the Finns; say, Tansys, for support. Perhaps in exchange for a seminar on our work here.'

'Interesting. You think you can raise more money for the Department? You act like a politician. Whether that's for better or worse, who can say? Burton had better watch out.'

'It's worth a try. I need to be out there because I know what to look for!'

'OK, OK! If you can get the Finns to come up with something, I'll see if we can match it from somewhere. But no promises, mind! It would need Burton's signature.'

Keir knew that would be no problem; his instructions in Paris were clear. But keeping his supervisor in the dark seemed like betrayal. Keir felt enmeshed in something bigger than both of them, Kirsti's warning ringing in his head.

*****

Monday 2 August, 11:15am local: Tansys.

Terve! Hello. You've made good time, Valentina!' Kirsti Kivi commented.

'Hello. Yes, no problems. Great to see you!'

After lunch, Kirsti and Valentina made their way back from the ground floor restaurant of the Teknia building of Kuopio University to the Tansys complex, situated among the trees on the other side of the main road which ran through the campus of Kuopio University.

'We should enjoy a fine weather walk, Valentina, down to the lake.'

They made their way past the collection of low buildings, which included Kirsti's laboratory, following an unpaved track in a forest of tall conifers, silver birch and spindly rowan trees. The air felt warm, with the odour of bracken.

'I didn't see you at the Paris conference, Kirsti.'

'I intended to go, but the meteorite fall and its consequences have taken up so much of our time here. The paperwork, too, for shipping out more of the samples. I think people must eat them! You know Brodie at Edinburgh? Well, he was on the phone continually. Tried to persuade me to part with another eight grams of material. Yes, eight grams! That's over a third of the amount we've managed to salvage so far, and more than twice as much as the amount we sent to Merriweather in the States.'

'That is a lot, considering the losses!' Valentina concurred.

'*Voi!* Perhaps if we give it all away we could get on with the backlog of our other research.'

'I think Edinburgh is making good use of it, though, Kirsti. I heard from Keir that Ilya and I missed a good paper by Clarke. Have you heard what they found?'

'Yes, fragments of DNA precursors.'

'Well, it's much more than that. Let's go over here and sit down; is that permitted here?' Valentina saw that they had arrived at a lakeside jetty with a large painted sign in Finnish: University Fish Research Centre.

'No problem, let's sit on these rocks by the jetty.'

The pair of them looked out across the lake, bordered by dense forest as far as the horizon, above which the cloud-flecked ice blue of the northern sky seemed strangely incongruous in the summer warmth. The water looked smooth as glass, except for patches of faint wind ripples farther out towards a distant tree-clad promontory, and for the occasional plop of small fish. Valentina stretched her legs, probing with a heel until she found a place to rest her feet among the rattling stones.

'Marvellous here, Kirsti. So quiet.'

Kirsti followed her companion's gaze across the water.

'To think it's just one of over a hundred thousand lakes in our country, but I think you'll know that already,' she said.

'Yes, I'm Karelian,' Valentina said, 'Are you from Kuopio?'

'I'm from near Pori, on the west coast.'

'You'll miss the jazz festivals, then.'

'I do. But it's good when we occasionally come down here to have lunch. Yesterday someone played a kantele while her friend recited from the Kalevala.' Turning over a pebble with her toe, Kirsti continued: 'I think you were about to tell me what the Edinburgh group is up to.'

'I had to leave the conference before Clarke's paper. Another delegate told me the essentials. As we expected, they're making full use of Pandora. They gave it all the relevant data from the organic content in the first batch of meteorite material you sent them. It came up with a graphical display of a bacillus like E.Coli. Tests confirm that it wasn't caused by contamination from the fall area or the laboratory staff. So it's almost certain that the E.Coli-like bacillus in the meteorite was extra-terrestrial.'

'Valentina, I'm no biologist. The only things I know about E.Coli are what they taught me at school - that it lives in the intestines of animals and helps digest their food. And through the media we've learned that some strains can cause serious infection.'

Valentina put a hand on her shoulder. 'Your first statement about E. Coli. Follow your reasoning through,' she said.

'You mean this bacillus was in something else's gut?'

'Maybe, if it's anything like the ones here on Earth.'

'You infer there are higher animals out there?' Kirsti raised her head, as if looking far out beyond the confines of the sky. 'You're claiming that someone's proved it at last?'

'Forgive me; I'm always suspicious of the word 'proved'. At present, it's mere speculation; at best, the evidence is circumstantial. And as we know, the meteorite is many millions of years old. Thousands of millions. It sounds far-fetched to me.'

'I'm inclined to agree with you,' Kirsti said, 'but I'm not in the driving seat.'

'Who is?'

'Here, it's Professor Tanskanen.'

Valentina picked up a pebble and rolled it in her fingers, regarding it intently: 'No wonder they want more of the stuff. They've decided to look for the host, haven't they? The animal carrier of this bacterium!'

'For our part,' Kirsti said, 'What do you think about practicalities? If I gave them the whole of our remaining stock of meteorite fragments it could only be a tiny proportion of what they'd need.'

'Possibly,' said Valentina. 'Even so, I suggest we treat Edinburgh on an equal footing to other investigators.'

As they climbed up the bank, Kirsti checked her watch. 'Our visitor will be at the airport round about now,' she said. 'He's expected at my office in about half an hour.'

'You've already met Keir Wilson?' Valentina asked.

*****

1:30pm. Kirsti's office.

Lauri Tiihonen knocked politely on Kirsti's door.

'Terve! Welcome, Lauri! Please - over here. I'll get you some coffee.'

Kirsti seated her guest, poured him a cup from the refreshments trolley and went through the introductions.

Lauri bowed his head toward Keir, who returned a quick nod and a smile. Lauri continued his observations, noticing that when the lad's eyes strayed to Valentina, he would look back to the table top again.

'Toivon ole hyvää matkaa!' Lauri said, extending a warm, firm hand. Keir rose and they shook hands.

'Lauri hopes you had a good journey, Keir,' Kirsti translated. 'He has very little English.'

'Kyllä varmasti, kiitos! Yes indeed, thank you,' Keir replied with hardly disguised surprise. Had Litchfield's computer programmed him with a Finnish phrase book?

But now that the ice had broken, Kirsti waited for Lauri and Keir to make themselves comfortable and asked Lauri to produce his map, which she then spread out on the table.

'This is the area on the west shore of Kolmisoppi which will be familiar to everyone except Valentina and Keir,' she said.

At the sound of these names in conjunction, Keir took an extra grip on himself, concentrating on Kirsti's voice. She addressed the meeting in her fluent American English, her accent quite different to Valentina's…

He snapped out of his reverie with an apology: 'Sorry Kirsti, I missed that. Did you say some of it struck the roof of the sauna hut? Is that here, near the south side of the cottage?'

'Yes. But I mentioned that a good twenty seconds ago. We're talking now about this demarcated area between the dry well and the summer cottage. Don't worry if you missed the details, I can see you're a bit tired from travelling, but we haven't much time. The important area for us tomorrow will be here.' Kirsti stabbed her finger at a zone north of the summer cottage.

'Lauri thinks he saw a splash near the actual shoreline,' she continued. 'We know that the level of the lake will be slightly lower now, because of the recent spell of dry weather. The splash was partly hidden by this reed-bed, but Lauri thinks the fragment landed where the shore is more stony. I believe there's a good chance of finding something tomorrow morning. I'll give you all copies of the schedule now and in a couple of hours we'll have something to eat round at my place. We'd better leave in ten minutes.'

'So soon?' Valentina asked.

'Yes. First, there's the sauna! Even now Kalevi will be starting up the stove. Then we join him for a drink.' Kirsti turned to Keir: 'And I can assure you, we'll all feel much better after the sauna!'

*****

2:30pm, Oakingwell University.

In the departmental tea room, Alan Menzies registered pleasant surprise when Burton handed him a copy of the signed leave-of-absence form for Keir's current visit to Finland. Even with Tanskanen's financial contribution, Burton had to find a significant top-up.

'Fortunately, Alan, there was no problem,' Burton said, 'I found some residue in the travel account which had to be spent by the end of this month, or we'd lose it. No point in trying to spend next year's money is there?'

'Thanks, Brian.' Alan tried to sound casual, playing down the event, but characteristically Burton had not quite finished.

'I'd like a full report, of course. Wilson must document everything. And I want to know about everyone he meets; where and when; what meetings are scheduled and between whom; what projects are running, who does what. The whole works.'

'Sure. But why this level of detail, Brian?'

'And I sent him a memo to that effect, so you don't have to say anything.'

Alan's jaw dropped.

'All right, Alan, I'll explain. My office in ten minutes?'

*****

Tuesday 3 August, 11:00am, Lake Kolmisoppi.

'*Ei kiitos,* Lauri! No thanks!' Keir politely declined to use the large pair of wading boots which Lauri had offered.

He said to Kirsti: 'Tell him that's just in case my big feet throw up clouds of fine silt from the bed of the lake. I'll start by observing from the bank with polarising glasses. Granted, it might be more difficult in places because of overhangs of tufted grass and tree roots near the water's edge.'

Kirsti translated his explanation for Lauri.

'*Eipä kestä!* No problem', Lauri said.

'By the way,' Kirsti said, '*your* Finnish is coming along nicely, Keir. It's marvellous what education you can have in the sauna, isn't it?'

Ten minutes into the search, Keir heard a shout:

'I've found something in the water!' Valentina had started to climb up the bank a short distance ahead. He ran forward involuntarily. When he grabbed her hand, she gripped him firmly. She leaped towards him, physically fit but light and agile; for Keir, an experience she could hardly have guessed. Or could she? Valentina looked up at him.

'Thank you, Keir!'

She stood, before him, framed by the lake, the sunlit trees and the sky. Her eyes were a curious warm grey, full of life and energy. An electric surge ran through him and he felt his knees weaken but rallied with an effort. He followed the direction of her find and heard himself say: 'Well done, Valentina.'

'I hope so, we shall see! You're an expert, Keir. You could climb down and identify it. But we'll be polite, shall we, and let Kirsti check it out?' Valentina laughed, giving him that sharp, darting glance he knew.

'It's down here; I haven't removed it,' she called across to Kirsti, who immediately came running.

'Let's see. Excellent work, Valentina!'

Keir stepped down the bank to where a disturbance among the stones below the surface suggested the point of impact. The crumbling mass had been an oblong object, but now had split into three parts. Keir estimated its total weight to be about two hundred grams, a very good specimen. He looked in Valentina's direction and nodded confirmation of her find. She returned him a wink and, with arms above her head, gave a cry of victory.

'Tonight we celebrate!' Lauri's voice reverberated above the shouting. 'Here, at my summer cottage!' he continued, evoking a roar of approval.

*****

7:45pm that evening.

It seemed to Keir more like late afternoon. The trees and lake were motionless. In the pale blue silence of the sky, the sun still above the northwest horizon, painting with its orange light a few slowly drifting strands of cloud. At almost eight o'clock, generous helpings of barbecued *muikku* fish from the lake were being served after the customary sauna; for Keir, the aroma of them was seductive. A few minutes ago, he had emerged from the sauna, accompanied by the other men in the party, in full view of the women who directed most of their attention to preparation of the meal.

After he'd dried off and dressed, someone offered Keir a portion of the lightly smoked salmon in its wrapping of *rieska*, a kind of soft, unleavened bread. Heikki, Kirsti's chief technician, attended to a well used smoke box of welded sheet iron, in which he'd previously placed a layer of juniper chippings before enclosing the raw fish and positioning it on the log fire.

'You like?' Kier turned at Lauri's heavily accented, rasping voice, accompanied by a glazed smile, as he held out what appeared to be a bottle of pale greenish wine.

'Sure, *kiitos*, Lauri!' Keir said, as the pale liquid swilled uncertainly into his glass. Lauri beamed affably and went around the other guests, charging their glasses in turn.

Keir eyed his glass carefully but unobtrusively. He recalled that even at the initial welcome before the sauna, when a litre of fine Finnish beer had been thrust into his hand, he'd noted from a distance the glazed grin that seemed a permanent fixture on Lauri's face.

'Kippis! Cheers!' Lauri raised his drink to the nearest of the assembled company, the firelight dancing and flickering on his beaming face with its three days of silvery stubble.

'Kippis!' They all replied in unison.

'The wine is really good,' Keir said to Heikki, 'the taste is quite subtle.'

Heikki's quizzical gaze alternated between Keir and his drink.

'Good. I'm glad you are enjoying it,' he said, raising his own glass of *Lapin Kulta*, Lappish Gold, beer.

Where Keir sat, the warmth and crackling of the fire were at his back and the cool of the evening on his face. The murmur of conversation rose and fell around him. Apart from the table talk and the sound of hissing and crackling logs, he relished the silence of the forest and the lakeside.

'I think this place, the smell of woodsmoke, the cooking and your excellent green wine will be unforgettable,' Keir said.

As he spoke he turned to Elena, Kirsti's laboratory assistant he had met on his previous visit.

'It's good to see you again,' she said. Her English is improving, Keir noticed.

'You too. Magnificent party! What are you planning for your career, Elena?'

'As you know I am helping Dr. Kivi in her laboratory just now, but I want to study at Helsinki, specialising in architecture. Dr. Kivi tells me that you are completing your Doctorate in planetary sciences.' Her voice sounded quiet and slow but the words were meticulously pronounced, with just a trace of a sharp edge to the consonants.

'That's right', said Keir.

'It sounds exciting', she continued, 'and you are very interested in this meteorite, of course?'

'I make no secret of that!' Keir replied with a smile as he drained his glass.

'*Anteeksi!* I'm sorry! Please forgive me for asking too many questions,' she remarked with an embarrassed smile. She started blushing.

'Oh, no! No problem at all - er - *eipä kestä,* Elena!'

'That was good, Keir! You are learning our language very well already!' Elena had regained her composure and they laughed together.

In the half-light of the late evening, augmented by the glow of the fire, he could see beyond Elena the full length of the table, now with stacked plates and empty bottles. As she continued talking, he could still make out the words but not their meaning. At the far end of the table, Kirsti and Valentina talked together. He watched as Valentina listened intently, the light of the fire dancing in her eyes... the last thing he remembered.

*****

The next morning started clear and bright, a light breeze coming in through a doorway that opened onto a forest path. As he awoke, Keir's vision adjusted to the searing daylight. Slowly he scanned the interior surroundings. Opposite his bed he saw a timbered wall, embellished with a child's drawing of someone on skis, a decorative poster with Finnish text and a photograph of a family group. There were voices outside.

'*Huomenta!* Hello, Keir! Welcome back to planet Earth!' Kirsti stood in the doorway carrying a small tray.

Keir sipped the black coffee, leaning on an elbow.

'I really am sorry, Kirsti! I must have had too much of that wine on top of the beer last night!' Keir said.

'What wine? Ah! You mean the Finnish vodka? Well, one sip of that is too much for me!' she laughed.

'So that was vodka? The green stuff I had.'

'Yes. A Lauri special, flavoured with mint.'

'But I could hardly taste it.'

'That's right. You have to be very careful. I'm sorry, I should have warned you. But I left you on your own when I saw you were having a conversation with Elena. I thought it would be a good opportunity for her to practise English. How do you feel now? Better?'

'Yes, thank you! It's amazing! No hangover at all. I suppose whatever it was must have been very pure. And thanks for the coffee. By the way, where are we?'

Kirsti smiled: 'We put you to bed in the *leikkitalo*, the childrens' play-house part of Lauri's summer cottage. You may be interested to know that it's nearly eleven o'clock, time for lunch.'

Lunch at eleven, Keir thought. I'll be just about used to it when I have to return to Oakingwell and go hungry until after mid-day. His deliberations were interrupted by Elena's attentive cries.

'Oh! Keir! Hello! Good morning - are you all right?'

He saw her look of genuine concern, one of her blue eyes hidden by a fallen lock of long blonde hair. He smiled at her and he noticed her cheeks redden slightly. He knew that she found him attractive, but his thoughts were elsewhere.

'Yes, thank you, Elena. And hello, everyone! Thank you for that marvellous meal last night. I hope I didn't cause you any problems. I don't usually drink that much.'

'*Niin*, well! You celebrated in style, Keir, but we're glad to see you've recovered!' said Kalevi, Kirsti's husband. He smiled as he stirred a large pan of reindeer stew, adding herbs, while Kirsti prepared the table. On another, smaller, table Keir saw a package with a Tansys label and an official looking document.

'Yes, Keir. It's another meteorite sample.' Kirsti said. 'You'll need to sign for it. And I'll have the clearance documents prepared by the time you leave for Manchester airport this afternoon.'

The departure arrangements took Keir by surprise. Also he noted; someone's missing from the lunch table!

'Where's Valentina?' he heard himself say.

'Oh, don't worry, Keir,' Kirsti said, 'She apologises for not saying good-bye. She had a slight accident.'

'What?' Keir felt icy cold as the blood drained from his face. The room fell silent. Elena looked at him awkwardly, her mouth trembling.

'Well actually,' Kirsti said, 'Valentina strained her back last night, when we were putting you to bed.'

'Could you please apologise to Valentina for me?' said Keir, weakly. He happened to be looking in Elena's direction. 'And tell her I hope she's all right soon.'

Elena looked back at him, and then to Kirsti, saying, 'Yes, of course.'

Keir reached across to the smaller table and placed his signature between the two crosses on the document.

*****

5 Edinburgh

Tuesday 10 August, Oakingwell.

L unchtime the following day found Keir again in the Gregson Bar. Alan Menzies sat opposite him. Sandwiches and ale were the fare.

'When I spoke to Brian this morning, ' said Alan, 'he wasn't exactly over pleased.'

'Really?' Keir said. 'Perhaps understandable, though. Most of my time was spent by the lake with Dr. Kivi.'

'But you had a good time, I hear. Opportunities for conversation. Unfortunately, you got stuck with one of the young ladies and then passed out.'

'I didn't know what was in my glass!'

'Don't get me wrong, Keir. This isn't an inquisition. I'd probably have reacted in the same way. It's just that Burton's impatient for information about... goodness knows what. Every detail, he said.'

'I'm glad he's told you why he wanted me out there again. How did he react to my report?'

'He said, "This is not quite what we asked for, but I expect it will do," then filed it away and asked me for my response.'

'If you don't mind my asking, what did you say to that?'

'I told him I believed you were more excited by the find than by anything else. He said, "All right. But for some reason Keir's changed. We need to find out why without making him nervous." Then I suggested we all talk informally at coffee. Perhaps we'd piece things together that way.'

'I'm quite happy with that, Alan. But I can't think of much more to tell him.'

'It would be odd, I must admit, Keir. I may be talking out of line here, so say nothing about this conversation.' Alan leaned forward. 'This business about you and the visits to Finland and elsewhere sanctioned by Burton: they don't exist, right?'

'Don't tell me. The military are involved,' Keir said.

'What makes you think that?'

'Come on, Alan. Are they involved or not?'

'We may be rushing things a bit here.'

'Please tell me what you're going to tell me!'

'OK. They are involved. But again, don't mention it to anyone.'

'I don't get it. At Oakingwell, we already have several student placements with the military! And there are companies like UK Defence Systems that send staff on our technical short courses. What's so unusual in this case, Alan? '

'Frankly, I don't know. I'm told to keep things under wraps and I don't know the reason. Something's going on. And he wants you involved. Don't ask me why.'

Alan reached into his pocket, pulled out a slip of paper and passed it to Keir.

'What's this?' Keir asked.

'This, Keir, is for your next visit. It's a return rail ticket to Edinburgh.'

'*You're* totally in on it, now?' Keir asked.

Alan didn't return Keir's smile.

'In effect, yes. All I can tell you is this: There may be others in on it, as you put it. But each of us operates on a need to know basis. It probably sounds weird, but you'll have to grit your teeth and be patient.'

'Aren't I entitled to know what it's all about?' Keir asked.

'Not until you're told.'

*****

Thursday 12 August, Edinburgh

At 10:05 am, as Keir's train drew in to Waverley station, he recognised Doug Brodie from his web Facebook image. Doug stood close to the barrier, sporting a tweed deerstalker and red tartan tie.

Doug pulled up outside his neat new apartment near Leith, at Portobello. Inside, out of the rain, Doug introduced his wife Ailsa. She had prepared some very welcome coffee with sandwiches and oatcakes.

'I've heard you've been to Paris, Keir,' she said. 'An old college friend of mine runs a B-and-B near there, not far from the observatory at Meudon.'

'That's right,' said Doug. 'She does a full English or Scottish breakfast and the price is very reasonable. I'll give you the address before we leave.'

'Thanks. Always useful to have a recommendation,' Keir said. He noticed that while their empty plates were being collected, a black vinyl document case had appeared on the table.

'Let's stretch our legs a wee bit,' Doug said, putting on a flat cap and handing Keir his coat.

The two scientists took a leisurely stroll down to the beach, rank with the smell of shell-fish and seaweed. Grey waves broke and rattled the shingle.

'Well, Keir. Shall we take a look at some images?' Doug stopped near an entrance ramp to the beach. He extracted a yellow envelope from his document case and handed Keir a pack of five A4 sized colour printouts, each in a transparent plastic wallet.

'I admit, it's not really the best place to study these,' Doug commented as a gust of wind threatened to bend the package, 'but we'll just have a quick look before setting off to the Institute.'

Keir took the folder, entitled 'Kuopio Carbonaceous Chondrite.' The contents included information about the view, magnification and other parameters for each of the enclosed pictures. The first picture showed a dark mottled stone and a ruler marked in centimetres to give an idea of scale. Keir immediately recognised the specimen of rock.

'What about age?' he asked.

'We're still waiting for confirmation. Probably around four thousand million years for the silcates, but I haven't received any indications yet for the carbonaceous components.'

Doug moved on to the third picture, which looked like a spiral arrangement of different sized billiard balls, packed together to form a complex chain. He looked closely at the caption below the picture, '[ST-4]. Series 239.'

'What does ST-4 mean?' Keir asked.

'It refers to the Savage-Tanskanen algorithm,' Doug replied. 'It's the latest in a series of techniques for rendering interpretations of genetic information in terms of image processing and graphics. It's not really an algorithm, though. It's a dynamic reprogramming software suite that uses a self-organising network-based system architecture. It was developed by Tanskanen after he was at Helsinki and while Savage was here.'

'To run on Pandora?' Keir asked.

'Yes, as an integral part of Pandora. You were at the conference?'

'Indeed I was.'

'Shortly, you'll meet Rosemary Clarke and Mike Savage. We'll show you Pandora - our version of it - which can connect via the internet with the other cloned machines of its kind, in nineteen different countries.'

'But I thought Edinburgh was the sole owner of Pandora,' Keir asked.

'No longer. We've sold licences to many other research groups internationally. It didn't take them long to build systems like ours and have them linked together. I thought we'd have difficulties with the military, but they appreciated the resulting increase in computer power and dropped their objections.'

'You have contracts with the military?'

'Of course, like most academic institutions. Don't ask me more about those, because I'm not authorised to say anything.'

'Fair enough. How much human interaction is needed for data input?' Keir asked.

'Pandora can do it on her own most of the time. The need for human assistance usually comes in bursts. We find that these requirements are getting less frequent as its information database enlarges, its network configuration evolves and its computing power increases.'

'You mean humans are getting too dumb to be of interest to it?'

'Well put, Keir. But we're making good progress in helping build up the shared genetic database. And Pandora's computational power has evolved enormously over the past eight months. Because it's a self-configuring architecture, much of the finer detail is tied up in Pandora's mysterious inner workings.'

'Couldn't you get Pandora to explain itself, Doug?'

'In principle, perhaps. But we do run a parallel monitor program which produces an abbreviated and sometimes inadequate description of events and processes.'

'In the face of these complexities how does Pandora remember the best way of doing a particular kind of task?'

'By learning as it goes along. We're certain it uses several memory modes. Not just primitive and associative, but methodological ones. Doubtless there are others as well. But like you, I'm a geologist, not a computer scientist - I'm still learning. So please don't ask me if it thinks or has consciousness and all that stuff! Mind you, Keir, it won't be long before artificial intelligence outstrips human beings.'

Keir recalled the dire warnings by other scientists in his future world; in particular, Professor Stephen Hawking's archived 2014 BBC newscast. 'Rather risky?' He ventured.

'I know!' Doug raised an eyebrow.

Keir faltered. *MUST NOT betray my future knowledge!* he thought. *How do I get out of this?* 'Er... can you see where Pandora might have weaknesses or difficulties in tackling the meteorites problem?' Keir asked, a bead of sweat on his brow.

'Not an easy question to answer! Perhaps the most serious weakness is in its very complexity. A few months back it would occasionally flip into chaotic modes, but it's learning to avoid these and they're getting much less frequent.'

Keir asked: 'What are the risks in letting it self-improve and evolve?'

'I'm not expert enough to say, Keir. Only three weeks ago, we ran the monitor program and concluded that Pandora had devised a revolutionary new architecture for itself. Way beyond the initial Savage-Tanskanen concept. We called it a crypton mode; from the Greek *kryptos*, meaning hidden. It's a very effective class of configurations which Pandora now uses as part of her regular tool kit. Very hard to describe, though. The representation produced by the monitor program was too simplistic. We think it involves recursion, a bit like several halls of mirrors. When we understand things more fully, we'll try writing it up for a journal article, or Mike Savage will, I suppose. I'm sorry, Keir, I'm going on a bit!'

'No, I'm interested, Doug!'

'Well, the long and short of it is, Pandora's reached a stage where it can recognise not just fragments of DNA and RNA. It combines this information with internal models it's built through countless learning processes and it's starting to predict, very convincingly in many cases, the structure and appearance of simple organisms in considerable detail.'

'Can humans intervene freely when it's working on something? Keir asked.

'An exceptionally well trained operator can intervene, but not always profitably, even on a good day! That takes a great deal of skill and even more patience. Most of us prefer to leave the machine entirely to itself. Only two of our team can claim to have come anywhere near taming it, and then only on rare occasions.'

'Mike Savage?'

'He's one, yes.'

'And yourself?'

'No, Rosemary! Take a look at Picture Five. It's like the outputs in Three and Four. Rosemary and Mike produced it using a crypton mode. They'll be joining us for lunch today.'

'Great, Doug. But what's this grey stringy mass pervading the whole image?'

'On closer inspection, you'll notice those strands are made up of minute billiard balls, arranged in similar fashion to those in the earlier images. It's no accident that some of the clustered strands are wound in the double helix arrangement familiar to cell biologists.'

*****

Keir looked down again at Picture Five. *This is a result of something way beyond machine intelligence and deep learning that we'd expect for 2010,* he thought. *Better play dumb!* Its caption confirmed that the sequence belonged to DNA in a chromosome of a cell nucleus. But what sort of cell remained a mystery.

'I'm not a computer scientist,' Keir lied. 'Just a humble meteorites man. Can you explain?'

'It may not be obvious, but it's an example of self-replication - an important property of living organisms.'

'Simulated by Pandora?'

'Yes. And there's more to it than these pictures. I couldn't bring you picture six because the printout isn't ready yet. But it might be by the time we meet up with Mike. If not, we'll email you the image and its caption via a link-set.'

OK, thought Keir, *you've convinced me - Pandora's a VERY smart machine. Does Galena have any record of it?*

Back in the house, while Doug got ready, Keir used his mobile link-set to interrogate the computer at his bed-sit in Oakingwell. He keyed a code number that gave him access to Bosworth's CMI node in Oulu. On entering the password, he was in. First, he keyed:

'Galena Database / Query / History / 2010 / computer / Pandora.'

Eight seconds later he saw fifteen results, all relatively primitive commercial gadgets of different kinds. He tried other Galena Database queries. None of them found a self evolving networked computer system resembling Pandora.

'Pandora shouldn't exist,' Keir concluded. 'History's been altered more than expected.'

Then he had an idea. The CMI node should have a backup copy of Galena's database for its VR projects. *Why not interrogate Galena's database for this very project, from 2003 up to 2010?* He did. The response took eleven seconds to arrive:

'It's good to hear from you, Keir. But I'm sorry. I don't understand your question.'

Keir felt his heart racing again...

*****

6 Blueprint

Dining Suite, Edinburgh Institute for Intelligent Systems.

Maybe Galena is having a bad day, Keir thought, as he tried to hide his perplexity. Perhaps the lunch to which he'd been invited would be a welcome distraction. He followed Doug, who shepherded his guests forward to a table with four place settings.

Mike Savage reached their table first. Thin for his height, which measured about two metres in sandals, Mike's gaunt face matched his physique. His sunken cheeks and beaky nose reminded Keir of a bald eagle - except that Mike had ample dark reddish hair, well washed but randomly distributed above and around his face. The straggly beard contrasted with his clean shaven upper lip, curled in a smile above slightly protruding teeth.

On being introduced, Mike responded to Keir's handshake with a soft cavernous voice: 'Hello Keir, had a good journey?'

Beneath low, shaggy brows, Mike's steel-grey eyes missed nothing as they scanned Doug's latest guest. The event passed too quickly for any interpretation as an aggressive stare. Instead, the smile broadened as its owner offered Keir the menu card.

'Thanks, Mike. Would you recommend soup of the day?'

'It's asparagus,' the eagle eyes had long since swept the other tables for visual data. His nostrils dilated almost imperceptibly. 'And it should be all right. Blame me if it's not.'

'Sounds fine.' Keir passed the menu to Doug.

'Thanks, Keir. By the way, the home-made steak pies do have meat in them and they're really good, if you like that sort of thing. But feel free to choose anything.'

'Yes, steak pie, please.' In Keir's line of sight a large picture window behind an opposite vacant chair caught his attention. 'It's a tremendous view from this room,' he said.

The city enveloped the hill upon which Edinburgh Castle perched, proudly overlooking its charge from rugged heights of grey volcanic rock.

'What was that?' Keir started at the thud of a distant detonation. It reminded him of the Oulu experience in the ditch.

'One o'clock! The next lot of images will be ready,' Mike remarked.

'It's the one o'clock gun on the Castle wall,' explained Doug.

'Of course. I'd forgotten about your pyrotechnic alarm. So clear, even at this distance!'

'Aye, probably because of the east wind today, Keir. And I bet we're in for a wee bit more rain before long,' Doug predicted, as he returned the menu to its plastic holder.

'The weather hasn't changed much since I set out,' Keir said.

'Brian Burton is your Head of Department?' Doug asked, as the soup arrived.

'Yes, but I try not to think of him while I'm enjoying good company.' Keir's smile barely took the edge off his comment.

'Indeed?' Doug persisted, 'Bit of an authority figure, then?'

Before Keir could respond, Mike asked, 'Has he published anything recently?'

'A year ago,' Keir said over a spoonful of soup, 'there were two papers with a research student of his. And again, just recently, he was a co-author with my supervisor on two more papers.' Then Keir recalled: 'Way back, before he became interested in planetary science, he was an electronic engineer. Radio astronomy systems, chiefly.'

'Jodrell Bank?' Doug asked.

'We've sometimes liaised with Manchester University, but no. Australia, I think.'

'Sounds like you don't approve of him very much.'

'Well, give him his due,' Keir conceded. 'He gets money into the department and fights our battles at higher levels. He's quite a strong leader.'

'But not one you respect, it seems,' said Mike.

'Things could be worse. I'm probably spoiled by my supervisor. Alan Menzies is a much more approachable guy.'

Keir trailed off, suddenly being aware of turning the conversation into a monologue on personalities.

'That's good in a supervisor,' Doug said. 'Glad to hear it, Keir.'

'Maybe I'm being unjust about Burton. He did support this visit.'

'Well, we must help you enjoy your stay,' boomed Mike. 'Let's have a bottle of wine!'

'Keir, you're our guest, you choose.' Doug handed him the wine list.

'Thank you. The merlot, please, if that's OK.'

Keir recognised one of Rowena's recommendations and he hadn't tried this particular vineyard.

The main course arrived and glasses were filled.

'To research, then!' Keir toasted.

'*La recherche*!' chimed Mike, raising his glass on high.

'His mother's French. Sorry I'm a wee bit late!' Rosemary appeared as if from nowhere, poured herself some wine and joined in the toast: 'To research and wherever it'll lead us!'

Their glasses met, and the group ignored glances from other diners as Doug introduced her to Keir.

'Soup, please!' Rosemary caught the eye of a waitress and exhaled a yawn. 'Excuse me, folks. No sleep. Been up wi' Pandora. I believe Doug's shown you his images, Keir.'

Keir nodded in confirmation. Rosemary looked probably in her late twenties, her dark hair short and naturally curled.

'That's right,' Keir replied. 'And we've had a very interesting discussion about Pandora.'

'Och!' Rosemary waved dismissively. 'That beastie's driven me roon' the bend a' nicht. Eh, Mike?' Without waiting for a reply, she deftly broke her bread roll with long nimble fingers. Keir noticed that like Valentina, she managed to look attractive without recourse to nail varnish or facial cosmetics; her manner now completely different to that adopted when giving her paper at the conference.

Meanwhile, Mike Savage responded with a toothy grin but said nothing, being well into enjoying his second course.

*****

After the meal, the gathering retired to the Green Room next door for coffee.

'Can I make a suggestion?' Mike motioned to the lavish seats in green leather. 'I'll download the rest of the pics here.' He placed his laptop on a low table.

'Let me order the coffees,' Doug said.

Mike nodded in agreement as they sat down around the table. Soon, four coffees with crisp chocolate mints were on its glass top.

Mike began connecting to Pandora from his laptop. In reverent silence they viewed the images and data on the screen. Coffee cups were withdrawn carefully lest any fluid spilled on the keyboard.

'This is for you, Keir,' said Doug, as Mike selected and enlarged a picture. 'It completes the set we were looking at this morning.'

Keir took it and stared. 'Don't leave me in suspense, Doug. What is it?' he asked.

The picture showed what looked like part of a sausage-shaped object.

Doug leaned forward. 'Here is the bacterium, according to Pandora.'

Keir took a moment to gather his thoughts.

'You're telling me this image was computed from genetic material found in the meteorite?'

'Results from the Kuopio meteorite are very similar to those for E. Coli. That's what's really so exciting!'

'Isn't there an interesting feature about E. Coli? I read somewhere it needs a host animal to live in.'

Mike responded immediately: 'Indeed! The most significant thing about E. Coli, as far as we're concerned, is that in order for it to survive and flourish, it usually has to live inside the gut of a higher animal host'.

Nobody spoke for several seconds. Keir's imagination raced, conjuring images of bizarre alien shapes. Would those become a future series of Pandora's output?

Mike drained his cup and set it down next to Keir's. 'Of course, there's always the chance that we could be quite wrong,' he suggested.

'You mean, about higher order extraterrestrial animals?' asked Keir.

'Yes,' Mike said. 'Take this apparent resemblance to E. Coli. It seems close genetically, but could still be significantly different. It's life cycle, for instance. It may not need animal hosts at all. We just don't know.'

'You don't sound very optimistic, Mike,' said Keir.

'Och! All Mike's saying,' Rosemary explained, 'is that we should concentrate on perfecting the technique for E. Coli type organisms before we hurl ourselves at wee green men and a' that.'

'When do you think you'll find that elusive host animal?' Keir asked, as the meeting neared its end.

Mike simply smiled. Then he rose and excused himself to return to the laboratory. 'See you later, Keir. Certainly before you leave.'

'Nice to see you here, Keir,' Rosemary said as she followed Mike.

Doug got up and walked across the room to chat with Mike near the exit, while Keir remained seated to gather his thoughts.

After a couple of minutes, Doug returned. 'Sorry about that, Keir. We're all ruled by the clock here. You'll see Mike before you leave. Meanwhile, here are some of our brochures to read at your leisure.'

Thanks Doug,' Keir said as he took the bulky folder.

'They include the work we've done already with Pandora. One of our recent tasks at the Institute was to find the solution to an environmental problem that arose in the waste disposal domain.'

'You mean the attempt by another company to biodegrade scrapped tyres?' Keir 'recalled' a report that appeared in the press eighteen months ago. He continued: 'Didn't public highways across southern Europe have to be closed off to traffic?'

'Yes, that's right. People were driving on tyres that disintegrated into a black slurry! In fact, anything made of natural or synthetic rubber was in danger of infection and degradation. Several plastics, too. The electronics industry was severely affected before things were brought under control.'

'You had a hand in the recovery, Doug?'

'Well, you could say that. In spite of the compensation claims to injured parties running into many millions, the manufacturers, including a large consortium, approached our group for a possible solution. The deals involved generous up front payments, to be doubled after six months, subject to delivery. We'd already anticipated this area of application. And with the aid of a prototype Pandora system, we produced a genetic engineering solution well before the deadline. The consortium, aided by the outcome of our research, has since gone from strength to strength and overtook, I should say took over, most of the competition. As part of our latest contract agreement, that consortium has provided this research unit with everything that it needs to support work on their genetic engineering requirements. Not just environmental protection. But more than that, the income has allowed purchase of hardware and software and a percentage of the equity in the Finnish computing company, Tansys Oy. We did try for sole rights of the Tanskanen-Savage computer system, but Tanskanen wouldn't play.'

Keir raised an eyebrow. 'You have a Tanskanen business connection?'

'That's right. Do you know him?'

'Oh, not really. Met him briefly during a visit to Finland.'

'He's a canny fellow, Tanskanen. He made sure that when he and Mike Savage applied for patents, he was unemployed.'

'Tanskanen unemployed? But he's a reputed genius!'

'Exactly! But he was technically unemployed at the time. Between jobs, actually. He left Helsinki University and set up Tansys Oy at Kuopio. The game is about intellectual property rights, Keir. Mike's share of the rights went to his university; he was a postdoctoral at the time. But Tanskanen's share was his own. When Mike came here, we bought the rights from his university while Mike continued the development work with us. The upshot of these agreements is that Tanskanen commands a sixty percent share of any profits that accrue from sales or licenses of the Pandora system. The institution, and hence our research group, have done very well from all this. But Tanskanen's personal fortune runs into many millions!'

'And your profitable collaboration continues?'

'I don't see any end in sight yet, Keir.'

'Truly impressive, Doug. Thank you. If you'll excuse me, I'll just have time to have a quick word with Mike before I leave'.

'I do apologise! It's three o'clock already. We'll go down to the lab right away.' As they descended the stairs, Doug continued: 'I've some phone calls to make, so I'll come and collect you at 3:45, OK?'

*****

Edinburgh Institute Computing Laboratory.

Mike Savage, wearing a headset, looked up at Keir from his workstation.

'Hi! Grab a chair, 'he said. 'Give me a few seconds to log out from Pandora,'

'Hope I'm not intruding. I thought I'd look in on the way out.'

'No problem.' Mike eased himself from his chair, reaching for a switch to turn on the nearby kettle. 'Like some more coffee?'

'None for me, thanks. Had enough to fill a tanker. You go ahead, though.'

'A typical aftermath of Doug's entertainment routine! Have you reached any conclusions during your visit here?'

'Well, if you're right about the E. Coli type organism, the implications are far reaching.'

Mike picked up a folder from his desk. 'I must show you this!' he said. 'Here's another of this afternoon's images, this time using data from a different particle of the same meteorite. It's unusual. Looks like a heap of manure, doesn't it?'

'Or a pile of sand?'

'Why did you say that?'

'Some time ago I heard of a newspaper report of an alien sighting in 2003,' said Keir, 'in Denmark.'

Keir appeared matter-of-fact, almost nonchalant, as he scrutinised Mike's body language and facial expression.

Mike's face had become expressionless, his speech clipped: 'Where did you first find out about us and Pandora?'

'At the recent meteorites conference in Paris. Do you have any connections with Karpov and Gazetny?'

'Well, sort of.'

'Do they know about this work you're doing; the E.Coli and now the sand pile looking images?'

'Apart from what we publish? Why don't you ask them?' Mike asked tersely. 'Sorry, I didn't mean to be irritated. And by the way, there's nothing that those two don't make it their business to know. Watch them, Keir. Just be careful.'

*****

Rail carriage on return journey.

The visit finished at 4:12pm that afternoon. Doug failed to appear. Instead, Rosemary drove Keir to the station. He reflected on the day's happenings while trying to relax on the southbound train. After transcribing some pencilled notes to his mobile, editing as he went along, he pulled Valentina's fax out of his coat pocket and found her number.

'English isn't her native language', he thought. 'Better spell it out in full'.

He sent a secure email: 'Thanks for your fax. Just left Edinburgh Institute. On train, Thursday 16:47 local time. Thought you might be interested: Saw Pandora results for

Kuopio meteorite. Image for reconstructed bacterium like E.Coli. Followed by conical shape with sandy texture. Size unknown. Pre-published, please treat in confidence. Possibly more to follow. Regards, Keir.'

Then he realised the train had drawn into Carlisle and pocketed his mobile. As the train drew out of the station, he saw someone making his way down the carriage gangway. The man approached, sat next to Keir and opened a newspaper. Their elbows touched.

'Sorry, mate.' The man said.

'No problem,' Keir replied. He leaned against the window and dozed off. Suddenly he awoke with a start. The train had pulled into Penrith. The man had gone, his newspaper neatly folded on the seat. Instinctively, Keir searched for his mobile.

'Damn!' he blurted, attracting some attention from neighbouring passengers. His link-set had gone!

'Are you all right?' asked a mother with a child at her side.

'Sorry about this,' Keir said. 'But could I please use your mobile phone for an emergency call?'

'Yes, hold on.' She opened her handbag and passed him her phone. Frantically, he dialled a number. Quite a long one. The woman looked on, bemused.

'Thank you!' Keir said. 'That was a free call.' He returned the phone and scanned the station platform as the train began to pull out. There he was! Under the station clock, a frantic figure; trying desperately to beat out the flames and billowing smoke rising from his jacket.

'You're welcome,' the woman said. 'You got through OK?'

'Yes,' replied Keir. 'I certainly did! Many thanks.' He smiled contentedly as the train picked up speed and the cloud of smoke became a grey wisp in the far distance.

*****

Professor Burton's office.

Professor Brian Burton, in clearly affable mood, gestured Keir to an easy chair.

'Hi! Please pour yourself some coffee or tea.' Burton said. 'First, let me welcome you to the fold.'

'Thank you. You mean, the extended research group including yourself and Professor Brodie?'

'Precisely.' Burton already had a coffee and took a noisy sip, then continued: 'Now, joining with us should not affect writing up your thesis, but you'll need certain provisions, mainly to ease communications between us and for making detailed records. These records, progress reports if you will, need to be delivered on time. But you're at heart a researcher and I won't bore you with those details now. When you leave here, take this information pack with you.' He patted a folder on the corner of his desk.

'Thank you. I don't know what to say, except that I'll do my best.'

'I know you will. I also admire your generosity. Although I wouldn't have chosen to do it, your action in covering for the assistant at Kirsti's laboratory did show consideration. At the time, you didn't know you were on CCTV. You'll find that being on camera is from now an occupational hazard, Keir.'

'Does that include all aspects of the research?'

'It does.' Burton's tone became a notch more serious: 'And that brings me to another thing.'

Keir felt a sense of foreboding. A well established Burton trade mark, Keir thought.

'If there's a problem, I hope I can put it right.' Keir said.

'So do I.' Burton smiled with his teeth, but his eyes remained cold like brown ice on a winter path. 'From now on, your interactions with other team members will be entirely professional.'

'Of course,' Keir said.

'For example, if I read the signs correctly, this ruling must also include people like Dr. Valentina Gazetny.'

Keir blanched. He felt nothing could be hidden from Burton. 'Meaning?'

'Meaning that for my remaining deep concerns to disappear, you should simply stick to the rules and all will be well. And this time I'll give you the benefit of the doubt and assume that when you emailed Dr.Gazetny about the Pandora scenario, you believed she was part of the same Group.'

'Isn't she?'

'In the command structure, she's Inner Echelon.'

So what? Keir thought, unsure how to deal with it. *And so much for secure emails!* He nodded assent.

'Ah. There is another problem.' Keir said, anxious to change the subject. A gambit no doubt also visible to Burton. 'My mobile link-set was stolen last week on the way back from Edinburgh.'

'Between Carlisle and Penrith?'

'Yes.' Keir, surprised but no longer fazed, began to feel immunised against whatever should come next.

'You did well to summon it to self-destruct, Keir. Especially in the pocket of an adversary. Yes, I like that.' Burton seemed genuinely pleased. 'But don't worry; I won't hold that slight breach of health and safety regulations against you!' He burst into infectious laughter at his own banter.

Keir joined in, cautiously, in case the atmosphere should change.

Burton continued: 'We'd better keep that little matter between ourselves. In the pack you'll find another mobile phone. To members of the fraternity, it's on the house.'

'Really? Thanks, Professor.'

'But lose it and you'll pay for the replacement. Presumably you've backed up most of your stuff?'

'Yes. And I can remember the rest.'

'Excellent,' Burton said. 'And good luck!' He held out a hand. Keir shook it and left with his package. He extracted the new mobile phone. An identical model to that he'd destroyed.

*****

7 Most Secret

Tansys Oy.

Dr. Kirsti Kivi reached across her desk to answer her mobile phone.

'Hello Valentina! How's your back? Where are you?'

'I'm fine, thanks. I'm in Moscow. Thank you for the meteorite sample.'

Kirsti could see on her phone screen Valentina in her laboratory. A heavily built man worked at a bench behind her.

'Have you had a chance to examine it yet?' Kirsti asked.

'My colleague is setting up the equipment now. Can I ask; do you mind if I come over to see you again at Tansys, say, next Monday?'

'No problem. Afternoon is best.'

'Good. See you at two thirty.'

*****

When Valentina arrived, she and Kirsti were joined by Jukka Tanskanen.

'Shall we go to my office?' he asked. 'It's rather more private and we may as well begin right away.'

'That's fine by me,' Valentina said. 'Have you discussed anything with Kirsti yet, Professor?'

'No. You know me. I don't do anything without permission.'

Kirsti looked surprised. Jukka of all people needing permission!

'This sounds very mysterious. And formidable.' she said.

'You're probably right, Kirsti,' said Tanskanen. He motioned Valentina to his swivel chair. 'Make yourself comfortable, Valentina. Ah! Here come the refreshments.'

Tanskanen stood aside while his personal assistant brought in a tray of coffee and cakes. As she left, he turned to Valentina. 'I bet you haven't eaten since lunch. When did your train arrive?'

'I got into Kuopio at ten forty this morning and you're right. I had a quick snack at the market hall in the town square at eleven. So thank you, this is most kind.'

'Ah, the *Kaupahalle*. Very good,' Tanskanen said. 'Let's begin then, could we please, Valentina?'

'Thanks, Jukka.' Valentina said, her clasped hands resting on the desk. 'This meeting is really about you, Kirsti.'

For the second time Kirsti raised her eyebrows.

'*Voi*! What have I done?' she said.

'Nothing to worry about at all,' Valentina assured her. 'In fact, it's because of your competence, experience and integrity that you're being head-hunted by our organisation. In strictest confidence, you understand.'

'Well, I'm flattered indeed,' said Kirsti. She turned to Tanskanen, 'Do you know what this is about, Jukka?'

'Yes.' Tanskanen gestured for Valentina to continue.

'We were hesitant at first,' Valentina explained, 'because you have family commitments. And if you think that may be a problem, or if there's any other reason, feel free to say no. But it's better to decide now rather than later.'

'Decide what?' Kirsti asked.

'It's about an extension of your work here at Tansys,' Valentina explained. 'Firstly, it doesn't affect your employment contract, and secondly, the time you spend doing it will, as much as possible, be part of your existing working hours.'

'Then why the concern about my family?' asked Kirsti.

'Because there are risks.' Tanskanen said.

'Like national service? Commandos? Or the police?' Kirsti asked, almost jokingly, expecting a negative answer.

'That's a pretty representative range of activities,' Valentina said. 'Roll them all into one and it's more or less the right picture.'

'*Voi!*' said Kirsti. 'Now tell me what it is!'

Tanskanen and Valentina exchanged glances. Tanskanen nodded, then said: 'Very well, Kirsti. To clarify. If you agree to sign on, you'll be a special agent of Electra. We're an organisation set up several years ago to oversee the well being of a minority group of extremely intelligent people and to ensure their non-exploitation by unscrupulous or criminal elements.'

'I don't understand.' said Kirsti. 'Why should this be a problem? Why can't the welfare service or police handle it?'

'Very reasonable questions, Kirsti,' Tanskanen replied. 'If we lived in a different society...'

'Are they children, or homeless?' Kirsti interrupted.

'They're not children. Not all, anyway.' Tanskanen said, glancing at Valentina. 'Homeless? Yes, I suppose they are, really.'

Then Kirsti put a hand to her face. 'Animals? Special animals? Intelligent ones, you say.'

'In a manner of speaking, yes,' Valentina said.

'Cloned for their intelligence. That's it, isn't it?' Tears welled up. 'Now they're all alone, at the mercy of humans!'

Again, Jukka Tanskanen and Valentina exchanged glances.

Valentina continued: 'If you bear in mind what you've just been saying, you may not be far wrong. We'll give you precise information at a later meeting when more of us are present. For now, let's concentrate on the idea of *protecting* this minority group. Do you think you're up for it, Kirsti?'

'Of course,' she said.

'Good,' said Valentina, 'Then if you approve, my colleague, Academician Ilya Karpov in Moscow and I, along with Professor Jukka Tanskanen, as joint North European Principal Conveners of the Electra Project, invite you to join with us as a first level recruit in the process. Our arm of the project is based near Oulu but you may continue working here normally for the time being. The second level selection happens at a plenary meeting to be held in two weeks time. Meanwhile, here's an information pack with more details. It doesn't disclose the particulars of the people we're protecting. That will follow at the plenary meeting. You see, we're soon to be bound by regulations of the United Nations, to whom we will be accountable. If, on what you've heard so far, you'd like to join, then you have a week to think about it. But it's confidential.'

'I'll join. Now, please.' Kirsti said.

'You're really sure?' Valentina asked.

'Absolutely!'

Tanskanen passed the forms: 'Please read carefully and ask any questions. Then, if you like to sign, by all means go ahead.'

Ten minutes later, Kirsti became a first level recruit of the Electra Project.

*****

2:30pm, Oakingwell.

Burton opened a window and returned to his swivel chair. The fragrance of freshly mown grass and the sound of birdsong on a lazy summer afternoon went almost unnoticed by the occupants of his office.

Drs. Smythe and Menzies and Professor Burton listened intently to the talking head of Doug Brodie on Burton's computer screen.

'There are too many gaps in the genetic sequences for my liking, but the computers have done their best with what was available.' Doug said.

'And what do *you* think, Rowena?' Burton asked.

'Yes, it's rather difficult, isn't it?' Rowena replied, knowing that Doug could see them all. Turning to the screen, she continued: 'Your so-called alien image looks like a heap of sand, Doug! In my view, your computer's probably found a false solution.'

Burton asked Doug, 'Did you try *exactly* the same input data on both systems, pooling the genetic information from MIT and Edinburgh and *then* running it on each of them?'

Doug said: 'We did. And then we repeated the whole experiment twice. The result was,' he continued, displaying Pandora images, 'not a lot of difference'.

'Could this thing be living, but incidental to the main goal of your search?' Alan Menzies asked.

'Contamination, either before or after the meteorite fall. That's always a possibility,' Rowena agreed.

'Look, I'd better go now,' Burton unexpectedly rose from his chair. 'I'll speak to you again, Doug. If you'll excuse me, I'm supposed to be meeting someone at three. Thanks for joining in the discussion and feel free to carry on with the others. Rowena and Alan, do help yourselves to the rest of the coffee.'

Burton silently closed the office door behind him and made his way down the stairway. Waiting for him in the lobby was a man in his mid forties, clean shaven with close cropped greying hair. He wore an immaculate charcoal-grey suit.

'Ah! Good afternoon, Leo,' Burton said while shaking hands warmly with the visitor, who had transferred the briefcase and gloves he carried to his left hand. 'I thought it best if we talk somewhere private, away from my office.'

Burton led his guest upstairs to a room with a round table and windows overlooking well kept gardens. He crossed the room to a computer workstation.

'Good of you to arrange this meeting, Brian,' Leo said, as he seated himself in a leather armchair. He glanced outside. 'And nice to see they've fixed the water feature in your pond. Yes, how very pleasant!' Turning to face his host, Captain Leo Bosworth came to the point: 'I think you know why I'm here, Brian.'

'Keir Wilson, isn't it?'

'Indeed. If you agree, I think that without further delay we should proceed with his assessment.'

'Assessment?'

'Yes, Brian. In preparing recruits for Project Electra, we both know the procedures. Before any disclosure to candidates can be sanctioned, we must be quite certain that they won't go telling anyone about it. As you know, at my suggestion to you last year, Keir spent some time with us during the Easter vacation, improving his health and fitness with those three other students who came along. Not a bad performer on the assault course. If you remember, he picked up the archery trophy. Indeed, I'm very glad you agreed to send him along to those training days; we got to know him quite well. But now we must be certain that the information we're planning to give him will pass no further. And thanks again for those copies of his reports, Brian. They're quite good on the whole, aren't they? The latest one about the Tansys visit in Finland was a bit of a rushed job, but never mind. It contains what we wanted to know about Jukka and Kirsti.'

Burton nodded. 'I'm very pleased to hear it. Shall we set up the test kit?' he asked.

'Yes, it won't take long.' Leo opened his briefcase and took out a portable head-up display helmet, which he connected to the laptop workstation. He inserted a memory stick, put on the helmet and tapped at the keyboard: 'That's a nice clear image. OK, we're logged in to Andover.'

'Very good. Shall I fetch him?' Burton suggested.

'Fine.' Leo removed the helmet and placed it on the table.

*****

Keir stepped into the room and noted the computer and its attachments.

Burton spoke first: 'Hello, Keir. Do take a seat. You've met Captain Bosworth before. We've got something over here which we hope you'll find rather interesting.'

'Why hello, Keir, old chap!' Bosworth effused, shaking Keir's hand vigorously. 'So nice to see you again. We were especially pleased with your performance during that recent training day you spent with us near Oulu. And we think you're the ideal person for testing this rather important piece of virtual reality software. Let me explain. At Andover, we've developed a role-play program intended for our recruits, and we'd like you to participate by trying it out.'

'What sort of recruits?' Keir asked.

'Oh, people we think might have special aptitudes. Well, let me put it this way,' said Bosworth, 'In it you'll find a lot of challenges and decision making. It's designed to test one's emotional, intellectual and moral fibre. And we hope that you'll become so absorbed that you won't notice us. We'll be participating, too, but in the background. Being part of the experiment is entirely up to you, of course, but we'd like you to give it a try, then afterwards there'll be a short evaluation questionnaire to complete.'

Keir glanced at Burton.

'It's OK, Keir,' Burton said, 'I wouldn't allow them to do it if it wasn't.'

'All right. Let's run with it.'

'Very good, Keir. But first, shall we all have some tea or coffee?' Burton motioned to a pair of stainless steel urns which were set out on another low table, along with a choice of biscuits.

*****

Friday 20 August, Keir's apartment.

A week later, Keir opened his mail to discover a letter from the Andover Military Academy. It had been signed by Captain L.F. Bosworth and carried the insignia of the Resources Development Corps. The letter thanked Keir for his help with the role-play game and for completing the evaluation questionnaire. The last paragraph of the letter caught his attention.

It invited him to a one day seminar, to be held at Andover the following week. The title aroused in him a mild interest: *Recent Advances in Space Biology III.* Admission by ticket only. He found a copy of the programme enclosed, along with his ticket bearing the number 17 in the top left corner. The meeting would be chaired by Professor Brian Burton, after a short introduction by Captain Leo Bosworth. Keir noticed that the principal speakers would include Dr. Rowena Smythe (Oakingwell, UK) and Dr. Valentina Gazetny (Oulu Base, Finland). The programme included a guided tour of Andover's 'new facilities', scheduled immediately after lunch.

'She's a high flyer, all right,' Keir murmured.

*****

Tuesday 24 August, 8:30am, Andover.

Rowena Smythe seemed happy with the audio-visual arrangements and Burton breathed a sigh of relief. He had asked for Bosworth's support in guaranteeing their perfection. The Andover technicians had obliged with competence and attention to detail, including the replacement of a video wall-screen which Rowena had criticised for lack of contrast.

'I wonder what Keir's reaction will be to the main subject of this meeting?' Burton mused aloud. He turned to Rowena: 'Do you think we're timing things right?'

'Too late now, dearest!' Rowena replied, 'He's due here in fifteen minutes and what would we say to him if we changed our minds? Quite apart from looking rather stupid!'

'Yes, yes!' Burton loosened his collar. 'But I can't help feeling a bit apprehensive. We all know how much is at stake.'

'Don't worry! I have the measure of the man,' Bosworth said reassuringly, 'and it's best that he finds out through us first, eh?'

Burton nodded in agreement.

'Of course!' Rowena concurred, 'And it certainly wouldn't be right if he learned of the situation by hearsay from someone like Brodie, or worse still, that Gazetny woman.'

*****

Bus stop, outside Andover Station, 8:40am.

In their concrete tubs, the dwarf shrubs were looking remarkably healthy, Keir reflected as he sat at a bus shelter outside Andover railway station. His train had arrived a few minutes earlier. He opened a magazine from the station kiosk and had started to read an article on the history of the omnibus, when an example of its kind eclipsed the morning sun as it trundled to a halt nearby.

'Military Institute?' he asked.

'Yes, mate!' the driver confirmed. 'We're not setting off for another eight minutes, though. You might as well walk. It's just over four blocks away, down the road on the right. Past the traffic lights and opposite the filling station.'

Half way to his destination, Keir suddenly sneezed. He glanced into a shop doorway, trying to find the source of the strangely pungent odour. He sniffed, but the air smelled fresh again. The shop sold office stationery; an unlikely candidate. *Possibly drains*? he thought, casting a suspicious glance at a manhole cover.

After a pedestrian crossing, he found the Institute a short distance ahead, a redbrick style building with high windows. Inside, he showed his ticket and driver's licence to the guard and entered a spacious reception area. The walls were adorned with rank upon rank of heraldic shields, the brilliant colours in stark contrast to the accompanying arrays of glinting metal armament pieces from many periods. Oil paintings depicted battle scenes and included several portraits in heavy gilt frames. A huge dark blue tapestry bordered with gold thread hung at the far end of the hall, dwarfing the doorway from which Captain Bosworth entered, his uniform immaculate. He walked with a brisk military step and greeted Keir with a handshake. A desk officer issued the necessary security pass.

'Welcome to AMI! Please come this way.' Bosworth said, leading Keir across the polished parquet flooring, their footsteps echoing, toward the door next to the tapestry. *If this is supposed to be a seminar, then where are all the others*? Keir wondered, as he looked back at the empty hall.

*****

9:00am, Andover Military Institute.

'Something bothering you, old chap?' Bosworth's voice startled Keir.

'Tell me, Captain Bosworth, where is everyone?'

'It's going to be almost entirely teleconferenced. There are just twenty of us here, including the support staff. Don't be deceived, though. It's a *very* important meeting. The other delegates will be on a battery of screens and far away, watching their own wall displays.'

Sixteen minutes later, Bosworth opened the meeting. He stood, holding his gloves and cap behind his back.

'Good afternoon,' he began. 'All communication is via a secure link, unconnected to any civilian network. Again, I must emphasise that any leakage of information beyond these four walls will compromise not only us, but could affect the other participants, and may put some of them in life-threatening situations. Right? We're going live in thirty seconds.'

Bosworth's head went back slightly as he theatrically jutted his jaw and lowered his voice at the same time: 'Be prepared for some surprising news, and remember, several other delegates out there are in precisely your position. They'll be experiencing these new revelations for the first time, so you won't be alone. New recruits have been selected for their abilities and personal qualities. Just relax now and take things as they come.'

A short phrase of digitised music preceded a soft, sonorous voice from the loudspeakers: '*All centres on line'*. There were twenty five active digital wall screens, arranged in a 5x5 matrix; the Andover screen central, as customary for the chairing institution.

Each screen now showed its group leader's face, including a young Singapore woman, Professor Midori Fung at top centre. A middle-aged black American, Dr. Clark Remington appeared left centre. Keir glanced up from checking through his papers. But on the screens he could recognise only two group leaders: Burton (Chair, Andover UK) in the centre screen and Tanskanen (Chair, Oulu Base SF) at centre right. Keir noted the 'on-air' light, a red unblinking square at top left, near the ceiling. Next to it, a green illuminated panel with the words: SECURITY LEVEL 3x ALPHA.

*****

11:00am, (local time) Oulu conference centre.
Professor Tanskanen occupied his desk to the right of two rows of seats, all of them facing the wall screens, but with the furniture angled slightly so that he could talk across to his four colleagues. Valentina sat in the middle of the front row, between Kirsti on her left and Ilya on her right. To the left of Kirsti sat another recruit, listed as Ms. Loma Korkangas, from Tallin, Estonia. Each wore a headset and all seats were equipped with a laptop computer.

The Finland delegation watched attentively as Burton's Andover screen logo became highlighted while he made the opening introductions. Each country's representatives were shown on their respective screens.

Then Keir felt his pulse race as Valentina panned into view on the Oulu screen. He couldn't mistake the headband and forced himself to remain expressionless, should his own image be recorded.

His attention switched to Burton's screen, highlighted again. In Keir's peripheral vision a small camera with a red light swung momentarily in his direction. If Valentina saw him, her expression remained unchanged.

Burton began his welcome:

'On behalf of the Principal Conveners of the Electra Project and its Committee, I welcome you all to this Plenary Meeting from our host's institution here at Andover.' Then, his face replaced with an agenda page, his measured tones continued:

'We all have access to the Proceedings, so I'm taking the Minutes of the previous meeting as read, because there is much to get through and only today to do it. Attention is therefore drawn to item 2 of this agenda.'

The item header filled the screen: *Induction of New Delegates*.

Burton resumed: 'But first, Professor Fournier, do you confirm that our team list is now complete?'

'Yes, Professor Burton. That is so.' Keir recognised Fournier, but with surprise noted the speaker's uniform; a French Army officer. A colonel, in fact.

Burton took over again: 'Fine. Any other comments or questions before we proceed?' He paused politely for a few seconds and then continued: 'We particularly welcome the *new* delegates in our respective groups and assure them of our support at all times. The pictures we'll be shown today will be already familiar to many of us, though not to the new membership. Also, not everyone knows about the recent meteorite fall near Kuopio in Finland and its subsequent recovery and analysis. The outcome of this and other meteorite work in our groups strongly suggests the presence of genetic material from space.' he paused to let his words sink in.

Keir nodded a greeting as Bosworth came to sit next to him.

'Hello, Keir. How's it going?'

'I wish he'd get on with it!'

Bosworth quietly ordered his papers. 'He will, don't worry.'

'This is not a new idea,' Burton continued, 'but many of us, let alone the wider academic community, still admit to surprise at finding such evolved material in carbonaceous chondrites. According to our present theories, this class of meteorites originates from accretion processes that involve mainly very primitive materials.'

Keir looked across the studio to where Burton sat and could see that he referred to an official looking pale green document on his desk. Burton addressed the camera again:

'However, the results from Massachusetts, Edinburgh, Tallin and Voronezh appear to confirm a very small percentage of more complex compounds identifiable as precursors of DNA. We, and the world at large, have heard about the E. Coli type of bacterium. But there is recent evidence for the existence of a similar *extraterrestrial* organism, obtained from computer processing of data from meteorite samples. There are three main points which I must now mention, specifically for our new team members.'

'This stuff's already common knowledge,' Keir whispered to Bosworth.

'Patience, old chap. Just listen…'

'The first point is this', Burton resumed, 'We all recognise the importance of collaborative projects between academic institutions, the military establishments and private industry, in which all benefit from cross-fertilisation of ideas and methods. And as we might expect, there are areas of science and technology which have progressed further under the auspices of the military than in either academia or industry alone. These include certain areas of computation and biosynthesis. In particular, since the Skagen event reported in the Læsø Nyheder in 2003, some high priority projects have been funded; in some cases, regardless of cost.'

A few faces on the screens smiled discreetly and Burton continued:

'But you clearly know what I mean. And, of necessity, much of the military work is secret.' Keir watched as Burton paused to adjust his spectacles in time-honoured fashion.

'The second point,' Burton looked across his spectacles at the camera, 'is that in consequence, some of the computing work now being reported in the technical and scientific press and which some of you believe to be novel *has already been carried out before - many times I might add*, on materials recovered in the past. For the benefit of our new delegates, I'm referring to meteoritic materials and in particular to joint work by some civilian research units and the military.' He paused again, maintaining his steady gaze at the camera. 'At the military establishments represented here, the DNA structures from these results have led to cultured organisms being grown in laboratories. Indeed, these have progressed well beyond the nursery stage. In fact, at five of our Electra sponsored bases, there are alien creatures approaching adolescence and adulthood. Likewise, the sandpile-like object of recent Edinburgh and MIT renown was a subject of covert investigation several years ago. As the work at Edinburgh, MIT and other centres continues, aided considerably by the Pandora super-computer network and data from other meteorite samples, I'm confident it will turn out to reveal an alien, similar in kind to the real ones in our care.'

Burton reached for his glass of water.

'I see what you mean,' Keir murmured to Bosworth. 'I did risk a cover-up of the 2003 report but this is big time. Is Doug Brodie involved?'

'I doubt it. His associate Tanskanen might be, of course.'

'Yes, possibly with Ilya Karpov and Valentina Gazetny! And perhaps Kirsti Kivi?

'Kirsti's a recruit. Level One, like you. Shh! Here we go again...'

Burton drew a breath and continued: 'The third point is that I'm talking about a predominantly *single* species of alien sentient beings. Their intelligence and inter-communication abilities exceed those of humans by wide margins. And their development shows no sign of reaching a plateau at adolescence. In fact, it shows every sign of increasing steadily with age and there is, as yet, no known upper limit, because none of the alien beings in our care has yet died of old age. Well, I think that more or less sums it up.' Burton folded his spectacles away and gathered his papers: 'Now there'll be a short intermission, while group leaders and their colleagues counsel their new trainees and prepare them for the tour of the new facilites here and at several other bases simultancously. And during the intermission, committee members will have opportunity to peruse the minutes of the previous meeting in their Proceedings. Thank you for your attention. We now have a short break and reconvene in fifteen minutes for the seminars.'

*****

Oulu Base.

Kirsti, her face pallid, turned to Valentina: 'You knew about the aliens and their incubation?' she asked, incredulously.

'Yes, I did. Most recently, Ilya and I had a long session on the secure link after the barbecue at Kuopio. That's why I didn't drink too much at the party. When we put Keir to bed, I sprained my back. But that gave me an excuse to get back to my room in time for a scheduled connection with Voronezh and then with Moscow. That's when I discussed your possible recruitment with Ilya. I had to wait until the following morning for a reply. Anyway, that gave me a couple of hours to organise my travel arrangements before setting off back to Oulu Base.'

'But Val, why didn't you discuss this *recruitment* side of it with me right away?'

'Would it have made any difference? Anyway, I wanted to discuss things with Jukka Tanskanen beforehand.' Valentina placed a hand on her colleague's shoulder and continued: 'Kirsti, by virtue of being so close to the meteorite work, you're already much more deeply involved than you suppose. And if you'd turned down being recruited in this way, you wouldn't have the full protection of the security services.'

'Protection? What for? I'm just a scientist!' Kirsti retorted, now flushed with anger.

'You're right. And as a scientist, it's only fair that you know about the existence of what Burton's mentioned. But at present this is highly secret knowledge for obvious reasons - you know what would happen if word got out!'

'True... unrest. Probably riots, and all that. But we scientists aren't to blame. We're just doing our jobs, aren't we? Well, I was, until you and Ilya enlisted me into your covert team!' Kirsti paused for breath, 'Sorry! That's not entirely true, is it? You and Jukka described things as best as you could at the time, given the secrecy. And you gave me a choice. What's next?' she asked.

'You still have a choice. Wait until this afternoon's tours before you think about recruitment to Level Two.'

When Kirsti sat down again, she realised why the minutes had been held over. They contained several explicit references to operations involving alien colonies.

'Are you all right, my dear?' Ilya pulled up a chair next to Kirsti and gave her something in a pressed clean handkerchief. She took the small glass of vodka as he continued: 'And I assure you that during your tour any resemblance between those blobby creatures and myself will be purely coincidental.' She smiled at him as he shook her shoulder and guffawed at his own joke.

'Er. Was there something from Finland?' Burton's screen re-activated briefly, whereupon Ilya grabbed the microphone on Tanskanen's vacated desk.

'No. Sorry for the interruption. Please continue.' Ilya hit the 'mute' button on his microphone and turned to his colleagues.

'Shhh! We'd better be good and get ready to watch the film show!' he said, as the laughter subsided.

*****

6:00am (local) Sloan Institute, Woods Hole, USA.

'Oh, my garsh!' Cindy Halford put down her half eaten apple and turned to her fellow rookie at the Sloan Institute, near Woods Hole in Massachusetts.

'Gee! I think I'm gonna be sick!' declared Eddie Schultz. 'This stuff's right out of a sci-fi video. It's just too wild, man!'

'Hey, you guys! We're on air,' Dr. Clark Remington hissed from his desk. He turned to his assistant: 'Try to keep him quiet, Cindy! Huh?'

'Sure, Clark. You OK, Eddie? Uh-uh! I'll take him to the rest room. Back soon, Clark.'

Cindy and Eddie departed via a side door while Clark started on his own apple, his eyes riveted to the Australian screen at bottom left. It showed a procession of wet and naked aliens under floodlighting lining up to be weighed and measured. They seemed to be in a vast, wet enclosure and were co-operating fully with their hosts. Sometimes, the aliens engaged in numerous intense communications between themselves. Various mobile patterns of colour and shading were evident on their bodies. The aliens varied widely in size but not shape, the tallest being about one and a half metres. These are definitely not humanoid, Clark noted, tapping his keypad.

Cindy returned at that moment and gazed at the same screen.

'You're a space biologist, Cindy. What do you make of it?' Clark asked.

'Excuse me? My degree in exo-biology tells me nothing about these critters. What on earth made me spend three years on that course?'

Her eyes raked the ceiling in frustration as she unwrapped a candy bar and began munching.

*****

11:05am, Andover Military Institute.

Following Burton's announcement, Keir arose with the others for the mid-morning break. In Finland it would be time for a late lunch and at Sloan for a very early breakfast. Meanwhile, the secure common channel remained open for informal dialogue between participants.

Keir got up to leave. He passed the Finnish screen and noticed the empty chair's desk about to be occupied by Valentina. He plucked up courage, switched his headset to a direct channel and voiced a greeting.

'Hello Keir! I saw you during the introductions.' Her manner had a formal edge. 'Ilya and I are very pleased to see you again. Presumably you will be staying on through the afternoon?'

'Yes, it starts with a tour of some kind. I think it's where we keep our aliens.'

'That's right, same with us,' Valentina said. She could tell that Keir saw her headband, and smiled. 'Oh yes, I was wearing it when we first met, wasn't I?'

Taken aback by her sudden openness, Keir faltered slightly and managed a wan smile. 'That's right!' he heard himself remark, 'It seems rather a long time ago.' He tailed off, not knowing how to continue.

'Well, Keir, I'd better get prepared. I'm chairing things here for the rest of the session. Jukka's taking notes and Ilya's gone off to sit with our two lady recruits.' She leaned forward a little, giving a glance off-camera. 'You know, I think he fancies them - both!' Keir heard a distant bellow in Russian, followed by laughter.

'I'm innocent!' Ilya's voice again, now in English. Then more sceptical laughter, with Valentina and other colleagues joining in.

'I really must go now, Keir,' she said, 'It's such a challenge keeping this lot in order. See you later!' she waved.

'Thanks for the chat, Valentina. And best wishes to everyone!' He walked tall as he headed off to join the others for coffee in an adjacent room.

*****

Andover Military Institute, conference room. 11:15am.

Burton called the meeting to order. He announced: 'All delegates are encouraged to ask questions at the end of each seminar. They may do this directly or via their respective group chairs. Now I hand you over to our first speaker.' Burton put Captain Leo Bosworth on the screen.

Bosworth's contribution dealt mainly with the technical aspects of keeping the aliens alive. He began: 'They're amphibious oxygen breathers, but on land it seems they only need 16 percent at most in their atmosphere. Here are the details.' Bosworth's face faded out to a text screen of statistics.

'Notice the high humidity they require,' he said, 'Ideally, their skins should be wet at all times. This is important for their respiration.'

Bosworth's talk continued with descriptions of the life support system within their enclosures and how most of the physical difficulties of keeping them mentally and physically occupied in their humanly hostile environment had been overcome.

'Actually, it ended up with *them* telling *us* how to do it!' he admitted. 'They're very social. In fact, as well as problem solving, they derive most of their emotional fulfilment through conversation between themselves. More about that on your guided tours.'

Keir noted the highly professional quality of his illustrations and his clear delivery. *Why isn't he a university lecturer?*

Bosworth finished exactly on time without prompting from the chair and used his jutting jaw signal to suggest readiness for some questions.

Dr. Remington spoke first, directing his question through the chair:

'Brian! Could Captain Bosworth explain to our rookies how these little guys feed?'

'Yes, Dr. Remington,' Bosworth replied, 'It's mainly by absorption through their skin, a very complex organ which I think Dr. Smythe will be discussing in her talk. So I won't steal her thunder.'

'OK, thanks. We'll wait for the details,' Clark said.

'Do your aliens show any need for seasonal variations in their requirements?' asked Midori Fung.

'Not very much, Professor Fung. They seem remarkably uniform and behave as if they are not used to seasons at all.'

'That is what we find also. Thank you, Captain.'

Bosworth returned to his seat next to Keir. Then Burton allowed two more questions before inviting Dr. Rowena Smythe's contribution: 'Please begin, Dr. Smythe.'

'Thank you. The aliens' physiology is by human standards unusual,' she began. 'And the new recruits will soon be seeing for themselves many of these features. Perhaps most obvious are their primary and secondary limbs.'

Rowena displayed a diagram.

'They have remarkable manual dexterity, if you can call it that. The reasons for this are structural.'

A new diagram depicted the complexity of their hands.

'It's probably best to think in terms of fractals. They have several levels of manipulation, all of which are co-ordinated by these special lobes in the cerebellum.' The next diagram appeared. 'And in their motor cortex...' Another diagram. 'Which is actually distributed like ganglia in a specialised nerve fibre network. As you can see, quite different to ours.' A series of further well labelled diagrams appeared. 'Respiration through their skin is similar to that of frogs but they also use well developed lungs... Now their sense organs... In common with us, they do have tactile sensitivity. They also have eyes, four of them, all sensitive to the same visible spectrum as ours but extended a little further into the infra-red and ultra-violet. They respond to acoustic stimuli like us, but again with extended ranges of sound frequency. We have found evidence of two other important types of sense organs. Like pigeons and certain other birds, they have a reliable navigation sense that we think is magnetic in nature. The other interesting sense is electromagnetic, a response to radio waves. We are not yet sure of the mechanism, but we think they can actually see the ionosphere, or at least its effects on the reflection or refraction of radio waves, and can detect lightning strikes many hundreds, possibly thousands, of miles distant. Finally, I'd like to emphasise that their methods of communication are mainly optical, a subject in its own right, and deserves a special session sometime in the future. As does their life cycle and methods of reproduction. But perhaps most interesting is recent evidence of their ability to modify their bodies through gene switching and to accomplish this by acts of will. Likewise, this deserves a future session.'

Rowena gathered her notes and commented:

'It would help if we understood a little more of their psychology and sociology, too!'

Two questions were permitted. Firstly from Remington:

'Cindy here would like to know how they react to narcotics.'

'An interesting question!' remarked Rowena. 'The aliens agreed to try some here, in a carefully controlled set of experiments. Not one of the substances had any detectable effects at the levels administered. We didn't overdo things and risk harming them, of course! But the reason for their resistance seems to be their biochemistry. There's a high degree of self-regulation, involving very complex and selective enzyme producing mechanisms. Within seconds of being detected, specialised enzymes are known to play a part in destroying the drugs, and the residues are excreted through the skin or in the urine. This may also explain why the creatures are so placid. But they can become excited at times. During mating, for example.'

There were a few smiles on the screens and titters in the audience, which Rowena pointedly ignored. 'Above all, they have a strong aesthetic response to sound, form and colour - in fact, anything sensory. But even here, there is a degree of control and we don't really understand the how or why of it.'

'Thanks, Dr. Smythe. We've observed this aesthetic sense as well, and one of our people is looking at the psychology of it. We'll keep you posted,' Remington promised.

'That's great. Thank you, Clark. Any more questions?'

'One from the Northland's dusky forests, I think, for Dr. Smythe.' Burton announced. 'Dr. Gazetny, please.'

Keir couldn't help being totally absorbed by Valentina's image on the Finnish screen. He knew she couldn't see him, as her British screen would hold Rowena's image. So he gazed fixedly at her, savouring every facial detail.

Her clear, slightly accented voice filled the room as well as the headsets of those using them:

'I sympathise with all the new delegates, as I'm as keen as they are to ensure the aliens have the highest quality care we can give. When you learn more about them, I'm sure you'll find the very word "alien" repugnant in this context.' Keir received her words with some relief.

'Even so,' she said, 'my question is this: When are these creatures to receive their freedom? Can their genetic engineering be steered towards compatibility with our environment, so that they can roam our forests and enjoy the things we enjoy?'

Keir wondered if others had detected the slight edge of emotion in her brief polemic speech.

'First suggestion of genetic engineering as a human intervention!' Keir whispered in Bosworth's ear.

'I noticed that, too,' he said. 'And it makes me uneasy.'

'Dr. Smythe?' prompted Burton.

Before replying, Rowena paused to gather her thoughts. 'I understand your concern,' she replied, 'but I assure you that we do all we can to ensure the aliens' comfort. And what you say might happen sooner rather than later.'

Keir detected a slight falter in Rowena's voice, and she had flushed slightly.

'Oops!' Keir murmured to Bosworth. 'It didn't take Rowena long to let that slip!'

'Thank you, Rowena,' Burton said, 'and everyone else for their contributions. The session is now closed.'

'A little hasty, Brian,' Keir murmured.

'Careful, Keir!' Bosworth whispered. 'Hope your headset microphone's turned off.'

Burton turned to look directly into the camera. 'We now have a one hour break. For lunch in our case. The sessions to follow the tours will be organised by Captain Leo Bosworth.'

Keir checked his microphone switch. Thankfully he had turned it off. He then looked carefully at Burton. If Rowena had committed an act of indiscretion, it didn't show on his face.

*****

8 Encounter at Andover

1.00p.m. conference room, Andover.

The lunch had been more like a banquet, Keir thought while spotting a vacant easy chair in the lobby. Before he could sit down a short, stocky sergeant approached.

'May I see your pass, please, sir?' he asked. '…Thank you, sir. This way. Come with me.'

At a flagged courtyard outside, Captain Bosworth was waiting.

'Keir Wilson, sir!' the sergeant announced, exchanging salutes with Captain Bosworth.

'Thank you, Sergeant. Hello Keir, this is Sergeant Hutchinson who will conduct you around the new facilities.'

Captain Bosworth pulled a clip-board from under his arm.

'Right, then.' he said. He looked at his watch and ticked a box on his notepad. 'We'll meet back here thirty five minutes from now, at 13:40 hours precisely.'

'Yes, sir!' The sergeant saluted stiffly. He then led Keir towards a row of parked all-terrain vehicles. They climbed into the nearest one, another elderly but pristine olive drab Defender 90. The Land Rover's turbo-diesel engine roared into life.

'How far do we drive?' Keir asked

'Not far,' the sergeant replied, curtly.

'Are any others coming with us?' Keir asked.

'No, said the sergeant. 'We show people round one at a time at each of the three viewing galleries. The tours are staggered as well. So as not to stress the aliens, you see,' he explained.

The vehicle pulled up at a perimeter gate and was checked through the barrier by an armed sentry. The sergeant steered a course through narrow lanes between buildings for a distance of about half a kilometre. The Land Rover passed through another checkpoint and stopped outside an imposing steel-clad building with impressively large sliding doors which were half opened. They disembarked and made their way, under a bright sunlit sky, across a concrete apron, towards the enclosure.

Keir peered into the gloom. Steel scaffolding surrounded the domed hull of the enclosure which almost filled the interior of the huge hangar. The outside surface of the inner structure was smooth and white. Glass-fibre reinforced plastic, he noted. Facing him was a horizontal array of five windows, about one and a half metres above ground level. He estimated that there must be room for about twenty such groupings of windows spaced around the dome. The warm, stifling air on his face carried a nauseating smell. He recognised it as the same odour he'd experienced earlier, in the street. The sergeant placed his right palm on a security pad and they entered a small room lit with strip lights. Items of protective clothing hung on a rack.

Keir and his guide slipped into bright yellow over-trousers and jackets, complemented by pairs of blue wellington boots, safety goggles and blue hard-hats.

'This gear is corrosion-proof,' explained the guide. He pulled a head-torch from a pouch on his belt. 'And you'll need one of these, just in case the lights fail. The switch is here. Strap it to your helmet.'

Keir tested it.

'Thanks,' he said, fixing it to his hard-hat.

'Next, we use the hand lotion dispenser and disinfectant matting on entering and leaving the airlock,' Keir's guide said. 'We have to maintain positive pressure in the dome.'

'Of course.' Keir appreciated the need for an interior free from contamination by terrestrial organisms. 'H.G. Wells rules OK,' he murmured.

'What did you say?'

'Nothing!' Keir's oblique reference to War of the Worlds was probably lost on his taciturn companion, who was making for a door to their left. It opened outwards and they squelched forward on wet flooring and more disinfectant matting into the brightly lit chamber. Their protective clothing glistened in the pallid glare of a strip light above another door immediately ahead. They approached it.

'In there. Let's go!' His guide gave a curt jerk of the head, motioning Keir to follow behind. It took about half a minute before their eyes grew accustomed to the more subdued light level of the enclosure. More panels of windows ran along both sides of an elevated narrow covered walkway that bisected the floor of the dome. Keir's guide extinguished the corridor lights.

The spatter of water on wet concrete grew louder and the air became intolerably oppressive. Keir felt perspiration trickling down his collar somewhere inside his plastic cocoon which seemed to stick and flex more awkwardly with every movement. But this was of minor consideration compared with the sickening feeling in the pit of his stomach. Was it the surroundings? The smell, perhaps. Or was it the knowledge that the seconds were counting down on what would be his first sight of the aliens? Beneath an air recycling duct, Keir found his breathing a little easier. A wall meter showed a pressure equivalent to just under one and a quarter atmospheres. He knew that beyond the viewing windows, the artificial atmosphere of the dome would be hostile to almost all terrestrial animal life. Nine percent carbon dioxide, sixteen percent oxygen. The rest was nitrogen, with lesser but potent amounts of hydrogen sulphide and other sulphurous gases, plus traces of methane and ammonia. He remembered being told that the artificial 'rain' which he could now see pouring down from sprinkler valves was rich in dissolved sulphur dioxide. The liquid appeared to steam as it trickled into a network of shallow sluice channels set in the concrete floor of the chamber. The atmosphere of the chamber was being circulated quite vigorously; mist and spray wafted against the windows, rather like a bad driving day in the outside world. It was proving quite difficult to see any sign of the expected alien creatures, as he moved from window to window. He could just make out the other two viewing galleries, one on each side of theirs. There were occasional clusters of unearthly looking tree-ferns about three metres high, whether artificial or real it was difficult to say. Had the aliens gone to ground somewhere or simply vanished in the haze?

Keir pulled a glove back to glance at his watch. 'Pity, I suppose we'll have to head back soon,' he said.

*****

Conference room, Andover.

Captain Bosworth returned to the chair's desk and waited with Burton for the time signal which would herald the next event, a closed session to be conducted in absence of the new recruits at the various viewing centres.

At the appointed time, Bosworth's image reappeared on the central screen: 'Welcome to the start of this Special Session. Now I join you all in extending a very special welcome the Secretary General of the United Nations, Ms. Zainad Masoud.'

Within the various conference centres, all eyes turned to the new speaker, her image on Burton's screen.

'Thank you, Professor Burton and Captain Bosworth of the British delegation, for organising this conference, and for allowing me for the first time to take part.'

The Secretary General spoke with formal dignity, and her dark eyes sparkled with a keen intelligence. She settled to a more relaxed composure and continued: 'You would be right in supposing that your work has become a matter of major concern for world peace and unity. Indeed, since April last year, when two of our governments, those of Argentina and France, requested assistance from the United Nations in directing their work in the nurture of alien colonies, a coherent strategy has evolved. By now, you will all be aware of the new powers of office which are vested in me, following last month's Council meeting in Geneva, at which the resolution was passed to amend Article W-1401. Following that meeting, I have formally accepted the recommendation under Clause 3 of that Article, which confers on me *de-facto* Chair-ship of Electra, your international project, in its entirety. This duty became effective from 12 noon UCT on Friday last, and each of the government bodies concerned are now accountable to me.'

*****

1.15 p.m. Downing Street, Defence Secretary's office.

At his office in Downing Street, Iain MacFarlane, the Defence Secretary, drained his cup of tea and crossed the room to close the window against the noise of a police helicopter patrolling above the buildings.

His headset automatically readjusted its sensitivity to match the sudden quietness of the room as he listened attentively to the UN Secretary General on his communication terminal. 'The code-name for the project remains unchanged as Electra,' she said.

'And trust the French and Argies to have put their oars in!' he growled to himself. He'd played a significant role in the emergence of Britain and the USA as joint leaders of the project. Now, in his view, they were being visibly sidelined. In spite of his misgivings, MacFarlane gained consolation from the notion of sharing his responsibility with the UN, should things go wrong. But these hopes were short-lived, as he listened further:

'In Project Electra, the sole agents acting on my behalf will be the heads of government of the countries concerned. It is my aim to maintain at all times an efficient, streamlined administration capable of flexibility, speed and effectiveness of response. This administration will operate at the highest levels of security. To this end, all infrastructure communications will be through secure, closed channels. Otherwise it will be largely unchanged. For the next three months, while we consolidate, constitution of the Inner Team will remain frozen, as will recruiting to the project. Administrative co-operation between bases will continue along present lines, but certain countries will need to follow others in tightening up their security.'

MacFarlane keyed into his netbook while listening.

'Some of you may be concerned at the news of my involvement. I emphasise that this is not bureaucratic imposition but one of the many duties conferred upon me by international agreement. In the circumstances which have arisen, the United Nations is to play an increasingly pro-active role in serving the needs of its member nations. This is especially the case now that these nations, and the world at large, have to adjust for the first time in history to the realisation that humanity no longer occupies its hitherto unique position as the most intelligent species on this planet. What the ultimate consequences of this adjustment will be is hard to predict, but one thing is certain. The initial phase of the adjustment process is crucial and must be carefully controlled. Above all, the human population of this planet must see their governments, the international community, and in particular, the United Nations and its member countries, as bastions of stability amid the pressures and changes that will inevitably occur. I use the word *inevitably* because, although a policy of complete containment has been implemented with all involved nations, we cannot assume that this will continue. Nor is it ethical. Up to the present, there has been no evidence of aggression or potential belligerence on the part of the alien population, and it behoves the United Nations to take a stand for good will and co-operation at the outset. That is not to assume that everything will go smoothly and we anticipate that some will feel insecure or threatened by the emergence of an alien intelligence and the development of its social, cultural and political structure.'

MacFarlane turned up the volume control.

'Certain situations and events may require my direct intervention. I mention this now in case my future actions should be misinterpreted by some as ill-considered or panic measures. During the next three days, I will be contacting separately your heads of government to discuss further details. Here, as in other areas of my work, I intend to carry out my official brief of service to the best of my ability, and look forward to your continuing co-operation in all aspects of our historically important endeavour. Thank you. That is all for now. I wish you well.'

Captain Bosworth thanked the General Secretary; then the screen went blank as the connection terminated.

Addressing the delegates, Bosworth announced: 'It is nearly time for the Inner Team members of each participating nation to convene, while the others will continue with an informal break at their respective establishments; all to consider the import of what has been said. Some of you will be joined by your recruits returning from their tours. Then we'll report back for the plenary session in forty minutes from now. This is intended primarily for the benefit of the recruits. Questions relating to the Secretary General's speech will be welcome. After that, I'll bring the conference to a close. We adjourn now for ten minutes.'

MacFarlane, in common with his peer officials in several other countries, had felt dazed when the image of the UN Secretary General faded from the screen. Within fifteen seconds, his telephone was ringing.

'Yes, David. On my way.' MacFarlane grabbed a folder from his desk as he headed for the Prime Minister's study.

*****

1.20 p.m. Alien Enclosure, Andover.

Suddenly, in the middle distance, Keir saw them. Feelings of nausea gripped him. He turned away and fought against his natural reactions, in the knowledge that any contamination of the enclosure by humans would be viewed with utmost gravity.

'Are you all right?' His guide looked intently through the droplets on his visor.

'I'm fine.' Keir turned slowly around and faced the window. Something like a slimy carpet, slightly to the left and close to one of the tree-ferns, occupied an area of about three square metres on the floor and extended partly up the trunk of the tree. Inside this, something was moving. He felt the plastic peak of his hard-hat scraping the window and took it off, along with the visor, in an effort to see more clearly.

The artificial lighting was dim, but sufficient to observe the rounded shapes of two hump-like objects emerging from the gelatinous mass. Then a third hump arose. A trio of turtle-like creatures was now standing erect on what could have been three hind legs or perhaps two legs and a stumpy tail. They were roughly equal in height; about one metre to the tops of each of their heads, which appeared to be scaly, dome-shaped protuberances devoid of any obvious sense organs or mouth.

The dominant colour of the bodies was brown, mottled with slate grey and orange. Keir found it difficult to tell. Everything was so wet and glistening with multiple reflections. He observed that the bodies resembled conical sand-piles. In spite of its wetness, the skin appeared scaly and tough. But there was another strangely contrasting aspect of their appearance which drew his attention.

The hands. Several of them, not in regular pairs, but on multiply jointed arms emanating from a flap or fold in the skin on each side of the body. These openings extended from where the shoulder would be, down to 'thigh' level. The hands themselves had incredibly long, delicate fingers. No claws or nails, but very prehensile. The total number and actual sizes of the hands were very difficult to assess, but Keir estimated that each creature owned at least three pairs of smallish hands and two pairs, if it was really right to think in pairs, of larger ones. All of these hands were being used, to a greater or lesser extent, in what seemed to be acts of gesticulation. The motions appeared sometimes rhythmic, sometimes random, but often very subtle.

Then the eyes. Keir knew they were eyes. One pair located on the front surface, just below each shoulder. They each erupted from a lid-like structure and were supported on short, retractable muscular stems. There appeared to be another pair of eyes, closer together, situated on the lower part of the body, where one might have expected to find sex organs.

'Amazing, aren't they?' Keir's taciturn companion came to life unexpectedly.

'I just can't believe it.' Keir heard himself say. Then, after a long silence: 'Look at those hands. They seem to be intense communicators, don't they?'

'Yes. But wait for the pictures.'

Keir recalled the series of colour illustrations in Rowena's talk.

'You mean photographs?' He again wondered how much Brodie and Savage already knew.

'I'm not talking about photos. I mean these, *here*.' The guide indicated another small group, nearer to the windows but well to the right of the first group. Keir hadn't noticed these until now.

'OK. Got them?' the sergeant continued, 'Now look at the abdomen!'

'Which one?'

'Any. Just keep watching!'

'Hey, look! There's a hexagonal pattern on it. Like a honeycomb. Must be about six to eight hundred little hexagons roughly equal in size. No! What? They've become a mixture of squares and triangles, the inner ones have, anyway. And slightly different colours, like a patchwork quilt.'

As Keir watched, he saw the design flicker and merge into other geometrical patterns. Sometimes the changes were too quick to follow. While this was happening, something else caught his attention.

'Look at the other one's abdomen!' Keir said. 'Some pattern changes are being shared! This might be their main method of visual communication.'

'We think so,' said the guide, 'but there's ultrasound, too. Like dolphins. That's usually for middle distances. For long distances they use radio. Very low power but narrow bandwidth. I'm in the Signal Corps, we sometimes pick them up on our sets. When they get closer, they use coloured patterns. For brief signals it's mainly hands.'

'Incredible! Do they form groups and have meetings?'

'We're pretty sure that for most involved discussions they use their patterns.'

Keir ignored the uncomfortable prickling of his scalp and the perspiration running down his face.

'Looks like graphics symbols,' he said. 'You don't see anything looking like a TV picture or a photo, do you?'

'Sometimes. Oi! Put your 'elmet and visor on!'

Keir complied.

'You *have* seen actual pictures, then?'

'Yes, but sometimes you can't be altogether sure. It all happens so quickly and the displays are usually faint, anyway, as you can see.' His guide seemed rather evasive, Keir thought, as he cast his eyes around the compound.

'Well,' Keir commented, 'there's not a lot for them to do here, is there? Wouldn't you think they'd give these creatures more stimulating surroundings?'

His guide shrugged, then beckoned with a nod. They both moved off towards the other end of the corridor, eventually reaching a place where one of the windows looked into a smaller chamber. Keir noticed that the interior was again dimly illuminated.

'Take a look at this!' the guide said, with his visor pressed to the glass of another window overlooking the same room.

Keir lowered his gaze, and was amazed to see immediately below the window two of the creatures standing about half a metre apart with their arms extended in a kind of mutual embrace. Their arms and hands seemed completely intertwined and their heads were only partly visible and like flat, scaly domes. But most of all, it was the abdominal display which preoccupied him. Furiously, the images flickered and moved; quite dim, yet distinctly visible through the gaps between their arms. The shifting fields of patterns and textures of both creatures seemed to signify an intimate dialogue of immense complexity. The eyes of the creatures appeared to operate independently rather than in pairs. He could just discern the faint glare which one body cast on the other, as the patterns grew and dissolved.

Abruptly, the pair of creatures paused then continued again for a few seconds. Another pause. This time, Keir caught a glimpse of something before the flickering patterns resumed. Undeniably it was an image of a human face. As he watched, the realisation dawned upon him that it was his own. His next thirty seconds were spent wondering if the face image had been specifically aimed at him, or whether he was merely an incidental part of their conversation.'

'I've just seen my own face on that one,' Keir said. 'And that's odd, because my visor's on.'

'You removed it a couple of minutes ago, back there.'

'You mean..?'

'Yes. When one of them finds something out, it's not long before they all know.' the sergeant said.

Keir saw no re-occurrence of the event. But the geometric patterns and shifting colours continued. Lines and surrounding edges of tinted areas were clear and sharp. Keir noticed that the dominant shades of colour being transmitted were reds, through orange and yellow. Green was rare and fainter and blue seemed to be absent, unless it appeared on its own. When that happened, it was a rippling network of electric blue, like dim lightning flashes. Recovering from the shock of a few moments ago, he began to feel drawn to the subtlety and sheer beauty of the moving designs.

'I'd like to know what they think of our abstract art,' Keir said.

'Probably same as I do, crap,' said Hutchinson.

Keir murmured: 'I wonder what Kirsti thinks. She'll be viewing something like this at Oulu Base.'

Curiously, the area containing this pair of creatures was dry, except for a few wet patches on the floor. In the background Keir could see digital displays of instruments in wall panels. There were several rows of touch pad switches, some indicator lights and three larger display screens on the far wall. A long desk, about half a metre above floor level, supported several desktop workstations equipped with 'QWERTY' keyboards and their own screens. A closed door indicated a possible adjoining closet or suite of other rooms. None of the low stools in front of the workstations was occupied.

'They type with those keyboards?' Keir asked.

'I was hoping for a demo from them, but they're not doing it at the moment,' the sergeant replied with a note of disappointment. He added, with a rueful smile: 'Most of the time they don't need to type. They can stick their fingers directly into the USB ports and send signals that way.'

'Digital signals with their fingers?'

'That's right! They learnt that in a few minutes. And it lends new meaning to the term *digital signals*, eh?' the sergeant chortled at his own joke. First time he's laughed, Keir thought.

The guide continued: 'And that's not all. They can receive through our equipment as well as transmit. A game their kids play is to grab image data through a USB or printer port and display it on their bellies. Bright little beggars, aren't they, sir? In case you think I'm 'avin' you on, the Captain's got photos back in his office.'

'I think I'm just about ready to believe anything,' Keir said.

*****

The blinding daylight and fresh air were most welcome as Keir stepped outside. It was already 1:36 p.m.

'C'mon, sir. Mustn't be late!' The sergeant walked straight past him and started up the Land Rover. Back at the rendezvous point, they arrived in time to see Captain Bosworth emerging from a doorway.

Bosworth returned the sergeant's salute and nodded a greeting to Keir before pulling the clip-board from under his left arm.

'How did you get on? Interesting, eh?' He began entering his updates. 'Sergeant,' he continued, 'Mr. Wilson's seen everything?'

'Yes, sir. Everything, except the gel chambers.'

'Fine. Thank you, sergeant.' He turned to Keir. 'Actually, I can think of better things just now. After that experience, let's see if there's any coffee left. Eh, Wilson old chap?'

Bosworth clapped an arm over Keir's shoulder as they made their way towards the atrium near the conference hall.

'Well, Keir,' Bosworth said, 'Project Electra is properly on the road at last. The UN has taken it over. That should mean better organisation and relative safety for the aliens.'

'Let's hope so,' Keir said. 'Tell me, why the name Electra?'

'It stems from the 2003 event. The first sighting took place on the Skagen peninsula in Denmark. Not very far from the tip at Grenen. The kid involved was wandering around a bird sanctuary at a location called Ellekrattet. As you'd expect, rather a mouthful for English speakers, who called it Electra.'

'Thanks. Now you've mentioned it,' Keir said,' I vaguely remember the district name in the report but didn't connect it. Can I ask you something else, quite different?'

'Fire away!' Bosworth said as he poured the coffee.

'You know, Captain, it's my impression after the shock of seeing alien life, I'm not convinced this is just a simulation.'

'Really? Why do you say that, Keir?'

'Back in our 2085 world, I studied several logs and reports of simulation missions, including diagnostics like rendering of skin textures and other complex surfaces such as rocks and vegetation. But in this world the level of detail is incredibly real, physically and emotionally.'

'I know, I know!' Bosworth replied, his voice now a whisper. 'Professor Litchfield thinks that something new is happening.'

'New?' Keir's mind flashed back to his recent view of the moon through binoculars and the missing crater Aristarchus.

'He admits the RIPE computer's having a hard time fulfilling the needs of this mission. It hasn't given up, though. He thinks that, as ever, it's adopted a novel approach. Rather than attempting an exhaustively precise simulation, it's been doing something else.'

'I know that lately it's been exploring theoretical physics.'

'Meaning?' Bosworth asked.

'Don't ask me how, but I think Galena's using Litchfield's laboratory to create a portal to a parallel universe.'

'One that matches and assimilates your 2003 event?'

'Why not? Some scientists think there are an infinite number of parallel universes. And perhaps there's no upper limit to what self-evolving computers can achieve! This is all conjecture, of course. Of one thing I am certain, though - I'm no longer strapped to a chair in Litchfield's lab! OK I admit, I'm biased. But it would be marvellous for me if this *is* a parallel universe and *not* a simulation. The people in it would be real.'

'Actually, Keir, if that's the case, your mission could perhaps help in clarifying...'

'That's all very well,' Keir interrupted, 'but how would it affect getting back?'

A bell rang. They joined the other delegates drifting towards the conference hall.

Bosworth said, 'Lichfield's brainchild *was* programmed to return us to our world of 2085, via the CMI route.'

'Then we can only hope Galena's been working on it!' On the other hand, Keir thought, *if Valentina's a real person, would I want to go back?*

*****

9 Electra

4:00pm (local time) Oulu Base.

The plenary teleconferenced session opened just as Kirsti had drained another cup of strong, black coffee; her third in succession. Gripping Valentina's arm, she still hadn't recovered from her tour of the alien enclosure at Oulu Base. Loma, on the other hand, appeared excited, with her attention riveted on editing her list of questions.

Ilya turned to both recruits: 'Loma, Kirsti. I need your questions now, please.' They each hit their *send* keys.

'Thank you,' said Bosworth's screen image. His cap and gloves were before him on the desk. 'Now that I have all your questions, I'll channel them to their intended recipients. If we run out of time here, answers can be relayed to your respective bases via secure link. All questions and replies will be recorded in the minutes.'

The image zoomed so that Bosworth's face filled the screen. 'Before we continue, here is another important announcement. Most of us will be aware that the name for this project is confirmed as Electra. Revised information about Project Electra and details of updated security procedures will be sent out in the near future to your various locations. Thank you.'

Bosworth read from a flat monitor screen at his elbow. 'Right! The first question of this session is from a recruit in the United States.'

The written text also appeared on the USA screen of the wall matrix, accompanied by a voice-over:

'Eddie Shultz, Sloan, for Mr. Bosworth. How long do you think it'll be before word of this thing gets out? I guess, someone somewhere stands to get a cool few million for the story'.

'Well, let me answer that one for you, Eddie,' replied Captain Bosworth, hardly concealing the irritation he felt over the omission of his rank. 'As a Field Executive for Electra security in my country, I'm well placed to give you and anyone else a strong word of advice. Don't even *accidentally* become party to such an act. I can only give you the British standpoint, of course. Any such relaxation of guard by recruited personnel would be regarded here as very serious indeed. If their *mistake* was confirmed, their protected status could be withdrawn, which means that their prospects for survival could diminish accordingly. As for the American equivalent of this scenario, I recommend that you put your question to your superiors in Massachusetts.

Bosworth's eyes dropped as he again read from his desk screen. 'The second question is from Singapore.'

'Professor Midori Fung, Singapore, for Dr. Smythe. Can these creatures be infected by any of our diseases, and if so, can they be immunised?'

'Rowena,' invited Bosworth.

'The short answer for both parts of your question, is yes,' Rowena replied. 'Their immune system is about as robust as their resistance to toxins and drugs, which means that it's very effective. But certain of our bacilli can be problematic for them. Tetanus, for example. We nearly lost two young adults last year from that infection. But they seem to adapt rapidly; and so far, their resistance to attack by terrestrial micro-organisms is remarkable. Their immune system is much more complex than ours. In fact, a group of them is liaising with our medical staff in developing quite novel techniques for prevention and treatment of disease, some of which may be effective in cases of human infection.'

'Thank you, Rowena,' said Bosworth. 'I'll have to cut you short, although I think you've stated the position clearly. The next question is from Finland.'

'Kirsti Kivi, Kuopio and Oulu Base. Where did you and your colleagues first find traces of the organic material that prompted you to look for life and regenerate these creatures? My question is for Professor Burton.'

'Thank you, Dr. Kivi. Brian?' prompted Bosworth.

'Brian Burton cleared his throat and scratched his left ear for a few seconds. Long enough time, Keir thought, to detect that he found difficulty in giving a straight and truthful answer. Nuances of body language, not apparent to the other conference viewers, confirmed his impression.

'Several years ago,' Burton began, 'I think it was eighteen to twenty, a colleague from the University of Hawaii showed me a carbonaceous chondrite from his laboratory. A fraction of it, about fifteen grams, was, he told me, being processed in the Ukraine. I asked him what he meant by *being processed* and he said, in very simple terms, that they were analysing the organic content and had found some particularly complex molecules.

He speculated that these were near precursors to nucleotide chains in the building blocks of life. There were other investigators, too, doing similar research.'

Keir felt certain that Burton, whose rambling story might have some foundation in fact, merely played for time. Bosworth glanced at the wall-clock.

'This was the inspiration behind the work, which was started in the USA, Britain and elsewhere, to reach the goal you've seen being achieved today,' Burton continued, casting a glance at Bosworth, 'and now we have access to part of the Kuopio meteorite ourselves, which you have been so diligent in locating.'

'I'm sorry, Brian; you've timed out. I apologise, Dr. Kivi, but perhaps the answer to your question can be completed in the manner I suggested earlier. Is that all right, Brian?' Bosworth asked.

'Of course!' said Burton, thankfully.

'Burton's up to his neck in something, that's for sure!' Keir murmured to himself. Then, with a start, he recalled the value of silent thought and again hoped that there were no active microphones, hidden or otherwise, nearby.

*****

3:30pm, Andover Military Institute.

Keir waited for his de-briefing in a small room adjoining the main entrance hall. Through the open door, the majestic arrays of heraldic shields again caught his attention. He would resist any temptation to press Burton with further questions about the early days of his meteorite experiments. Instead, he resolved to watch and listen very carefully for anything he could add to the sparse jigsaw puzzle in his mind. Surprisingly, Rowena Smythe entered and sat beside him.

'Hello, Keir. What's *your* impression?' she asked. 'That is, about the conference and seeing the aliens for the first time?'

'Quite mind blowing.'

'You're taking it very well and I'm impressed.'

'Thank you. I'll probably have a few nightmares for a fortnight,' Keir said.

'Hmm. Well, I hope it isn't too pushy of me; how would you feel about moving to Level Two?'

'What's involved?'

'Just a small task. And I think it's right to tell you, you're well on your way to becoming material for the Middle Echelon.'

'I do feel rather ghost-like,' Keir declared, 'and the prospect of becoming material intrigues me.'

'Let's get on, shall we? This means, in practical terms, that you are to return to Oakingwell, but first you have to carry out this small mission on the way, as part of your ongoing training. Now that you've seen everything, well, almost everything, you should leave here as soon as you can and if anyone asks, you've never been here.'

'Thanks Rowena, I suppose it's good to be in line for promotion but what have I done? Nothing as far as I can tell! And from your perspective, why is it necessary for me to avoid mentioning this place?'

'Being part of Project Electra changes a lot of things for all who are involved, Keir. I understand you also attended that army training exercise near Oulu.'

'It was only a short one.'

'Doesn't matter. From now on, mention of your overt connections with the military has to be minimised. As in my own case, most of your responsibilities will be realised from the *academic* arm of our organisation, rather than the military one. Also from now on, under Project Electra you will be my responsibility. At least until the remainder of your time at Oakingwell. Your immediate priority will be to complete your thesis under Alan's continuing supervision.'

'I was wondering when somebody would mention that!'

'I'm sure you were, Keir. Quite rightly! You can't be expected to follow through your new duties with an unsatisfactory academic record. The military are just as keen for your success as I am, and we're confident you can do it, otherwise you wouldn't have been recruited in the first place, let alone be on a path for promotion.'

'But just say, what if..?'

'If you didn't complete your thesis? Keir, that would be deemed a *mistake*, perhaps not quite in the sense that Leo mentioned to that young American this afternoon, but we would have a problem deciding what to do with you.'

'There's nothing like a bit of pressure, I suppose!' Keir said.

'You'll be OK. If you've been to Finland, you'll know what they mean by *sisu*.'

'I've still a long way to go with my Finnish.'

'I'm talking about guts and determination to succeed. And there's no harm in telling you that your aggregate test score is the highest yet. But don't get over-confident. That could also lead to mistakes, and now I *am* talking about the Bosworth definition.'

'Thank you. I'll be careful.'

'That brings me to another point. A moment ago it sounded to me as though you actually *intended* to go further with your Finnish. Is that so?'

'It's an interesting language and culture.'

'It is, I don't deny it. But come on, now!' Rowena inclined her head and gave him a sidelong look. 'You don't have to bullshit with me, Keir. You're quite interested in other things, too.'

Keir dropped his gaze. 'I like the people.'

Rowena gazed up at the ceiling, then fixed her eyes on him.

'And one person in particular, Keir? You're quite far gone on Valentina, aren't you?'

A brief silence.

She continued: 'It doesn't take much feminine intuition to see that if it had been possible, you would have leaped into that screen and ravished her!'

Keir felt dissected by this uncalled-for barrage. But a resolve crystallised within him. He gathered himself and calmly looked Rowena in the eye.

'Rather a heavy way of putting it, Rowena. If you're suggesting that there's something between us, well yes, I feel that I'm in love with her. Is that a problem?'

'It may turn out that way. Does she feel the same way about you?'

'Unfortunately, I've no reason to think so. Anyway, what does it really matter to you?'

'It matters a great deal to this organisation. They already know you're a good agent, or the makings of one. Now they know that you're human as well. But it could be your undoing.'

'You don't mind?' *And for agent, do I read spy?* He thought.

'Personally, dearest, it doesn't matter to me in the least. But as far as Project Electra's concerned, your relationship with Valentina really could make you vulnerable. And perhaps her as well. So you'd better make sure you apply your skills in preventing a minor complication becoming a major disaster. OK? End of lecture!'

Now maybe it's my turn, Keir felt: 'Are questions allowed after this lecture?' he asked.

'Well, I suppose so.'

'What's the full answer to Valentina's earlier question about setting the aliens free?'

'There isn't one. I'm lying, of course, but I think you're smart enough to understand why. It's an Inner Echelon question. As far as even the Middle Echelon are concerned, the matter remains closed until it's decided otherwise.'

'It's not out of the question?'

'It would be a *mistake* for me to say anything more on that subject. We'll move on to consider your itinerary, shall we?'

'Itinerary?'

'Yes, where you go when you leave here,' Rowena said. 'We don't like new recruits being followed, and we vary their exit patterns as much as we can. Now I want you to memorise all of this.' A small blue notebook had appeared in her hand. She opened it, glanced at her watch and continued: 'In fifteen minutes from now, we'll have some afternoon tea. Then, when I tell you, you'll go to Car Park B at the rear, where Sergeant Hutchinson will be waiting. You've met him already, right?'

'Yes.'

'He will take you to Winchester, where you'll board the Glasgow train from Southampton. Actually, you must leave the train at Crewe Junction. Then you'll catch a bus for Stockport from Crewe station. Got that? You'll get off the bus at Holmes Chapel and take a cab to the other end of the village. You'll ask the driver for the Cabbage Inn, where a room has been reserved for you in the name of Jonathan Sykes. Say it: *Jonathan Sykes.'*

'I'm Jonathan Sykes.'

'Good. In the morning, after breakfast, you check out and pay the bill in cash to a guy called Andy. You make sure it's Andy and nobody else. He'll give you a receipt and on the back of it you'll find your next instructions - for which you'll need more cash, which I have here. When you've read them, get rid of the instructions in the toilet. Don't use your credit card or any cheques, only cash. Here it is, seven thousand in used notes, with the issue form.' She opened her handbag and gave him an A5 buff envelope.

Keir glanced at the contents. 'What do I do with this form?' he asked.

'Satisfy yourself the cash is all there, sign the form and give it to me.' She watched as he checked the amount and signed. 'Thanks. Left handed, too. Like me. All the best people are left handed. Now in the back of the plastic wallet, you'll find your rail ticket. You'll use cash for the bus fare.' She reached in her bag for another item. 'This looks like a standard mobile telephone, unlike the fancy looking job Brian gave you. It's called an S4B and sets up a secure link with a password. If there's any irregularity whatsoever, you are to key in the code sequence I'll give you before you leave. If you lose this link-set, you go to any public call box and key 8831 followed by the same sequence. You'll hear three beeps and then nothing. That signifies destruction of the S4B link-set and its supporting electronics. But... loss of this link-set is a category-one mistake. Right?'

'Right! Is that it?' Keir asked.

'Ah! Hang on!' Rowena took from her bag a small piece of paper. 'It's your first password. Use it to make a call to the number that's written underneath and you'll see another password on the LCD screen. You're *au fait* with throw-away passwords?'

'Yes. Part of my military training.'

'Fine. At the start of each day, key in the expired password and use the telephone number you're given to get the password for that day.

'Just one small thing.'

'Yes?'

'If there's a technical problem?'

'Then contact Leo Bosworth. But be careful, dearest. He suffers fools less gladly than even I do.'

'I know. By the way, what will happen to me after my PhD?' He wondered if Bosworth is the only other person in this 'virtual' - possibly parallel - world who knows that his RIPE project is due to terminate in less than four months.

'You have a choice. To stay with Electra or leave. But you will still be bound by contract. We expect most people will stay. If they do well, they'll be looked after.'

'What contract?'

Rowena's face remained expressionless. 'The one which is about to be drawn up in the next few days. Now let me go through the travel arrangements once more with you, and then we'll go for our well-deserved tea.'

*****

Wednesday 25 August. Holmes Chapel, Cheshire.

Eighteen hours later, after breakfast at the inn, Keir's footsteps echoed on the empty forecourt of a garage not far from the town centre. As instructed, he'd put on a cloth cap and chequered scarf. The memorised list of instructions from Andy included a rendezvous at the garage. *Is it the right one? Arkwright's, yes. But where's the car?* He looked in vain for the second hand Mercedes saloon he needed to buy. Recalling Bosworth's fluent handling of the Defender, he muttered: 'Let's hope Galena's programmed me OK to drive a vintage car.'

'Yes, mate?'

Keir turned to meet the inquisitive stare of a middle-aged forecourt attendant. 'Is Mr. Lewis about?' he asked.

'That's me. Who are you?'

'Jonathan Sykes,' Keir replied.

'You've come about the Merc, then?'

'Yes. Do you have a silver-grey C-Class?'

'Round here.' The man calling himself Lewis opened a roller shutter door at the front of an outbuilding behind the garage.

Keir saw that there were three cars. Interestingly, two Mercedes, one of them on a ramp.

Lewis answered his mobile telephone: 'Hello Mr. Hartley. Yes, it arrived yesterday. I don't know. Hold on, I'll have to check in the office. Can I call you back in half an hour?' Lewis turned to Keir, 'Sorry, Mr. Sykes. I'll be with you in a couple of minutes.'

He left Keir looking at the cars and wondering which one had been earmarked for him. There were no price labels on them and the instructions had stated clearly that his car would have an advertised price of six thousand five hundred pounds. He remembered Rowena's parting words: 'If there is *any* irregularity whatsoever' and felt in his pocket for the reassuring plastic case of his secure new link-phone. *It's missing!* He tried other pockets, but in vain. He felt a trickle of sweat running down his cheek.

'Are you all right, Mr. Sykes?' Lewis had returned, and he walked over to a workbench inside the repair bay.

'Caught a cold, I think.'

'You look a bit rough, if you don't mind my saying so. Sorry to keep you standing around like this. Here, would you like some tea?' he extracted a vacuum flask from behind a large open tool box and poured some of the contents into an oil-stained mug.

'No, thanks. I'll be fine.' Keir said.

'It's going about, you know. The 'flu jabs don't seem to work around here. Are you from these parts?' Lewis drank from his mug.

Keir paused, pretending to blow his nose. 'Which of these Mercs is mine?' he asked.

'Oh, neither. While in the office, I double checked the sales list and yours is in the bay at the far end. I'll open the door for you. We finished servicing it late last night and it's ready for the road. Drives like a dream. We'll get it onto the forecourt, and then you can have a test run.'

Keir noticed the price stickers as specified. Any relief he felt being swamped by anxiety over the missing link-set. He watched as Lewis removed the stickers.

'There. Let's climb in,' said Lewis, 'now that we can see where we're going. By the way, is this yours?' From his overall pocket, Lewis produced a rectangular plastic object, which Keir recognised at once. With profuse thanks, he returned the link-phone to his anorak pocket, but not the one in which he'd kept his scarf. Keir zipped up the pocket and climbed into the driving seat beside Mr. Lewis.

When they returned to the forecourt a few minutes later, a few more customers had arrived. Some were looking at the other cars.

'Well, it's ready to drive away, said Lewis.' As I said, a full set of new tyres and shock absorbers.'

'Perhaps six thousand one hundred? I'd have to spend a couple of hundred on the interior and the spare wheel could be better,' Keir haggled.

'Tell you what. I'll do it for you at six three.'

'Six two? I'd be happy with that.'

'Very well, then. You've got a bargain, Mr. Sykes.'

The sequence of price figures matched those of the plan and they shook hands on the deal, Keir agreeing to pick up the car after lunch when it had been valeted.

At 14:05 hours, Keir nosed the Mercedes out of the garage, pulled over to the kerb and entered his destination into the satnav. Then he dialled a number Andy had given him and accessed a message on his link-set:

'Acknowledged, your destination is Liverpool, L13, Old Swan. Location is 47 Cranmer Street. Distance is 39 miles via the M6 and M62 motorways. Major road works after Junction 19, M6, estimated delays of up to 10 minutes. This is still quicker than alternative routes. Do you wish to confirm?'

'Yes,' Keir said.

'Confirmed. Your estimated time of arrival is 15:33 hours. Have a pleasant journey'.

That's odd, Keir thought. He entered another code into his link-set.

'Bosworth here.'

'Hi Leo. Do you know about my Cranmer Street mission?'

'Yes. Any problem?'

'Just left Holmes Chapel and I've felt another 'memory' being called into play. This time it isn't a pre-programmed one. Back in my 2085 world I was a frequent visitor to the city of Liverpool and I happen to know that Cranmer Street isn't in the Old Swan district, but down by the River Mersey.'

'Really? Thanks, Keir. I'll classify that finding with your missing Aristarchus one and let Bryant know. How's it going?'

'Thanks. I'm on the road heading for Liverpool now.'

'OK cheers. Have a good journey, old man. Over and out.'

Heading out towards the M6, the motor purred gently as the vehicle picked up speed. The Cheshire countryside rolled past at a leisurely pace. On the motorway, the weather began to change as banks of ragged nimbus clouds rolled in from the north-west. He hardly noticed as the cruise control compensated for the increased headwind. He turned off the M6 onto the M62, heading for Liverpool.

After leaving the M62 and negotiating moderate urban traffic, Keir guided the Mercedes north along the dual carriageway at Queens Drive and turned west at the Prescot Road traffic lights. The satnav took him through Old Swan and he turned into Cranmer Street as predicted, soon after half past three. He peered through the steady drizzle outside, observing the lack of numbers on most of the houses. He continued to count the doors to his left as the car slowly edged forward.

Opposite number 47 there should be a newsagent's shop. Keir checked his notes on the link-set. Then he donned a purple woollen bobble hat, locked the car and crossed the road. In the shop he bought a paper, three Mars bars and a tube of Smarties.

'Can I have a receipt, please?' Keir asked.

On the back of the receipt he expected another address. This time, 13 Bramble Street. On the satnav, the postcode would take him a few miles north.

After 9 minutes, he arrived. Suddenly, as Keir pulled into the kerb, the deserted street echoed with a loud crack. The rear window of the car imploded. Cubes of shattered glass were scattered everywhere throughout the interior. At the same time, he felt a blow to his right shoulder that pushed him into the steering wheel. Partly restrained by the seat belt, he swung round as he fell forward, his head catching the sun visor.

His ears were still ringing as he pulled himself straight in his seat, not knowing what to do next. Then instinct took over and he gunned the car towards the far end of the street. He noticed a shiny smear on the bezel of the dashboard and a crimson patch spreading out through the fabric of his sleeve.

'No! I've been shot!' Keir heard himself say. By now the car had reached a T-junction with another equally dismal street. It ploughed onward into the facing wall, Keir already unconscious.

The paramedical team stepped nimbly through glass splinters and the tangle of metal. They carried Keir on a stretcher, with drip, to their ambulance. The police made repeated sorties to the cordoned area, moving bystanders out of the way while taking photographs and examining the wrecked vehicle. A recovery wagon then removed it for further forensic examination.

*****

Thursday 26 August. Andover Institute, Major Bradford's Office.

Captain Bosworth saluted briskly as he joined the briefing meeting, the ever-present clipboard under his left arm.

'At ease!' said Major Ron Bradford. 'Looks like they managed to get to Wilson.'

'It would appear so, sir. Most unfortunate. But he's out of danger now, I'm told.'

'That's better news, Leo. Help yourself to coffee.'

'Thank you, sir. Having one yourself?' Captain Bosworth poured two cups. 'You'll remember he was a former trainee of ours. Didn't he do some training sessions with you?'

'Yes, that's right, Leo. Five university students in that bunch. Not nearly enough time to throw the whole works at them but Keir was fairly good by the end of it.'

'That's right, sir. He's still doing his PhD. His supervisor is one of Brian's men, Menzies.'

'Brian Burton?' The major raised the cup to his moustache. 'With a little effort, I can just about remember when he first became interested in meteorites, professionally, that is.'

'I didn't know that was another of your fields of expertise, sir.'

'Oh, hardly, Bosworth,' the major said. 'I'm an engineer, not a planetary scientist.'

'It's eleven thirty hours, sir. Shall I fetch Captain Evans?' Leo asked.

'Give her another minute. Ah! She's here now. Our resident queen of politics, logic and war games.' Major Bradford concealed the fact that he still smarted from being beaten by her in an online war game that had lasted for a month. He looked up from his desk as she entered.

'Sorry I'm late, sir!'

'All right, come on in, Jenny.' The major returned her salute. 'Have some coffee while it's still hot.'

'Thank you, sir. Have I missed anything?'

'No. We're about to begin. Please sit down. Here are today's briefing papers. Jenny, Leo.'

Captain Jennifer Evans sat in an easy chair next to Bosworth. At a nod from the major, they each opened brown envelopes. While they perused the contents, the major leaned back and lit his briar pipe. He turned to address his colleagues.

'Normally our meetings are fairly routine and relaxed affairs aren't they?' He followed the rhetorical question with a few puffs at his pipe, seemingly gathering his thoughts. 'However, we're here this time to consider a very serious, I'd say extremely grave, matter. It'll be some time before we can talk properly to Wilson. He'll be rather indisposed from his ordeal for several days. And the police will have already questioned him enough.'

'Doesn't he come under the project's Northern Administration now, since leaving Andover, sir?' Bosworth asked.

'Leo.' The major cast an irritated glance at his pipe and re-lit it. 'I feel certain, now that the UN is more involved, that Project Electra *will* have a more centralised administration. But I feel bound to support him any way I can. After all, he was one of our trainees. First, we need to assist his speedy recovery by ensuring he's not subjected to further stress. And if any media people do arrive here, we'll field the questions while deflecting attention away from the real purpose of his visit to Liverpool. The yellow sheet contains guidelines for your responses to the media. By the time this misinformation, if you will, has percolated through the news channels, we'll be ready to send someone else to Bramble Street if necessary.'

'I don't understand it, sir,' said Bosworth. 'As we know, the security level for his visit was triple-alpha and ostensibly he was just an anonymous member of the public visiting a friend. Regrettably for our security image, we don't know *how* the incident happened or who perpetrated it.'

'Sir?' Captain Evans asked.

'Yes, Dr. Evans?' The major unexpectedly used her academic title.

'I have a theory, Major. And with respect, both the publicity and planning of our training courses for civilians need revision.'

Captain Bosworth shifted uncomfortably in his chair.

'Go on,' the major said.

'As things are at present, it only needs a few on the outside to have over-active imaginations. We know there are still those who believe that when we sent trainees running around retrieving information from dead-letter boxes last year in all sorts of urban and rural sites, it was for a real secret operation. I know it's tempting to think that a reporter picked this up and also found out that Keir had attended one of our courses. However, I do believe that his visit to Andover and his exit were unobserved and that security has not been breached. Unless Keir himself has given the game away; although that to me appears unlikely.'

'Well, Leo, how do *you* account for the Liverpool affair?' the major asked.

'The car incident could have been an unrelated robbery attempt, or a case of mistaken identity in a gang-land feud. As soon as I heard about it, I re-researched the street and its immediate surroundings through police files and from as many other sources as I could.'

'Hmm! How do you know he wasn't followed? At Holmes Chapel, his link-set was mislaid for several minutes. A lot can happen in that time. Do we have a file on Mr. Lewis, the garage man? Even if you're right, Leo, it's still very unfortunate for everyone concerned.' The major motioned with his pipe stem towards the tabloid newspaper on his desk. 'It's a pity some fools can find no better way of earning their daily crust than writing this!'

A banner headline ran: 'TERRORISTS GUN DOWN SAS MAN.'

'In the face of this nonsense, what do you suggest is the way forward, Major?' asked Captain Evans.

'If there's to be a press conference,' he replied, 'then so be it. We read them the story that's on our yellow sheets and re-educate the public. Gently, no knee-jerk reactions. We must be very careful, or several undesirable things could happen. One, Keir and other operatives could be put in jeopardy. Two, we'd become scapegoats. Take a look at the Ministry of Defence Memorandum in your info' packs.'

Papers were shuffled as the major waited. He re-lit his pipe for the third time while his subordinates followed the typescript.

'It's clear from Item Five,' Major Bradford continued, 'that if there's any more adverse publicity of this kind, then our mission training courses will be cut from the budget. It goes on to say that the staff involved could face disciplinary procedures. That means us. Apart from these obvious warnings, the rest seems to me intractable unless you have a degree in law or English. How about you, Jennifer? Does it make any sense?'

'You've distilled the important points, sir. I'm more concerned about Item 19.'

'Yes. More gobbledegook, but I don't like the look of it. Could you paraphrase for us?' the major asked.

Jennifer scrutinised the document again.

'I don't like it either, Major.' she said. 'What bothers me most is the veiled threat, not just to Keir's mission, but to Keir himself. Items 13 to 20 are a list of governmental security support decisions in decreasing order of priority. Item 19 mentions a requirement for protective support on Type B missions from Andover. It's unusual to find mention of bases by name in this kind of memo and although Keir's mission isn't referred to specifically, it is Type B and I find its low position in the list disturbing. I think that Keir's mission could already be in danger. I mean, by default.'

'By default?' asked Bosworth.

'Yes, Leo,' Jenny continued. 'The wording of this document suggests, although it doesn't say so explicitly, that you might as well draw a line two thirds down the list and ignore the lower part. Put simply, low priority support here could mean risk of termination through withdrawal of protection.'

'Termination? Surely not!' exclaimed the Major.

Captain Leo Bosworth licked dry lips, not daring to pour himself another cup of coffee. As if reading his mind, the major arose from his desk, took Leo's cup and refilled it.

'Thank you, sir,' said Leo. 'Well, it's clear that we have real problems. And I feel that you shouldn't have been placed in this awkward situation, but now that it's happened, it's my responsibility to sort it out.'

As he handed Bosworth the cup, almost symbolically, the major's steel grey eyes were unwavering.

'Yes. Thank you, Leo,' he said. 'Let me know when you've drafted your suggestions; say, by four o'clock this afternoon?'

'Yes, sir.'

Bradford took a thoughtful pull on his briar. 'Bosworth, you may delegate, but keep a tight rein, won't you? Thank you both for coming. Dismissed.'

The door squeaked as Captains Bosworth and Evans exited.

'He wants to get some damned oil on those hinges!' Leo said when they were out of earshot. 'It'd be a start to putting *his* house in order!'

'Nice to get into the fresh air, though, isn't it?' Jennifer remarked.

'Indeed. I don't know what he smokes in that wretched pipe. And I'm surprised we didn't discuss the nature of Keir's mission.'

'Bradford may be no academic, but he's very logical, Leo. The reason is that Keir never reached 13 Bramble Street. In fact, you probably know more about the place than I do. From what I've found out, it's one of the Northern Administration's communication centres.'

'That's right, Jenny. The basement is full of electronics. On the chimney there's a seemingly crooked TV dish aerial, like many others in the neighbourhood, only this one's aligned towards one of our geostationary satellites. You know why they put the communications station into Bramble Street, don't you?'

'Because anyone visiting knows, or ought to know, that they're being watched. Like Keir, I suppose. Who occupies number 13, Leo?'

'Penny and Baz live in. They're well established there and look like a couple of poverty stricken elderly pensioners, so they get left alone. You don't mug anyone in Bramble Street without asking the local gang bosses first. Penny and Baz, and their three cats, give the place an air of normality and respectability.'

'What was Keir supposed to do, Leo, if he'd made it to the rendezvous?'

'He'd have received his final mission directive, which was to use his link-set to update Penny's. Keir's mission was simply to provide Penny and Baz with information about a new satellite that was put in orbit three days ago. Oh, yes - and the car would have been delivered to Oakingwell for use by Burton and Smythe.'

'What will happen now?' Jenny asked.

'Penny and Baz have already received the information by other means. If all had gone according to plan, it would have been part of Keir's exercise dreamed up by Rowena.'

'And now, Leo, you're carrying the can!'

'Part of the line of duty, I guess.' His jaw set, Leo thought: *Surely, even in this world, the buck stops unltimately at the Ministry of Defence?* 'But I'm more concerned about Keir's safety when he's released from hospital,' he added.

*****

Friday 27 August. Whitehall.

'You know what this means, Iain?' the Prime Minister returned his sherry decanter to the walnut topped table and offered his Minister of Defence the re-charged glass.

'Increased protection for all operatives. Subject to the usual criteria of competence. Will there be a budget allowance, David? I'll draw up a costing for you...'

'Really, Iain! You know we can't afford an incremental budget this year. And I'd have to wait for further details from the SG before I could consider a release of top-up funding. She contacted me yesterday by blue telephone,' the Prime Minister waved at the device on the corner of his desk. 'That was exactly twenty four hours after her speech about Electra. In practical terms Iain, it means that security of operations and safety of personnel, from Inner Team to field operatives, remain your responsibility. For which the existing budget should be adequate.'

'Are there any new directives on how we are to deal with problems, David?'

'Is there something specific you have in mind, Iain?'

'Well, a suitable illustration might be the Wilson case.'

'Oh yes. The one that's in the press at the moment. That was rather unfortunate, wasn't it Iain?'

'Yes, but we can handle that.' The last syllable rose an octave and MacFarlane cleared his throat. 'I'm more concerned about what the press are *not* aware of. The breach of security at Holmes Chapel. He almost *lost* a secure link-set. It was *out* of his possession for at least ten minutes while he was hanging around a garage.'

'The facts of the matter are already in my possession, Iain. But as of now we must not lose *any person*. By *frozen*, the SG means no more recruits to the Project, but she also means no *less* as well. You see, she also chairs the UN Human Rights Commission and Ethics Office and if anything untoward should happen to any of the workforce within Project Electra, which is now her baby, as it were; well, I don't have to spell it out, do I?'

'No, David. I quite understand.'

'That's good. Now Kate made me this fruit cake last night. Would you like some?'

*****

10 French Disconnection

Monday 6 September. Paris Observatory.

brown envelope lay unopened on the polished mahogany table in the deputy director's office at the Paris Observatory, Meudon. Mme. Geneviève Seurat, his personal assistant, opened it. She glanced at the contents and placed the letter on the professor's desk. Next for her attention, she opened his diary. *The only appointment this morning is a M. Alain Faubert at 10:15am for thirty minutes.* She closed the book. The wall clock now showed four minutes past nine and the professor had not yet arrived. In the absence of telephone messages from him, she checked her computer screen: no email. Perhaps he'd been involved with one of the observatory's telescopes during the night? Yes, it had been a good night for seeing, although most of the important work tended to be done abroad with remote access from computers. But Professor Fournier had always enjoyed making use of the on-site equipment and had successfully arranged funding for its renovation and maintenance.

No doubt he's catching up on his rest and his car will appear at any minute, she reassured herself.

At ten fifteen precisely, Mme. Seurat invited her guest into a small adjoining lobby. She felt flustered and could not disguise her embarrassment at the deputy director's absence.

'It's most unusual, M. Faubert! I'm sure he hasn't forgotten. But for some reason, it seems that he has been unable to contact us. Would you prefer to wait here or perhaps see one of his colleagues?'

'No thank you, it's quite all right.' M. Faubert, his white raincoat over one arm, stood with his back to the window. Mme. Seurat took note of his appearance: tall and neatly dressed in a brown tweed suit, but not shaved for about three days. Designer stubble, she guessed.

'Would you like a cigarette, Madame?' He held out a freshly opened packet of Disque Bleu with his free hand.

'No thank you, Monsieur Faubert. I'm afraid there's no smoking in this building.' She rearranged a pile of magazines on a nearby table, and then fussed with the curtains a little.

'Are you sure you don't mind if I wait?' he said, putting his cigarettes away and looking through the window.

'Of course not. Please sit down,' she said. 'May I take your coat?'

A most attractive smile, thought M. Faubert.

'No, thank you. It's all right.' He smiled back, 'I'll hold on to it while I wait.'

At 10:30, Mme. Seurat brought coffee and two croissants on a plate. A further fifteen minutes later, Faubert knocked on the office door and with a brief word of thanks announced his intention to leave.

'I'm so sorry that Lucien has not arrived and you have to go, Monsieur,' said Mme. Seurat with obvious concern. 'Can I book another appointment date for you?'

'Thank you. But would you like to contact me on this telephone number?' he said, handing her a business card. 'Say, tomorrow at half past three? And we can fix an appointment then, perhaps.'

'Yes, of course. I'll ask him to ring you, if you like.'

'That would be excellent. Thank you very much for the coffee. You have been most kind.'

'The pleasure is mine, M'sieur. Again, I'm most sorry that Lucien isn't here.'

M. Faubert politely made his exit. As the automatic doors closed behind him, he made a brief telephone call.

'Phase one appears to have gone ahead without any problems,' he said.

He put on his raincoat and descended a short flight of steps, then made his way across the tarmac apron to a waiting Peugeot limousine.

As the chauffeur turned right at the gate-house, Faubert reached unobtrusively for the weapon he carried in the raincoat pocket and slid it into an open briefcase at his feet. They drove quietly through the suburbs of Paris and joined the city traffic.

The car stopped just within sight of the Seine. Faubert got out, without the briefcase, and began walking towards the bridge of Les Invalides while the Peugeot veered off down the

Quai d'Orsay. A few spots of rain were falling. Alain Faubert turned up his collar and continued on his way.

*****

Tuesday 7 September. Oakingwell.

The group of visiting researchers at Oakingwell followed Keir to a reserved evening table in Arundel College.

'I hope you'll enjoy the meal,' said Keir. He'd heard from Frank that Burton looked forward to being seen in the distinguished company of the Edinburgh group. *Then where has he gone?* Keir thought.

'Brian will be back shortly,' he added, as he hung up their coats.

Keir needed some help, as his shoulder still ached from his injuries. He joined the others as they waited. A further three minutes passed as hunger and impatience conspired to diminish casual conversation.

Then the swing doors opened and a familiar face appeared. With mild surprise and the thought of food dispelled for a moment, Keir watched Brian's kilted legs propel their owner towards the gathering.

Burton exchanged smiles with the guests. 'Shall we have a drink, before we dine?' he suggested.

He offered the first round as the party sat around the table.

'It's a fine kilt! I didn't realise you were a fellow Scot,' said Doug.

'Thank you. It's my mother's side of the family, actually.'

'Good grief!' Doug's expression had changed to one of horror.

'What?' Burton's response registered total perplexity.

Keir suppressed a smile when he realised that Doug's remark had been triggered by something totally different.

'No! Nothing personal, Brian. It's just that I've noticed this.'

Doug held up part of a tabloid newspaper that had been left on his chair. A small banner under Foreign News read: *Top Astronomer in M-way crash*

'Sorry, everyone,' Doug said. 'Friend involved in an accident.' He handed the paper to Burton.

Burton paraphrased the short article, about six column-centimetres long, for the group:

'Looks like Fournier was in his Citroen when it was crushed between two wagons. They say he's in intensive care, condition stable. Awful news, but at least he's still alive!'

During the meal, Doug in particular couldn't talk with enthusiasm about his research. He excused himself early:

'Sorry, I've underestimated the effect of the journey,' he said, arising from the table just as the dessert arrived. 'No reflection on your excellent cuisine,' Doug assured the waitress, 'Just tired, that's all.' He turned to Brian. 'G'night. Glad to meet you again. Thanks for the meal and see you all in the morning.'

'Yes, of course,' Burton looked over his spectacles at his departing guest. 'You do look a bit whacked, Doug. I hope you feel better tomorrow.'

Doug Brodie climbed the stairway of the accommodation block and entered his apartment. He shivered. Maybe the cold, or shock of the news? He sat on the bed and buried his head in his hands.

'Oh no! Not Lucien. God, please let him live!'

Doug grieved actively for a long time. Then he took off his shoes and slid fully clothed under the duvet cover. 'Please let Lucien live,' he whispered, then entered into fitful sleep.

*****

Wednesday 8 September.

After breakfast, Keir bade farewell to Doug and his colleagues and then joined Frank, Alan and Rowena in a morning coffee.

Shoulder still giving you gyp?' Frank said.

'Sure is. Can't concentrate on anything.'

'Why don't you ask Alan here if you can recuperate for a while?'

'I agree with Frank,' Alan said. 'What do you say, Rowena.'

'I know where you can chill out,' Rowena said. 'Come and see me in my office.'

Chill out. More research needed into period vernacular, Keir thought. He had a good idea what she meant. 'OK, when? Now?' he asked.

'Yes. Please excuse us,' she said.

'You need to get away from here, dearest,' she continued, on closing her office door. 'So I'm sending you to Paris.'

'Under the Electra umbrella?'

'Of course. You've been there before, so it'll be less stressful than our other European bolt-holes.'

'Is it a hotel?'

'A safe house actually, Keir.'

'How long?'

'Let's say, a week. That should do the job nicely.'

Keir contemplated her 'do the job' phrase.

'Is there anything special to be done?' he began.

'Actually, there is, Keir. Just a small task while you're there.'

*****

After the Eurostar sleeper, Keir arrived at the Gare du Nord and took the Paris Metro network to Meudon station. He found the address of the small guest house which had turned out to be the one Doug and Ailsa had recommended.

Claudette and Guillaume made him feel welcome with a glass of red wine. And Keir discovered that the Sauvignon grapes in the hands of Guillaume Fabrice Bouchemal, master vintner, produce claret that is incomparable. Keir's thoughts were interrupted by a phone buzzing on the chair next to him.

Claudette picked it up. 'That's marvellous, Doug! Yes, we'd be glad to see you. That would fit in nicely, because Keir's due to leave on Saturday. Yes, he's right here. Keir?'

'Hi Doug!' Keir said, taking the phone. 'What are you up to?'

'Hello Keir, I might ask the same of you. I'm coming down to stay at Claudette's place for a few days, just after you leave, it seems.' He paused. 'Have you heard anything more about Lucien?'

'No.'

'Well in that case, please forget the subject. It's better for you that you know nothing further at this stage.'

'That sounds all very mysterious, Doug! Actually, before leaving I'd like to visit Meudon Observatory again. It's quite near here. You can see the buildings from my window. And they've received a sample of the meteorite.'

'No!' Doug interrupted. In measured tones he added: 'That's to say, in the present climate, it really would be best if you kept away from the observatory. Just take my word for it. It'll become clearer later. For now don't ask any questions, just lie low and enjoy the rest of your break.'

The urgency of Doug's voice Keir felt unwise to ignore.

'OK,' Keir said. He paused for further information without avail.

'Hope you feel better soon, laddie. Could you put Claudette on for me?'

'OK, Doug. If there's a chance we might meet as I leave, cheers 'til then.'

Keir returned the telephone to Claudette, allowing their conversation to resume. He pondered Doug's inhibitory words about the observatory. Claudette had already mentioned in passing that Meudon had an observatory that employed Lucien Fournier. He didn't mention his previous visit, as he recalled the appearance of the distinguished greying haired Frenchman he'd met at the conference. He turned to Guillaume, unable to resist the temptation to satisfy his curiosity.

'Guillaume, s'il vous plait, comment ça va avec Lucien Fournier?' Keir hoped that his broken French would be understood by Guillaume as he tried to ask him for news about Lucien.

'Lucien? *Oui! Quelle horreur!'* he began. Then he saw that his wife had finished with the telephone.

'Claudette!' He beckoned her to carry on with the story.

'That's terrible!' Keir remarked, as the tale unfolded. The story resembled the newspaper report at Oakingwell, apart from added detail about Lucien's condition. No broken bones. Severe concussion, mainly. But what were the connections between this tragic accident, Doug's avoidance of the issue and his concern about the observatory? His mind raced. Why should Doug want to keep this under wraps? Maybe it's that dreaded need-to-know principle,

'What's the matter, Keir?' asked Claudette, 'You look very pale.'

Another possibility had crossed Keir's mind. *What if it isn't an accident?* And what if the French authorities suspected him of being involved because of the common link with the meteorite work? That's assuming they're aware of my research area and my connections with Project Electra, he thought. They might know by now that he'd arrived in France, but would they be concerned enough to find out where he stayed? *Yes, I'm uncomfortably close to the observatory.*

'Cognac, M'sieur Keir?' Guillaume interrupted him by thrusting a charged glass into his hand.

'*Merci*, Guillaume,' Keir said, moving towards the window.

At that moment, Keir saw someone in a white raincoat on the opposite side of the street. He had a mobile phone. *Is he taking photographs?* Keir wondered. A minute passed by and the man walked away to a parked car. The slight limp. Slight but peculiar.

'It can't be Viv, surely?' Keir murmured to himself.

'Please sit down, M'sieur Wilson,' Guillaume said, pulling up an easy chair.

'Thanks.'

'Anything the matter? Are you OK?'

'I think we're being watched.' Keir replied.

By the time his host reached the window, a Peugeot limousine had pulled away from the kerb.

*****

A hospital in Paris.

Jacqueline Fournier clasped the hand of her husband, as he drifted in and out of consciousness throughout the night. A tall slender woman in her early forties with dark eyes and black hair flecked with grey.

Lucien, a little older, tough and wiry, normally with a twinkle in his intense grey eyes. That's exactly how she remembered him when they were on their last outing in the old Citroen Light 15, on a picnic with their two teenage children.

Now he appeared moribund, head and face heavily bandaged, with a drip into his left arm and a mask with an oxygen tube in his right nostril. A characteristic odour of disinfectant pervaded the small room, in which a battery of electronic equipment kept its impassive vigil on the silent patient.

She felt so amazed and thankful that he had survived the accident and believed it to be a miracle. The rescue team had taken one and a half hours to cut him free from the wreckage. He had lost a lot of blood in addition to sustaining head and facial injuries. According to witnesses, a heavy wagon in front had stopped suddenly. Another wagon behind failed to slow down and pushed the Citroen into the back of the first one. The wagons had become almost locked together, with the wreckage of the car pinned under the cab of the second. She shuddered at the memory of the newspaper and television pictures. Only a week had passed since the accident.

Among the get-well cards on the bedside locker were some from friends of the family; Doug's card in a prominent position. She recalled the accompanying letter, in which he had offered to come over to Paris at the weekend. She must ask her children Robert and Vivienne to get some Friday shopping.

Jacqui clutched her husband's right hand, the only part of him free of medical apparatus and bandages, but she must leave him now. She placed his hand under the covers and gave him a tender kiss on the bandaged forehead. Then she made her way out along the sanitised corridors.

On the way, she met André Leclerc, the consultant surgeon in charge of her husband's case. They exchanged smiles. André placed an arm around her shoulder.

'Well, how has he been with you this morning?' he said.

'The same, really. But I think he tried to say something about an hour ago. Perhaps it was just my imagination.'

'Oh? I'll be along to see him on my ward-round in half an hour. It's a long drawn out business, isn't it? You are a brave woman, Jacqui.'

She began to cry. André tightened his hug a little.

'Look, Jacqui! I have an idea. It's really against the rules but I'll bring a flask of his favourite burgundy with me. We'll try holding a moistened swab of it under his nose. Every familiar stimulus can help, you know. All right?'

'Yes, if you like, Monsieur Leclerc, thank you. And tomorrow, can I bring a guest, another friend of his, from Scotland?'

'Of course! I'll be pleased to meet him. See you later, Jacqui.'

*****

Meudon. The guest house.

The buzzing telephone sounded again under a cushion in the lounge.

Keir picked up the phone.

'Hello?' A very English voice on the line.

'It's for me, I think, Claudette!' Keir said, 'Hello!'

'My dearest! I hope you're having a good rest and not asking your hosts too many awkward questions,' piped Rowena. Keir could visualise her facial expression and gestures, probably sweeping back that lock of golden hair. They had agreed not to address each other by name on the telephone.

'Well, can I be of assistance?' he asked.

'Not really. I want to talk to Claudette, please!' Rowena said. Claudette took the telephone and the ensuing conversation in French lasted for about five minutes.

Claudette rang off. 'Come through here!' she said.

She led Keir down a flight of stone steps to a cellar full of radio equipment. A large white plaque above a short wave transceiver on a workbench bore a French amateur radio call sign; the station being licensed in Guillaume's name according to the log-book cover. On the same bench, near a corner of the room, Keir saw a separate short wave receiver switched to standby. Several other items of electronic equipment were connected to it and another notebook next to a computer contained a list of short wave frequencies.

Claudette selected five of these and the receiver hissed into life. She looked at her watch. Keir also noticed a wall clock coming up to the hour. At one minute past precisely, to Keir's amazement, he again heard Rowena's voice, this time coming from the receiver.

'Hello again, Keir!' The message continued: *'It's all right. This transmission is a thoroughly scrambled frequency-hopping job and is as secure as the link-set you nearly lost. Sorry to rub your nose in it, but you really must be very careful now. Your kind hosts are part of our scene, as you might have guessed. I want you to give Claudette your electric razor. Don't worry, you can have it back when Guillaume has extracted her updated link-set SIM card. Doug has briefed me about Lucien. And as you know already, as deputy head of the Meudon Observatory, he accepted a fraction of the Kuopio meteorite and nearly paid for it with his life. Yes, Keir. Things are hotting up and Lucien will be out of circulation for some time. Officially, that is. Doug is going to visit him in hospital and arrange for his transfer to a clinic in Besançon. When he's strong enough, he will cross the Belgian border in unmarked United Nations transport, ostensibly to take a holiday at the resort of Frederikshavn in Denmark. That's enough about Lucien for now. Just keep out of his way and don't go near the*

observatory, or anywhere near the Sacré Coeur Hospital. Behave normally and don't attract attention. See you. Bye for now.'

The receiver returned to a continual hiss and a red light on the transmitter winked on for about half a second, followed by a musical *ping* from the receiver. Guillaume closed down the system as Claudette led Keir back into the lounge, where croissants and black coffee were waiting.

*****

Oakingwell.

Burton signed the form on his desk. Alan Menzies scowled, reluctantly adding his signature.

'Don't worry, Alan. It's just in case,' Burton said.

'Isn't it up to the student to ask for an extension to his thesis writing-up period?' asked Alan.

'Normally, yes.' Burton moved across the room; an involuntary act, as he almost invariably interviewed people whilst framing himself in the glare from the window: 'But times are not normal, Alan. Giving Wilson a one year extension for completion is quite reasonable, on the grounds that it's going to be effectively part-time from now on.'

'He's really in it up to his neck, isn't he?'

'How do you mean?'

'You know very well what I mean, Brian. This Project Electra thing!'

'Keep your voice down, Alan!' Burton hissed, '*They* want him. The UN, the military. We're just onlookers in all this.'

'It's a damn shame! Nearly ready to submit his thesis and the poor laddie has to go roaming around Europe. As if they couldn't wait a couple of months before they have him pissing about doing their errands!'

'Anyway,' Burton continued, 'Wilson's time in France has been a brief respite, of sorts.'

'I'm glad you said "brief" and "of sorts", Brian.'

'And he can have a little longer, but not in France. At the end of the week he flies to Copenhagen.'

'Copenhagen?' Alan's jaw sagged.

'Yes. He then takes an internal flight to Aalborg and catches a train to Frederikshavn, on the north-east coast.'

'Go on. You're just waiting for me to ask. What for?'

'To look after a very important person, Alan. Someone else who is due there to recuperate from a road accident, or incident, as it almost certainly is.'

'Fournier?'

'Hole in one, Alan. Fournier! The old boy can recover in the company of someone he can feel at home with. They've both survived recent assassination attempts and have mutual scientific interests. It'll do the pair of them a power of good, and there's a fair chance that Wilson's thesis will benefit from the arrangement.'

'Your idea?'

Burton paused for a moment: 'Actually, it was cooked up between Rowena and someone you might have heard of in connection with your work: Valentina Gazetny. An unlikely alliance probably brought together by concern for Keir.'

'They don't get on, Rowena and Gazetny?'

'Apparently not, normally. I don't know the details.'

'I can understand Rowena's concern for Keir, but why is Gazetny so interested?'

'Search me, Alan.' Burton shrugged. 'Probably part of her job. She's fixing up the security through Commander Lars Nielsen. He's on the UN approved list. Wilson and Fournier will be looked after by the Danish equivalent of our SAS.'

'Two things still bother me,' Alan said.

'Yes?'

'First, Keir still needs constant protection. That's really heavy considering he joined us as a research student. Second, given that Project Electra information is divulged on a *need-to-know* basis, why tell *me* about security details?'

Burton adjusted his spectacles on the bridge of his nose, and then regarded Alan impassively.

'Let's deal with that last point first,' he pointed to a brown envelope poking out of Alan's jacket pocket. 'Things will be clearer when you've seen that letter. Delivered by UN approved courier half an hour ago and hopefully to be read before you lose it. On your first point, Wilson's been assessed and now he's UN property. You'll just have to accept that.' Burton sat down at his desk and continued, flatly: 'Don't let me detain you, Alan. Please go to your office and open the envelope.'

*****

11 Meeting of Minds

Monday 13 September, North Jutland.

Keir stepped out of the railcar at Frederikshavn station. A fresh, cool wind blew in from the Kattegat under a cloudless sky. He wheeled his baggage to a drop-off point.

'Hi! Jonathan Sykes?' the Lancashire accent came as a surprise.

'Are you collecting anyone else?' Keir asked.

'Sykes and none other.' the driver replied. A rugged man, possibly in his early forties, Keir judged.

Satisfied with the correct wording, he handed over his bags, which were loaded into the rear of the vehicle, an old but well cared for Series 2A Land Rover. Adorned with several club stickers and the name "Belerophon" traced in gold lettering on each of the bronze green front wings.

Keir climbed aboard. The vehicle chugged into life and lurched ponderously towards the main road.

'How was the journey?' the driver shouted, above the sound of the 1950s technology diesel engine.

'Fine. I'm getting used to travelling,' Keir replied.

'Good. By the way,' said the driver, 'I'm Rollo Swift.'

'Hi! Is that your real name?'

'Yes. And yours?'

'Keir Wilson,' he shook the offered hand briefly, allowing it to return as quickly as possible to the steering wheel.

'If you don't mind my asking, why such an obtrusively British vehicle and number plates?'

'That's true. There aren't many drivers from the UK in this part of Denmark, but plenty of farmers. And the Land Rover Club image attracts interest without arousing suspicion. In fact, I find that Belerophon can drive anywhere in Europe without problems.' Rollo clouted the dashboard affectionately.

'Why Belerophon?'

'It's a name my uncle gave to the oldest and noisiest steam traction engine in his collection.' Rollo laughed raucously above the roar of the engine and the incessant whine from the gearbox.

The road appeared smooth, but somehow the vehicle found excuses to pitch and jolt, eliciting further comments from its owner: 'Tough as old boots, Keir. And it starts on the button, in any weather!'

'Have you ever considered soundproofing?' Keir shouted.

'Wouldn't give it a thought, mate. It's music to my ears.'

'Isn't it more expensive to run than modern turbo diesels?' Keir shouted.

Rollo laughed again: 'The firm's paying. Look, we're here!'

They turned into a gravel path, which continued for about half a kilometre and ended at a farmhouse with white painted stone walls dressed with timber. The red tiled roof had several gables and two satellite dishes adorned a chimney at one end. At the door stood a well dressed woman in her early forties.

'This is Lisa Holmboe. Lisa, Keir Wilson from England.'

'Pleased to meet you, Keir. Come with me. Rollo will attend to your luggage.' Lisa led Keir up a flight of stairs to an upper lounge. They continued through a door at the far end. 'There is a bathroom along the corridor,' she added, 'and this is your study-bedroom. In about ten minutes, the Professor will join us in the lounge for something to eat.'

*****

Oakingwell.

Despite security regulations, Alan Menzies had taken the military courier's letter home over the weekend. Now, back in his office, he scrutinised its contents yet again. He scanned past the United Nations emblem and went through the opening paragraph:

Dear Dr. Alan Menzies,

Major Ronald Fitzwilliam Bradford has taken up other duties and Dr. Sharon Rowena Smythe has now been appointed as Senior Principle Scientific Officer, Biological Executive. In consequence, you have been assigned as United Nations appointed Guardian (designate) of the Field Operative Keir Peter Wilson (alias Jonathan Sykes) with details of duties as defined in Appendix D2 and any Notice of Variation thereof. A training course has been arranged at the Andover Military Institute to enable you to expedite the duties listed in Appendix C of this memorandum. Subject to successful completion of this course, you will be notified of your new appointment. Meanwhile, you are to continue under the direction of your Co-ordinator, Brian Hamish Burton.

'No doubt as general dogsbody!' Alan muttered cynically. He waded on through the document, yearning for the less complicated life of an academic researcher in a provincial university. The frustration of being locked into a system which operated in ways beyond his comprehension welled up within him. He thumped his desk with a brawny fist. A physical expression of the mental effort needed to gather his thoughts together.

Keir, his hapless research student, seemed now even more vulnerable and must be protected. With a shrug of resignation, Alan penned his name in the appropriate box and walked over to Burton's office for the counter-signature.

On the way, he laughed to himself. 'Hamish! I never knew that. What poor Scot had been the ancestor of such a...?'

'Alan! Ah. Were you talking to me?' Burton stood in the corridor.

'Hello, Brian. I said here's something for you to countersign.'

*****

Frederikshavn.

'Great!' Keir said at the sight of the table before him. And the enticing smell of Danish pastries. Traditional confectionery, complete with cholesterol, he thought.

'Hello! I'm Lucien Henri Fournier,' the professor introduced himself in near perfect English, 'Of course, you know that already, apart from my middle name, perhaps!' his eyes glittered in the firelight of the hearth.

Keir had learned of Fournier's friendship with Doug Brodie and guessed he might know of his visits to Edinburgh.

'I remember you from the Paris Conference, Professor,' he said.

'That's right. Please call me Lucien, Keir. You have met Rollo before?'

'No, we've only just met on the way from the station,' Keir said.

'If you want the CV info' Keir,' Rollo said, 'I'm third son of a Manchester brewer, a former Chief Technician at Manchester University and Corporal in the Territorials. That's how I became roped into this. Someone in the TA knew of my job with the university and I was visited by some guy called Boswell.'

'Bosworth?' suggested Keir.

'Yeah, Bosworth, that's right! Smooth talking beggar, isn't he? Thought I'd be too old but that didn't bother him. Drafted my wife in, as well. Can't leave her on the outside, he said. He knew she'd been to unarmed combat classes and he'd arranged extra training for us both. We took a fortnight's holiday and spent most of it playing commandos at Andover and Salisbury.' Rollo and Keir laughed together.

'*Eh bien, mes amis*! Now that we know each other I'll tell you my story. It was quite different!'

Lucien poured the coffee and waited for his companions to relax. The flames in the gas-fired hearth cast a flickering light on their faces. Keir's thoughts strayed back to the barbecue in Finland, to the gentle giant, Lauri. To Kirsti, Elena and Valentina.

'You're tired, Keir, *mon brave*! Perhaps later.'

'No, Lucien! Just a few passing thoughts. Please continue.'

The professor stretched in his chair, the flickering firelight accentuating his craggy features.

'*Eh bien*! Well, you have both seen things in the media, and perhaps I should begin with the first events I remember on that day. In the morning, I had breakfast with my family. It was raining. And when it rains I drive to work. I took the car out of the garage. Thinking back, it was the brakes. They still worked, but as I told the police after I left hospital, the travel on the pedal was not the same. They were a little softer, also. But it was not a long time since the car was serviced and I decided to take it to the main dealer near my destination. I'd planned to telephone my office and ask a colleague to collect me. On the way, a heavy wagon pulled up in front of me. I pushed my foot on the brakes. They worked at first, and then suddenly stopped working. The windscreen hit the overhanging tail of the wagon in front, but fortunately the car stopped with the wagon a few centimetres from my face. The glass was everywhere inside the car. The driving mirrors were smashed, so I looked around. Another wagon was coming from behind - *accelerating*! Then - ouff! It was all over for me. I remember only waking up in the Sacré Coeur Hospital.'

'Here, have some of this!' Rollo offered the professor a Napoleon brandy. 'Not much left. He turned to Keir. 'It's Lucien's favourite;' he explained, 'so, for you, some Scotch perhaps? Single malt, of course.'

'Thanks Rollo.' said Keir.

Rollo poured for Keir and himself and toasted to his colleagues' convalescence. Then he handed Keir a tourist map including the district surrounding the safe house.

'May not be much use to us yet. We're confined to barracks for a short while.'

'Doesn't bother me,' Keir said. 'I'm sure we've got plenty to talk about and I've brought some books and CDs. Is that machine available?' He nodded towards the computer workstation on a corner table.

'Sure,' Rollo said.

'Thanks, I won't use it now, though.' Keir rose from his chair, 'Well, it's been a long journey and if you'll excuse me, I'd better hit the sack.'

'Hit the sack? That is something you say in England for going to bed, I think. Well, it's been very good to meet you, Keir. *Bon nuit. Au revoir bientôt*!'

'*Au revoir*, Lucien!' Keir left them both looking absently into the gas burning surrogate coal fire.

'Rollo, my friend,' said Lucien, at length, 'As you have to leave tomorrow, perhaps we should talk now about whether we should share our thoughts concerning Project Electra with Keir.'

'You mean, the meteorite conspiracy?'

'Yes, Rollo. I don't really see why we shouldn't discuss it with him. My sources tell me he's trustworthy. On the other hand, he has connections. He knows several people elsewhere. You see, he attends conferences and it is so easy to get talking at these places, especially when the wine is flowing, yes?'

'I see what you mean,' said Rollo, 'but I believe Tanskanen in the Finnish group has met him. So has Valentina. She's well placed to advise us of anything dubious, now that she's responsible for arranging our security.'

'I thought that was Sven Sigurdsson's domain.'

'He's gone, Lucien. Promoted. More UN inspired musical chairs. Now it's Valentina Gazetny and Ilya Karpov who cover the UN Northern Europe Sector.'

'Fascinating, my friend. It's really becoming quite complicated, *n'est ce pas*?'

'True. Anyway, I'll leave the decision about Keir in your hands, Professor. I'm just the driver, Belerophon's dutiful slave!'

'With a first class brain, if I may say so. It is a tradition in both of our countries to have excellence in technical and engineering matters. Eh, Rollo?'

'I won't disagree with that.' Rollo offered Lucien the last Danish pastry.

Declining politely the professor asked, 'Any more news about your father?'

'He's holding his own thanks, Lucien. They're going to try nanotech intervention. Invasion of the tumour cells. To get them to self-destruct, hopefully. You've had some success in France, from what I've seen on the Web.'

'That's true. I hope it goes well. Rollo. I will pray for your father and for you, my friend.' They looked at each other, eyes level.

'Thank you, Lucien. Thank you.'

*****

Tuesday 14 September, Oakingwell.

Alan arrived early at his office to find a group of four undergraduate students waiting.

'Excuse me, Alan,' asked Jane, spokesperson for the group. 'We can't find Keir. Would you please come down to the lab and see our demo? We think we've got it right, this time.'

'Aye. Certainly, Jane. Keir's away for a wee while,' Alan explained. 'But no problem at all, let's go.' The students led the way and after fifteen minutes Alan headed thoughtfully to his office. On the way, he met Burton in the corridor.

'Honestly, Brian! How can I be Keir's minder, when I'm a thousand miles away looking after his laboratory classes? I'm really convinced these damn Whitehall nutters keep their brains in their backsides!'

'Let's go to my office, Alan.' Burton suggested.

Once inside, Burton vented his displeasure. 'Please, Alan, listen, to me!' he said, through clenched teeth, 'And listen hard! First, it's the UN and *not* Whitehall who sent you the letter. Secondly, keep your feelings under control and your voice down. Don't mention *anything* remotely to do with Electra outside this office while you're on campus. Is that understood?'

'Oh, c'mon, Brian!'

'And you know that mentioning unpalatable words within earshot of students can be a disciplinary matter!'

'As can physical assault!' retorted Alan, breaking free of Burton's grip on his elbow.

They glowered at each other like sparring animals. Burton retreated to his desk while Alan moved towards the door, his face florid with rage.

'Look, Alan! Please sit down. Please!' Burton's plea had an edge of desperation, but Alan complied. He eyed his opponent stonily.

'Oh, damn! Sorry Alan. I lost my cool.' Burton found it hard to apologise by nature. He deserved some admiration, Alan conceded.

'OK. I lost mine, too. Sorry about that,' Alan said.

They both waited.

Burton broke the silence: 'It's pointless to be arguing like this, especially as we've both worked together for so long in Keir's interest.'

'Is there any significance in your using the past tense, Brian?' asked Alan, still with a cold edge to his voice.

'As you mention it, there is.' Burton pulled up his chair and leaned forward, theatrically. 'You were not the only one to receive a directive - here's mine.'

He took out a letter from the top drawer of his desk and gave it to Alan.

'It's OK,' Burton said. 'Not restricted. Between people of our rank, that is.'

Alan raised an eyebrow at the implication. The letter looked similar in format to his own. The second paragraph being of particular interest:

Following Captain Leo Fenton Bosworth's transfer to other duties, you are appointed Convenor for your group's staff and trainees and for meetings between the various Bases participating in Project Electra. This is effective as of noon on the date of receipt of this memorandum, and carries with it the Inner Echelon rank of Executive Officer Grade IEO3. In compliance with line-management policy, you are accountable to Officers of Grades IEO2 and above, as specified in Appendix B.

'Congratulations, Brian.'
'That's not all. Read on,' Burton prompted.
Alan turned the page:

Details of your duties are as defined in Appendix D1 and any future Notice of Variation thereof. Your brief does NOT cover those duties assigned to personnel of similar rank which include Guardianship *NOR any duties listed in Appendix E.*

'Note that 'Guardianship' is highlighted in yellow,' Alan said. 'What it boils down to is that in the Electra hierarchy, I'm now Keir's official Guardian while you are Convenor. And, subject to outcome of my training course, we would be of similar rank.'
'Precisely.'
'But I thought there was a freeze in special appointments and promotions for another few weeks,' Alan commented.
'You're right, Alan. But they've invoked an exception clause. It's all in the fine print: Appendix F. In a nutshell, it means that in reality they can do anything they want, anytime. But it's reasonable for you to be surprised, and so was I. Something pretty serious must be afoot down at Andover and I think it's all linked with Keir's unfortunate incident in Liverpool. I mean, that it should never have been allowed to happen.'
'But it was totally unforeseen, wasn't it?'
'Unforseen or not, heads have rolled because of it and we've been selected for promotion, so congratulations in anticipation, Alan.'
Burton sat back again in his chair, in an attitude of relaxation. He continued: 'As you say, *your* formal promotion will depend on the outcome of that training course.' His transient enjoyment of the caveat decayed to a shrug of resignation. 'But no doubt you'll come through with flying colours,' he added.
'Noting the distinctions between our duties,' commented Alan, 'it looks like we'll be alone in our respective castles.'
'Or dungeons,' remarked Burton, with a sardonic smile.

'So the good news is that I'm going up two notches and the bad news is that Keir's problems are all my responsibility and cannot be transferred to you.'

'Exactly right, Alan. And the amusing news is that neither of us gets paid any extra for it!'

'Apart from travel, accommodation and subsistence expenses, perhaps.'

'We're hardly going to get rich on those, Alan, are we?'

The two exchanged rueful smiles and Alan departed for his office, reflecting that financially Burton would be the heavier loser because there would be less time for his consultancy work, quangos and other extracurricular sources of income. His own position seemed no less problematic. There would be further pressures on his family life. *Designate*, his letter had said. He could be called upon to expedite certain new responsibilities *now*, ahead of maybe passing the course leading to formal confirmation of his office. And until his new rank could be confirmed, he would be answerable to Burton. *Some big deal*, he thought, as he closed the door behind him.

*****.

Frederikshavn.

Keir heard the Land Rover's wheels crunching on the driveway. The engine stopped and a door slammed. He waited with Lucien for Rollo to join them for breakfast, Danish style. The buffet again impressive, with its selection of cereals, freshly baked breads of various kinds, pastries, cookies and all manner of cheeses. There were fruit juices, tea and coffee.

'Full English breakfast, if you like?' Lisa offered.

'Oh, no thank you - this is just fine!' said Keir as he entered.

'D'accord,' agreed Lucien.

'Actually, I wouldn't mind that, please Lisa!' Rollo said.

The trio occupied a table in the corner of the room. Their window overlooked the main road in the distance, beyond the wide driveway where the Land Rover waited. Between mouthfuls of toast and honey, Keir admired the rugged functionality of the vehicle as it glistened in the driving rain. Wouldn't mind one like that, he thought.

'It's the only time it gets cleaned, Keir.' Rollo said. He looked at his watch. 'Regrettably, it's about time for me to leave!'

He grabbed his leather driving jacket which reeked of diesel and donned a green baseball cap. 'I'll see you again soon, Lucien, if you're still here. *Mange tak,* Lisa! Cheers, Keir! Perhaps we'll meet again, soon.'

'*Bon voyage*, Rollo, my friend,' Lucien waved from the door.

The staccato roar of the engine receded down the path, to merge with the general sounds of commuter traffic.

'An energetic man, is he not? And he has eaten *all* his English breakfast!' Lucien commented.

He returned to the lounge and reclined in one of two sumptuous armchairs near the fire.

Keir sank into the other chair as the professor continued: 'Indeed, I know very little of his comings and goings. His assignments are largely a mystery to me. He's like the Lone Ranger of the classic movies!'

'You'll get used to all that, Lucien. It's all part of the 'need to know' preoccupation with security.'

'*Eh bien.* There is certainly something I need to know. It concerns the motivation of my would-be assassins and their parent organisation. I believe that such an organisation exists. In the hospital, I have had time on my hands to think much, my friend. My poor wife and young ones. When they visited me, they could see only this heavily bandaged man in bed, doing nothing. But, *mon ami*, I was thinking. In between sleeping and being attended to by the staff, I was reflecting hard about the whole business of the meteorites, the aliens and the attempt on my life.'

Lucien shifted his position slightly, as if easing some residual discomfort.

'What I tell you now, Keir, is the distillation of my thoughts.'

*****

Oulu Base.

Ilya Karpov guided the cross-hairs cursor on his screen to the map of France and zoomed the image to show the conurbation of Paris and its outlying districts, including Meudon.

'Valentina!' Do you have a trace on the ambulance?'

'Yes, Ilya,' she replied, 'In spite of false plates, it was registered in Lyons, four years ago.'

'Good. And I've just confirmed that it was stored overnight, immediately before the incident, at a warehouse near Paris, twelve kilometres from the Gare du Nord. Here are the GPS coordinates.'

'It's amazing, isn't it, what has become available to us since our appointments when the UN took over?' Valentina remarked.

'Makes our job easier in some ways and more detailed in others, doesn't it? Feel like some tea? What are you doing now, by the way?'

'Oh, just intrigued. Northern tip of Denmark. I'm plotting the progress of a vehicle driven by one of our field officers. It's travelling towards the Skagen peninsula. Oh, damn! There's some cloud cover moving in from the north east. His tracker's turned off, so I'll have to switch to radar and lose definition, I suppose.'

'Who's is it?'

'FO23 and his Land Rover. Yes. Got it. You can talk to him, if you like. He left SH5DK about twenty minutes ago. You know, where Lucien is holed up.'

'*Da*! Poor Lucien! A safe house. It must feel like house arrest! Is his wife joining him?'

'Not for another week at least, Ilya. But now that FO25 has arrived safely he will have some company for a while.'

'Ah, Wilson. The Oakingwall man?'

'Oaking*well*, Ilya,' replied Valentina. If the burly Russian heard a trace of irritation in her voice, he didn't register it.

'Well, Lucien and Keir should get along fine. And it would be nice for us to have some sabbatical leave in a secluded country *dacha*,' he said resignedly. 'I'd get a lot more research done. And stop laughing, I mean it!'

'Was that an indecent proposition? What about Tonya? But what you say is true, Ilya. We do spend too much of our time not writing our papers. When was our last publication, nine months ago? I feel ashamed!'

'Indeed, and we are both getting into such deep involvement on the security side of this project that we will not be allowed to publish any of our findings, even if we accumulate a wagonload of manuscripts!'

'I know, Ilya! The samovar's ready. Pass me your mug.'

'Thanks, Valentina. I'll talk with FO23 when he's reached Skagen. I'd like to know what he's doing up there. Is it on his itinerary?'

'None that I've given him, Ilya.'

'Indeed?'

*****

10:00am, Frederikshavn.

Lisa had cleared the breakfast things and closed the east-facing windows against the freshening wind.

'Help yourselves to more coffee when you need it, and please let me know when you're ready for lunch, gentlemen,' she said, her head round the door.

The professor thanked her and turned to Keir, who asked:

'Lucien, about the meteorite situation; how many types of alien do you think are encapsulated in the material floating around in interstellar space?'

'If it's meteoritic material we're talking about...' he paused to adjust the position of his back, which still occasionally pained him.

Keir gave Lucien a cushion for his chair.

'Thank you, Keir. I would say, none, whatsoever.'

In the silence which followed, the professor stroked his beard and regarded Keir with concern, as he had clearly caused some surprise.

'Do you mean, all this talk of aliens from outer space is a blind alley?' Keir asked.

'In my view, it is totally unfounded.'

'But what about the reports of evolved organic matter in some of these meteorites? You only need one genuine exception to tilt the balance in favour of extraterrestrial life.'

'Well, Keir, I'm not convinced that there have been any genuine exceptions.'

'It's a pity we can't get answers from the aliens themselves!'

'D'accord. If they are first generation, all they know must surely derive from what we've taught them.'

'Anyway, what about Kuopio?' Keir recalled the flash of joy in Valentina's face, by the lakeside in Finland, as she found the historic fragment. 'And the findings at Edinburgh?'

'I have an alternative proposition, my friend. What do you think of the idea that a proportion of observations could be not inaccurate, nor misinterpreted, but actually falsified?'

'What?'

'I've no personal stake whatsoever in this argument, apart from getting a little nearer the truth, whatever that may turn out to be.'

'You must have good reason for this!'

'Bien sûr! What first aroused my suspicions was a close examination using a mass spectrograph at the Sorbonne. A very small portion of the interior of the meteorite contained a compound which could only have been produced here, on Earth.'

'Where? In the Earth's crust or mantle?'

'No. In a laboratory. Possibly a nanotechnology laboratory, somewhere on this planet.'

'You mean. someone's used nanotechnology to tamper with a meteorite?' Keir asked.

'Well, just parts of the meteorite. Those parts containing so-called biological material. Even so, to create this and be convincing, I think the laboratory would belong to a well equipped establishment.'

'What about motive? What do *you* think, Lucien?'

'Always there is the loner with an ego and wealth to pay for such an enterprise. Or it could be a group of such people. To ask why, you have to ask another question, Keir.'

'OK, what have you in mind?'

'Well, if materials linked with aliens were found to come from space, where would cash and resources start flowing? Most likely, in the direction of those working for programmes involving space monitoring and exploration, not to mention exobiology.'

'There is something else. It did seem to me too much of a coincidence that the meteorite fell where it did: almost outside Tanskanen's back door!'

'Eh bien, Keir. I agree. It is very convenient and worth noting. And Professor Tanskanen being so involved in Electra.'

'Here's another thought. The Andover teleconference, Lucien. Project Electra was organised, among other things, to prevent harmful exploitation of the aliens by humans.'

'Indeed yes, Keir. I felt honoured to be involved in such an enterprise. Please go on.'

'But the aliens themselves, Lucien. What if exploitation was the very reason for their creation? I mean if it was from human or animal DNA and genetic engineering?'

'A bizarre thought, Keir. But there is nothing wrong in brainstorming with it. Go on.'

'And the aliens-from-space fake evidence is part of a cover up?' Keir suggested.

'We must think of motivation. Why do it with such elaboration, energy and determination, my friend?'

'If the aliens were believed to be from space, they're more likely to attract respect and be undisturbed.'

'On the other hand, what you're suggesting is, if they are artificial mutants derived from humans or animals, we expect riots in the streets, *mon ami*. They and their creators would be hunted down and attacked. The scientists responsible and their support staff put at risk, along with the aliens themselves. And all without any fear of reprisals from an extraterrestrial race.'

'So we're agreed. It benefits the aliens if they're believed to be extraterrestrial!'

'*Oui, mon brave*. Which could lead to another possibility: the aliens themselves being the perpetrators of the deception.'

They both paused. Keir broke the silence.

'Even so, Lucien, we seem to be no nearer to solving the mystery of your Paris incident or of my wounding in Liverpool.'

'One thing is clear, Keir. An organisation exists and I don't wish to sound paranoid, my friend. But I believe that any individuals who pose a threat to it are in danger of liquidation.'

'And that's why you were attacked?'

'Perhaps, Keir. At least we're almost certain of one thing. We agree, a dangerous organisation exists. We don't know its identity or the true extent of its resources.'

'And suppose this organisation sets out to perform a specific task and has the necessary resources? Who knows what might happen to anyone who gets in their way?'

'You mean, Keir, they thought you were onto them?'

'Possibly. Piecing things together, I had suspicions, but nothing concrete. And my security was so tight, overseen by the military. How about your situation? You're convinced that someone's trying to warn you off?'

'If my so-called accident was a mere warning, we are dealing with some very ruthless people indeed.' Lucien paused briefly. 'Shall we have a coffee? There are still some cookies left over from breakfast. The reasoning faculties, as well as an army, marches on its stomach, if I may misquote our Napoleon Bonaparte!'

Keir suggested a short walk outside.

'Ideal, Keir! But first we should tell Lisa how long we will be gone, in case of problems.'

Their route led away from the front path, beyond the rear of the property. Under a grey sky the wind had changed. It blew warm and moist. There were few trees visible, but the rolling downs were verdant and fresh. They set out across a field bordered on the right by a wooden fence aligned at right angles to the main road behind them.

'Keir, my friend, what are your views on extraterrestrial life?' Lucien asked.

'As a kid I enjoyed Star Wars and all that stuff. But in time I had doubts about ET. On the other hand, I'm willing to accept either ET or terrestrial origins for the aliens. How about yourself?'

'As an astronomer, I never tire of contemplating the stars and galaxies. I believe that a percentage of stars, however small, may have planets that support life.'

'Ah, but if we do the thought experiment for an infinite universe, surely that would also mean an *infinite number* of planets could support life!'

The professor laughed. 'Well, *mon ami*, that's more likely than zero, *n'est ce pas?* And even if the universe is finite, in my view the result is still non-zero.'

'OK Lucien. Regarding the matter in hand, let's imagine we have this organisation, alien-inspired or otherwise. And it wants to convince the world that there are alien DNA traces in a meteorite. Ideally, the organisation would have to get to the meteorite specimens first. The composition would have to be adjusted immediately, before someone else was able to classify it as a normal meteorite. Let's say they have the meteorite processed in some laboratory. What would they do next? My guess is that they'd take them to a site and publicise a meteorite fall. Maybe even drop them from an aircraft.'

'An interesting thought, Keir. Also, the organisation could substitute part of an existing meteorite. For example, one recovered from the remains of a Dutch museum damaged by fire last year. I believe that the so-called Kuopio find could be part of that same meteorite. The petrological analyses are so similar. The curator in Holland was a friend of mine and he felt the fire was deliberate. He died in a car accident two months later. Except I do not believe that was an accident, either.'

Lucien's eyes clouded as he looked down at the ground.

'A fine man, Keir. One of the best. His grandchildren still come to visit us in the school holidays. Luuk is the image of his grandfather. But I digress, my friend!'

'Not very pleasant people we're up against,' said Keir.

At that moment, a gust of wind caused a green turbulence to race fitfully through the coarse grass around them.

*****

12 Skagen

11:00am, Skagen Peninsula, Denmark.

In the Land Rover, Rollo's link-set burst into life with a series of short vibrations. He pressed the acknowledge key.

'Fox Oscar Two Three from Oscar Bravo.' Rollo recognised Ilya's incoming voice from Oulu Base.

'Roger. How's it going, Ilya?'

'Fine. Where are you located?'

'Three point seven five kilometres north east of Skagen railway station.'

'Confirmed. There are three other vehicles, but you can't see them from your location. Stand by; I'll transmit our satellite images to you. You'll see that there's some broken cloud, but it's dispersing now.'

'Roger. Is the weather going to be fine here, Ilya?'

'Fairly pleasant,' Ilya said. 'How are things at the house?'

'Fine, so far. Lucien is making a good recovery. Just a minute, Ilya!'

'Is everything all right down there?'

'I'm not so sure. Hold on a moment.'

Rollo raised his binoculars and allowed the autofocus to bring into crisp relief the distant dark figure on the sand. He pressed the record button. But too late, it had gone.

'I'm sure there's someone out there. Standing near the water.'

'What's wrong with that, Rollo? It's a beach, isn't it?'

'Yes, but this is Skagen peninsula, Ilya! Notices all over the place in several languages. Danger, no bathing, paddling or wading. The tides can be treacherous. In the holiday season, they bring tourists out here in tractor-trains. Mainly just to watch.'

'To look at what? I see nothing special. No monuments. Ah! Your nearest building is between you and the railway station. It's probably a small café, judging by its thermal signature.'

'Hang on... I've just sent an alert to the coastguard on my other phone. And you're right, Ilya; there's a new bistro in the sand-dunes about a kilometre behind me. I drove past it.' Rollo panned his binoculars. 'It's called *Den Sandsvæsen*. I think it means sand-people.'

'Really? What's in it for the tourists? Perhaps a strip tease show and a well stocked bar, eh? Of course! That's *why* you're there!' Ilya's gusts of laughter took on a curious mechanical quality, as the audio auto-gain control tried its best to cope. Rollo could hear Valentina's words of admonition in the background.

'The tourists come to look at the sea, Ilya,' Rollo continued: 'It's really where *two* seas mix together and cause spectacular turbulence, even on a calm day. The Kattegat to the east and the Skagerak to the north and west. They meet right here, on the northern tip of Denmark. That's why there's no bathing. The patterns in the water are visible on the satellite imagery.'

'*Da!* You're right, and I'll believe your story, dear friend Rollo, but there are many who wouldn't!'

'Rollo!' Valentina spoke now. 'Don't listen to him! He is a descendant of Ivan the Terrible!' More laughter, some crackling noises, and then:

'Rubbish!' Ilya again, 'I'm a good-living Russian Orthodox Muscovite!'

'Liar!' Valentina said. Either she had switched to a desk mike, or activated another set on the down-link channel. Her voice sounded as clear as Ilya's.

'Are you two having a vodka party up there at Oulu Base?' Rollo joined in the continuing entertainment.

'Nobody believes me,' Ilya said, 'not even you, Rollo! Never mind.' Then his professional concern came to the fore: 'Perhaps you should tell me what you see now. Is that person or object still there?'

Rollo scanned again with the binoculars. 'No. It's gone... Hang on! It's there again.'

'The waters are dangerous, as you say. Sounds like somebody might be in trouble. Can you get any closer?'

'Maybe. The tip of the peninsula goes out much farther. My first binocular reading was a range of nine-nine-zero metres, just at the tip of the peninsula. The water looks really rough out there, Ilya! I think even an expert swimmer or surfer would have real problems. The tide's going out, so I'll go forward in four wheel drive as far as I can. I'll call you back when there's something to report.'

'Roger, Rollo. Catch you later on. Closing the channel. Over and out.'

'Cheers, Ilya.'

Five hundred metres from the tip of the peninsula, there appeared to be a firm, flat bed of wet sand. Then suddenly, Rollo felt Belerophon drop about fifteen centimetres and tilt forward ominously. He resisted the temptation to deliver more power to the wheels, and paused. The vehicle seemed stable, for the moment.

'Are you still there?' he called the coastguard again. 'Mayday, mayday, my vehicle is in quicksand, quicksand, do you understand? Charming! They must have rung off!'

With one hand trying the operator again, Rollo used the other on the horn button to sound the time-honoured sequence SOS in Morse code. By the tenth SOS, the coastguard line still engaged? *Possibly organising the swimmer's rescue*, he thought.

'SOS, SOS...' The horn continued for what seemed like an aeon. He saw a flash of fluorescent orange in his driving mirror. The hovercraft! It passed him, along the north east margin of the peninsula, skirting the water's edge. Either they could not hear him, or they were intent on maintaining highest priority for the swimmer. That's only reasonable, Rollo conceded, as he continued pumping SOS messages into the void.

The hovercraft appeared ahead, an orange blob methodically sweeping the far coastline and occasionally dipping and bobbing in its broiling waters. He realised that the wind would carry his sound away from them, but wondered if he dared flash his lights to attract their attention. They wouldn't let him interfere with their search, but they might call up another patrol. He resorted to alternating the signalling modes, horn and headlight. Then, at last, another moving object caught his eye.

'Hooray! Here they come!' In his driver's door-mirror he saw a greenish, rust covered amphibious vehicle swing into view. He looked down at his watch. Amazingly, it told him that only about seven and a half minutes had elapsed since his first distress call. The vehicle drew level with him, about twenty five metres away on his right. There, the ground looked firm. *They're old hands at this game, and they must know this place inside out*, he thought. Suddenly, a young blonde girl stood up on the platform of the rescue craft, yelling at him in Danish. He opened his driver's door, being careful not to fall out.

'English! English!' he called.

'*Mange tak*! OK. I not speak *Engelsk*. Tro! Tro!' She called to her companion, a German Shepherd dog. Within fifteen seconds, the animal had picked his way skilfully towards and around the Land Rover and jumped onto the bonnet, with the end of a lanyard in his mouth. Keir reached around and grabbed it. The girl beckoned to him.

'You come now! Come! Come!' she shouted to Rollo.

'What about my car?' he protested. But he must obey, hoping there'd be time to rescue Belerophon from a horrible grave. He scrabbled around the cockpit area and the passenger seat for his secure link-set. *Got it*!

'Let's go!' he shouted to himself. He paused for an instant at the open door, noting the dog's tracks. He aimed for a light set of prints, near the limit of his range. He jumped and immediately sank up to his ankles in the silt, but no further. He fed the rope through his hands, taking up the slack as he freed himself, almost losing his shoes. With a sucking noise at each step, he made for the firmer sand where the craft stood, avoiding several jellyfish basking impassively in the sunshine.

'Thank you!' he called to the girl, 'And thanks, Tro!' The dog cocked his ears, acknowledged him with a gentle whimper and licked his hand.

'You have!' the girl motioned him to take a plastic mug of coffee, which she had poured from a flask.

'Many thanks!' he said.

'You welcome!' she replied, smiling. She looked about nineteen or twenty. Extremely attractive, he thought.

As a counter to temptation, he imagined his wife June being present at his side: *Enough of your nonsense, Rollo, and get that wretched Land Rover out of the sand*! He heard her say.

He motioned to the girl the need to rescue his car. She in turn motioned Rollo to stand clear of the craft. Its diesel motor blasted his eardrums as she guided it into position about twenty metres behind Belerophon. Rollo watched as Tro bounded his way over with the rope in his mouth. Incredibly, he began using his muzzle and a front paw to thread the rope through the circular aperture in the rear cross-member, which by now had sunk just above the sand. He returned to his mistress with the free end of the rope. She patted him and secured it to a large cleat on the front of her amphibian, then drew the twinned rope taut, folding the slack around a shiny, well used capstan. With the hand brake off, Rollo hoped he hadn't left his trusty vehicle in gear.

'No matter, it'll survive!' he said to himself.

A loud squelch greeted his ears. The most beautiful sound in Denmark, he thought. The Land Rover half slid, half lifted, as it lurched out of the mire.

'Wonderful!' he cried, jubilantly. He ran across to the amphibian as the girl climbed down to recover the rope. His inhibitions banished, he went forward to embrace her. But he backed off, as Tro growled menacingly. She smiled again at Rollo and shrugged.

'It is nothing,' she said.

'But it's everything, to me. Here, please take this!'

'No! Can not take!' she protested.

'OK then. Buy some biscuits for Tro instead!'

She looked at him with a puzzled frown.

'Buy for Tro? OK. *Mange tak*! Men-ee-thanks!' she said, gratefully. Suddenly, the dog barked excitedly.

'Else! Else!' A middle-aged man approached them.

'Papa!' the girl shouted, as her father climbed nimbly aboard their amphibian. He waved and greeted Rollo in Danish. Tro raced around, leaping with excitement, and eventually stood on the prow of the craft, like a Viking figurehead, wafting his huge tail from side to side.

'*Engelsk*!' Else explained. The man paused and then smiled, as his short-cropped greying blond hair tremored in the north east wind.

Else felt relieved that her father had arrived on the scene. After all, who is this stranger from England who had alerted them?

'You're obviously new to the Skagen area. Welcome! My name is Niels. You have met Else, and Trofast, of course!' Niels spoke in accented but clear English and the dog cocked his ears again. 'You look exhausted! Can you drive your car?'

'Thank you, yes. My name's Rollo.' They shook hands. Rollo then shook Else's hand. A warm, sensitive hand, supple, yet firm. She smiled at him again.

'Very good,' Niels said. 'Bring your wagon down to the café. But before you do, we'd better check it out.' He leapt down onto the sand, and began grovelling about underneath Belerophon. 'There! I've wiped the clutch housing and the transmission brake is clean enough. The front swivels are dirty, though. It'll be OK to drive off the beach, but we'll need to give everything a good jet-wash back at the garage.'

'Thank you, Niels. And your English is excellent!'

'Thanks, Rollo. To cope with the tourists, I speak seven languages, four of them fairly fluently. My daughter Else doesn't normally work here in the tourist season, though. She prefers animals and horticulture. Next year she starts agricultural college, and her English will no doubt become much improved.'

At that moment, the orange hovercraft sped past them about three hundred metres away, retracing its path along the northern side of the peninsula. Niels and Else waved to the crew, and the brightly coloured craft continued on its way, receding from sight until hidden from view by the extremity of the dune field.

'You seem to know a bit about classic four-by-fours and how to look after them, Niels.' Rollo said.

'I should do! I used to look after a few of the old ones like this, during my service in the army. That brings me to a question, Rollo. Why haven't you got one of *our* club stickers? Not yet in the Danish 4x4 club? Then I'll have to sign you up.' Niels glanced at his watch. 'If we make it snappy, we'll get a good choice for a snack at the café. Come on!'

*****

11:15am, Frederikshavn.

'Have you been here before, Lucien?'

'To Frederikshavn? No, never. It seems a beautiful place, if only they would let me get out of here to look at it! Pardon me, Lisa! I meant no offence.'

'That is all right, Professor, Lisa said, 'I know perfectly well what you mean. But that's what a safe house is for, yes?'

In characteristic fashion, Lucien shrugged resignedly.

She continued: 'Don't worry, my friends. Today, you might be allowed a little more freedom.' She checked her watch and then called up Ilya Karpov on her link-set.

The others looked on as Lisa gave her status report:

'The health of our principal client is good, status four and improving. Health status of Fox Oscar Two Five is three and improving. Here, we're totally secure with no change since the last report.'

'I have an update on that,' said Ilya.

'Please say again'

'A security update, Lisa. Your security status is now three. I repeat, three. Yellow alert. Is that understood?'

'Yellow alert? Yes, understood, Ilya.' Lisa said, surprised.

'I will explain,' said Ilya, 'This morning, Fox Oscar Two Three reported a sighting at Skagen, which is to be regarded as suspicious until further clarification is obtained. Just a precaution and no cause for alarm.'

'Can you tell us what Field Operative Two Three is doing at Skagen, Ilya?'

'Negative. I'm not authorised to say, at this stage.'

Ilya's voice didn't betray that he had no idea why Rollo had taken that route .

'Thank you, Ilya. Nothing further to report from here. Bye! Over and out.'

'Bye, Lisa! Channel closing.'

Lisa replaced the set and continued with her tasks, clearly disappointed for her two guests.

'Well, Lisa,' said Keir, 'we'll just have to sit tight until it blows over. How often do you have yellow alerts?'

'I was assigned here six years ago, by Danish Army Intelligence. During that period and the recent United Nations take-over, the highest security status has been two, just on one occasion. No yellow alerts.' She crossed to the window and opened it, looking up at the sky to locate the source of the sound. A helicopter flew steadily past the house, heading south.

Keir got up from his armchair to have a look. As he approached Lisa, he saw a small spot of red light gliding across her left cheek.

He charged, bringing her down with a rugby tackle, and they both crashed into a small antique card table in the corner of the room, splintering it in pieces. Almost simultaneously, a loud report! The top window shattered and a small cloud of dust flew up from the carpet near Keir's right foot.

'Blood and sand!' he exclaimed.

'*Sacré bleu*! It very nearly was, my friend!' cried Lucien.

'I think Lisa's hit her head, Lucien. She's out cold!'

Keir fumbled in her tunic pocket for her link-set. Then he realised that it would be useless without Lisa's personal ID code. He went to the sofa, where his jacket lay, and used his own communicator.

'Ilya! Ilya!' he called.

'Fox Oscar Two Five from Oscar Bravo,' came the reply.

'Ilya! Sorry, Ilya! We want a doctor down here, quick! Medical assistance, right away. Security personnel, too. We've been shot at!'

'Your status is red alert, code five. Give me the details.'

'Details follow! Lisa sustained blow to head, unconscious, suspected concussion. No others injured. Ballistic projectile embedded in floor, believed to be fired from passing helicopter.'

'Roger. I have the helicopter. Receding, now four kilometres south. Exit drill! Leave the building. Carry Lisa outside. Proceed quickly to rear of property and take refuge at least one hundred metres distant. Wait for Commander Nielsen, keep together and leave the rest to me. Is that understood?'

'Roger. Understood. We're leaving now.'

'Roger, over and out.'

'I've got Lisa's keys - I'll open the doors. Lucien, off you go. I'll bring Lisa.'

'*Oui, mon ami*! Anything else?'

'We grab our link-sets and coats on the way out. That's all!'

They followed the same route that Keir and Lucien had taken on their earlier walk. Keir had Lisa in a fireman's lift in spite of his injury. At last, they arrived at the recommended distance from the rear of the house.

'I'm Commander Lars Nielsen.'

Keir turned his head at the sound of the newcomer, who seemed to have arrived from nowhere. His face daubed with camouflage, he stood like a Guy Fawkes effigy; exuding grass, twigs and leaves, which quivered in the wind. Otherwise his battledress appeared to be standard issue.

'Thank goodness!' Keir said, 'Have you any medical staff?'

'Of course. Sergeant Berg will assist.'

Another uniformed soldier had appeared:

'Give her to me.' she said, crisply. Keir obeyed, with Commander Nielsen's help.

'*Tak!*' she said. She made Lisa comfortable on a portable stretcher. 'Please tell me precise details of what happened,' she added.

Meanwhile, three other soldiers had approached the house. One of them moved closer and stood to one side of the broken window. He dropped a small object into the room and moved away again. One of the other soldiers appeared to be reading from a device in his hand.

The third member of the group carried a flat box, painted drab brown, about the size of a briefcase. He sat on the ground by the garden fence and opened the box.

Keir joined the Commander again, while Sergeant Berg attended to her recumbent charge. She arranged Lisa's transfer to a military ambulance in the care of paramedics.

'What are your men doing near the house?' Keir asked.

'Chemical trace analysis of the projectile,' the Commander replied, 'The opposition use a variety of weapons. We're making sure what type it is before deactivating it, if necessary.'

'Opposition? Who are they?'

'Not at liberty to say.'

'I didn't think it was still active when Ilya told us to get clear of the house,' Keir said. 'I thought it was a bullet they fired at Lisa, not a grenade.'

'It looks like bullet damage,' Nielsen said. 'We'll check it out to make sure.

'By the way, I'm sorry. I didn't introduce myself. The name's Keir Wilson.'

'I know. And don't be sorry,' the Commander said blandly, 'it's better than being called a number, isn't it? Anyway, I already know your identity, and it's best to use *Jonathan Sykes* while you're outdoors. Been in Denmark long?'

'A couple of days.'

'It's a pity you can't look around the town yet. I hope you get the chance, perhaps when all this returns to normal.'

'Thank you. You know Lucien?'

'We had some afternoon tea here on his first day at the house.'

'All clear, Commander,' the soldier with the measuring instrument reported.

'Sergeant Berg, proceed with recovery of the projectile. And tell me if Corporal Knudsen needs to deal with it.'

'Sir!' with a salute, she turned on her heel to organise the recovery. Nielsen's team had donned protective suits of a tough, highly reflective material with the appearance of aluminium foil. Their silvery visors resembled welding masks.

'Lisa's coming round!' Lucien said. Keir saw with relief her eyelids flickering.

'I'm sorry, Commander,' Keir said, 'I feel it's my fault. I pushed her away from the window and we fell.'

'Always you are sorry, Field Officer! That is nonsense. You saved her from being killed, with little regard for your own safety. I will be citing you for a commendation.'

Keir looked surprised. 'Thank you, sir!' he said, weakly.

'It's all been a bit of a shock for you, hasn't it? Don't worry, we'll soon have you back inside when my people have finished. It seems that when Lisa opened that ground floor transom window, the projectile came through the adjacent pane of fixed glass. It will have gone straight through the floor boarding and buried itself in the concrete beneath. From the residual gases results, it looks like standard issue ordnance. But we must make sure that everything is safe.'

'One of *our* bullets?' Keir asked.

'Almost certainly. We witnessed the incident as well. The helicopter was one of ours returning from a rescue operation near Skagen.'

'What rescue operation?'

'This morning FO23 wisely contacted the duty coastguard patrol on seeing a person in the water there. They sent out a recovery craft and the crew raised an alert after recovering someone from the Skagen peninsula. The helicopter was called to ferry that person from the coastguard team.'

'Why was a military helicopter called, instead of a police or ambulance one?'

'The situation required it,' Commander Nielsen replied glibly. 'The coastguard station acted correctly. Shall we see how Lisa is getting on? Look, she's sitting up!'

Keir pressed the more immediate question: 'Why on earth did one of our own helicopters fire on us?'

Commander Nielsen paused for a moment, his pale blue eyes unblinking as he turned to Keir. 'I really have no idea. Perhaps we will find out after the inquiry.'

*****

11:35am, Café near Skagen.

'This soup's really good!' Rollo commented, 'And thank you again, Else, for pulling me out of the quicksand.'

'It was what I must do!' Turning to her father, she spoke a few words in Danish, then turned to Rollo again. 'Nice to meet you, must go now.'

'See you later, Else!' Her father spoke deliberately in English as she left the table.

'Bye, Else!' Rollo said, but she didn't look back at them. Tro had waited obediently outside the cafe and Rollo heard him padding at her heels before soft sand muffled the sound of their departure.

'She has her work to finish,' Niels explained, passing Rollo the basket of bread rolls. 'Your call came through just as she was in our conservatory. You were lucky to catch her. She's usually a long way from the buildings, looking after the outdoor plants. I keep telling her to carry the mobile phone around, but she hates interruptions, even from me!'

'But I didn't make the call.'

'The coastguard patrol must have spotted you, then. By the way, how did you come to get stuck out there? We don't normally take vehicles that far out.'

Rollo described his sighting, watching Niels carefully, while trying to look casual.

'Interesting,' Niels commented, as he munched his roll.

Is that all? Rollo thought. He needed to explore the matter further. 'Why d'you think it's interesting, Niels? Don't you get the occasional odd-ball bather, as we do back home?'

'Indeed. You must have many dangerous beaches in Britain,' Niels remarked. 'Such a lot of coastline.'

I've let him digress, Rollo realised, trying to keep calm. He tried again: 'Were you suggesting that there was something special about what I saw this morning?'

A voice from the serving counter heralded their main courses. Niels got up to collect them, while Rollo fetched the cutlery and paid.

They sat down again and Rollo waited patiently, hoping for an answer without further interruptions. His hopes were short-lived, for the cafe door had swung open and they were joined by a friend of Niels's. They greeted each other and began a conversation in Danish.

Rollo glanced at his watch. No time for the niceties. He had to get an answer quickly. He waited for a gap in the conversation.

'Excuse me, Niels!' he blurted, managing a glassy smile, 'I'd like to meet your friend! Please tell him his lunch is on me.'

'I'm sure he'll be grateful! Let me introduce you. Carl, Roland.'

'Rollo. Nice to meet you, Carl.'

They shook hands.

'Carl's wife runs a newsagent and general store next to the railway station,' Niels said. 'He speaks very little English.'

'Niels! I'd like you to ask him something.'

'Yes, Rollo?'

'Has Carl ever seen anything strange on the beach around here, like I did this morning? I'd be grateful if you would ask him for me.'

Niels frowned slightly before addressing him in his native Danish. 'Carl, my visitor Rollo thinks he saw another *sandsvæsen* today. He wants you to say something about them, like how many you have seen on our beach, perhaps.'

Carl seemed familiar with the expression. Niels translated as Carl explained his view of the phenomenon:

'They were called sand-creature because, from a distance, they looked more like the sandcastles which children made, or perhaps like snowmen, but brown coloured. People who reported these rare but curious sightings would sometimes call the coastguard, or alert Niels and his amphibian. But so far, they had always vanished before the rescue craft reached the scene. They were very rare, almost non-existent, during the tourist season. And when they appeared at night, they sometimes glowed and flickered faintly. The official explanation was that they were probably a strain of mutant marine life, migrants from British coastal waters, possibly related to the whale or porpoise; brought into being perhaps through contamination caused by dumping of radioactive waste.'

'What of the secrecy that seems to surround the topic? Rollo asked.

Carl continued through Niels, his translator: 'It was better not to speak of the *sandsvæsen*, because any connotation of radioactivity could be bad for tourism. Carl remembered an article which his wife had read to him from an English newspaper, last year. It had been written in the corner of an inside Travel Page, but unfortunately headed, *Denmark:*

Glowing Reports of Skagen. Curiously, though, the local tourist trade had since improved, especially from British visitors.'

Turning to Rollo, Niels said, 'Carl concludes that such articles might indeed have a slight beneficial effect on trade and also prompt a clean up of the environment. On balance, he's happy to talk of the sand-creatures. Just to his friends, of course.'

'Thank you, Niels,' said Rollo. 'Thanks to you both.' The Danes shook hands in turn with Rollo, who added: 'Please let me know, Neils, how much I owe you for the rescue.'

'You paid for the lunches, let's call it quits,' said Niels.

*****

Oulu Base, Finland.

Ilya rarely felt perplexed, and even less often allowed it to show. Valentina also felt concerned. They had eaten a hurried lunch, breaking their own rules by bringing food into the communications room. But things were threatening to get out of control since Keir's emergency call from the safe house and confirmation of the helicopter incident by Lars Nielsen.

'I know why Rollo's at Skagen,' Ilya said. 'He's talking to the locals about something, and it can only be this!' He flashed an archived image onto his screen; a cartoon sketch of a snowman-like object, but more conical in shape. 'While you were monitoring Rollo's position, I've been doing some homework on Skagen. Since Rollo's detour up there, the database has given me some very useful information which ties in with the helicopter incident at SH5. Well, it might possibly tie in. We need more evidence.'

'What have you got, there, Ilya?' Valentina asked.

'Take a look at these newspaper articles! There are two which refer specifically to separate sighting incidents of happenings on the beach, rather similar to Rollo's. The first one is almost seven years ago to the day, in this North Jutland newspaper. The English translation tells of two sand-creatures, as the local inhabitants call them, who were seen bathing in impossibly treacherous waters on the Skagen peninsula. The local coastguard team examined the scene, but they found nothing.'

'Have many people been washed away and drowned in that area?' asked Valentina.

'Almost certainly, although I haven't checked the official casualty figures. But it says these *sandsvæsen* vanished without trace. The reporter mentions several similar stories in the locality, including two of sand-creatures which glow in the dark. In fact, an article appeared with the headline, *Loch Ness Monster at Skagen*? Another article is from the British paper, the London Evening Clarion, dated two weeks later and called, *Glowing Reports of Skagen*. It tells a similar story, probably drawing on the Danish reports. It's all here if you want to take a look! I'll put the database references in your area, Val.'

'Thanks, Ilya. You don't think we've got a *breakout* situation on our hands, do you?'

'It pays to be suspicious of strange new events. Has the helicopter arrived yet?'

'The one with the Skagen casualty? It's landing now Ilya, on the hospital roof. I have their radio messages. Their main priority must be to get the injured coastguard crewman into the hospital. They're disembarking on the roof-pad at the Aalborg Sygehus now.'

'Sygehus?'

'It means hospital.' Valentina said. She continued: 'The helicopter will then take the prisoner to Blokhus for forensic checking.'

'After Blokhus,' Ilya said, 'it'll go on to Aarhus for the interrogation. I'll bet you an hour's pay they'll ask me to fly out there and do it!'

'Ilya, I'm not some kind of fool. I'm not betting you anything! As co-ordinator for safe house security in Scandanavia, I've already been asked by the Chief Security Executive for Denmark to arrange this interrogation. And yes - that means *you*, Ilya!'

'OK, Lars Nielsen,' Ilya murmured, 'you owe me one!'

*****

13 The Prisoner

Wednesday 15 September. Oakingwell.

Alan entered Burton's office, a collection of unmarked student assignments under his arm: 'Are you suggesting I should fly out there, Brian?'

'It's up to you, Alan.'

That was not exactly very helpful, Alan thought. 'Well, I feel that I can't really leave my students to fend for themselves. Not the first year ones, certainly!' he commented.

'You'd only be away a short time,' Burton said, leaning back in his swivel chair as if addressing a small insect on the ceiling, 'Perhaps just a couple of working days, if you don't count the weekend.' He turned to Alan again: 'I suppose you're thinking that Wilson will be back here in ten days, anyway.'

'Yes, but I do realise this is the second shooting incident he's experienced within a month,' Alan said. *And trust Burton to suggest the weekend*, he thought. *The family gets short-changed again.*

'As I say, it's up to you. If you really want my advice, I suggest that you take your new brief very seriously indeed. And provided it doesn't conflict too much with your job here, I suppose you can still draw full salary.'

'Thank you *very* much for that, Brian!'

'All right Alan! You win, on this occasion. I'll arrange the necessary cover for your teaching. But I'm not disposed to authorising musical chairs with class timetabling on a regular basis. In the circumstances, I suggest you leave as soon as you can. Make use of Thursday and Friday and be back here by first thing Monday morning. And if there are any other likely periods of absence, I suggest you find external funding.'

*****

Alan returned to his office and checked his email. One of the messages had an address unfamiliar to him, but he guessed it might be a ciphered 'pointer message' in connection with Project Electra. On reading it, his thoughts were confirmed:

Hello Alan!

Hope all is well. There's plenty of interesting things to do over here, but the weather is not so good, so we're going to try some indoor hockey in the new octagonal stadium. Do have fun. Best wishes, Jon.

Alan knew the message to be entirely redundant apart from one throw-away codeword *'octagonal'* which happened to be eighth word from the end. Using a look-up table, this signified Alan should read his Project Electra email. He went on line with his link-set and the first of the two unscrambled messages read:

Proceed to SH5DK. Discuss with OBSF.

Alan recognised the now familiar abbreviations for the safe house at Frederikshavn and the Finnish base near Oulu. The second message, headed *General Conditions of Service: Update* he found less terse and occupied several pages.

'Not more red tape?' he asked himself. But as he began to browse through the large formal document, he unexpectedly felt much better.

'Hey! Looks like we're getting paid on top of our salaries!' he exclaimed to himself while scrolling down the job list. He paused at *Convenor*, Burton's new appointment. Sifting through the fine detail and under *Rates of Pay*, payment would be hourly, proportional to the duration of the tasks or meetings, plus an expenses allowance for travel and daily subsistence. *Those rules aren't bad at all*, Alan noted, but in small print a clause stated: *'Wherever possible, time should be saved by conducting meetings over the Secure Link, from the Convenor's local Access Point using the Project's officially approved software application package, which is designed for handling these aspects of the administration and communication.'*

Moving on further, he arrived at *Guardian*. His pay would be along the same lines as Burton's, with one exception.

There would be an additional monthly flat rate: *'in recognition of ongoing responsibility for welfare of an individual assigned to essential duties incurring high personal risks.'* Alan did some quick mental arithmetic. That made his expected annual income about twice Burton's figure! The final clause stated that *'there is no commensurate increase in rank attached to any further responsibilities which may from time to time arise therefrom.'*

'Who cares!' Alan cried, jubilantly.

The document concluded with some details about taxation, and with the statements:

'*All income specified herein is additional to whatever the incumbent may earn from any other source, and this entitlement over-rules any existing pay agreements with any specific employer, within United Nations countries, which would otherwise preclude their employee from accepting additional income from elsewhere.*'

'Nice one!' he shouted. At that moment, Burton knocked and entered. Peering over Alan's shoulder, he recognised the contents of the screen but didn't comment.

'Just to confirm the cover for your classes, Alan'

'Thanks, Brian.'

'You'd better get on with your travel arrangements,' Burton said glibly, closing the door again.

*****

Frederikshavn, North Jutland.

The ambulance took Lisa to a military hospital near Blokhus for overnight observation. Back at Frederikshavn, Lucien tugged his beard, deep in thought, while Keir sat opposite him, near the fireplace. Corporal Petersen crossed the room towards them.

'Here you are, Keir. I've put one sugar in for you,' the Corporal said, 'I'd better turn up the fire, it's getting chilly.'

'Thanks, Søren.' Keir took the mug of black coffee. 'Any news of Lisa?'

'Nothing further, but I think she'll be fine. It's just a routine precaution. Can I top you up, Professor?' He took the cup and replenished it.

'*Merci*, Søren! I'm sorry. My head was in the clouds.' Lucien placed his cup on the tea trolley next to his armchair. He still looked slightly pale from his ordeal.

'Keir,' he said, 'you must not keep blaming yourself! The Commander was extremely impressed by your selfless response to the danger.'

'Very kind of you to say that, Lucien. Don't worry, I'll be fine. But I keep asking, why were we shot at by one of our own helicopters? I couldn't get any real sense out of the Commander. How about you, Søren? What d'you think?'

'I'm just as puzzled as you are, Keir. But off the record, I was wondering if it's one of our soldiers with a grudge. You see, not everyone likes Commander Nielsen, and this helicopter thing is a great embarrassment to him in his position of being in charge of local security here.'

'I not so sure,' said Keir. 'The soldier in question wouldn't put himself in such a serious position just for that reason, surely?'

'Unless, perhaps, he is being granted a substantial favour, or being paid a very large sum,' Lucien ventured. 'Let's consider, we are not at war, so the worst that can happen to him is that he is court martialed and goes to prison. If he pleads insanity, he may at the very worst be dishonourably discharged instead.'

'But Lucien, how does that make sense?' Keir protested, 'If Lisa had been killed, the guy would surely get life?'

'I think that's true,' agreed Søren.

'It is possible, of course,' Lucien suggested, 'he deliberately aimed to miss.'

'In which case,' Keir said, 'he must be a crack shot, to take such a close risk that he did.'

'He would have to be a crack shot either way, *mon ami*, whatever way he had planned the outcome!' Lucien commented.

'Not necessarily, gentlemen.' said Søren, 'It could have been an image-seeking rifle.'

'Indeed?' Keir said. He scanned his memory archive for early twenty first century ordnance. It didn't add up. Reliable service weapons of this kind weren't around until after 2020.

'You may be right, Søren,' Lucien said, 'I understand there are a few experimental versions around.'

'They're improving all the time,' said Søren, 'Our sniper friend could have programmed one from a digitised image, perhaps using a photograph and GPS data, and when the helicopter flew past the target, he wouldn't even have to take aim, so long as the rifle was pointing roughly in the right direction; its servo motors would do the rest.'

'Like a robot arm?' asked Keir.

'Yes,' Søren agreed. 'Of course, the weapon could have encountered some difficulties at the time it was used,' he suggested, 'like the approach direction and sun angle.'

'And Lisa might have changed the image of the window by opening it!' Keir said,' The target image would need to register precisely with the rifle's stored image for successful recognition and lock-on.'

Keir stopped abruptly. One step further and he might mention what he knew from his future world.

'Of course, the target might be smaller but still well defined, like the fixed transom window up there.' Keir continued, as he walked over and pointed to the top left corner of the window, which had been very quickly and professionally re-glazed.

'Possible, I suppose,' Søren said.

'But there was still a risk of killing someone, *n'est ce pas*?' Lucien asked.

'Quite so,' Søren agreed, 'I daresay the sniper will claim that he didn't intend to kill, but merely protest at something or other.'

'*Alors*! We won't really be any the wiser until after the inquiry, as Commander Nielsen says,' Lucien said. 'Therefore we may as well relax until we're told what to do next.'

He noted the nods of assent, picked up the remote and turned on the television.

*****

Aarhus Military Base, Denmark.

'What rank is the prisoner?' Ilya asked the desk sergeant at the Aarhus Military Base.

'Lance Corporal, sir.'

'What uniform can I wear?'

'Well, sir. We normally wear the UN colours here. If you want to wear your Russian Major's uniform, sir, that should be no problem, so long as it bears the UN insignia.'

'I do, and as you can see for yourself, it does, Sergeant!'

'Very good, sir. You'll need this.' The sergeant handed Ilya a recorder.

'I know the procedure, Sergeant!'

'Very good, sir!' The sergeant opened his book and verbally announced the item of equipment being issued while he ticked the box: 'One off, recorder, portable type V44K, interview for the use of. Please sign here, Major.'

Ilya signed the page using his alias, the one embroidered on his uniform, and they saluted. Guided by an orderly he descended down a flight of stone steps. The damp-smelling and dimly lit corridor led to Cell 19, the Interrogation Room; its door flanked by two armed guards, who stood to attention at his arrival.

'Here's my pass. At ease, gentlemen!'

'Thank you sir!' The guard on the right of the door handed back his papers and the one on the left opened the door.

'Thank you!' Ilya said.

'Sir!' said the second guard, closing it behind Ilya.

Ilya pointedly ignored the prisoner and addressed the other man sitting at the bare wooden table, above which a shadeless lamp shone.

'Major Sergei Borodin, sir!' Ilya saluted.

'Good afternoon, Major Borodin,' the other man said, returning the salute. He took Ilya's recorder and turned it on. 'Major Borodin has entered and introduced himself. He doesn't speak Danish. Neither does the prisoner speak Russian. They both speak English and the interview will be conducted in that language. This is Brigadier Stanislav Topolski now leaving the Interview Room at 14:27 hours. Thank you, Major.'

'Sir!' Ilya saluted again and then sat down, removing his gloves as the Brigadier left.

'Ah! I see they've left us some water. Would you like a glass?' The prisoner remained silent. Ilya poured himself half a tumbler and continued:

'Perhaps we should get to know each other. What is your name?'

There followed a silence of a few seconds before Ilya resumed, with a smile:

'You are quite right, of course. I do know your name, already. It is Lance Corporal Mads Erik Gade, is it not? You did well at school, and at university quite brilliantly. First class joint honours in computing and temporal logic. You plan to follow an academic career when you have completed your military service. But for the present, you are still in the army and, as you may have heard, I'm Major Sergei Borodin.' Ilya paused for a further few seconds. 'Until quite recently, I was assigned to the Noginsk Military Prison, have you heard of it?'

More silence.

'Let me tell you something. I used to be in it once. As a prisoner. You see, I committed a misdemeanour when I was a young officer. So to some extent we have something in common, my friend. Of course, I regret it very much. By now I might have made it to Brigadier, like our colleague who has just left. But there it is. They will still pay me a reasonable pension when I retire and some would argue that little has been lost except my honour.'

Ilya looked down at his gloves, his face hidden in the resulting shadow. 'But that means a lot to me,' his tone changed ominously. Looking up, his face now fully illuminated, he stared at the prisoner squarely in the eyes. 'You see, to my family, it was a disgrace! My dear father taught me so much, and wanted me to do so well. He served under Andropov. *The* Andropov, General in the KGB. Forgive me!'

Ilya's mouth quirked very slightly, the trace of a tear visible in the corner of his eye, as he stated: 'He never spoke to me again.' He took the prisoner's glass and filled it, placing it within easy reach.

'Here!' he said, waving brusquely at it. He immediately continued: 'There was one consolation for my dear old father as he lay dying in Kiev Infirmary. I was still too ashamed to visit him, but my mother convinced him that by admitting my guilt and resolving to be a loyal soldier, I had restored the family's honour. My mother always believed in me, you see. But it took her many years to convince him. And like yourself, I never knew my *real* father'.

The prisoner's hand moved uncertainly towards the glass. His teeth clinked on the rim as he took a sip of the water. Ilya's expression relaxed and he allowed himself the trace of a smile.

'There, my friend. There is no need for discomfort. There's no need for disgrace, either. If you meant to do something significant and meaningful, by what you did, then tell us. We're here to understand and help each other, Mads.'

'I did it for Denmark.'

'Yes, I am a patriot, too. I can see you had good intentions, Mads. Tell me about it.'

'You aren't like the other person, Major. You seem to understand. So I'll tell you.'

'Thank you, Mads. There's no hurry, please take your time.'

'All right. Can I do this in confidence?'

Ilya faced the instrument. 'Turning off recorder at 14:38 hours for a confidential phase of the interview which has been requested by the prisoner. Right, that's it.'

'You know about Skagen, Major?'

'Skagen! Ah! You mean Skagen peninsula. That is in the north of your country, I think. Remember, I am from Russia. Go on.'

'Well, towards its tip, it's nearly all sand dunes. But there's something there! I mean something very odd, which is being kept secret.'

'What is the nature of this thing you speak of?'

Mads' fervent expression turned to uncertainty and he averted his eyes.

'You are not from here, so you may not believe me.'

'Let me tell you this, my friend! Before I joined the Russian Army, I was a student at St. Petersburg University, or Leningrad as it was then. I studied biochemistry and had many hobbies and interests, like Astronomy and Space Science. I can describe the atmosphere of Jupiter and the building blocks of life itself. So nothing is too strange for me. Yet when you think about it, Mads, it is all so very strange and wonderful. But now, here I am! A soldier! It would make me feel good to hear of new and interesting things again, so please tell me.'

Mads listened intently, watching the heavy features of this big Russian with the gentle, deep voice. Evidently a sensitive man with a yearning for knowledge. He took another sip of water and repositioned himself in his hard chair to resume his story.

'Please don't laugh at me, then. What I'm going to tell you will sound unbelievable.'

'You can be assured, Mads. I won't laugh.'

'Very well. It all started when I was at school. Seven years ago. A friend there told me about an article in a local paper on the nearby island of Læsø that his father had seen. The article described conical shaped creatures on the Skagen peninsula, about the size of a small man. They came to be called *sandsvæsen,* or sand-creatures in English. Some called them sand-men but political correctness prevailed.'

'Of course!' Ilya said, 'Please go on.'

'They were reported to appear near the tide-line and then disappear, always around the same location, near the tip of the Skagen peninsula. This may not seem out of the ordinary, but if they were actual people and they tried to swim they would probably drown because of the treacherous waters there. Anyway, we went to the library to view the paper in detail and anything else we could find in the library's databases on this topic. There was nothing, so we went to the area itself during the holidays. We drew a complete blank but we were told by the locals that the best times to come were November and

February, outside the holiday seasons. So my friend and I played truant from school. That's because I didn't want to upset my mother and young sister at weekends with tales about strange men on a lonely beach.'

Ilya listened intently from his chair. 'This is interesting. Carry on, Mads,' he said.

'Sometime later, I was on a similar visit. It was mid-November. Pieter and I saw one for the first time. We hid in the sand dunes and I was using a reasonably good pair of binoculars. It was very well defined, glistening and brown, with many arms and strange looking hands.'

'It must have excited you both after waiting for so long,' said Ilya, 'Do you think you could draw it from memory?'

'We did better than that. On our next expedition we took a decent camera with us which Pieter borrowed from his dad. That was the following week. We saw and recorded *two* that time, both near Grenen, the tip of the Skagen peninsula. We were positioned in a dune-field just east of a region called Ellekrattet, which happened to be clear of bird spotters at the time.'

'Do you have the pictures?' Ilya asked.

'Yes, we do. We promised each other not to show them to anyone until the matter came to light officially, in case we were accused of faking stuff. Also we heard of another person who'd taken pictures being got at by officials who visited her.'

'Got at? Can you explain that, Mads?'

'Yes. Put simply, her reports were suppressed for some reason. We don't know why. The whole thing has been subjected to a quiet but persistent debunking campaign and the story is being put around that, if anything, the sightings are probably of a school of porpoises. At the more bizarre end of the spectrum, some have suggested migrant Loch Ness monsters.'

'Who do you think is debunking it?'

'At first, we thought it was you guys. Sorry, Major! I mean the military, or government. We went to the local authorities, but they just didn't want to know. So when I went to Copenhagen to visit my aunt, I spoke about it to her best friend, who's a civil servant. At first, she listened. Then she became sheepish and closed up. She didn't want to know either.'

'What do you think you really saw, Mads?'

The prisoner took a longer draught of water and Ilya replenished his glass.

'I've studied the pictures, Major. In fact, I did a computing course in image processing at university and secretly enhanced them in various ways. These sightings influenced my other subject choices, as well. I've read elective courses in marine biology and planetary science. I've since made several more sightings and have a detailed library of pictures. I think that if you're as genuine as you seem to be Major, I ought to give you a copy of the full collection, processed images as well. There's so much stuff it takes up nearly two whole DVDs. And in answer to your question, I truly believe that we have a colony of aliens at Skagen. But I also believe that these creatures are *not* extraterrestrials.'

Ilya remained impassive. 'You appear to have become quite an expert, Mads. I'd like to know what your view is,' he said.

'Very well. If you're considering extraterrestrials at our level of development, or just a little beyond, then you're talking about a tiny time-slice in vast geological or biologically evolutionary timescales. The probabilities are simply far too small. If there are beings out there in space, they're either very primitive, or technologically so far advanced that they could pass easily for one of us if they wanted to. We have to face it, Major, someone here on Planet Earth has been playing around with genetic engineering and produced something that now needs covering up. My experience in the Army, although short, is long enough for me to suspect there are people in high places responsible for suppressing that information.'

Ilya eased himself in his chair. 'Mads,' he said, 'what you have told me is more interesting than you could possibly imagine. Yes! I am most grateful that you have shared this information with me, and I would very much like to examine your pictures and maybe take them away from here, perhaps to Moscow, and study them there. But now I have to ask the more painful question of how it was that you came to be aiming a rifle at a cottage window from a helicopter.'

Mads sat in silence for about half a minute. Then he broke down, burying his head in his hands.

'I've ruined everything, haven't I?' he cried, 'By being stupid. So utterly stupid. You must believe me when I tell you this, Major.'

'Go ahead, I'm listening, Mads.'

'It wasn't pre-meditated. OK, I spent twenty minutes thinking about it, but it wasn't a long-term thing. The trouble is, when they examine the weapon, they'll think it was!'

'Why should they think that, Mads?'

'Well, we had a choice of weapons and I opted for the imaging rifle because I'm such a lousy shot. They told me they were still under development and not in regular service. I put up with being taunted about it, because the technology of it is so interesting. The few imaging rifles that were issued could hit an orange at 100 metres. But my modified one can hit a fly on an orange at 100 metres. I didn't brag about it because it was a personal challenge. Although these improvements were completed several months ago, they'll think I was doing it to plan something.'

'Your rifle is now in my possession, Mads,' said Ilya. I admire your skill and ingenuity!'

'Thank you, sir. It was back at university, with my image processing and computing knowledge, that I first took an interest and actually built an imaging weapon system around an old .22 sporting rifle. I kept improving the target locating accuracy and modifying the servo system in our garden shed. From the astronomy and physics courses at university, I learned enough to improve the gun-sight optics, too. Eventually, that gun would shoot anything, within the limitations of its range and calibre, if the original image data was right. And now I've modified an issued weapon.'

'I appreciate what you're saying and it's very interesting. But you still haven't told me what made you fire that shot.'

'It's true, I *was* wondering for some time how I could attract the attention of people to the Skagen situation. I made a tentative approach to Commander Nielsen three weeks ago, telling him in confidence about some of my pictures. He said he would return them to me in a week, but when I asked him, it was as if he'd forgotten all about it. I still haven't seen them but fortunately they were just back-up copies. It's the same old cover-up campaign, Major. I kept thinking long and hard about the so-called sand-creatures and the denial over the reports, and it was all bottled up inside me. It came to a head when we had to ferry the rescued coastguard crewman to the hospital in the helicopter. He'd been attacked by something in the water. We were told not to say anything, but I saw his injuries, Major!'

It appeared that Mads might vomit, but Ilya resisted his inclination to interrupt the story and the Major paused for several seconds, while the prisoner recovered his composure.

'I knew that I had to find a way of forcing attention on the issue,' Mads continued, 'so I decided there and then to bring myself to trial for a suitable offence, so that I could testify about what I know. I did the best thing I could, with the resources to hand, and fired that shot, as we passed the safe house.'

'Who said it was a safe house?' Ilya asked evenly.

'One of Commander Neilsen's men, er, women, sir.'

'Yes, forgive my interruption. Please carry on, Mads.'

'This will sound terrible to you, Major. But I don't care about my Army career, so long as the truth is told. To be in prison is a disgrace, I know. And the worst of it is - I could have killed someone if it had gone wrong. But I was so confident in my modified rifle, and the shot went exactly as planned. Although we were cruising quite slowly, I had to act quickly. I moved to the mid-section of the helicopter and aimed through the open door. On the approach to the cottage, I used the rifle-sight itself to take and store a picture of the house. Then I programmed the sight to fire the rifle at the top corner of the window. That was because the white paint on the frame made a good contrast image and the shape of the corner would be easily recognised by the rifle's aiming computer. At full zoom, the rifle detected no person in its immediate target area, even when someone opened the adjacent window. Such was the precision of my system.'

'Wasn't that a little risky, though? Without a tripod or other anti-shake measures? You must have had good servos to operate at full zoom.'

'I agree, Major. I'd tested them and was confident they wouldn't let me down.'

'As I said, I was impressed by your ingenuity and perhaps one day we can discuss things further.'

Mads felt pleasantly surprised by Ilya's obvious technical interest, and he wondered if he dare draw encouragement from the Major's oblique reference to his future.

'I'm quite happy to cooperate with the army on improving their weapons,' Mads said.

'That's all very well, Mads. But in spite of your technical capabilities, your knowledge of law and regulations appears abysmal! From your training, you should know about the extensive trials new weapons undergo before approval and certification. Indeed, you could be in more trouble from using an unauthorised firearm than for the shooting incident itself.'

'Sorry, sir.'

'But now that you've succeeding in attracting the attention you wanted,' Ilya continued, 'we have to think of where we go from here.'

'Yes. I know. I've been irresponsible and deserve what's coming to me. And now I feel spent. I no longer want to testify in court, because it will be behind closed doors and kept secret anyway. That was another illogical mistake which I overlooked in my haste, Major!'

Ilya could see tears of despair welling in the young prisoner's eyes.

'Well, Mads! Instead, you've told *me* about it, and I am honestly grateful for that.'

'What will happen to me now?'

'I'm going to ask the Brigadier in,' Ilya saw Mads wince, 'but I'll have a few words with him first. What follows may involve you being transferred to another cell for a short time under armed guard, but don't panic. It's procedure here. You have to give me time to talk to people, you do understand?'

'Yes, Major Borodin.'

'Right, here we go.' Ilya gave three taps on the door. One of the guards opened it.

'Sir?'

'Get me Brigadier Topolski, would you?'

'Sir!'

The Brigadier entered the cell, surprised to be greeted in fluent Polish.

'We are still under conditions of confidentiality,' said Ilya, 'We've been a long time, I realise that. But certain things have come to light which are of a maximum security nature. And I mean three alphas! As of now, I'm invoking my privilege, as the envoy of the United Nations Joint Chief Security Executive for the Northern Europe Sector, to request, in fact to demand, that the prisoner accompanies me forthwith to a classified destination for further interrogation by appropriate agents whom I will appoint personally. Meanwhile, please put the prisoner in one of your cells, under guard, until we've signed the transfer papers.'

'I will comply, in the name of the United Nations, but this is very irregular, Major! And I will have to report it to my superiors.'

Ilya lowered his voice. 'So long as you comply first, that will be deemed in order from the UN standpoint, Brigadier. And there is a degree of urgency which becomes more extreme with each second that passes.'

Ilya half turned, his UN shoulder flash now plainly visible. His pale eyes like splinters of blue steel, he added: 'Please say so if you understand me, Brigadier.'

'Of course. No problem, Major.'

'Thank you, Brigadier.'

Ilya replaced his cap and they saluted. He then donned his gloves.

The Brigadier turned to the guards:

'Take the prisoner along to Cell 27.'

'Sir!' they said in unison.

The Major and Brigadier, ignoring the prisoner, climbed the stone steps together.

*****

14 Mads

Thursday 16 September, Oakingwell.

The spectators were on their feet. Alan's monumental slam-dunk in the final seconds of the basketball match had given the staff team the victory they needed, after five years of student domination; the event made even more incredible by his relatively small stature. Even the students in the audience cheered Alan wildly as his colleagues hoisted him shoulder high and pressed though the chanting crowd towards the changing rooms. As they lowered him, beads of sweat rolled off his forehead.

'I can't move!' Alan Menzies cried; his face contorted in agony.

'It's his back!' someone said.

Burton knocked and entered Alan's apartment:

'Your travel arrangements are cancelled. I'll ask Brodie to cover for you instead,' he said.

'Thanks, Brian. And I'm sorry about all this.'

'Can't be helped, I suppose,' Burton shrugged with a humourless smile. 'Just rest yourself and get well. Meanwhile, I'll manage the classes that you and Parker can't cover, and then I too must leave.'

'Are you going somewhere, Brian?' Alan tried not to sound too enthusiastic about the prospect.

'Er, yes,' Burton replied, as if taken slightly off guard. He eased the door closed and returned to his office to flick open his link-set and contact Doug Brodie at the guest-house number in Paris.

'Go where?' Doug's voice bellowed from the instrument.

'Denmark. The safe house at Frederikshavn. My man here is sick.'

'I've got some business to attend to, but I could be there by this time next week.'

'That's very good of you, Doug. You couldn't possibly manage to be there in three days, by the end of *this* week?' Burton ventured.

'You're right, I couldn't. So please don't push it, Brian!' came the irritated reply.

No command structure in this outfit? Burton thought. 'OK, thank you. A week's time it is,' he agreed icily. 'Here are details of the itinerary...'

However, Doug interrupted him: 'Please send the info' by secure email, Brian. Sorry to cut you off, have to go now. Cheers.'

Doug nodded politely to Claudette who had passed him a welcome cup of coffee. He rang off and took his coat from the rack, the cup still in his hand. Within a few minutes, he had set out by public transport to the Sacré Coeur Hospital.

*****

Paris. Sacré Coeur Hospital.

Jacqueline Fournier thanked M. Leclerc for helping her find Lucien's spectacle case and returned to the hospital entrance, where Doug met her exactly on time.

'Just a wee something,' he said, brandishing a bunch of flowers. 'How are you? You certainly look better than you did a week ago!'

'Thank you, Doug! They're so beautiful! Lucien telephoned me last night from Denmark and he sounded very well.'

'That's good news indeed, Jacqui!' Doug lifted his umbrella against the rain and they walked together to the bus shelter.

Twelve minutes later, Vivienne opened the front door just as Jacqui found the keys. They all went through to the lounge, where Robert played with his birthday present. He'd plugged the virtual reality headset into his computer and became totally engrossed in an intergalactic adventure and oblivious to his mother's return.

'Could you please give this to Lucien, Doug?' asked Jacqui, handing him the spectacle case.

'No problem, Jacqui. And I'll give him love and best wishes from all of you! Eh, Robert?' The boy seemed remarkably tolerant, considering Doug's pat on the back had brought about the total loss of control of his space cruiser. It had then collided head-on with a rotating arm of Platform Omega-Nine: '*Game over.*'

'Sorry, Robert!' said Doug. 'Could I have a go?'

'Of course, Monsieur Doug! *Voilà!*' A few seconds saw Doug fully kitted with a visor and handset.

'OK, laddie, what have we got loaded?' Doug asked, scanning the catalogue of titles which flashed before his eyes. Intent on the headset display, his elbow had swept the spectacle case and half a dozen miniature SD memory cards onto the floor.

Jacqui picked everything up and tapped Doug gently on the shoulder. 'Here, Doug. I'll put the case in your jacket pocket, where it's safe!' she said. 'And Vivienne, could you please bring these big boys and me some coffee?'

*****

Monday 20 September. Frederikshavn.

Keir stirred as he heard Søren activate his link-set.

'It's all right,' Søren said, 'Just a routine call to Ilya.'

'Long time for a red alert!' Keir commented. 'It must be the sixth day.'

This time, Ilya requested to put Lucien on the line.

'*Bonjour,* Lucien! Søren tells me you're making an excellent recovery!'

'Yes, thank you, Major Karpov. I feel much better, in spite of recent events! But dare I ask if you have everything under control, yes?'

'Well, we do our best. Glad to hear you're continuing on the road to good health, Professor. That brings me to my next topic, that of your departure from Frederikshavn.'

'We have to leave?'

'Yes. The day after tomorrow. Your transport will arrive, care of Doug Brodie from Edinburgh. You've known him for some years, I believe.'

'Ah! It will be wonderful to see him. Where is he taking us?'

'He's bringing you here, to Oulu. Keir is coming with you. I'll confirm the details to you through Søren this evening. So if you could please put him on again, I'll say *au revoir* for now, Lucien.'

*****

That afternoon, Søren announced that Doug had arrived at the safe house from Oakingwell. After the welcome, exchanges of news and surrender of the spectacle case, Doug produced a bottle of champagne.

'Ah!' said Lucien, 'This is one to be lightly chilled!'

'Well, gentlemen,' Søren said, 'I'll certainly miss you all when you leave. Ilya tells me that Lisa will be back here tomorrow, and we can all have a party. He's asked Commander Nielsen to arrange everything.'

*****

Lisa looks stunning, Rollo thought; amazed by the transformation. Gone were the drab attire and perfunctory demeanour of her backstage role. She took control with charm and attention to detail.

'Look,' she said, 'the professor can sit here at the head of the table. And Doug, you sit here on his right, with Keir opposite.'

'Just one small thing, Keir,' Rollo said. 'Here is my report of the Skagen scenario and my meeting with those Danish guys.'

'Great. Thanks, Rollo.' Keir folded the three page document and tucked it into his inside jacket pocket.

Rollo and Søren were quite happy to go with the flow. They all sat down to the magnificent meal that had been prepared by Commander Nielsen and his colleagues.

Doug volunteered to pour the wine and as he filled one of the glasses, he leaned forward between Keir and Lucien. 'Remind me to show you something afterwards,' he said.

When the commander had left, along with his group of helpers, Doug and Rollo moved across to a smaller table and turned on the PC workstation. Lisa elbowed Keir gently: 'Are you and the Professor ready?' she asked.

'First, some background details,' Doug said. 'Here's an SD card I've brought from Jacqui in France.'

'Indeed! Is it of scientific or technical nature, or perhaps a piece of light entertainment?' asked Lucien.

'It's not entertainment, but first let me tell you where I found it,' Doug continued. 'In your spectacle case I discovered two of these cards. One of them is Robert's flight simulator game, but the other is rather more interesting. Keir, I'd like you to view it first.'

Keir put on the virtual reality headgear and attached the handset to the computer as Doug slipped the card into a slot.

'OK. Let's go!' Keir said. He began to use the gloves to orient himself in the scene before him, but without response. Instead he found himself already in a scene, without any control options. He became part of a 3D movie, without music, but with the surround-sound providing all the support needed for the happenings. A motorway scene enveloped him, with tall trees on either side as he drove a black saloon car past a route sign in French, following a large wagon.

Suddenly the wagon stopped. He heard, and almost felt, the splintering of glass, with his head ending up a few centimetres from the tail-gate of the wagon. With shock, Keir recognised this as a precise re-enactment of Lucien's description of his accident experience, including the collision from behind. In this new knowledge, he decided to continue, noting every detail until he heard the sound of a vehicle siren and everything melted into a black silence. He took off the helmet and wiped his brow with a shirt sleeve.

'No need to ask me what I make of it, Doug!' Keir commented.

Lucien came across to the computer. 'I'm clearly at a disadvantage, my dear friends,' he said, 'Do tell me, Keir, what is this movie you have been watching?'

'Be prepared, Lucien. It concerns the incident of the motorway collision.' Keir said, uncertain how to continue.

Doug quickly intervened: 'Lucien, let me first suggest an explanation for what you are about to see. In that way, it may lessen the actual trauma.'

'*Mon Dieu*! What have you in store for me?' the professor looked apprehensive. He re-charged his champagne glass and allowed himself a generous sip, then raised his head in expectation: 'Go on, Doug. What is this about?' he asked.

'When you were in the Sacré Coeur hospital, Lucien, do you remember any unfamiliar visitors or anyone placing a VR helmet, like this one, over your head?'

'*Non, mon ami*. But I was in great pain, until they gave me the drugs. Then I was heavily sedated and bandaged from head to foot. If anyone tried to show me a film show, I would know nothing about it, I'm sure! But afterwards, I was told that Jacqui and Monsieur Leclerc the consultant had tried familiar stimuli, like odours and recorded music. But I don't recall any of this, and certainly no other audio-visual effects.'

'Well, here's my opinion for what it's worth, Lucien. From your account of the events, I'd say that you were *programmed* to remember the incident as you described it. I think that this was done while you were in a suggestible state, either before or after you were admitted to hospital. This VR sequence corresponds so closely to your description that I can think of no other explanation. Only *you* can tell us how close the correspondence is with your memory of what happened. Would you like to see it now?'

Lucien watched the VR playback impassively, apart from wincing at the collision, and confirmed the sequence of events shown on the headset as being exactly as he remembered them, along with some fresh minor details of which he had only hazy recollection.

'But how about the feeling of body movements?' Keir asked. 'Like being pushed forward in your seat, having your foot on the brake pedal, or seeing all the glass inside the car?'

'That's right,' Rollo concurred, 'These are important details, and I don't see how they could possibly be contrived if you were fully bandaged.'

'What about while I was being transported to the hospital?' Lucien suggested. 'Perhaps we're looking for a special ambulance, which conveniently arrives on the scene?'

'We can check that, of course,' Rollo affirmed. 'The hospital admissions records should show who brought you in. After our next report to Ilya, he'll probably do that for us.'

'Just one thing, Lucien?' Keir asked.

'Yes, my friend?'

'Did you notice any *differences* between your recollection of the event and the playback we've seen?'

'Hard to say, but I'm sure it's very close to how I remember it.'

A few moments later, Lisa activated link contact with Oulu Base. Valentina answered:

'Hello, Lisa! I'm on the evening shift,' she said. 'Your red alert status is sustained and we suggest you remain indoors until it's time to leave. Repeat, remain indoors. Commander Nielsen will continue to organise your supplies. Any news?'

Lisa mentioned the VR playback and handed the link-set to Lucien.

'Hello, Lucien,' Valentina said, 'Could you please upload me the contents of your SD card? Ilya's back and he'll join me in watching the replay. Then I'll call you again in about half an hour.'

*****

Valentina and Ilya studied the video files from Lucien's SD card with rapt attention and used their UN authorisation to access other relevant files. Within two and a half minutes they were able to confirm that the ambulance in question had not been sent from a Paris hospital, but from one of the outlying districts.

'According to the records at Sacré Coeur Hospital admissions,' Valentina said, 'Lucien was brought in that day at 09:38 hours by an ambulance from Esternay which was staffed by a relief crew. I've checked the Esternay District Hospital files and interestingly the entries for that day do not refer to any journey near Paris around that time. But Ilya thinks the ambulance was genuine, as it aroused no suspicions at Sacré Coeur. He also says that the radio communications log at Sacré Coeur Hospital for that day looks normal.'

'*Merci*, Valentina. Keir has a question for you.'

'Hello Valentina!' His nerve held as he concentrated on the information content of his message. 'I think there's still a possibility that an ambulance was taken without the knowledge of the Esternay authorities. We need to know whether at least one of their fleet vehicles was in for repairs.'

'Ilya can hear you, Keir. He's starting to check the service logs for the Esternay ambulances during that week, and we should expect that information any second. Ah, thanks Ilya! It's on my screen already. There were two ambulances off the road. One was having a routine 20,000 km service at the Esternay depot and the other was away in a body repair shop at Coulommiers, not far from the Paris-Reims motorway.'

'That could be the one we want!' cried Keir 'If it was still roadworthy, it could have been borrowed for the morning without being missed by the hospital at Esternay. Can we trace the vehicle's identity and movements?'

'No problem. I have its registration details, fleet number and equipment inventory right here,' Valentina replied.

'Presumably it's repaired and in service again?'

'Yes. It was on call this morning at 11:13 local time. Ilya intends to follow things up, including any available CCTV footage, through our colleagues in Paris. Thank you for the possible lead, Keir. We'll keep you updated.'

Keir turned to Doug: 'Presumably she means Claudette?'

'Just one more thing, Keir.'

'Yes, Valentina?'

'Have *you* any thoughts about Lucien's alleged accident?'

'It's another jigsaw, all right. One bizzare but not impossible scenario does occur to me. Blame it on my experience in Liverpool if you like.'

'Please, go on.'

'Let's imagine. Lucien has an arranged collision accident. An ambulance rolls up, then crooks disguised as paramedics collect Lucien and whisk him away to a place where he, in a dazed state, can be drugged, interrogated and otherwise maltreated. They'd have to do it quickly, bandage him up as necessary and take him to the hospital.'

'Well, Keir, there were no traces of drugs when Lucien was admitted. We've had access to his medical records.'

'OK. Let's say the captors pretend to be a relief crew, pick him up, hand him over and disappear. When he's well enough, at least one of them visits him in hospital, possibly disguised as a medic, and replays that video we've seen. Their idea being to reinforce the collision experience, rather than any memories of other ill treatment.'

'It seems to fit the picture, Keir. What do you say, Ilya?'

'*Da!* We should take that on board. What do the others think?'

'Affirmative nods at this end, including Lucien,' Keir said.

'Thank you Keir,' said Valentina. 'And so sorry to hear you're another victim, Lucien. We'll continue looking into that. Meanwhile, Commander Nielsen will be in attendance until you leave the safe house. But your departure has been brought forward. The Commander and his team will be using the safe house from the day after tomorrow. Have an early night and commence departure preparations in the morning. Stand by with your link-sets, Rollo and Keir, to receive details.'

For a further half hour, they studied the downloaded maps and plans for their itineraries. Rollo would take Keir and Lucien in the Land Rover to Aalborg, from where they would fly to Helsinki. Rollo would return to the safe house and await further instructions. Keir and Lucien would travel by different routes to Oulu, arriving at different times. The plan for Lucien: he would take the next available internal flight from Helsinki to Oulu and be collected by an identifiable but unmarked car. Keir would travel by rail, taking the night train out of the Finnish capital. Valentina had other business to attend to but would join the train near the end of its long journey, at a place called Oulainen, but she would not meet him explicitly nor acknowledge him. Even so, he looked forward to that part of the journey, but tried not to show it. He hoped they would meet together in whatever road transport had been organised at Oulu. It hadn't been mentioned whether she would be sharing the road transport with him. And after the events of the last few days, Keir had a feeling in the pit of his stomach that something would almost certainly go wrong.

*****

Tuesday 21 September.

Rollo climbed out of Belerophon and crunched across the gravel toward the front door. Lisa welcomed him in.

'So they're away all right, are they?' she asked. 'I saw on TV that Lucien's flight was delayed by fog.'

'By thirty three minutes. Shall I make us some tea and coffee, Lisa?'

'You know I always have it ready for you, Rollo! Go on, tell me that you're still not used to having me around,' Lisa chided, with a hint of a smile.

'We'd better get down to business right away,' suggested Commander Nielsen. He pulled some maps out of a brown folder and laid them out on the lounge table. 'I've obtained a record of your excursion onto Skagen beach from Ilya. Perhaps you could fill in some details for me on this chart?'

Lisa passed the commander his cup of coffee. It rattled in the saucer as she lowered it carefully to the table.

'Are you OK, Lisa?' Rollo asked.

'Sorry. Just a slight tremor as a result of my fall. I'm told it'll be fine in a few weeks.'

'How I'd like to get my hands on the guy responsible for that shooting incident!' Rollo said.

'You'd better be on your best behaviour, Rollo!' commented Nielsen.

'How do you mean, Commander?'

'The person to whom you refer is on his way *here* as a guest.'

'What?' Lisa and Rollo chorused in astonishment.

'Ilya told me that Lance Corporal Gade will arrive this evening at around 20:00 hours. And we are to treat him with due courtesy, just as if he were an ordinary Lance Corporal.'

'A tall order, if you ask me!' commented Rollo.

Lisa placed a hand on his arm in a gesture of restraint.

'Yes, Commander,' she said. 'But are you going to tell us the background to this, er, situation?'

'What you need to know for the present is that Lance Corporal Mads Gade was interrogated by Major Borodin.'

'Ilya?' asked Lisa.

'Correct, but let's get used to alias names! When Gade arrives, Ilya doesn't exist. He's Major Borodin at all times until Gade leaves here - unless Ilya thinks otherwise.'

'How long's he staying?' Rollo asked.

'Technically, he'll be under house arrest while he's here,' the Commander said, leaning back in his chair with his hands clasped behind his head. 'But in practice, Gade is here to help us with the Skagen matter for as long as he remains useful. And he's no idiot. His IQ is 216.'

'A mad genius with a rifle!' Rollo commented.

Lars Nielsen ignored him and continued: 'I've been given two weeks to collate a report on the sand-creature sightings and offer suggestions about their significance. Rollo, you're to work closely with Gade on logging as much detail as you can, in chronological order, making use of these charts or any other materials which I can obtain for you.'

Nielsen reacted to Rollo's open mouthed response with a casual wave of his arm towards the net-curtained window on the opposite side of the room.

'My team is on standby to offer assistance with such things as carrying out fieldwork and exploring other ideas which you consider relevant for completion of the report.'

Rollo downed his coffee in one long gulp. 'Whatever you say, Commander!' he said bitterly. *We'll need a copy of the report I gave to Keir,* he thought.

'It's not what I say but what Major Borodin says,' Nielsen said, 'He and Gazetny are running this show. Her alias is Olga, and she'd like us to use it while Gade is here.'

*****

A cool wind blew in from the coast and bore a fine drizzle which permeated the uniforms of the group crossing the wet gravel to the door of the safe house. Lisa opened it and Commander Nielsen stood behind her.

Mads Erik Gade raised his eyes to meet Lisa's. 'I'm very sorry for what happened, it was inexcusable,' he said, his voice faltering.

'Please come in, boy,' said Lisa, doing her utmost to hide her discomfort.

'Thank you, Miss Holmboe.'

In the hallway he faced the Commander, who returned his salute laconically and looked past him to address the guard detail. They saluted in unison and with the sound of crunching boots returned to their parked vehicle.

Lisa ushered Mads towards the lounge. Rollo's gaze bore solidly into the youthful face of the Lance Corporal as he stood in the doorway. Lisa followed him in, looking pale, but in full control.

'Welcome,' she said with a faint smile. Then, indicating Rollo, 'Andy Sutton; Andy, Lance Corporal Mads Gade.'

Rollo looked around momentarily before recognising his own alias. He rose from his chair and extended a stiff hand. The Lance Corporal's fingers were cold, wet and limp.

'I'll leave you with the Commander. Supper will be at eight thirty,' Lisa said, drawing the door closed behind her.

Nielsen's face remained an expressionless mask. 'At ease, Lance Corporal. You may sit,' he said.

Mads sat down some distance from Rollo. The Commander stood with his back to the fireplace, his stature and unblinking pale blue stare accentuating his dominance. For a few minutes he briefed Mads on the security arrangements and then activated his link-set.

'Hello Olga. Please tell Major Borodin that everything is in order and we commence tomorrow as planned.'

*****

Wednesday 22 September, Skagen Peninsula.

Fine drizzle persisted through the following morning. Just before mid-day, the sky brightened. Mads sat in the front passenger seat of the Land Rover, which Rollo steered carefully across flat sand below the dunes as they followed the Skagen peninsula along its northern side, driving east and then south east towards the tip at Grenen. Mads looked out of his side window, noticing that a second vehicle had joined them.

'Another military wagon, Mads,' Rollo said. 'It looks freshly painted in camouflage brown and green drab, with several radio antennas.'

'I once thought of joining the Signals, Andy,' Mads ventured.

'One can't help wishing you had, Mads. A radio aerial is rather less lethal than an imaging rifle!' Thus Rollo yielded to the temptation of demonstrating his low esteem for the passenger. He still felt anger at having to tolerate the presence of someone who had come so near to killing his friends and colleagues. *'But if this is the line of duty, so be it,'* he thought.

'I've been stupid, but I'm grateful for the chance to help in the investigation of the sand-creatures. Not that this compensates for my crime, I know,' Mads replied.

'But will your information be reliable?' asked Rollo tersely. 'How are we to know that what you say won't be tainted with crazy notions and political fantasies?'

Mads bit his lower lip in silence.

Rollo realised he might be close to insubordination and recalled the admonishments of Commander Nielsen that the Lance Corporal is to be treated reasonably. But he persisted in making his point:

'It's just that all the fanatics I've met have this amazing inability or unwillingness to put themselves into other peoples' positions and to think about the consequences of their actions...' he stopped himself abruptly from going farther over the brink. 'OK, I'm sorry!'

'You are right, of course,' Mads said calmly.

Rollo suspected Mads of a mere gambit to defuse his animosity. He gripped the steering wheel firmly, in a deliberate gesture of pulling himself together. *Otherwise, I'll be ending up paranoid, too*! he thought. *It's time to concentrate on the task in hand.*

*****

'Let's stop here and look at the charts,' Rollo said. 'Perhaps you can try remembering your exact position in relation to your first sighting?'

'I recognise the general area, but the dunes have changed since then. It was over six years ago.'

I know it was over six years ago! Rollo fumed silently. *I've been through this guy's CV notes half a dozen times before we set out this morning*! He swallowed hard and voiced a more restrained version of his continuing thoughts:

'Yep. Let's mark up the relevant charts in pencil as well as we can, then compare our estimations with what Major Borodin has for this area in his satellite imagery archives.'

'If you like, Andy,' said Mads.

'Well? Have you any better ideas?'

'Frankly, yes. You don't mind me making a suggestion?'

'Please do.'

'First we take some initial scene shots. Then we combine them with the imagery I have, including some drawings, plus any satellite data for the past seven years from Major Borodin, and create a virtual reality animation of the scene changes on the computer back at the house. That would help me to estimate positions of the sand-creature sightings more accurately and relate them to the present. We'd both get a better idea of how to continue this survey. Then we come out here again and get the filling-in shots we need to refine the VR sequences.'

'What about the software needed to process the image data?'

'I've brought most of my graphical and image processing programs with me. They're in my haversack hanging up in the closet. The rest I can get by logging in to my home computer through the network, if that's permitted. The output can be made compatible with any of the popular VR display programs on the web or in the high-street stores. You probably have a standard display capability already.'

Rollo recalled that the VR playback of Lucien's incident had run satisfactorily. He also knew of Mads' work on enhancing the capability of an imaging rifle. *The guy is clearly a crazed genius, with the occasional flair for commonsense*! Rollo thought.

'OK Mads,' Rollo conceded. 'Let's do it.'

About three hours later and just before lunchtime, he swung the Land Rover through a wide arc, leaving the military truck to carry on with its work. They retraced their journey to the main road and began their forty minutes drive back to Frederikshavn.

*****

After lunch and with Rollo flushed with initial success at mastering the animation software and producing some preliminary runs, Rollo and Mads returned to Skagen for their final shots. The military truck had left. Now mid-afternoon, a different sun angle prevailed, but the software would deal with that.

They worked together during the remaining daylight, with Mads visibly heartened by Rollo's appreciation of his usefulness.

'I have something for you,' said Mads.

'Yeah?'

'In my bag there's a diagram and description of my imaging rifle.'

'Oh...OK. That should be interesting. Thanks.' In spite of the lingering bad taste that Rollo felt for the subject, he couldn't hide his fascination.

As they approached the safe house, Mads felt the time is not yet ripe to tell Rollo about his most recent interview with the Major, this time by phone. He wondered if the Commander knew, but there'd been no mention of it. Major Borodin's message via Rollo's link-set lingered in his mind. He had listened as the Major made him an offer he couldn't refuse.

*****

Thursday 23 September. Oakingwell.

Rowena Smythe stared fixedly at the document on her desk. Abruptly, she keyed a number into her telephone and waited for a reply. When it came, she recognised the tones of a fax machine and hung up. *Burton*, she surmised, *is curiously inconsistent when it comes to matters of communication.* She needed to see him right away. She swept out of her room and began the cross-campus walk to Burton's office. The A4 sheets tugged at her hand in the stiff breeze. This information Rowena thought too sensitive to deliver by fax or campus email and she assumed the unwilling role of courier.

'Come!' hailed Burton, his teeth embedded in a salmon sandwich.

Rowena entered, eyed the ceiling and then lowered her gaze to the spectacle of gnawing mandibles and falling crumbs. The owner of the snack looked incongruous in his pressed suit. He swivelled his chair to gain improved access to the top drawer of his desk.

'Ah! Rowena, I've got something for you here, somewhere.'

We're not being very methodical today, are we? Rowena thought to herself, as she waited with undisguised impatience.

'Here it is!' he cried jubilantly. These are some results from Andover. A few minutes ago I received a faxed reminder to read my secure email, which contained the results printed out on this sheet.'

'Same as mine?' Rowena asked. They confirmed that the contents of their sheets were identical.

'OK. Let's talk about it. I presume that's why you're here?' Burton sputtered, between mouthfuls. As if it had become an embarrassment to him, he gulped down the last vestige of his meal, chasing it with a residue of lukewarm coffee.

'These creatures seem remarkably adaptive, don't they?' Rowena commented.

'I see what you mean, but I don't think adaptive is the right word. It's a kind of metamorphosis, isn't it?'

'I agree with you, Brian. The interesting thing is how rapid these changes have taken place since the aliens were first let loose on Pandora. The Edinburgh people are getting quite worried that there are simultaneous changes taking place within the Pandora system itself, which they are unable to monitor.'

'But Rowena, that's a logical consequence of the system structure. Right from the start there were lots more hidden layers than in conventional neural networks. Being able to see what's going on internally has always been very difficult indeed. And being able to *interpret* what's going on at any particular time and place in the system network is even *more* difficult! Remember how, twelve months ago, chaotic instabilities within the system were a nuisance? And how the system turned this around to its advantage and used chaotic instabilities to improve its performance? Mind-blowing! Now it actually *relies* on multi-level instability patterns to augment its genetic algorithms and create short cuts to its optimisation processes! And not just for the complex problems we throw at it, but also the ongoing one of its self-evolution.'

'I know all that, Brian!' Rowena sighed impatiently. 'And its resemblance to biological systems has always interested me. But what are you driving at? What are you trying to tell me? *Please* come to the point, Brian!'

Burton smiled a humourless smile: 'Well, the *first* point is that Pandora has gone well beyond those stages in its self-evolution where its behaviour is understandable by humans. You would agree?'

'Yes! OK, next?'

'Right, second point. Look at the results on your Andover sheet again. What do they suggest, Rowena?'

'You're being very patronising today, Brian.'

'All right, I promise to do something about that. Perhaps if I change the filling in my sandwiches it will help.'

'I'd be happy to make suggestions.'

'I'm sure you would. But for now, let's both take a look at these performance test figures for the aliens and Pandora. What have we? Game of chess at level ten, starting with various standard openings. Look at the game completion time using the King's Gambit Declined for various combinations of opponents. The aliens are not bad at all, are they? Good humans can take around fifteen minutes to develop an interesting game with Pandora.' Burton stood in his usual place with his back to the window, rocking gently on his heels as he considered the statistics before him. 'Amazing, isn't it?' he said.

'Certainly is! The trends over the past three months show considerable improvements for the aliens,' Rowena observed. 'They've won more than half of their games with Pandora, whereas the last reported success by a human player was four months ago, if you can call a draw by a Grand Master a success.'

'Pandora's processing time is getting shorter, too. And I've got some news which doesn't appear on the sheet. The aliens lost one and drew two yesterday, which clinches the argument that Pandora's rate of improvement really has increased since their arrival on the scene.'

'And I note our colleagues in Beijing use the Chinese game "go" to report similar trends,' remarked Rowena.

'Yes, the aliens are learning off each other, too.'

'And apart from chess and go, the other performance measures show marked advances in conceptualisation, pattern recognition and outcomes in all the usual problem solving tests. Not to menion some unusual ones, as well.'

'Many of which the aliens themselves have devised,' Burton added.

'And look, Brian! There are five games-scenario tests which were devised jointly by the aliens and the computer. I'm quite blown away by the increasing mutual co-operation between machine and aliens.'

'That brings me to another point.'

'Meaning?' Rowena asked.

'It looks as if the aliens have acquired some understanding of Pandora's workings. Knowledge which is denied to us by its sheer complexity.'

'There's more to it than that, though, isn't there Brian? What about the gross physical changes taking place in certain individuals of the alien population? I've noticed that they're trying very hard to adapt to our planetary environment.'

'Yes, Rowena. Obviously, if they can feel comfortable here, that'll enhance their performance significantly. I'm hoping that with your biological expertise you might throw some light on the mechanism of what's happening.'

'Well, Brian, I've little doubt they've gained increased control of their own anatomical structure. To some extent they can plan and carry out alterations to their bodies without surgical intervention.'

'And almost certainly they're using Pandora to help find optimal solutions. Do you think they're attempting a transition to humanoid form?'

'Yes, I think they are.'

'I can see that their big problem will be to make the change via a smooth transition without compromising their existing physical and mental advantages and all the benefits of interaction with Pandora.'

'I agree with you about retention of mental factors, but the change itself doesn't *have* to be gradual, Brian.'

'How do you mean?'

'On our own planet,' Rowena said, brushing a lock of hair from her right eye, 'Look at caterpillars and moths, maggots and flies, and all the other examples of abrupt anatomical transitions in the insect world.'

'I'd hate to tell my grandmother how to suck eggs, Rowena, because you're the genius biologist. But wouldn't that kind of change be too drastic for the aliens? In the hierarchy of organisms, they're surely far too complex, and imagine the psychological trauma!'

'Thank you for the compliment, Brian, but I don't think we're related. In response to your argument, if you'll pardon another cliché, I'd say necessity is the mother of invention. These creatures have every intention of operating as freely as possible in our environment. They won't feel like waiting for a few million years or even a few years, having recognised the obvious competition from us humans. So they need to adapt at the earliest opportunity. We know they're extremely bright, resourceful and highly communicative, and they have the ever increasing power of the Pandora system at their disposal. I'd lay two to one odds that before long they'll demonstrate a feat of adaptation that will make our attempts at genetic engineering look like a child's first encounter with kindergarten building blocks!' Rowena tossed her head as if competing for a university debating society prize.

Burton's eyes narrowed to slits as his mind raced onward, trying to anticipate the strategy of the aliens. After several seconds, he spoke.

'Rowena, have you noticed that the recent changes in the aliens' appearance seem to have slowed down? Some of them were starting to look a little like us in some ways, but if that *is* the direction they're taking, they're still a long way off. Can any of them breathe our atmosphere unaided yet?'

'None that I know about, Brian. For all their intelligence, I think that they may struggle with that. But I believe their breakthrough will come and when it does, we'll certainly know about it.'

'Just one thing, Rowena. Down at Andover and the other facilities abroad, the aliens have been given access to computer power and used it to full advantage. But in spite of their incredible manual dexterity and excellent sense organs, they've shown no inclination to set up a workshop or laboratory of their own, where they could do experiments to serve their scientific interests, including their adaptation. Maybe this shows a need for equipment and specialised biochemical facilities to progress the change.'

'I think they'd ask us, if they needed to,' Rowena said.

'Well, up to now their interactions with humans have been limited to co-operation in answering questions, being weighed and measured, playing games and solving puzzles. They seem to get on better with Pandora!'

'And themselves, of course,' she added.

'Quite so. But I just can't understand why they don't take advantage of our other technologies. Without them, I find it difficult to imagine how your breakthrough will come about.'

'In truth, Brian, so do I. But then, I'm only human.'

'You think it will, though?'

'As I indicated at the Andover meeting, I expect it to be sooner rather than later.' Rowena got up to leave.

'I thought that issue concerned their freedom?'

'For them, it would amount to the same thing. Think about it, dearest.' She moved towards the door.

'Rowena?' Burton called her back. 'Do you suspect, ever so slightly, that it could have already happened?'

'You mean the sand-creatures of Skagen? Brian, we covered this ground a couple of days ago. To me, it doesn't look like a breakout pattern. More likely, the phenomenon belongs to the time-honoured class of events which includes sightings of UFOs and their occupants. I realise Ilya and Valentina are quite excited by the sand-creatures idea, but I think it's just another part of the low level background noise which occurs throughout reporting history.'

Brian Burton rose from his chair. 'I'd be inclined to agree with you,' he said. 'Although we both have to face the possibility that we may be wrong. After all, we're scientists, aren't we?

*****

15 On the Beach

Thursday 23 September. Frederikshavn.

Rollo and Mads had slept well. In the morning, after breakfast, they compared the previous day's work with the sighting reports Mads provided. Søren followed their progress and Lisa provided light refreshments. At 11:00am Mads led Rollo through some animated sequences he'd prepared.

'Here's the picture of my first logged sighting. This one my friend and I saw in 2003. I've tried to render it as objectively as possible, trying not to be influenced by other reports,' he said. 'See, there!' He drew Rollo's attention to a distant shape near the horizon.

'Frustratingly small, isn't it, Mads?'

'Yes! And enlargement won't work too well because we're limited by the distance and an old 5 megapixel camera,' Mads explained. 'The first guy to report one, the previous year, provided more detail on body shape but less on location, as we can see. And none of the other individual reports on their own give us accurate locations either.'

'Sure Mads, but statistical analysis of enough sightings might reveal some clues as to where we should start probing.'

'I hope so. I must admit, in the past, I was mostly interested in details of their anatomies rather than precise location, but I'll try to remember, given how the landscape has changed.'

.

Rollo and Mads continued working together, logging every detail as they searched for patterns in the sighting events.

'How about estimating grid references and distance readings and entering them manually into the statistics program?' Rollo asked.

'It'll take a while, but let's do it,' Mads agreed.

After another two hours they had the results they wanted. They created a graphical display of their data and superimposed it on a military survey map of the Skagen peninsula. Then Mads circled an area on the map.

'The locations of the sand-creatures fall within this zone with a probability of about seventy percent,' he said.

'We'll need a very low tide to investigate this area,' Rollo said. He fired up his link-set. 'Let's see... There will be a low tide tomorrow morning. Although the tide forecast is quite small in this region, every little helps.'

'We'll be digging,' said Mads, 'Does your Land Rover carry a spade?'

'Of course.'

'Right, Andy. Tomorrow morning it is, then.'

*****

Friday 24 September. Skagen.

Belerophon avoided the patches of quicksand as Rollo, considerably wiser than on his first expedition, drove closer to the dunes as they rounded the peninsula.

The tide was half an hour to full ebb and the weather forecast accurate: A sunny morning with cotton clouds chasing each other towards the pale north-east horizon. Ideal! Rollo and Mads climbed down onto the sand and donned their bright fluorescent yellow life-jackets. Other safety procedures had been arranged by Ilya, following Rollo's earlier contact with him, including an extra rescue craft on standby.

They moved slowly forward in heavy wading boots, prodding the ground ahead with canes. Shading his eyes, Mads scanned the dune landscape that they'd left behind, Belerophon a distant green shape against the nearest of the dunes. He turned to his left and led Rollo thirty metres north-west. A crosswind tugged at their clothing and Mads turned with his back to the wind to view the landscape again. Using Rollo's binoculars, he followed the profile of the dunes and noted the compass readings on its graticule.

'Here we are,' said Mads. 'At the exact centre of the circular zone. A few jellyfish, but that's about all, Andy. The water's covering part of our circle, but things should improve before long.'

'There's something I didn't mention before, in case it delayed your work with the imaging.'

'Yeah?'

'You know on my last trip down here there was a military vehicle with a lot of radio aerials?'

'Did they find something?' asked Mads.

'Yes. Major Borodin spoke to the Commander. He told me the ground where we're standing now has a different kind of response to radio waves.'

'Something under the surface?'

'Quite the opposite, really. It's as if this part of the beach is hollow, or honeycombed.'

'No cavities would last more than a few seconds near the water table.' Mads argued.

'Sure,' Rollo said.'I'm just telling you what they detected. I've no idea what it could be, either.'

Mads passed Rollo one of the thin poles and continued visual observation of the ebb tide.

'So far, it feels quite normal,' said Rollo, 'down to about half a metre.'

'Let's work our way outwards in a spiral,' Mads suggested, 'and leave a rod in the sand as a marker.'

'Fine. Could you wait a moment, Mads?'

Rollo entered a code on his link-set and thoughtfully began reading his electronic mail.

'There's some good news. Sykes is safe in Finland!' he said. 'And bad: I'ts from Major Borodin, unclassified because it's in all the newspapers.'

'What's happened?'

'It's started! Riots and mayhem. In the UK, the Andover Institute's been under attack.'

'How does that affect us?'

'You wouldn't know what's at Andover, but it seems you can pick up any newspaper.'

Mads looked down at the sand, and then at Rollo.

'I understand there is, or was, an alien colony there. What if the aliens anticipated the threat of their own destruction and found a place to hide and survive?'

'An interesting possibility, Mads. It wouldn't take them long to assess human nature and the results could provide a motive. If they've been around for seven years, they'd have enough time to develop a strategy for their survival and even perhaps retaliation.'

Rollo's gaze swept the deserted shore.

'I suppose if a colony of aliens is around here,' Mads said, 'we might expect an area of concentration or emergence. But we're probably wasting our time if whatever the ground radar detected is deeper than the length of these poles.'

For a good half-hour, they continued their search.

'The tide's already turning, Mads.' Rollo said.

'Never mind, let's both keep going...Hey!'

Close to the water, Mads gave a shout.

'What is it?'

'I've hit something! Just over half a metre down. It feels firm and like rubber.'

Rollo came alongside and also prodded the area.

'OK. Hang on. I'll fire off a yellow flare.'

The boat crew arrived within four minutes.

'Hi there, I'm Knud Hansen,' the skipper introduced himself.

Mads completed the introductions and explained the excavation plan in Danish.

'You'll need more manpower!' said Knud, 'We may as well beach the dinghy and use spades. I'll call up the other boat and that should make a gang of at least six. We carry two spades in each boat and you have one, so if we all work hard but carefully together I think we have a good chance of building a crater around the object and lifting it out, in spite of working below the water table! Added to that, the other boat has a portable generator and a jet-wash.'

'Like a car wash hose?'

'Yes, Mads. And we'll probably need it.'

After arrival of the second boat, it took half an hour for the gang to clear a crater, underwater work increasingly impeded by restless waves and clouds of suspended silt.

'Got it!' cried Rollo, as he, Mads and two of the crew with ropes helped to work the object free and drag it out of the water. The gentle lapping of the waves sounded about five metres from the semi-transparent hulk. They stood back, amazed at what they saw.

'What do you think it is?' Asked the skipper

The rest of the crew members joined Mads and Rollo, standing in a circle gazing down at it. The brownish white cylindrical shape measured about two and a half metres long and eighty centimetres across at its widest point. The crust had a rough texture and bore indentations on its upper surface, so that it looked like a giant French loaf, but semi-transparent, tough and layered, with a feel like plastic or rubber. This was not the only source of wonderment. Deep inside they saw what looked like the body of a man.

'Good grief!' Rollo heard himself break the silence.

The pallid body appeared to be a tight fit, its shape constrained by the contours of the casing, through which a fine network of what appeared to be blue and purple blood vessels was just discernible. The eyes and mouth were half open. But the figure lay perfectly still, the scalp covered in matted brown hair and with bluish grey nails on the toes and fingers. Rollo grabbed his phone camera and began to record some views from various angles.

'Andy, we must move it from here!' Mads glanced at the sea.

'Where? I don't think we should put it in the back of the Land Rover. I've got too much junk in there. Maybe Knud could take it to the coastguard station while we plan the next stage.'

'You speak as if it's dead, Andy. I think we should arrange to have it taken to a hospital for observation by experts,' Mads suggested.

'That's a good idea,' Knud said to Mads. 'We'll leave you to attend to that, but if you need any assistance, let us know.'

'Thanks for your help!' Mads shouted after the crew.

'If we're looking for an expert helper with security credentials, we should try Major Borodin,' said Rollo.

An unfamiliar voice came through on the link-set as he tried to contact Ilya.

'Major Karpov is not available at the moment,' the voice announced. 'Do you wish to leave a message?'

Rollo hoped Mads hadn't heard that.

'This is FO23 at Skagen,' he replied. 'Tell Major Borodin we have condition code Triple-X in grid square Golf-Nine.'

'You did say Triple-X?'

'Affirmative. Would you please patch me through to... Helen?' asked Rollo, remembering Rowena's alias.

*****

Oakingwell.

Rowena thanked Burton for giving her a lift to the far side of the campus in his car. But suddenly her link-set burst into life from inside her document case. Burton thought it better not to voice his opinion of the security implications of such a repository. *If she commits a mistake, she commits a mistake*, he thought.

'FO23, I presume,' she chimed. 'What are you up to, Farmer Giles? Are you still cruising around Denmark in that museum piece of yours?'

'Hello, Helen! I'm at Skagen with, er, Major Borodin's new assistant.

'Well, I hope it's a nice day for you on the beach!'

'Not much time. We have a Triple-X near the water line at the tip of the Skagen peninsula. Is that understood?'

Rowena slid forward against her seatbelt as Burton braked hard.

'A close encounter? Give me that thing!' he demanded.

'Charming! Here, take it!' she demurred, passing him the link-set.

'Hello! CO3 here. Say again, please,' Burton called.

'It's a Triple-X. A single occurrence but there may be more. The subject is comatose. Shape is like a human male in early twenties. It's encased in a kind of outer shell.'

'A chrysalis!' Rowena blurted. 'Give that back to me, please!'

Burton relinquished the set as quickly as he'd grabbed it. He felt his world-view changing as he listened and wiped the beads of perspiration from his forehead.

'Hello! It's me again!' Rowena continued. 'If it's been in sea water, you must *not* let it dry out. Do you understand?'

'Yes!' Rollo acknowledged.

'Get it to the isolation ward of a hospital. I've a contact at the Aalborg Sygehus. Ask for Dr. Chris Dorn and tell him the patient is code Triple-X. Tell him I'll arrive at Aalborg tomorrow. He'll know what to do because I'll explain to him shortly. Meanwhile, email me some pictures. I take it you have some?'

'Yes. Eight different shots.'

'That's good. Now listen. Sergei and Olga are not available, so Clifford here will arrange the transport logistics. There'll be a helicopter which needs to be fitted immediately with a sea-water tank. My colleague will arrange for a small inflatable dinghy and a bucket to be brought to the scene. It'll be an adequate improvisation.'

Burton frowned at the mention of his alias name.

'Aliases!' he said. 'I see little point in playing games in this situation.'

'Quiet!' Rowena said, 'People could be present who aren't triple vetted. Here, take it!' She thrust the link-set into his open palm.

Poker-faced, Burton continued the transmission: 'Hello, Clifford here. I'll get on with that, immediately. Just keep the subject thoroughly wet with sea-water as Helen says, and wait for the helicopter. Is that understood?'

'Understood,' said Rollo.

'Cheers from both of us, then. And well done!' Burton signed off and stretched back as far as his car seat would allow. His eyes burned with a strange light as he turned to face Rowena.

'Truly fascinating! Marvellous, isn't it?' Gripped by euphoria, he leaned sideways to embrace her, but she promptly backed away.

'Get that helicopter called up, Brian,' she said. 'And let's keep our love-hate relationship strictly professional, shall we?'

Tight lipped, Burton keyed a message sequence to Denmark into the link-set, turned the car around and gunned it in the opposite direction.

'Where are we going now?' Rowena asked.

'As you said, Aalborg. We should make Warton Aerodrome within the hour. Please make sure there's a fuelled aircraft on stand-by.'

'Courtesy of the UN? You don't hang about, do you, Brian?'

'Here,' he said, returning the link-set.

'Thanks. After that, it might be an idea to get those pictures of Rollo's downloaded!'

As Rowena feverishly prodded the keypad, Burton indicated the glove compartment.

'Rowena, for goodness sake, please help yourself to some liquorice all-sorts and try to relax,' he said.

*****

Saturday 25 September, Aalborg.

Dr. Born, in his early thirties and almost two metres tall, scratched his short blond hair. He smiled down at Rowena through rimless spectacles.

'Would you like some more coffee?' he said.

'No thank you.' She looked pointedly at her watch.

'Of course! It's time for me to introduce you to our client. Let's go downstairs and find out how my team is getting on.'

Burton winced as he followed them both into a brightly lit operating theatre. He'd never been a willing spectator of things medical. A variety of tubes and cables connected the recumbent figure to several racks of electronic equipment. The subject, still encased, lay in a shallow tank of saline solution.

Rowena looked transfixed at the sight.

'Yes, it's a chrysalis!' she declared from behind her surgical face mask. The aliens have solved the problem of radical transformation in a most natural way. Like caterpillar to moth. They're masters of gene switching!'

Burton, astounded and sickened in approximately equal measure, listened nervously to the sound of a gurgling drainage tube somewhere behind him.

'How long do you think it was submerged, Rowena?' he whispered.

'Maybe six months, or just a few days. Difficult to estimate without the results of tests and it's equally hard to say when the occupant might emerge. Naturally, so to speak. Let's hope it survives the trauma of excavation. What do you think, Christian?'

'As you say, Row... er, Helen, we need more information. This must be the first known case of its kind.'

Dr. Born methodically surveyed the console of instruments.

'This looks encouraging; I believe he'll survive the ordeal. Until a few hours ago I thought his emergence would take several days. Now I think his time could be much sooner. Some fissures are opening along the underside of his capsule. Difficult to see from here, as we decided to lay him on his back in the position he was found.'

'Yes, I see them,' Said Rowena through her surgical mask.

'It's hard to judge whether the experience of being excavated is inducing the change,' Dr. Born said. 'Of course, if there are any signs of movement, my colleagues and I will make the necessary adjustments to his instrumentation and try to ease his passage into this world in the most humane way.'

'Good, good,' said Burton, edging towards the door. 'He's in capable hands.'

'You do realise,' Born continued, 'we have little idea of what exactly to feed him on, but DNA evidence should confirm whether he is close to human. Our scan of his abdomen suggests that his diet could be compatible with ours. After some allergy tests, we intend to start him off on milk, if his swallowing reflex is in order.'

'What about breathing?' Rowena asked, 'We know that the aliens in their original state needed quite a different atmosphere to ours.'

'His lung capacity and structure seem human and his blood likewise,' Dr. Born explained. 'We're going to assume that the transformation is as intended and that he will breathe normally.'

'Well, thank you for showing us,' said Rowena quietly.

'My pleasure. I think that we'll now return to my office. If something happens, I'll be on call. Otherwise we should let the team continue with their work.'

At 5:45am the following morning, Rowena awoke to the sound of several knocks on her door. The nurse's voice, quiet but insistent, betrayed her excitement: 'Come, Dr. Helen! Dr. Born is waiting for you down in the theatre.'

*****

Sunday 26 September. 6:05am.
Dr. Born and his team were already busily engaged when Rowena entered the theatre.

'Welcome to Harald. I'd like to make use of your biological expertise, if you could help us,' Dr. Born said, his persuasive smile mostly hidden by his green face-mask.

'Of course,' Rowena said.

'It took my team a good five hours to stabilise the alien after careful removal of the covering layers of translucent membrane,' Dr. Born explained. 'Shortly, we'll take Harald to Ward E9, which is secure.'

Dr. Born ushered Rowena from the theatre and they removed their surgical attire in the ante-room of the operating theatre. He continued: 'One of our nurses chose the name Harald in honour of the recent birth of her sister's baby. When Harald's had some rest, we'll pay him another visit. Say, around eight o'clock this evening? That gives you some time as well.'

'Sure,' Rowena agreed. 'I'll tell Clifford. By then, Mads and Andy should have driven down from Skagen. We're expecting them around six.'

'No problem, Helen. I've arranged for all four of you to stay overnight at the staff apartment block next to the Conference

Centre. Two flights to Helsinki are already booked for noon tomorrow.'

'What about Mads and Andy?'

'I understand Commander Nielsen will be meeting them at Frederikshavn tomorrow afternoon.'

*****

Several plantations of ornamental grass swayed lazily above one of many sheltered rockeries in the gardens of Aalborg Sygehus.

'Here we are, then,' Rollo said. 'Question is, when we can see Harald?'

Rollo and Mads pulled into the car park and jumped down from the Land Rover.

'Wonder if he's awake yet?' said Mads. 'I guess Helen will be waiting for us, but first I'm having a shower!'

'Me too. Then hopefully we can find some food. I'm starving. By the way, early this morning I was notified of your clearance and so have the others. No more aliases, thank goodness. Rowena, that's Helen, said that we're sharing a room on the ground floor. This looks like the entrance.'

When suitably refreshed, Rollo and Mads joined Rowena and Brian Burton in the ground floor TV room.

'Hi! Good journey?' Without waiting for a reply, Rowena continued: 'News looks ghastly, doesn't it? Riots in Canada now. And in Paris. I'm glad Lucien is out of it. Jacqueline and the children flew out to join him in Oulu last night.'

'How are Doug and Keir?' asked Rollo.

'Doug is at Oulu Base,' Burton said, looking over his spectacles as he placed a journal back on the coffee table. 'Obviously he's very concerned about Edinburgh and the safety of Pandora. Keir's still on his way to Oulu via Helsinki, by rail.'

'I'll bet Doug's worried!' Rollo said.

'Yes,' Rowena agreed, 'He knows it's really a matter of time before Pandora and possibly the whole of the Edinburgh Institute will be sacrificed to appease the anti-alien fanatics and their followers.'

'What?' Rollo stared uncomprehendingly.

'That's probably true, or soon will be,' Burton said dryly, 'The thing is, the population, or rather, a select sample of its more vociferous fringe groups, are looking for someone, or something, to blame for the advent of this new threat to civilisation, as they see it. In spite of the efforts to publicise extraterrestrial origins, any institution which has been involved in nurturing the so-called alien menace is fair game. I believe the UN are holding on to the secret bases and letting the governments leak information about more dispensable sites in the hope of preserving stability.'

'But surely the Pandora nodes at Edinburgh and Andover are indispensable!' cried Rollo.

Burton adjusted his spectacles, then changed his mind and folded them away to an inside pocket:

'Remember,' said Burton, 'In truth, the Edinburgh node is quite minor compared with the extensive facilities which have been developed elsewhere. Whenever you heard about Pandora doing something, it was really the network. In a nutshell, the Pandora network has a fault-tolerant architecture and can probably look after itself several times over!'

'It seems regrettable to sacrifice *any* network nodes,' Rollo said.

'It was Pandora itself, the network, that is, that suggested it,' Burton said. 'Don't worry, the Pandora node at Edinburgh may seem to the general public to be an important target, but compared to the network as a whole, in time it will seem very minor.'

'I disagree!' Rowena said. 'Anyway, how does this affect what we do now?'

'It doesn't, in the short-term,' Burton replied. 'Tomorrow morning, Rollo makes his way back to the safe house at Frederikshavn, to be joined later by Mads, when his old friend Commander Nielsen will have a chance to chat with him.'

Mads grimaced.

Burton continued: 'I understand Rollo and Mads will carry on for a week supervising any further excavations at Skagen. The rest of us will go on to Oulu.'

'I think we're all aware of the itinerary,' Rowena said tartly.

At that moment, Burton's link-set vibrated in the pocket of its owner; a message from Ilya.

Burton eased himself out of his chair. 'It seems there's a change of plan', he said. 'Ilya's booked flights for Mads and Rollo to join us at Oulu Base. Something brewing, I think. Anyway, let's find some place to eat,' he suggested.

Mads beamed with relief.

At 8:00pm, Dr. Born ushered the party into Ward E9, a small room with two beds, one empty and the other containing the new patient, Harald, laying flat on his back with the covers rolled down. His pyjamas fitted quite well, Rollo observed.

Harald appeared to be sleeping, his chest rising and falling in a natural breathing rhythm.

'How long will he stay connected to this rack of instruments?' Rowena asked.

'We may have a better idea by the end of next week,' Dr. Born replied.

Harald, in his pale green pyjamas, lay with his jacket open to the waist. The skin appeared healthy and unmarked. With a start, Rollo noticed something unusual. His breath caught in his throat as he realised Harald's skin looked smooth right down to the waistline. He had no umbilicus. Earlier that evening, in the shower room, he hadn't known whether to comment, and had decided against it. The same feature was missing from Mads.

*****

16 Night Train to Oulu

Sunday 26 September. 6:00pm, Oulu, Northwest Finland.

Under a darkening sky, Valentina stepped out of the Communications Building and climbed into the cabin of the waiting Sisu truck. She waved at Ilya as the driver revved the engine. After five kilometres the forest tracks near the Yli-Ii region gave way to a paved road and twenty minutes later she arrived at the northern outskirts of Oulu. At a filling station, Valentina accompanied the driver inside, where she remained, browsing through the magazine racks until the truck left. Almost immediately she saw a blue Volvo estate car nose its way onto the forecourt. She paid for a newspaper and after checking the number plate made her way to the waiting Volvo. The driver filled it from one of the pumps and acknowledged her with a curt nod as she opened the passenger door. When he emerged from the garage shop, he didn't introduce himself. Valentina pulled up her coat collar. They drove through Oulu as far as the Linnanmaa campus of Oulu university and picked up another passenger, a young man with a ginger beard who introduced himself as Yrjö. Possibly in his late twenties, Valentina thought.

'Hello, I'm Olga,'she said.

They continued south west for another two hours, until they reached the main street in the town of Oulainen.

'*Missä on ravintola, Yrjö*? Where can we find a restaurant?' the driver asked.

Yrjö wasn't sure but Valentina directed them to a small hotel with a bar just off the high street and near the railway station. They pulled in and ordered some food. Her companions ate mainly in silence.

Eventually, Yrjö spoke to her: 'The train from Helsinki will arrive at 4:15 in the morning. Have you fixed up your hotel accommodation? Can we take you anywhere before we go back?' he asked.

'I'll stay the night here, thank you,' Valentina said, 'I don't think there'll be a problem.'

As the two men left, she went to the bar and paid for the meals. When the car had driven off, she left the hotel and walked two blocks toward the railway station. In the shadow of a cottage doorway, Valentina reached in her coat pocket for a key, opened the door and went inside. She checked each room and all its appliances and fittings. Another routine safe house check completed. She called up Ilya on her link-set to leave a message:

'Hi! Everything here's in order,' she said. 'I'm going to get some sleep, if you don't mind. Up early to catch the train for Oulu.'

*****

Valentina set her alarm for 3:45am and curled up beneath the duvet cover, listening to the gentle sighing of the wind in the timbers of the building and the occasional swish of trees outside. Soon she drifted off to sleep.

When she awoke, the trees were still bending before a breeze blowing in from the west. She dressed in the darkness and drew back the heavy curtains. The sky looked clear, with a few stars. But she blinked as the bright yellow sodium lights near the railway station illuminated the room. In the yellow light, the reflection of her face in the dressing table mirror looked back at her like a pale mask. She felt half awake, cold and lonely. She drew comfort from the link-set in the palm of her hand, but refrained from using it in voice mode. Ilya could be paged in an emergency, but the rational part of her mind told her there was none. *Not yet, anyway*, she thought.

*****

Monday 27 September. Oulainen.

At 4:05am, after a breakfast of crispbreads and coffee, Valentina let herself out of the safe house, one of four maintained by Oulu Base, and locked the door. She walked slowly towards the unblinking yellow glare of the sodium lamps. Near the station, the lighting changed to the bluish harshness of mercury vapour lamps. Her soft shoes made hardly any sound as she padded along the concrete walkway to the platform.

Suddenly, her heart missed a beat. A movement near the corner of the station building. The hem of a coat? Now it had disappeared. Valentina looked behind her at the lamplit emptiness and then ahead at the tall fir trees beyond. She heard the rumble of an approaching train and watched the star-like headlamp grow in size and intensity, poised astride its needle-like reflections in the cold, clattering rails.

*****

4:10am, Night train from Helsinki.

Keir's sleep broke abruptly with the vibration of his link-set alarm. Dark shapes of trees swept past the carriage window, some singly, others in tight clusters or extended ranks, their evergreen foliage black against the starlit sky ragged with occasional broken cloud. The steady droning of the engine deepened as the train began to slow down. Keir started in anticipation at the sudden courteous announcements in Finnish, Swedish and English confirming the impending arrival. He looked about the carriage, waiting impatiently while his heart pounded in his chest, so loudly that he felt sure it would be heard by other passengers. Wheels squeaked and clicked on the track as the carriages protested mildly at running over some points. He looked outside again as the first concrete slabs of the platform drifted ever more slowly past his window. Then silence, as the train glided steadily towards its halt at Oulainen Station.

In spite of the orders he'd received, Keir had to consciously resist the overwhelming temptation to get up and look for Valentina. The flagstones now seemed to be drifting forwards, but it was an illusion. The train had stopped. Above the gentle murmur of the idling motor, he heard a carriage door slide shut and eased himself back into his seat. A door latch clicked behind him.

'*Tiedan lippu, olkaa hyvä*? Your ticket, please?'

Keir produced it.

'*Kiitos, hyvää matkaa.* Thanks, have a good journey.' The uniformed man continued on his way to the front of the compartment. He exited through the connecting door, continuing to the next carriage.

The train began to glide forward and Keir settled back in his seat. The last of the station buildings receded and soon the yellow glare of street lamps gave way to the dark shapes of trees again. The carriage swayed gently and someone ahead of him coughed. *Where's Valentina*? Keir asked himself. He hadn't seen her board the train. *Probably in one of the forward carriages*, he thought. In his carriage, he estimated that there were about eight other occupants, all asleep except perhaps for the owner of the cough. The high-backed seats made it difficult to judge for certain. Quietly, he got up to go to the toilet at the rear of his carriage, trying not to disturb anyone. He thought he'd succeeded, until he noticed one of the passengers stir and shift position as he neared the toilet door.

On his way back to his seat, he glanced down at an abandoned copy of the *Helsingin Sanomat* and read the headline. He had some difficulty with the Finnish but the scene in the picture looked vaguely familiar to him. *It's the Andover Institute, in ruins*! he realised. He almost collided with someone coming towards him; the same person whom he had disturbed before. Keir returned to his seat and watched the reflection of the receding figure in the window of the forward interconnecting door.

*****

Keir pulled out his tourist map and studied the section of the railway line between Oulainen and Oulu. A stretch of about 100 kilometres. He carefully reached for his link-set and attached a pair of small headphones which conveniently made it look like a personal stereo. Forbidden to contact Valentina directly, he decided to page Ilya from the hidden corner of his seat and adjusted the brightness of the screen. He opened the secure channel for text transmission.

'Sorry to wake you, Sergei,' he typed.

'No problem, FO25. I'm not asleep,' the display replied.

'We've just left Oulainen. Tell Olga I think I'm being followed,' he typed. 'Should I get off the train, somewhere up the line before Oulu and draw him after me? Can you arrange transport from there instead of Oulu?'

'No need to panic, my friend. We have two of our people on the train.'

Keir breathed a sigh of relief. 'Thank goodness. I thought we were in for some hassle.'

'Just the same, perhaps you could describe your man for me?'

'Purple anorak, dark eyes and thin black hair, rather greasy. He's coming out of the toilet now,' Keir replied, glancing at the reflection while pretending to doze. 'Prominent nose, medium height and build.'

'Not one of ours. You may have a problem.'

Keir felt the hairs rise on the back of his neck. 'He's coming closer. Have to stop now.'

'You and Olga will get off at Vihanti, understood?'

'Roger. Ah, Sergei!'

'Yes?'

'He's sat down two seats behind me.'

'OK. I'll tell our guys and give Olga the arrangements. Contact me again in ten minutes if you can. Otherwise just send two short bleeps. Understood?'

'Understood. Is Vihanti where I meet up with Olga?'

No reply. The link had been broken by auto cut-off, or possibly by conditions. He tried to re-establish contact. The call got through, but with Ilya's device in voice-mail mode.

*****

As Keir settled back in his seat, he wondered: *Is Valentina also being watched?* He looked intently at the reflection in the far door again; the man behind him still outside his field of view. At that moment, the door ahead slid open. Valentina! *What on Earth is she doing?* He watched, transfixed as though carved in stone. Without hesitation, she came over and sat down beside him.

'Keir!' she whispered. 'I'm sick of playing games. I'm scared.' She moved closer and held his arm. A different Valentina to the one he knew, or imagined he knew. She looked pale, worn out. Their eyes met and her dry lips mouthed the words: 'I need you Keir. Please stay with me.' She buried her head in his shoulder and he took her hand in his. With great effort he kept his voice steady, utterly unable to comprehend this new turn of events.

'Did Sergei contact you just before?' his whispered question muffled by her hair.

'Yes. He said we get off at Vihanti and look for the Volvo estate car which brought me to Oulainen. That was all.'

'Why are you frightened, Val? Is there anyone following you?'

She told him about the near encounter at Oulainen railway station. He wondered if the after-shock of that event, followed by Ilya's recent warning, might be responsible. She lapsed into a long silence. Keir searched for something to say, when she spoke again.

'I suppose we must learn to accept these things, Keir. Being watched, or even hunted down. I saw it happen many times to others because of the nature of my work, but this is my first personal experience of it.'

'Why was it necessary for you to join the train at Oulainen? We could have met on my arrival at Oulu.'

'For now Keir please accept that it *was* necessary. I can't tell you more yet. You've heard about the riots?'

'I saw a picture of Andover in yesterday's Helsingin Sanomat, but I couldn't follow the text.' Keir found himself gently running his fingers through her hair.

'Yes, Keir. Your Andover Institute; now it is completely destroyed. Everything, even the aliens' compound. It is all so horrible, so frightening. And I'm sick with the shame of it, that the human race could carry out such genocide on impulse!'

He felt her shoulder quiver beneath her thick overcoat and the pressure of her gentle sobs against his anorak. She turned her head slightly, so that he could see a brown curl of hair sticking to her wet cheek. She turned a little more, looking up at him with weary reddened eyes through a mist of tears. He felt no embarrassment, but met her gaze fully. She knew that he loved her and squeezed his hand. Suddenly, as he tried to distance himself from the surging maelstrom within him, Keir's attention switched to other matters close at hand.

'Did Sergei tell you what I told him?' he asked.

'Yes, I know that you, that *we*, are being watched.'

'Did he tell you the guy's in the second seat behind ours. Now he'll know that we're together in this.'

She looked at him with an expression which caused a landslide in the pit of his stomach. It was a synthesis of many facial expressions and signals he had seen, and yet entirely new.

'It's certain that they know already, Keir. But I think the job of our protectors is now easier. Either one or both of us stand a better chance if we are together. And there's no other way I would want it to be, Keir,' she said softly.

He watched in dumbfounded silence as she licked her dry lower lip, and he tried to stifle the alarm at his own arousal.

'We've got to get out of this, first!' he whispered in her ear, attempting to orient himself with a gesture of pragmatism. He looked again, this time at eyes of soft grey which did nothing to assist the steadying process. She drew herself up kissed him resolutely on the mouth, but with a gentleness which had his senses reeling again. Then she was on her feet.

Mesmerised, Keir could only watch as the dim carriage lights threw her face into stark relief, her brown hair wildly swept to one side. She had become as Boudicca, or perhaps more appropriately, as Luonnotar, the heroic nature-maiden of Finnish antiquity. *What's she doing now?* He heard a voice say somewhere in his mind.

Valentina picked up the folded copy of the Helsinki newspaper and unfolded it. She rounded on the man sitting two seats behind them and threw it into his lap. He looked ahead, avoiding her gaze, as she articulated clearly and deliberately: '*Sinä*! *Ja sinä olet toinen muurhaaja*! And you are another murderer!'

Keir felt the carriage, although sparsely occupied, reacting to her accusation and he tensed in readiness to spring to her defence. Her opponent raised an eyebrow and glanced up at her with a laconic smile.

'*No niin, kukaan ei ole täydellinen*. Well, nobody is perfect,' he replied.

Two or three passengers looked on with interest, while others hid behind what they were reading or remained in attitudes of sleep. Keir heard a child shouting:

'*Katsoa, äiti*! Look, mummy!'

Keir noticed a man in a brown leather jacket move adroitly nearer the scene, while another man wearing blue denim overalls returned from the toilet to a position much nearer than his original seat. Who are they? Keir wondered, Ilya's men or this guy's cronies?

Keir reckoned there was something odd about the man being addressed by Valentina, but he couldn't be certain. Then it dawned on him. The accent! He spoke Finnish, but the American accent should have been obvious. He turned to face the man squarely.

'You're following us, right?' Keir asked. 'We're bound for Oulu, what about you?'

The man's eyes levelled to meet Keir's: 'This *is* the Oulu train, I hope! Now d'ya mind if I finish my book?'

Probably New Jersey, Keir thought.

'OK, babe?' The man winked cheekily at Valentina, who glared down at him. She pulled away under Keir's prompting and returned to her seat beside him.

'Why did you mention Oulu?' she whispered.

'Because in 20 minutes we're making a hurried exit at Vihanti. And don't worry. I think the two other guys are Ilya's people.'

'I don't recognise them,' she said.

'We'll just have to hope so. All we can do is sit here and wait until the very last moment and then clear out fast.'

'I have to use the toilet!' whispered Valentina.

'OK. Be careful. I'll keep watching.' Keir squeezed her arm as she left her seat. It seemed like an age before she returned.

'There's a man standing by the toilet door!' she whispered.

'Hmm. And another up front there, too. Never mind. Just look as if you're relaxing with all the time in the world. Do you have your bag handy? You leave first, on my signal.'

Valentina felt no reservations about handing over control of their planned exit to Keir. On returning, she curled up with her head on his shoulder for the remaining 10 minutes of their journey. The carriage pitched and yawed ever so slightly as the train continued to glide almost silently over the rails. Keir watched the interconnecting doorway, behind which the one in the next carriage gently bucked and swayed. He focused on the reflections in the glass, waiting for signs of movement from behind him. Now he began to feel tired and his attention strayed away from the door to the advertisements behind the transparent panels on the end wall. To the left of the door a poster displayed a grim road accident: 'This could be you!' the banner proclaimed in Finnish. The amazing introductory bonus offer by a leading motor insurance company failed to interest him. The advert on the right panel showed one of the more sober and ubiquitous adverts for VR. Not Virtual Reality, but *Valtion Rautatie*, the State Railway.

Eventually, Keir saw their adversary steady himself as the train began to slow down. The same multilingual announcer declared the train's imminent approach to Vihanti station. The suspect now had a bag over his shoulder and began moving towards the exit at the rear of the carriage. Keir observed the man next to the toilet standing at the rear interconnecting door, barring the American's way. The train had slowed to almost walking pace and Keir watched through the window at the slow procession of concrete fence posts heralding the brightly lit station which yielded its identity on a painted signboard above its entrance.

In verification, the announcer called: 'Vihanti.'

The train stopped.

'Let's go!' Keir whispered.

He felt the tension in Valentina's hand relax as in one movement she got up and hefted her small bag under her right arm. He followed her to the forward exit. The man there yielded to let them pass. Thwarted by the obstruction at the rear of the compartment, the American had returned to follow nearly at Keir's heels. Ignoring him, Keir hastened through the doorway and stepped down to join Valentina on the platform. He glanced back, to see their pursuer still inside the carriage, in heated argument with the man who had let them pass. As the American raised what could have been a mobile phone or link-set to his mouth, the doors slid shut in front of him and the train purred northwards into the early morning light.

*****

5:33am, Vihanti.

In unison, Keir and Valentina sighed with relief and made their way to the station exit.

'Can you see the Volvo anywhere?' Keir asked. The sky had now brightened sufficiently for them to examine the road in both directions. To the south, it ran parallel to the railway track and towards the town centre. To the north, the road curved away from the track just before a bridge over the railway, which, judging by the traffic on it, supported a main highway.

'No, Keir. I'd expect it to be parked somewhere near here at the roadside. I do hope there's no problem. You saw the American use a radio?'

'Yes, I think he'd already left his seat before us. He'd anticipated that we might get off here, in spite of my explicit mention of Oulu, and now he's passed confirmation to his accomplices.'

'They'd need accurate information about the car and its occupants in order to stop it getting here, Keir. It was the same civilian car which brought me to Oulainen.'

'Unmarked?'

'Yes. Well, it was a taxi. Just like any other.'

'Looks like an inside job, then, doesn't it? That's not good, Valentina. Not good at all. We could be sitting ducks, even at this moment. Sorry to sound so cheerful.'

Valentina let him take her hand. He squeezed it gently and looked carefully around.

'I think we should take cover,' he said, 'There are plenty of trees on both sides of the railway track going north.'

The wind had dropped and the tops of the tallest trees were beginning to reflect the orange light of the eastern sky, the stillness being broken only by the sounds of birdsong and their own breathing.

'Any of those stronger branches could be a sniper's perch. And he wouldn't need an imaging rifle,' Valentina said.

'Yeah. Likewise, any of those dark spaces between the trees could give cover for an assassin.'

'Let's tell Ilya what's happened, and see if he knows anything,' Valentina suggested.

'Well, I hope the opposition can't detect the signals from our link-sets. They may have seen us already, of course.'

They both moved steadily and quietly northwards, to the right of the rail track under cover of the trees. The bridge they saw earlier also crossed the railway ahead of them.

'They're unlikely to try anything if we can get in amongst those houses,' Valentina suggested, indicating part of a housing estate just discernable about three hundred metres beyond the bridge and close to the left of the track. They must try to draw level with it without incident.

'Keir, if they're using radio contact, couldn't we detect *them* with our link-sets?'

'You mean in scan mode?'

'Possibly. But first let's see if Ilya can give us positions of any suspicious infra-red signatures in our vicinity.'

Ilya's voice became a welcome lifeline to the outside world. He took details and warned them that he'd not raised contact with the Volvo for over two hours.

'Keir, you ask about scanning mode on your link-set,' Ilya said. 'OK, ready?'

While they listened to Ilya on Valentina's set, Keir applied the relayed instructions to his own and immediately heard a lively hiss from the tiny loudspeaker. The display ran through a wide range of frequencies and stopped at a local TV channel, treating them to the early breakfast newscast in Finnish.

'It works! Thanks Sergei. And you too, Olga, for the idea!' he gave her a kiss on the cheek.

'Keir!' she cried in mock dismay. That had worked, too, breaking her tension.

'Now then, you two!' admonished Ilya. 'You'll have time later to play in the forest, but first we've got to get you out of trouble. There's some good news: the next military infra-red satellite with sufficient resolution is due any time now for an almost overhead pass in your area. I'll be able to look for signs of activity around you. The important thing will be to start moving on my signal. Any assailant will probably follow you, and I should catch his trace as he moves between the trees.'

'Thanks for your help, Ilya.' said Keir.

'Pleasure's mine, old chap,' Ilya's unconvincing imitation of a British aristocratic accent continued: 'The satellite is now over the horizon, so stand by.'

'Standing by.' said Keir. He tried to recall the American's handset and judge the size and shape of its tiny aerial. *Helical whip, probably around 450 megahertz,* he thought, as he reset the scanner. He picked up several data channels and selected one, following it with an auto-detect decoder sequence. They eavesdropped on a conversation about the best route to a farm outside town and then tried other channels, none of which sounded particularly sinister.

'Keep moving north,' Ilya said. 'I've got both of your images, faint of course, but clearly visible. Very close together, if I may say so.'

'Behave, Ilya!' chided Valentina, her spirits lifted by the banter with her colleague. Keir continued to operate the scanner.

'Don't be alarmed,' said Ilya. 'but there are several other infra-red bright spots in your area. Probably animals, some deer, perhaps. Ah! I see some interesting movement.'

A cold chill ran across Keir's shoulders and down his spine. Valentina tensed, and they both cast apprehensive glances towards the trees, through which the railway sliced a corridor.

They listened, moving forward as Ilya continued: 'It's all right. I think some animals must have heard you or picked up your scent, they're moving further away among the trees.'

Keir and Valentina began to draw level with the housing estate on the left side of the railway line.

'The satellite's moving away to the north-east now, but the image is still fairly good,' Ilya commented. 'Hey! We have other movement. Two bright spots about twenty metres apart, one behind the other, moving parallel to you. They're about two hundred metres behind you and two hundred metres to your left and keeping their distance. The leader has stopped. Keep going, both of you!'

'Can you tell if they're armed?' Keir asked.

'Can't say. The image isn't sufficiently clear for that. And now the satellite is starting to move out of range and your part of the image is getting very noisy. The leader is starting to come towards you. Now the picture's gone.'

Keir saw a movement between two trees about a hundred metres distant.

'Come on!' he whispered. 'Into the estate!'

'It might be a trap!' Valentina said.

'We've no alternative.' They started running. 'Look, there's a gap in the railway fence!'

Keir glanced back. Now on their side of the track and behind them, a man in grey jeans and a brown roll-necked sweater ran towards them with the speed of an athlete. Keir and Valentina saw the gap simultaneously and hurled themselves through the trees and scrub towards it.

'You first!' Keir gasped.

He followed her through the gap. They stumbled on, acutely aware of their vulnerability, the openness of the railway contrasting with the cover afforded by the trees. As they zigzagged away from the tracks, they heard a loud report, but the bullet spat a cloud of railway ballast into the air just behind Valentina. They could hear the crunch of feet on gravel as they slid down the slight embankment.

'Get to the houses!' Keir hissed.

'We need to get over the next fence first!' Valentina said, her eyes darting along its length as she searched desperately for an opening.

'Over there!' Keir pointed to a slender rowan tree standing about two metres from the fence that bordered the housing estate. 'Quickly, you climb it first!'

'It won't stand our weight, not even one at a time!' Valentina protested.

'Exactly! It'll bend as you climb higher, then you can swing over the top of the fence.'

'What about you?'

'Do it!'

This is a different Keir. So like Alexandr, she thought. But there wasn't time to think! She climbed nimbly to where the trunk thinned and it began to yield, her slim figure partly masked by the foliage. She needed more height than she'd anticipated before the tree would bend sufficiently. As she reached higher, grasping the narrow trunk, the tree creaked as it bent like a war bow and she felt the topmost wire of the fence touch her ankle. She transferred her weight to the wire. The tree tried to right itself and threatened to pull her off balance. She sank towards the wire again, then let go and jumped. The tree swished back to its upright stance as Valentina dropped to the ground on the other side of the fence.

'Run for it!' Keir cried, as he saw the enemy come into sight over the top of the embankment. The man aimed his weapon at Valentina as she darted for cover round the corner of the nearest dwelling.

The bullet whined past her head and shattered a toilet window of the house. A dog barked and the burly resident, unaware of the danger, opened his front door and cursed loudly as he sent his animal after the offending children he thought were responsible.

The gunman mouthed an obscenity and quickly retraced his steps to avoid being seen, ignoring Keir completely. This gave Keir time to use the tree and follow Valentina over the fence.

'Not yet! Hold your fire,' the accomplice of the first man whispered harshly from the railway track.

He raced to the tree and climbed it. The tree had helped two people that day, and it was enough. It snapped under the man's weight and he had to cling to the railway side of the fence before dropping to the ground before his enraged colleague.

Around the corner of the house, Keir and Valentina froze, expecting to be confronted by the angry householder. Instead, the owner followed his dog into the back garden to investigate the commotion.

Valentina remained still, trying not to show any fear, as the animal stood snarling, cutting off any hope of retreat. Although cornered by the animal, she noted its fine condition and recognised it as a cross breed. He had the rich golden coat and Husky-like appearance of his Finnish Pystykorva forebears, but larger, the size of a full grown Alsatian.

The swarthy owner approached and stood behind his dog, mouth agape at the sight of Valentina.

'*Voi*! *Anteeksi*!' he apologised, scratching his forehead. 'Come here, Simo!' he called off the dog and helped Valentina out of the flower bed. 'Who are you? And why, may I ask, are you in my garden? And can you explain that?' He motioned to a net curtain which flapped gently behind the broken window and then abruptly turned around at the sound of more furious barking, and the sight of a weary figure crawling from a bush.

'Er, he's my companion, Keir,' she said. 'And I'm Valentina.'

'Simo, come here, at once!' The man brought his dog to heel for a second time.

'Keir! Are you all right?' cried Valentina, alarmed at the way he held himself. He must have been in the way when the tree snapped back. She suppressed a smile.

As if reading her mind, Keir explained: 'No, it's my wrist!'

'Whatever's going on here?' the man studied Keir, 'You need a bandage, perhaps? Virpi!' He called to his wife who, in spite of being alarmed by the course of events, brought out a first aid box and fussily began to attend to Keir's wrist laceration. The dog took up station next to his master.

'Simo! On guard! That means that if either of you try to leave or do any tricks, he'll have you. You understand?'

Valentina nodded her assent.

'I'm really past caring,' Keir shrugged. 'Thank you for patching me up, Virpi.'

Valentina translated and Virpi looked up at her patient; smiling for the first time: '*Olkaa hyvä. Han on vakaa nuorimies*! That's all right. He's a sturdy young man!'

Virpi spoke too quickly for Keir, but he felt caught off guard by the expression in Valentina's eyes as she looked across at him from several metres away, leaning against the wall and not daring to move lest Simo should switch to attack mode. Her face registered an unmistakable look of yearning and Keir found himself responding in like manner. Virpi smiled even more. As if on cue, the man went inside and returned with a tray of small tumblers, in exquisite Finnish cut glass.

'Koskenkorva for each of you!' he announced, serving the drinks. 'This will make you feel better.'

'Thank you.' Keir smiled nervously and Simo growled at the movement as he took his glass from the tray.

'*Rakastavat*! Lovers!' Virpi elbowed her husband with a grin.

'*Hei*! *Kippis, kaksi rakastavat*!' the man beamed and raised his glass in toast to 'the two lovers'.

'*Kippis*!' they all said, as their glasses touched.

'What is *rakastavat*?' Keir asked.

'We drink to young love, my friend! *Anteeksi*! My name is Paavo, and you know my wife's name, she is Virpi, from Lapland. *Minun pieni pohjois-kukka*! My little flower of the North!'

'Shut up, you big daft thing!' his wife replied in Finnish.

'Well, you were first to mention the subject, my dear.' Paavo said. Then he turned to Keir. 'Now you've had a little time to recover, could you please explain our broken window?'

As Valentina translated, Keir appreciated the ever present danger, against which even the redoubtable Simo could not prevail.

'We thank you for your hospitality and understandable concern, but we must warn you that we're fugitives.'

'From the police?' Paavo puckered his brow.

'No. We are agents of the United Nations. Here are my credentials.'

Keir and Valentina showed him their ID cards. Paavo smiled again.

'It's OK, Virpi.' Turning to Valentina, he said: 'Who is pursuing you?'

'We don't know. But they're armed, and that's what caused the damage to your window. Inside the house you'll probably find a bullet, which could be recovered as evidence.'

'Please come inside, both of you!' Paavo insisted. 'Simo, Come!' the dog followed obediently as his master continued: 'Why didn't you tell us you are from the UN? And where have your attackers gone?'

'Thank you, Paavo!' Valentina, able to move freely at last, shook the soil out of her shoes as she spoke: 'When you appeared, they decided to back off, so you have almost certainly saved our lives. But they won't be far away; they're almost certainly biding their time until we leave here.'

*****

17 Cornered

Vihanti: Home of Paavo and Virpi.

They entered through the back door. 'We'd offer you a sauna,' Paavo said, 'but the hut outside is a risky place for us all just now. You're both welcome to an early breakfast and coffee instead.'

It feels strange being a prisoner in such hospitable surroundings, Valentina thought as she helped Virpi to clear the table. Events at the home of this suburban couple seemed so normal, so domestic. The dog lay curled on a rug in front of the log fire and a washing machine whined intermittently in the kitchen area. She could hear the breakfast news from the FM radio set on the window ledge.

'What's it saying?' Keir asked.

'Sh-h! Wait a moment!' Valentina said. The Finnish announcer continued for half a minute longer before the broadcast continued with the station's call-sign jingle and a commercial break. 'Keir, the news from Britain is not good. And in the United States the National Guard has been called in to protect the alien compounds. There is increasing unrest in other countries, too.'

'No doubt including this one, Valentina! I wonder if those two stooges are still wandering around the railway embankment.'

'Why not try the scanner?'

Keir complied and soon detected a strong series of chirps on his reconfigured link-set.

'Do you think it's them?' asked Valentina.

'Don't know.' Keir glanced in the direction of his host. 'Could you ask Paavo if he has a portable TV antenna we can borrow?'

Valentina acted as interpreter.

'Yes. They have one from an old analogue TV in the back room, if you want to give it a try.' Paavo unplugged the antenna and passed it to Keir.

'Thanks, Paavo. Now this will take a few minutes. The plug is not compatible with the socket on the link-set.'

Paavo appreciated the problem and fetched a spare piece of cable and some tools. When Keir had finished he held the portable antenna clear of the walls and aimed it in the general direction of the embankment, allowing the scanner to do its work.

'The direction may not be accurate,' Valentina warned. 'The antenna is tuned for the local TV channels.'

'I know,' Keir said, 'Any ideas?'

'Virpi,' Valentina asked, 'May we borrow your frying pan, and do you have some PVC tape?'

Valentina took the antenna and attached the rear of it to the frying pan, which now became a disc-shaped reflector.

'I didn't know you were into telecommunications, Valentina!' Keir commented. 'Will it make the antenna more sensitive?'

'Probably not, but when you turn it around to face *away* from the transmission, you should get a very sharp *drop* in signal. In that way, we'll be able to judge the direction of the transmissions much better.'

'Lateral thinking. I like it! But does that mean we won't be able to hear what they are saying some of the time?'

'Well, Keir, ' Valentina said, 'they're on foot and hardly likely to be moving at the speed of Superman. We only need to check their direction occasionally.'

Suddenly their scanner bleeped.

'The auto-decoder's giving us something and it's in English.'

The sounds were crisp and clear. To Keir, it suggested close proximity. The tiny loudspeaker on the set clicked into life:

'*Target Two visible through window on left.*'

Keir resisted the urge to obey his instincts. He did not duck, but slowly moved to one side of the window, without looking through it.

'*Target Two occluded. Target One just becoming visible again at right.*'

'That's me, Keir!' said Valentina.

'Yes. Now tell Paavo and his good lady to move to the opposite side of the house away from windows. And please ask them for a pencil and paper.'

When their hosts were safe, Keir sketched a diagram. From the geometry of their previous positions in the room, he worked out an approximate location for his adversary.

'It won't be an accurate triangulation, because the window is only one and a half metres wide, but I'd put the enemy in that clump of bushes behind the tree and two thirds up the embankment.' Keir whispered.

'Why are you whispering?' Valentina asked. 'Do you think they might have listening devices?'

'If they have Doppler laser kit aimed at this window, they can probably hear every word we're saying. But then maybe not. Look, that triple glazing might prevent it.'

Keir noted the window, built according to standards prevailing for most Finnish homes. He turned to face the wall opposite the window. 'But I suppose lip-reading is still a real possibility. We know that our own link-sets can decode a video sequence quite well. We don't know what kit they've got. Trouble is, if we draw the curtains in the absence of direct sunlight they'll become suspicious.'

'Let's draw them anyway, Keir,' Valentina suggested, 'We've nothing to lose. They already know we're here.'

'No, wait!' Keir said quietly, still away from the window. His general air of innocence often belied a mischievous, sometimes devious, streak in his nature. 'Let's play dumb and see if we can feed them some mis-information. First, we'll try to confirm whether they *can* lip-read by suggesting something that will evoke a response on the scanner.'

'OK, Keir,' Valentina said. 'Then we can try directing some speech at the window to test any Doppler laser capability they may have.'

'Sure. Before we do anything though, I'd better find the channel frequency of that guy's accomplice. Then the multiplexer can let us hear both transmissions.'

Within a few seconds, Keir's link-set had picked up both assailants in conversation:

'Epsilon to Kappa, keep your position this side of the nearest track rail at the top of embankment and line up behind me. Then drop over to join me in the bushes when I give the word. Understood?'

'Kappa to Epsilon. Roger. I need another visual on your location. Tell me when it's clear to go. Over.'

'Epsilon to Kappa. Check it now. Nobody's looking, but be careful.

'Kappa to Epsilon. Roger. Got you. I'm level with you now. Standing by.'

'Epsilon to Kappa. Roger. Wait. Go! Do it now!'

Keir turned his head imperceptibly, looking up the slope out of the corner of his left eye. He saw opponent number two slide into position. Both were now hidden behind the same group of bushes.

Valentina moved closer to listen to Keir's link-set.

'Look, Max. We've got them both. Let's take 'em out and go!'

'Not yet, Brad. You're too impulsive. You shouldn't have fired at the bitch during the chase back there! We must have the information first. Don't you see? This is the best thing that could have happened. Pass me your Cuthbertson... Now we just sit tight here with it trained on the window glass until they blab sufficiently. And then take them out with one shot each. Yours is Target One and mine's the feller, right?'

'Thanks!' Keir whispered on hearing their probable real names and he turned the volume control down on the scanner, making it barely audible...

The two gunmen were closer together now, still using radio contact for flexibility of deployment. The bushes giving them cover were spaced about two metres apart, one above and behind the other.

'Yeah, but I was only thinking of the time. We should have been out of here and half way to Oulu by now! What if they've called the police or UN Security?'

'No, they'll think we've cleared off. And the information has priority, right? We tell Gamma it took a bit longer, that's all. If we do clear off without it, he'll have our balls, you can bank on that!'

'They're using a Cuthbertson!' Valentina whispered. 'Triple glazing is no obstacle. It's sufficiently sensitive to read the scattered infra-red light from the inner pane, and its on-board signal processing is state-of-the-art technology. We'd better be very careful. They might even be able to hear our whispers. '

As if to confirm her suspicions, Max's voice came over the scanner.

'I think they're talking again.'

At that moment, the gentle slopping noises from the kitchen became a high pitched whine.

'No - it's a damned washing machine.'

Keir sighed with relief and cautiously increased the volume control on the scanner to counter the level of background noise.

Disconcertingly, the washing machine entered a quiet part of its cycle. Then he noticed Paavo's portable digital TV on a corner table. He crawled across the floor, turned it on and grabbed its remote.

Keir returned. He hit a button and the TV set promptly delivered a pop concert at a respectable volume. Whereupon, a voice erupted from his scanner:

'*Tchah! Too much TV sound. Better try the Bermak'.*

'Did you hear that?' Keir looked at Valentina. 'What do they mean?'

'As you guessed before, they've got an imaging lip-reader. So there's no need for that part of our experiment, either.'

Keir asked, 'What information are they waiting for us to give them, Valentina?'

'We may never know. As soon as they have it, we'll be dead.'

'You must have some idea!' Keir whispered.

'There are several possibilities,' Valentina said, 'the first one being the precise location of the Finnish base.'

'They'll know that from satellite imagery. Anyone who browses the Web can find out.'

'Not necessarily. There are five decoy sites in the north-west of the country, and we don't publicise any of our Triple Alpha classified sites on Web pages.'

Keir reflected silently on the fate of the Andover Institute, where the alien compound had been a closely guarded secret, but clearly not guarded enough.

'Then which site do we fool them with?'

'Rovaniemi,' Valentina said without hesitation.

'Fine. But it's highly probable that once we've given them that information, and they see us together behind this window, we're dead ducks. And why Rovaniemi?'

'Because our aggressive friends outside seem anxious to leave in good time and keep to their schedule. Rovaniemi is the farthest north of the decoys, and the least convenient, unless you fly from Oulu. But I don't think they'd take that risk. And Ilya could arrange a nice surprise for them when they eventually got there.'

'What sort of surprise?' Keir asked.

Valentina paused, smiling back at him. 'I'm sorry, Keir, that's something I'm not allowed to say.'

'Neither of us will be saying anything if we don't get away from here. We must find some transport. Could you ask Paavo what's available?'

'You mean, commandeer their car?'

'If it comes to that, then yes.'

Valentina crept cautiously through the doorway and found Paavo seated in his study, trying to look calm. She explained the need for transport.

'Our son Janne is on his way here with his van,' Paavo said. 'It's fortunate for you that we live in a corner house. He'll very soon pull into the driveway over there, out of sight of the railway. You can both get into the back of the van and he can drive you to wherever you like. But can you keep the enemy in place without them suspecting that you're leaving? I can call the police as soon as you give the word.'

Valentina found Keir busy on the floor with some scissors and the remains of a cardboard box, as he started to make a pair of head-sized shapes.

'Where's the masked ball being held?' she asked.

'Right here,' he said without looking up.

Keir continued his task as she watched.

Then she whispered: 'I'll go and ask if they've anything to colour the card.'

Within six minutes, they had a pair of reasonably lifelike heads attached to crude wooden handles made from sticks which Paavo kept for the sauna stove.

'Not enough time for a flattering effort. I hope you don't mind too much.'

The hair had been drawn in and coloured using brown sauce. The card looked a bit dark as well, but it would do, Keir thought. In silhouette against the pale cream wall, they were as near perfect as he could make them.

'They're good, Keir. I must remember to tell Kirsti she has a rival artist in our group.' With horror, Valentina realised that the TV set had paused at the end of a programme. *I hope they didn't hear that*, she thought.

Admiration of the handiwork ceased at the sound of an approaching car. Keir grabbed the cardboard silhouettes and carried them unobtrusively into the kitchen.

'What are you doing?' Valentina asked.

'Back in a moment. Must warm them a little, over the cooker hot plate. Our friends out there may be using infra-red gear for imaging - almost certainly on their gun-sights. These cut-outs will have to be at around body temperature if they're to be convincing!'

'Nice, Keir!' She realised that they would have to work quickly as the TV resumed pumping out its background entertainment. Keir returned to the room and they prepared to use their normal voices for the benefit of the Cuthbertson laser eavesdropper, which the enemy would almost certainly be using in preference to the lip-reader, should the TV be turned off. They knelt, facing each other beneath the opposite edges of the table and out of sight of their assailants. They carefully aligned their cardboard replicas and moved them steadily into view, each trying not to shake their respective handles in their excitement. Keir had forgotten to turn off the television.

'Hold it there,' he whispered harshly.

He shifted slowly backwards and reached for the TV remote, knowing that with each passing second the temperature of the cardboard would fall away from its credibility threshold. He switched off the TV and carefully resumed position under his edge of the table.

'*Max*! *It's them. Can you see?*'

'*Yes*! *I can just make them out at the table. Looks like they're discussing something. Let's take aim. It's definitely them. Anyway, Brad, we'd better shut up and keep listening.*'

Keir began the voice-over.

'How long, do you think, before we can make it back?'

'We're expected at Rovaniemi Base in about twelve hours from now,' Valentina replied.

They could not have wished for a more speedy response; glass shattered and Keir felt the impulse a split second before they heard the first shot. The second followed almost instantaneously and Valentina needed all her strength to prevent her replica leaping from her hands, as the bullet punched a neat hole just above the painted ear and tore through the handle. The wall spat two gouts of dust and plaster fragments showered into the room.

From outside, both targets appeared to jerk and fall backwards out of sight. The assailant's listening device picked up a shrill scream and a deeper groan, accompanied by a crash, which could have been a falling chair.

'*Two hits. We've got what we came for, Brad.*'

'Yep. Let's stow our kit and piss off out of here. There's a delivery van coming.'

'That's handy, lets take it!'

'Don't be a fool, Brad. The police might be here any second. We'd better stick to the plan and get back over the railway.'

Keir and Valentina waited. A vehicle door slammed, in the direction of the driveway. And the scanner remained silent.

'Sorry about the mess we've left behind!' Valentina said, as they made for the back door. 'We're very grateful for your help,' she added. 'Hope my scream didn't alarm you. You're taking it all very calmly.'

'All in a morning's work,' Paavo commented. 'You see, I'm a retired Major in the Finnish Army. By the way, I trust that the UN are replacing our windows and replastering our wall?'

'I'm sure my colleagues will be pleased to help an old soldier, Paavo!' she said.

'Valentina?' With a smile Keir hefted his kitbag onto his back. 'Here's our transport! Let's hope the two stooges haven't intercepted Paavo's messages to Janne.'

'I think they'll be too occupied with clearing off,' Valentina said. 'They were in a hurry, remember.'

'Go quickly. Now!' Virpi guided Valentina through the back door towards the van. 'Here are some sandwiches and drinks in case you need them.' She turned to her son and added: 'Drive carefully, Janne!'

The car slid out of the driveway.

'Let's make for the main road and take Route 86 heading north-east to Oulu,' Valentina said.

They had hardly left the house when a problem arose.

'Heads down! It's them! They must have changed their minds.' Keir hissed, as he pulled Valentina against him. Their assailants had emerged from trees on their left about a hundred metres ahead. They were flagging down the driver.

'Keep going. They mustn't find us!' he shouted to Janne, who had braked slightly in hesitation.

'Keep going. Don't stop!' Valentina translated into Finnish.

'Brad's obviously very persuasive!' Keir commented.

With a roar, the van accelerated past the two men. They swore audibly as they jumped aside.

'Bastard!' Max bellowed after them, raising his fist.

'Max, you don't think they could have escaped?' Brad said.

'I'm not sure. We'd better go back and check.'

'Look! We can't. It's the police!' Brad tugged at Max's elbow. 'You know the cottage we passed a few minutes ago? There's a motorcycle parked by the log-pile.'

'You're right! It's a Harley Davidson. Good thinking, Brad. At least we can check the van, there'll be no problem catching it up. And I'm looking forward to sorting out the driver. Let's go!'

*****

Janne's electrician's van 7:10 am.

The back of the cream coloured Saab van carried a load of electrician's tackle, which made it uncomfortable and noisy. Keir had to shout to make himself heard.

'There's a motorcyclist coming up behind. About half a kilometre.'

'It might be the police,' Valentina suggested. 'Any flashing lights?'

'No. Just headlights. They're gaining on us.'

'Let's have a look.' Valentina shifted herself into a better viewing position. 'It's difficult to make out how many are on the bike; if only they were wearing helmets.'

'You're right! No helmets. So they're probably on a stolen machine, either joy riders or our two friends.'

'Oh! It's not *them* again, is it, Keir?' Valentina cried.

'Janne! I think we're being followed!' Keir shouted.

'*Anteeksi? Ei Englanti*!' Janne bellowed over his shoulder.

'He doesn't speak English, Keir.' Valentina said, 'Don't worry. I'll handle it.'

Janne glanced at his door-mirror and abruptly steered the van left into another road. A few seconds later, the motorcycle followed.

'What do you want me to do?' Janne asked. 'It looks like a powerful machine and I can't shake it off. We've the weight and air resistance of the roof rack and ladders to cope with. Look out! They've nearly caught up with us already!'

Had it not been for the glint of morning sunlight on the steel muzzle of Brad's' weapon, Janne might have allowed the motorcycle to draw level, in the hope that the riders wanted to pass. The image in the door mirror dictated otherwise. He shouted: 'One of them has a gun!'

At the screech of Janne's brakes, Keir and Valentina slid forward, colliding with the metal bulkhead behind the front seats. They ducked instinctively in anticipation of the rear impact. When it came, they were flung back again. Keir's shoulder took their combined momentum and the nearside rear door burst open. Tools and cables spilled out onto the road, amid the debris of the collision. In trying to swerve away, the bike had impacted the offside corner of the van and its riders were no longer visible. Keir had slid half way out of the back of the van, with Valentina laying across his legs and preventing him from actually falling out. He reached up to grab the handle of a swinging offside door severely dented by the collision. His gaze swept upwards to the top corner of the van, where the cream paintwork had been deeply scratched and smeared ominously red. He followed the traces of the smear to what looked like an item of luggage above him. To his horror, silhouetted against the bright sky, he saw the shape of a human head, jammed into the metalwork of the roof rack and overhanging ladders. Keir freed himself and slid out of the van.

'Valentina! Are you all right? Don't come out, just stay right there!' He jumped to his feet with a gesture of restraint.

'I'll be fine Keir. Are *you* all right? You look terribly pale. Get back inside and let's get away from here,' she urged.

From a kneeling position in the back of the van, Valentina offered him a helping hand. As she bent forward, Keir experienced an ambivalence of desire and respect which caused him to avert his eyes.

Valentina smiled. 'Come on, let's go!' she said, hauling him in beside her.

Janne accelerated cautiously, lest the occupants behind him should slide out. In the driving mirror, he could see that the doors were too distorted to close properly, but he felt disinclined to stay around and fix them.

Bracing himself against the side of the van, Keir peered out behind them and saw a headless body stretched out on the grass verge, with one of its arms draped over the lower bar of the roadside fence. He could find no sign of the other person. Their van driver, unaware of his recently acquired payload, had already reached a steady cruising speed. Keir flopped back beside Valentina.

'What's the matter, Keir? You don't look so good. Are you hurt?' she asked, drawing herself towards him.

'No, I don't think so. Listen, Val. That crash we had. We've got the head of one of those guys up here on the roof.' He pointed upwards as he spoke.

Valentina regarded him with a puzzled frown as she tried to work out what he said. *Is this a nuance of the English language or is there really a human head on the roof?* As if reading her thoughts, Keir continued: 'It's somebody's head, Valentina. Jammed tight in the roof rack!' As Keir spelled it out, she grasped his hand and turned deathly pale as her imagination took over.

'Hadn't we better stop and do something about it?' she heard herself say.

'Yes, when we're a couple of kilometres clear, we'll find a place to sort it out,' said Keir, in an effort to assume control.

In businesslike manner, he concentrated on preparations for some video shots. *Ilya might like to know who we've got on board*, he thought, glancing up at the roof. He recalled that the head lay face down, its half open eyes looking into the metal. With the bright sky behind, it would make a poor camera shot and he was not looking forward to readjusting the subject.

'There's a car coming up behind us!' cried Valentina.

'I've seen it,' said Janne. He slowed down and pulled over to the grass verge.

As the van stopped, Keir grabbed Janne's yellow hard-hat from a hold-all on the floor. He found an orange plastic bag and emptied its residue of ready-mixed cement into the grass. At the same time, he wrenched the rear door wide open to hopefully conceal the crimson stains on the bodywork. As he tied the bag over the grisly cargo, the car sped by, its driver believing that he'd passed a contractor who'd stopped to adjust his load.

The three glanced at each other, wondering what the driver might have seen further back along the road. As if reading their thoughts, the driver of the same car now reversed. He stopped in front of the van and walked over to Janne.

'There's been a rather nasty accident back there!' the stranger said. 'Did you see it?' He trembled visibly.

'Oh, yeah?' Said Janne, innocently.

'Yes, a motorcyclist I'm afraid. Must have been a tradesman like yourself. Tools and things all over the place. Just thought you might have noticed. I've left my mobile phone at home. Do you happen to have one? We'd better call the police and an ambulance, not that anything can be done for one of the riders.'

They spoke quickly but Keir guessed the subject of conversation. He peered from behind the rear of the van in time to see the newcomer being sick on the road. *Poor guy, delayed shock*, he thought.

'I'm sorry. I'll be all right,' the man said. He studied the dented rear doors of their van.

'Don't worry,' Janne reassured him. 'We'll deal with everything. Just take it easy. Keep warm and have a drink!'

'Thanks, I will. 'The car driver climbed back into his vehicle and cautiously drove off.

'Where's he gone?' Keir asked.

'Janne's dealt with him,' Valentina said.

'Good. Before we leave I must record some shots. Don't look if you don't want to.' Keir pulled aside the orange plastic. He angled the link-set and recorded several frames of high definition video. 'Fine so far, now I need a full face shot, but I can't dislodge it. Not without tools of some kind. And I'm certain we lost the hacksaw in the collision.'

'Here's an adjustable wrench and a screwdriver,' Valentina handed him the tools. 'Why not remove the roof-rack?'

It took Keir and Janne several minutes of precious time to lift the rack clear. As they set it down on the grass verge, Keir wondered if he should turn the frame over so that the face would be uppermost, but dismissed the idea with a shudder. He stood for a moment, swaying slightly.

Janne took over, using his boot to apply pressure in the right places and the head rolled clear, disappearing into the long grass. Keir regained his determination and rolled it into position with a stick for the desired final shots. When Keir had finished, Janne packed the object into a plastic bag and laid it in a ditch. He then cleaned his hands and boots on the grass.

They hurriedly restored the roof rack at a minimum number of attachment points to make it secure. As they set off again, Keir thought he saw a distant movement in the trees.

*****

Oulu Base.

Ilya tried firing up his link-set to contact Valentina's device. No answer, just a pattern of bleeps. 'Its status is still scanner-mode, after all this time!' he said to himself.

As Ilya keyed in the interrupt sequence, he reflected that he felt quite lonely without Valentina. He missed her calming influence, remembering how she punctuated it with girlish laughter. His thoughts drifted to Tonya and lazy summer afternoons in their favourite spot under the trees in Izmaylovski Park. And the flour on her clothes after working in the baker's shop near the university in Moscow. *Another six months and I should earn enough to buy us a better car*, he thought. *But I dare say she'll want me to save it, for what? For when we get married?* He let out a raucous laugh that startled himself.

Ilya's attention returned to the lidless stares of the monitor screens displaying an assortment of satellite images. From his control computer, he selected one, magnifying its gossamer trace of the highway which ran north-east from Vihanti. The van showed as a tiny dull speck. Switching to infra-red, the speck became a pin-prick of light as the satellite's onboard sensors picked up the heat from the engine. He detected another cluster of activity, further back down the road, as service vehicles attended the scene of the collision. Ilya tried Valentina again and Keir answered:

'Ilya! Can you see us?' Keir's voice barked urgently. 'We're in a van, about eight kilometres north-east of Vihanti. I'm about to send you some images taken with my link-set. Ready?'

'Roger. Go ahead!'

The pictures weren't professional shots. Ilya would have to be content with what he could see, a gory mess taken from difficult angles with partial occlusion by roof rack spars. Two hurried shots of the head on the ground weren't much better, but the shape of the right ear appeared almost perfect. Ilya zoomed this part of the image and sent it to the database for matching with known suspects. Nothing?

'Wait please, Keir. Still trying to trace the ear.'

He wasn't satisfied. Years of training told him that he recognised that ear. He moved across to activate Valentina's workstation and began another search. He found a video sequence of one of the vehicles used in the Lucien incident, but the people in view were far too small to provide the detail he needed.

'Keir? That head on the roof. Are you free to give me a description of the body? Especially I need to know his height.'

Keir remembered how the body lay; straight, with an arm stretched out on the fence bar. 'Tall. About one metre eighty with the head, and dressed in a dark brown jacket and grey trousers.'

'Think, Keir. Do you recognise that man from anywhere else, like on the train? Take your time.'

'Not the train. I do recall a man standing over me at the conference. It could have been him.'

'Interesting! OK, Keir. Thanks. Could you put Valentina on? Hello?'

A loud report cut short Valentina's reply. Something had struck the body of the van as it climbed a shallow gradient. The van kept moving and no sooner reached the top of the hill when it began to sway erratically. She and Keir were thrown sideways as the vehicle slewed across the road out of control.

*****

18 Problem in the Forest

Janne's van.

With a rending crash, their van collided with a tall silver birch tree at the roadside.

'Janne! Are you all right?' cried Keir.

Their driver sat pressed back into his headrest by the deployed airbag, while Valentina found herself wedged between the driver's and passenger's headrests. She saw a trickle of blood oozing from Janne's leg. Easing herself into the back of the van, she found Keir at her side nursing a bump on his head but seemed otherwise uninjured.

She gripped Keir's arm.

'Janne's been hit in the leg. Not that he'd notice just now. He's out cold.'

'See? It's gone straight through,' Keir said, peering between the driver's door and Janne's seat. 'Yes, it looks like the bullet has exited into the centre console behind the gear lever.'

'We've got to get him out of here, and quick!'

'There's a wagon coming! It's pulling over.' Keir said. A groan from Janne indicated his return to consciousness. 'Easy now, Janne. Help is on its way.'

Meanwhile, Janne began cautiously holding his leg.

The wagon had stopped where it might act as a convenient shield. The driver approached them.

'Could you please help us?' Valentina asked him in Finnish. 'Our driver needs to go to hospital. Casualty department; we've stopped most of the bleeding with a generous first aid kit.'

'No problem. But there is only room in the cab for two of you. And the wagon has a full load.'

'You go with him, Valentina!' Keir shouted.

'No, you go. Keir,' Valentina said. 'That's an order.'

'If you stay, so do I!' Keir said, as she and Keir helped get Janne into the wagon.

'And Janne,' Valentina said, 'Don't worry about your van. We'll get you a replacement.'

'Better keep Ilya updated,' Keir said, resuming his link with Oulu. 'Ilya! Janne's being taken to hospital, he's on board a wagon, but we're OK.'

Ilya had been following the images, the communications equipment switching satellites as necessary 'Glad you both escaped injury. But you must leave the area. Your remaining pursuer is about three hundred metres from you. Moves as if wounded, possibly waiting for that wagon to leave. His position is...'

The roar from the wagon's engine drowned Ilya's voice as the vehicle began to resume its journey.

They heard Ilya finish the call: '...And I'll arrange for the van to be collected and replaced. Over and out.'

*****

'What now?' Keir asked. 'With a dead van, we're back to being sitting ducks!'

'Quick! Before he gets over the brow of the hill. We need to cross this road and get into the forest!' Valentina whispered harshly as she pulled Keir after her.

They crashed through the thickets, which tore at their clothing, and kept going until the ground under their feet gave way to a seamless carpet of compacted bracken.

'How d'you know he's on the other side of the hill?' Keir asked.

'I don't. I'm just guessing,' she said.

Tall trunks of conifers loomed skyward, disappearing into the interlocking canopy of needle covered branches. At ground level, the pattern of rough bark and fallen twigs repeated itself with distance. The air felt very still and their footfalls sounded loud in spite of the cushioning effect of the ground.

'If we carry straight on for about a kilometre, with the sun on our right,' Keir whispered harshly, 'there should be another road. I saw it branch off earlier, after we left the scene of the bike collision.'

'Yes, I saw the T-junction as well. It should carry on in a north easterly direction. Ilya would tell us, and he might give us a fix on Brad.'

'Brad was the pillion rider and he's dead. It's the other guy who's following us. And as we know, he's much more professional.' Keir said, pulling out his link-set. 'But you're right about the road. Let's ask now in case we make a wrong decision.'

They found it strange to hear the calm clarity of Ilya's voice. Keir turned the sound down to the limits of audibility:

'From your GPS fix, the road in question is one point one five kilometres from your position. I'll send a rendezvous car to it. Then we can get you onto Route 86 for Oulu. As for your assailant, I can only guess because I cannot see him any more. For him I have to rely on infra-red and the trees are too dense. I'll tell you when our enemy breaks cover. Understand?'

'Understood,' said Keir.

'Keep going, then!'

'Thanks Ilya!' Keir grabbed Valentina's hand. They sped on, trying to avoid branches and twigs in their paths which might betray the sound of flight. Ahead of them a natural avenue between the columns of trees promised a clear run with a substantial increase of speed, at least for seventy metres or so. They approached the lone trunk near the end of the avenue when they realised their mistake. As he heard the sound, Keir felt the sudden and painful loss of a tuft of hair. He saw the bullet smack into a trunk just above eye-level a few paces in front of him. Chips of bark and wood fell as they dived past the tree.

'Now we know his direction, Val.'

'Low velocity impact! Near the limit of his range,' Valentina said. 'I think he's a hundred metres behind us.'

'Right! Let's split now. You go right. We'll meet further on.'

Their assailant seemed unperturbed and fired another round, but the aim had been slightly over-corrected for lateral movement and the projectile whined past Keir's left ear. Blood from his scalp wound trickled down his right cheek as he disappeared into cover of the trees, which had resumed a more random configuration. The ground began to descend and he realised that he'd cleared the crest of another mound. He could hear Valentina's progress, now some distance away, but couldn't see her.

'This time, I'm the main target!' he thought. 'The bastard wants me out of the way first, and then he'll catch up with Val at his leisure.' With extreme reluctance, Keir accepted the idea that they should stay separated, but hoped she might not come after him into the line of fire.

*****

Valentina stood rigidly behind one of the larger trees, listening intently. She picked up the sound of Keir's movements again, somewhere ahead but well over to the left of the direction in which she ran. Cautiously, she began to set off again. Then she froze. Above her, on the mound, a blur of brown passed between the trees as the irregular footfalls of their wounded pursuer crunched on some twigs. Then he vanished, presumably over the far side of the mound. Valentina dared not move until she felt sure of her safety. She decided to call up Ilya on her own link-set while she waited.

'*Da*? Olga! How's it going?' sounded Ilya's welcome but rather loud voice.

She fumbled for the keypad to reduce the volume and confirm her navigation fix. 'Can you help us?' she said, 'We've split up, but still heading for the road!'

'That might confuse things a little,' Ilya replied. 'But I've located Yrjö at last and he's leaving you a car, a maroon Mercedes. You'll see it when you go due east. There are some buildings nearby. If *you* reach it first, your priority is to escape *immediately*. Wait for nobody. That includes Keir.'

'But I can't...'

'You must. That's an order from UN Operational Command. They're monitoring this. There's no room for sentiment. You must return here at all costs. Report to me again when you've reached the car and driven out of range of your attacker.'

'Yes, Sergei. Over and out.'

With utter anguish, Valentina felt caught up in a monstrous and merciless machine. Ilya must surely understand the human side. But he had to obey orders, this time from the top.

A sound took her by surprise. She looked up in time to see the barrel of a weapon being aimed at her from a range of about twenty metres. She heard the loud report as the link-set leaped from her hand and fell to the ground in several pieces.

'Don't be afraid, I won't kill you, immediately,' said Max. 'First, I'd like you to know something.'

'There's nothing you say that can interest me!' Valentina said.

'That's where you're wrong, I'm afraid. Your man is not as he seems, you know. You see, he and I share something in common.'

'How on Earth is that possible?'

'I thought you said you weren't interested.'

'Carry on, then, if you must.'

'We're both from the future: July the 3rd, 2085 to be precise.'

'You're insane!'

'Maybe and maybe not. You'll never know, anyway. After that unfortunate motorcycle incident, I deserve a little amusement, don't you think? No! Don't move, my dear, or I *will* take you out. And it won't be to a place of your entertainment. However, our little interlude together may amuse some *voyeurs* I know. Then I can concentrate on dealing with your friend.'

Her adversary used his free arm to hang his mobile phone from the branch of a tree, with its camera pointing at Valentina. He then smiled and took a step towards her. Valentina instinctively dropped to the ground and as she rolled behind another tree, a second bullet whined above her head. She nimbly leaped to her feet and, like a gazelle, darted away between the trees, speeding onward down the incline. Two more shots rang out in succession; one went wide but the other ripped a lock of hair from her temple - the pain excruciating. Next, she noticed that a shard of black plastic from her link-set had entered the palm of her right hand, which had begun to bleed. Her arm nagged with the referred pain, but she pressed ever forward, praying for sight of the road and the waiting car.

Sight of the roadway beckoned her and with a renewed spurt of energy, Valentina vaulted the fence and nearly fell into the ditch behind it. She could hear the advancing tread of the gunman and scanned the open road for sign of the car, and also Keir. The car! About a hundred metres away, to her right. She realised that Keir must still be behind her, perhaps near the road, but certainly still in the forest. She turned and dashed towards the vehicle, noticing it appeared empty, and painfully but resolutely heaved the door open.

'*Very obliging of someone,*' she thought. *Ready to go. Engine ticking over.* Escape in the direction of Oulu would involve driving past her pursuer, who would emerge from the forest at any second. But Keir might also emerge somewhere. She gunned the vehicle forward; if it had not been fitted with traction control, she would almost certainly have crashed it. As Valentina snaked violently away from the grass verge, she heard a deafening crack. A pockmark appeared in the windscreen in her direct line of vision. *Thank God! Bullet-proof glass.* She swerved at her assailant in an effort to run him down. He dived clear as she accelerated and then stood on the centre line of the road to take aim at the receding vehicle.

At that moment, Keir appeared fifty metres ahead. He saw Valentina on the far side of the road, the car still accelerating. Then he saw the gunman and scrambled back into the undergrowth. As he did so, he heard another shot, immediately followed by an explosion. *He's got one of the tyres!*

Keir moved as swiftly as he could through the forest and parallel to the road. He saw the car through the trees. It went past him, weaving erratically. Then it came to a halt. Keir's heart missed a beat as he saw Valentina roll out of an open door and fall into the bushes on the opposite side of the road. Something else tumbled out behind her. Possibly a cushion or seat cover. She staggered to a crouching position and limped off into the forest. Another shot ricocheted off the car's open door. Keir assumed that Valentina would keep running in the same direction and he broke cover to cross the road and join her. But she'd vanished completely. The sky now overcast, without the sun as a guide, he hoped she would keep the road in sight to avoid going round in circles.

The attacker followed Valentina into the forest. Slowed by her throbbing hand and an injury to her shoulder on hitting the ground - her pace no match for her pursuer - she turned defiantly. Her assailant renewed chilling eye contact with her. This time, without hesitation. He raised his weapon from a distance of about ten metres.

Exhausted, she sagged against a tree. *Well, perhaps it's fitting that I die among the trees I love*, she thought. *Good-bye, Keir. I hope you make it safely. If not, we'll be together again soon, perhaps.* She remembered her Lutheran parents in Karelia and began reciting the Lord's Prayer. She stretched out her uninjured hand to caress the pine needles on an overhanging branch. '*He's taking his time, isn't he? Go on, amuse yourself and gloat over your kill.*'

The delay before the final percussion which would send her to eternity seemed an eternity in itself. Then she saw a most unexpected thing happening. Her assailant fell back, screaming and clutching his eyes. Valentina heard the thud as his weapon fell on the soft turf.

'Is that you Keir? Where are you?' she cried, renewed hope surging through her and banishing the pain. But she heard only silence, punctuated by the whimpering of her attacker, who had fallen to his knees, groping for his armament. '*He can't see!*' Valentina realised. She rushed forward and carefully kicked the gun clear. Then she began to back away cautiously and silently.

She paused, watching from behind another tree. *I daren't pick it up,* she thought. *What other weapons might he have? I must get back to the road, and find Keir.* Valentina moved silently between the trees, making her way around the stricken gunman, towards the dim light in the direction of the road. Then she felt sick. '*What if this is an elaborate game he's playing? Perhaps he wants me to make for the road so that he can get Keir as well.*' Her mind raced and her heart pounded in her ears. '*Yes - that's it. He wants to force us into the car and dispose of us together. Nice and clean*; *no bodies to hide or drag anywhere.*' Any second, she expected him to look up at her; that leering face with its beetle brows and small, perfect teeth. The pain had returned and she felt thoroughly confused. The trees swam before her eyes and with an effort, she cleared her vision of the myriad speckles and from her new vantage point she discerned the man still kneeling on the ground, and apparently still looking for his weapon. '*What's in the knapsack he's got on his back?*' she wondered. The speckles came again and a roaring filled her ears. But unaware of her knees giving way as she fell to earth, she yielded to the gentle green ferns and soft bracken.

Keir nearly missed seeing her. A protruding foot betrayed her position. He brushed the ferns aside and looked into her white face and noticed her blood-caked hand and the red trickle from her right temple. He feared the worst.

'Valentina!' he choked.

'She sleeps,' said a voice. 'Be not anxious, Keir.'

A few metres away, a knapsack-like object had detached itself from the prostrate form of the gunman. Keir recognised the shape with astonishment.

The alien came towards them. For an instant Keir felt he'd returned to Andover. Then suddenly, its frontal regions developed a striped pattern, which danced and wavered, changing in structure and colouring as he watched. The voice belonged to another specimen of the same alien life form, presumably better adapted to the Earth's atmosphere. Its abdomen shimmered and flickered in vibrating pulses of colour, as if in response to its alien companion. It turned to face Keir and spoke again:

'My mate tells me that your adversary has been effectively subdued.'

'Thank you!' Keir heard himself say, as if in a dream. He couldn't see any mouth speaking. *Is it an illusion, or are the words inside my head?* Perhaps he'd find out later. For now he felt so relieved at this unexpected rescue. He listened, if that's the correct word, while the conversation continued:

'She also tells me in considerable detail how it was accomplished, but that would take at least an hour of your serial audio speech communication to explain. Therefore, I summarise by telling you that the subject's optic nerves in both eyes have been disabled by micro-manipulation. Partial motor paralysis was also induced. He will be able to walk under escort, but any violent or threatening gesture will cause him extreme pain. His weapons have been confiscated. Keir, may I introduce my colleague, Ar-y'naa?'

Keir offered his hand. The handshake felt cold and almost adhesive, as if brushing against the feet of a thousand flies. He turned his gesture into a nervous salute.

'Honoured to meet you, Ar-y'naa,' he said. 'And thanks for dealing with that guy over there.' He saw Ar-y'naa flood her abdomen with orange, radiating from a pulse of yellow at the centre, and assumed this to be an acknowledgement of his gratitude.

'It was necessary, Keir, as is the recovery of Valentina,' said Ar-y'naa. The words in English came over near perfect, perhaps slightly clipped with measured syllables. 'You may return to the car with Mir'leor while I attend to your mate,' she added.

'Mate?' Keir asked in surprise.

'I apologise. Perhaps I misunderstand the strong feelings of attachment that you have for each other,' Ar-y'naa responded, with a gesture which could have been a shrug.

Keir looked at Valentina. She tried smiling back at him through her obvious pain. Clearly, she could also 'hear' their speech. He felt she knew more about these people than he did.

'Come!' said Mir'leor, 'It is required to re-activate the car and proceed to Oulu.'

'Is this man, Max, coming with us?' Keir asked.

'No. He will be collected separately,' Mir'leor stated.

Through the trees, Keir noticed that a white ambulance had parked in front of the car. 'Tell me, Mir'leor, do you have a language of your own?' he asked.

'We have no difficulty with your speech, but you may be interested to know that your name has a meaning in our language. But more about that later, perhaps.'

'Really? How about Valentina?'

'To us, *v'ar-l'n-ti-naa* means our-breath-stirs-the-field.'

This astonished Valentina.

'Where I was born,' she said, 'the fields stretched to the horizon, all around. I used to sit at my bedroom window watching the rippling patterns of the wind!'

'I'll bet not all of our names find interesting translations,' Keir said.

Mir'leor quivered and flickered pink and yellow patterns. 'One day, I will tell you what *b'ur-t'n* means!' he promised, effusing a deep, rhythmic belly-laughter. He coughed, having hyperventilated himself slightly in the oxygen-rich atmosphere.

'Are these coincidences meaningful?' Keir asked.

'We have to admit, we just don't know.' Mir'leor replied.

Keir wondered what other revelations were afoot, or whether it could be another strange trick played by Galena.

Perhaps both, he thought.

At the roadside, he watched as the ambulance crew went about their business, seemingly oblivious to the aliens.

'Perhaps it's fortunate that Max can't see the occupant on the opposite bunk,' Keir commented.

Part of the brown clothing would be visible, with the body mainly hidden by a green sheet which extended short of the pillow. Beside the bunk he saw a plastic container, like a large picnic box. Keir shuddered as the rear doors were closed. He watched as two of the gloved crew attended to the puncture with the car's spare wheel, while the other two replaced the windscreen. Then the crew left in their ambulance.

*****

11:47am, Oulu Base near Yli-Ii.

Keir awoke to find their car parked outside a long hut in a forest clearing. Valentina still slept soundly, curled up on the rear seat. The aliens had disappeared.

'Looks like we've arrived,' Keir nudged her gently.

They both yawned and stretched.

'You're right, Keir. They've pulled up outside Block 3A, the communications centre. Ilya is probably waiting for us.'

'Why didn't he send someone to the car to fetch us? We're both really knackered after that ordeal!'

'Don't know. We'd better get in there and find out. You see that door on the left? That's where we check in and confirm our IDs.'

Keir followed Valentina out of the car and shielded his eyes from the daylight glare. He hadn't appreciated how deeply tinted the car windows had been. The alien in the driving seat would have been almost invisible from the outside. But as he watched, the tint began to fade and within several seconds the windows appeared normal.

'Did you see that?' Keir whispered.

'Yes, I didn't know we had cars like that.'

Strange, Keir thought, as he pondered the seeming incompatibility of her remark with her position in Security. They passed through clearance without difficulty and entered the hut. Ilya came out into the corridor to greet them with one of his all-embracing bear hugs.

'Welcome back, Valentina! And Keir, it's your first time here, yes? This calls for something special.' Ilya said, producing his hip-flask with a flourish. 'And for you, Valentina, I have hidden away a bottle of best Finnish Koskenkorva. Come!'

'You roguish drunkard!' Valentina riled as Keir looked on in surprise. 'It's a good breakfast we need,' she continued, 'and with some decent coffee!' Then with a wink to Keir: 'Don't worry, we're like this all the time, you'll get used to it!'

Keir could not avoid a pang of jealousy at the obvious rapport between the pair, and hoped that his smile didn't appear too forced.

'Let's have a look at your hand, my dear!' Ilya grabbed Valentina's wrist in a most unmedical manner and scrutinised the wound. 'You'll live. In fact they've done a good job. Ar-y'naa, was it? Typical minimal scar effort. Does it still hurt?'

'I haven't noticed it at all since we woke up in the car.'

'She's an excellent micro-surgeon, isn't she? *Da*! Absolutely marvellous.' Ilya answered his own question, nodding with satisfaction.

As Ilya fetched their breakfasts from the dispenser, Keir voiced one of the many unanswered questions circulating in his mind.

'Ilya, did *you* deploy the two aliens to come for us?' he asked.

'Yes, I agreed to it following Mads' suggestion.'

'Mads?' Keir added another question to the growing list.

'Indeed. Mads arrived here yesterday from Denmark, with Rollo and two of your own colleagues.'

'Yes?'

'Burton and Smythe.'

Keir swallowed at the thought of Burton, from whom it seemed there is no escape. 'Is Lucien here?' he asked.

'Lucien and his family are all here. He and Burton will be joining us for lunch. Rowena Smythe and the others are busy; we'll see them perhaps this evening.'

'Have we time to take Keir around before lunch?' Valentina asked.

'I don't see why not, if you don't mind waiting for my shift to finish in one hour twenty five minutes from now. Things have been rather busy since the news in the media. I'm sorry I neglected to meet you at the car.'

Keir felt pleased about the site being named Oulu Base because he could pronounce *owe-loo* perfectly. His pronunciation of its precise location, nearer to Yli-Ii, usually evoked smiles. This he attributed to the same mysterious physiological problem which prevented him from articulating the French 'u' sound, the Finnish 'y' being approximately the same. In the far distance he noticed the UN flag over the gatehouse of the military training area, bringing back memories of his entrance to this VR world that had now become so much more real than his 2085 world. He switched his attention to the morning sunlight which cast dappled patterns as it slanted through the trees. The still air bore the subdued fragrance of the forest. *Regrettably, time to go back indoors,* he thought resignedly.

The party of five entered a large log cabin. Its functional structure, with square floor-plan, reminded Keir of a summer cottage. A double door opened onto the veranda and a stout exterior wooden ladder led to an upper balcony. They pulled up four chairs and Keir used the remaining stool as they arranged their places around a pine table in the largest of three ground floor rooms. They helped themselves from refreshments on a corner table, which bore a generous salad bowl and plates of various Finnish breads. Keir, quick to notice the portions of lightly smoked fresh salmon neatly wrapped in *rieska*, allowed his thoughts to drift back to the forest barbecue hosted by Lauri near Kuopio.

He remembered how the Finnish vodka had begun to cloud his vision of Valentina at the far end of the table, the firelight flickering on her face as she spoke inaudibly to her companions. Was it from that moment that he knew that he'd fallen in love with her? Or was it at the meteorite find, or even as far back as that first encounter in the throng at the Paris conference? *Anyway, it was certainly confirmed at the barbecue,* he thought.

'Keir!' As if in answer to prayer, Valentina stood beside him. 'I know you like these!'

He took the plate from her. 'Thank you, Valentina.'

Keir felt uneasy in the gathering and yearned that he and Valentina could be alone. But other matters, including an important unanswered question, competed for his attention.

*****

2:00pm.

'Well, we don't really need to introduce ourselves again, do we?' Ilya said, opening the briefing discussion. 'So now to business. In a few moments, you'll be joined here by Jukka Tanskanen, now the North European Co-ordinator for Project Electra. Don't worry about the present lack of space around the table. I won't be here for a while. I have to go and talk with Mads in my office near the Genetics Block. I'll meet you later at the four o'clock break and after that at the evening meal. You all have copies of the agenda sheet? I see that Brian and Lucien have. Here are a couple of spares. Keir and Valentina?' He passed one to each of them.

'We've never been called that before!' Valentina said.

Ilya smiled, but briefly; his underlying manner grave. He extracted the meeting's papers from his briefcase, checking each document curtly before laying it on the table. There were footsteps outside.

'Here is Professor Tanskanen,' Ilya announced. He made a round of formal introductions for protocol's sake and then picked up his briefcase.

'Over to you, Jukka,' Ilya said. He nodded politely and left.

Tanskanen looked around briefly at each member of the group in turn. Jukka Tanskanen's pale blue eyes dwelt on Lucien a little longer, the contrast between them striking. The new chairman stood incredibly tall. His immaculate suit, straight and well groomed blond hair with the clean shaven, almost boyish, complexion would have made him pass for a keen young business executive. But the thin-lipped square jaw and depth of his gaze told of other qualities.

Keir decided that Burton and Tanskanen were equally impassive. All the while, Burton had said very little, and seemed to have hardly noticed him. He'd smiled when meeting Valentina, but like Ilya's smile of a moment ago, it had vanished to give way to an even more sombre countenance than usual, as if beset with grim preoccupation. Keir glanced across at the open window. The tall trees stirred outside and faint cadences of birdsong filtered into the room. *It'll take more than that to cheer those two up*, Keir thought.

Meanwhile, Valentina doodled on her pad, waiting for something to happen. *After what she's been through, nothing much will bother her*, Keir mused. He stretched himself and leaned back. He'd forgotten that he sat on a stool and corrected his balance just in time.

'Oops!' Lucien said.

The event seemed to act as a trigger to the proceedings. Tanskanen tapped his pen on the table.

'This meeting is convened,' he began, directing his clipped voice to a microphone on his lapel, 'at fourteen ten hours, local time.' He went on to address the gathering:

'Academician Karpov is regrettably unable to be with us at this discussion. I'll try not to make it a monologue. Firstly, there's an obvious and serious *threat* to the human population of our planet. I take it we're all agreed?'

There were immediate murmurs of dissent in some quarters.

Keir continued keying his notes on his link-set:

T. Threat assertion taken for granted.

T. Surprised at responses. Trying not to show it.

Tanskanen believed that he betrayed no emotion as he listened.

'Are the aliens *really* a threat?' Burton asked. 'If advanced extra-terrestrials wanted to enslave us, they'd have done so long before now.'

'Surely these aliens are of our own making?' Lucien interrupted. 'Forgive me, Professor Tanskanen, please address Professor Burton's question first.'

'I will. Professor Burton, I didn't say the *aliens* are a threat. But we've seen how our peoples' reactions to them have had a de-stabilising influence, and it's the world's major powers that have experienced this the most. Some of the under-developed countries have felt that they had little to lose by these external disruptions, but in reality their economies are linked to those of the developed nations, particularly the super-powers. Sooner or later the developing nations must be affected. In the majority of these cases, measures have already been taken with skill and due consideration for their neighbours. But in a few cases things have gone differently. Opportunities have been taken to settle scores and create conflict, a situation exacerbated by the former impressions of weakness of the United Nations.'

'Thank you, Professor Tanskanen,' Burton smiled icily. 'But with respect, this is nothing new, is it? We've all been following the media commentaries and news updates.'

Tanskanen's pale steely gaze, unblinking beneath his blond eyebrows, turned to Lucien:

'And I realise, Professor Fournier, that you adhere strongly to the view that the aliens are products of our own genetic engineering experiments.'

'I'm always happy to consider alternatives, if there's sufficient evidence,' Lucien remarked. 'I mean real evidence. But to suppress information until there are inevitable leaks, rather than manage the situation from the beginning, can lead only to disaster!'

'Of course,' Tanskanen continued, 'we can't deny there's been much confusion associated with these unprecedented events. Meanwhile, it matters little whether the aliens are terrestrial or extra-terrestrial in origin. They are of superior intelligence and highly gifted in so many ways as to make them appear a subject of delight and fascination to some, but an overwhelming threat to others. Unfortunately, the latter group predominates and includes most of the world's general populace, its politicians and military leaders. That's why we're here, in this meeting. I want you all to drop your contemplation of the ultimate origins of these aliens for a moment and consider the known facts and how we should respond.'

Keir's scientific curiosity clamoured for an answer, and his experiences during the past twenty four hours had numbed any inhibitions.

'Excuse me, Professor Tanskanen,' Keir said, 'would you mind telling me just one thing before we proceed?'

'Go ahead, Mr. Wilson.'

'You just said "drop your contemplation". Does this mean that you already *know* the origins of the aliens?'

'I'm not prepared to give my views at this point in time,' he replied blandly.

'Come on, Jukka!' Burton almost sneered, 'It's a fair question. Are we in this thing together, or aren't we?'

Keir felt pleasantly surprised by Burton's act of support, but equally surprised to notice that Valentina looked cautious, almost uncomfortable.

'I really must ask you all to be patient,' Tanskanen remained unruffled. 'I promise you that the matter of origins will be dealt with more fully, but not now. It isn't my brief to discuss it, yet.'

'Thank you,' Keir said. *For nothing*, he thought. *Who did brief you then? Perhaps we need to find out.*

*****

269

19 The Oulu Connection

2:30pm Sunday 26 September. Oulu Base.

When helping to set up Oulu Base, Ilya had designed and procured materials for a desk of polished wood, its inlaid marquetry around the margin incorporating several flush keypad switches and indicator lights.

Normally, he would enjoy how the many neatly positioned items on its expansive surface were enhanced by reflection, like the buildings across the waters of the River Neva in St. Petersburg, or the ice floes near his childhood home in Arkhangelsk. His most ornate item, a rare traditional samovar crafted from hand beaten Russian silver, resided on a side table. He relished how the spangled light from its intricately curved and angled surfaces caught the eye from any part of the room. Opposite his gloves and cap, that he always kept at the far right corner of his desk, four portable workstations were stacked on the left far corner with their lids closed, like books; a fifth nearer to hand, its flip-up screen display replicated on a large wall-panel. Counterbalancing the electronic functionality of his office, Ilya's samovar had the assistance of several Chagall prints and a few well chosen items of traditional style furniture. To one side of the large picture window fitted with photochromic glass, he had a cluster of pleasantly arranged potted plants. As if celebrating its size and shape, the tallest of three cacti wore a crown of golden trumpet-shaped flowers.

On this occasion, celebration was far from Ilya's mind, in spite of the apparent breakthrough at Skagen. The recent plight of his colleagues at other UN Electra bases distressed him and far too many questions were unanswered. The heavy carpet muffled Ilya's boots as he paced his office. Mads sat at another small table, which had ornately carved legs. He sipped his tea nervously.

'A bit like old times, eh, Mads? Here I am, asking the questions again. I'd like to focus on several matters we mentioned in the Genetics Block a few minutes ago.'

Mads stiffened perceptibly.

Ilya continued: 'And this chat will be a little less formal than the one we had at Aarhus, but I do want answers.'

'I tell you, Major, I can't remember the details.'

'Listen!' Ilya moved closer. 'I got you off the military hook and brought you here to render service because of your expertise and technical ability. It may be difficult, time is running out, but if I really tried hard enough, I might be able to find someone else to fill that role. I'm sure that Commander Nielsen would be only too happy to look after you back in Frederikshavn.'

'There's no need to threaten me, Ilya, or Major Borodin, if you prefer! If I could remember, I'd tell you. I'm just as keen to see a resolution to this whole business as you are.'

Ilya paused to light a cigar. That morning, following an earlier tip-off from Rollo Swift, he'd contrived to have a pre-breakfast sauna and shower with Mads. He had needed to see for himself the missing umbilicus, and note any other peculiarities of Mads' anatomy.

'I had an operation when I was a child,' Mads had said, 'to remove a cyst.' But Ilya's additional training in the Medical Corps and the total absence of an operation scar told him otherwise. The similarity between Mads and the new arrival from Aalborg was no coincidence, he concluded.

'A resolution to the whole business is clearly beyond us at present.' Ilya seated himself in his swivel chair, taking another pull on his cigar. 'We nibble away here and there, don't we? Hoping for patterns to emerge.' He nodded in the direction of his computer. 'I admit, you did a very good data analysis job with Rollo, which led you to Harald.' Ilya paused to exhale a plume towards the ceiling. 'Yes, a remarkably good job. But as you can appreciate, it helps to know exactly who's who. And I intend to find out.'

'I know what you're thinking, but I don't see how Harald and I can have anything in common!' pleaded Mads.

Ilya extinguished his cigar with slow deliberation. He tapped a keypad on his desk and a drawer slid open. 'Have you heard of someone called Pieter Borg? I can see that you have. Perhaps you should read this, Mads. Then tell me what you think.' He handed Mads a pair of sheets from the drawer.

Mads had recognised the name of his school friend who had accompanied him on past joint expeditions to look for the sand-creatures. He read through Pieter's hand-written statement. It recounted with vividness and accuracy many episodes of their adventures together. But half way down the second page an alarming claim began to unfold:

'Mads had torn his shirt on the barbed wire, and his right arm was bleeding. The sand-creature came towards us and put out a long arm with tendril-like fingers. Anyway, when this arm gripped Mads' arm, Mads fell down and lay on the sand. I was terrified, but watched as the creature's fingers seemed to divide into lots of smaller fingers. Some of these tiny fingers entered the wound and then withdrew again after a short time. Perhaps ten or fifteen seconds. The bleeding stopped, and when Mads came round, the creature had shuffled away into the dunes. I climbed the nearest sand dune, which was quite high, but saw no sign of the sand-creature. Mads was rubbing his arm, but it was completely healed. By then, my memory of the event had been erased, but I did remember being worried about his torn shirt, his mother being rather strict. Mads got up, thinking he had simply fallen over. If it hadn't been for my car accident a few months afterwards, I'm sure I would never have recalled the details of the encounter. I kept it quiet because I now have a responsible position with the Danish government. I'm only telling you now because of current events and your position with the UN. But like I said, why don't you find Mads and ask him? He did tell me about his arm being healed by a sand-creature, but I had no memory of it at that time. He also told me that his belly-button was getting smaller and it eventually vanished. That would be about two to three weeks after the barbed wire incident. He never told his parents, and even went to the trouble of either painting one on his belly or using a plaster when we went swimming.'

'Well, Mads?' Ilya said, 'Surely you would connect this with the gathering pace of events, including Harald's arrival on the scene and then later, the micro-surgery performed on Valentina? But you've said very little indeed and I know you too well, you're not stupid. What else have you found out?'

'I can't say. I don't know.' Mads' eyes had a strange, fixed look. Ilya picked up his link-set.

'Frederikshavn? Hello Lisa. Is the Commander there, please?' There followed a brief pause.

'No, no! Please!' Mads alternately clenched and unclenched his hands several times and then gripped the sides of his chair. 'I'll tell you everything I know!' he blurted.

'Nothing urgent, Lars. I'd just like another status report from you at 16:00 hours. Thanks. Over and out.'

Ilya returned the set to his tunic and used his foot to activate a recorder from behind the desk. He leaned forward and checked he had extinguished his cigar in the ash tray, stirring the butt until all signs of combustion had ceased.

'Good man, Mads. I'm waiting,' he said.

*****

Back at the group meeting, 2:55pm.

As coffee appeared on their table, Keir and Valentina were pleasantly surprised to see another orderly bring in some more food. Someone else brought a stack of additional chairs.

Jukka Tanskanen announced the next item on the agenda; the completion of a fresh form which he handed out.

'You all have your illustrations of the aliens?' he asked. 'Please note there is only one illustration of the Type II alien, but we suspect there are variants, at least one of which can deploy whip-like tendrils. Check your papers and if you're still unclear about anything, then please ask me.'

Keir perused his copy. It contained two illustrations, one bore the caption, *Alien Type I* and showed a picture which could have been that of Mir'leor, or any of the aliens he he'd seen back at Andover. The second illustration, *Alien Type II* appeared humanoid in form, with a question mark above the picture. As Keir checked his answers, at least one of the questions still bothered him:

Have you at any time of your life been exposed to physical contact with a Type I alien? YES/NO: Type II alien YES/NO

He thought to answer NO to Type I, but hesitated. He'd slept during the car journey, so alien contact without his knowledge could have happened. He explained the matter to Tanskanen, eliciting the response:

'If you were asleep in their presence, you must play safe and put YES. And so should Valentina.'

The door opened as Ilya returned to the meeting: 'Sorry I'm a bit late,' he said.

Tanskanen's mask-like face nodded almost imperceptibly. 'Good afternoon, Ilya,' he said. And addressing the meeting:

'I've asked Ilya to explain more fully some of the matters already raised.' He arose and offered his chair to Ilya, handing him the top sheet of his writing pad.

'Thank you, Jukka', Ilya said as he sat down.

'I must leave you for the remainder of this meeting,' Tanskanen added, 'and shortly you will be joined by Dr. Kirsti Kivi and Mr. Rollo Swift, who are on their way over from R-15, the New Projects Laboratory. Rollo's main brief is to explain Project Icarus to you. Right, I'll leave you in Ilya's good hands.' As he opened the door to leave, Kirsti entered. She sat in a place next to that vacated by Tanskanen, who slipped out as if he hadn't noticed her, closing the door behind him.

'Welcome, Kirsti!' Ilya looked at her with a fleeting smile.

'Thank you!' she replied. 'Rollo will be here in a minute. He's been talking with Dr. Orville Bonar.'

'My friends,' Ilya said, 'you haven't yet met Dr. Bonar, except for Kirsti, who met him by chance on an incoming flight to Kuopio. He's an environmental engineer from Woods Hole in Massachusetts. Also, he had been a top gun fighter pilot.' He leaned across the table to whisper in Burton's ear: 'I wonder, Brian, if could you please fetch another chair for Rollo from the stack behind you? Thanks.'

'Of course!' Professor Burton tried to conceal his grimace at the thought of fetching a chair for a technician. As he placed it in position, Rollo entered.

'Oh, thanks Brian!' he said, jovially. Then he discerned the formal atmosphere of the meeting, became poker faced and winked at Keir, who responded in like manner.

Burton detected the communication and grimaced again.

'The meeting will now hear two discussion papers,' Ilya began, 'one by Dr. Kirsti Kivi and the other by Mr. Rollo Swift.' Ilya swept the assembled company with his glinting beady eyes. 'Time is short, so please reserve all questions until the end of each paper. Kirsti, please proceed.'

'Thank you Ilya.' Kirsti began by ignoring her notes and addressing her colleagues informally. 'You all know my lifelong interest in meteorites which I share with many of you. As a geologist, I've become acquainted with the work of many specialists, including the output of planetary scientists like Brian and astronomers like Lucien. The work of Ilya and Valentina has also widened my horizons and now Keir is beginning to contribute. And, not least, Rowena, our exobiologist who's helped me draw the threads together most conclusively regarding the question of alien origins. I've also had opportunity to discuss with Lucien the evidence he's uncovered surrounding the circumstances of some meteorite finds. While my recent studies of these matters progressed, culminating in my visit here to Oulu Base, two things became clear to me.'

Kirsti paused for a sip of water from a glass which Ilya had passed to her. She picked up her notes and continued:

'Firstly, there are undoubted traces of organic material in several meteorites from different reported finds, containing enough genetic information to allow scientists to incubate at least one type of alien life-form in the laboratory. Secondly, and this is the thrust of my argument, we must accept that the alien life-form which has become known to us as the "Type I alien" has little or nothing to do with meteorites.'

'What? Surely the evidence must be overwhelming!' cried Burton. The meeting became turbulent as members began to exchange comments.

'Please, everyone!' Ilya's voice boomed, 'Let's have order. We'll all get a chance to talk later. Please continue, Kirsti.'

'The last assertion I will deal with first. It stems not only from my close reading of the scientific evidence, but also from a bulletin released by the United Nations as an act of openness in the face of the present difficulties. This information is being released gradually and selectively. Along with two surviving sister bases, in Australia and the Canadian Rockies, we are the first to be informed.'

Kirsti paused to let additional murmurs subside. She glanced at Ilya and continued: 'The full document is available through Jukka Tanskanen, but I'll give you an outline of the main points. Here we go: One of the initial aims of the Project, in its pre-Electra period, was to promulgate the idea that the aliens were from outer space, so as to direct attention away from experiments which were being conducted in several, mainly military and commercial, establishments around the world. This network of bases had been at work for several years in the quest to synthesise a specialised life-form, using genetic engineering methods. The intention was to produce a life-form that would be super-intelligent and be tailored to work as an interface between humans and advanced computer systems. The Pandora networks are recent examples of this involvement. Computer scientists were rapidly losing track of how their computers worked and self-evolved. Particularly, they needed some linked entity which could not only help them monitor what was happening, but contribute to raw computing power. As I speak, these computers are becoming totally reliant on the intervention of alien intelligence and their pattern recognition capability.'

Burton leaned forward, saying: 'Surely this isn't the right place to discuss this matter.'

'Order!' said Ilya. 'Kirsti, please.' He gestured her to continue.

'Thank you,' Kirsti said. 'To placate the objectors, the official reason given was that this was a temporary but effective short cut to the understanding and development of advanced computers, many of which were already saving human lives, until the day came when such systems could again be built entirely from inanimate materials. But secretly, the participating governments assigned the job to the military, on the understanding that the information and accruing benefits would be shared between the experimental bases of each country. A secret co-ordinated military project would also take care of security problems.'

'You mean it's now official that these aliens are not from space at all?' asked Burton. Meanwhile, Lucien stroked his beard thoughtfully. Keir studied Valentina's face, trying to appear unobtrusive. Her placid smile didn't inform him.

She knows more than she admits, he thought.

'Please!' Ilya called the meeting to order. 'Kirsti, could you draw your contribution to a conclusion?'

'Very well. Historically, 'Kirsti continued, 'the early experiments at alien creation ran into difficulties. Several governments were on the verge of agreeing to de-commission the work, when suddenly there was a remarkable breakthrough. A group in France had produced not just a proto-being, but a complete, sentient life-form. It was indeed intelligent, but had other attributes in addition to those in the original specification. Extreme manual dexterity, for example. Information was shared between the bases, followed by a number of alien nurturing compounds being set up.'

'Where did you get all this from? What report?' asked Burton.

'Brian, please!' Ilya admonished.

Kirsti took another drink of water, pausing deliberately to allow her information to be assimilated. The meeting became silently expectant.

'The aliens, as we know,' Kirsti went on, 'had a high capacity for intercommunication between themselves, flourished better, and were more productive, if allowed to continue in their own kind of social environment. But they continued to co-operate in the development of computer systems, often adding innovations of their own. The formation of alien communes continued, but the arrival of so many aliens on the scene, at secret bases, was unlikely to remain secret for long. It could not be admitted that these aliens were produced by banned experiments. So, as Lucien has already foreseen, it was the project organisers who orchestrated and promoted the "aliens from space" idea. Indeed, the aliens themselves didn't deny it, but were happy to leave the handling of administration and publicity to human military and commerce, which had the resources to bring the work to fruition.'

'That's deception on a grand scale!' Keir could no longer restrain himself. Ilya eyed the ceiling in resignation.

'And besides,' Rowena joined in, 'you'd need far more than DNA to produce, let alone design, an organism of such complexity. This would require a *lot* of industrial and academic collaboration! Sorry Kirsti, I'm messing you about.'

'No problem, I don't really mind being interrupted,' Kirsti said.

Ilya buried his head in his hands and then looked up abruptly with a broad smile. 'Very well, my friends, if you prefer it that way. But I think our question time at the end will have to wait until *after* the meeting, OK? *Please* can you conclude, Kirsti?'

'Thank you, Ilya. The UN document goes on to describe the elaborate concoction and planting of false evidence to support the "meteorites" line of explanation. This failed to convince some of the scientific community. In fact, a few of the more outspoken ones did disappear under questionable circumstances, and we are indeed fortunate that Lucien has survived to be with us. In fact, we also have two other survivors present.'

'You mean, Valentina and myself?' Keir asked. 'But we didn't make any public statements about the aliens, one way or the other!

'For the past twelve months,' Kirsti continued,' Valentina has spearheaded the investigation, which was under way in Northern Europe even before Project Electra was underpinned by the Secretary General. Indeed, UN adoption of the project was a consequence of her initial findings. Valentina was forbidden to tell this to anybody, and her name does not appear in the document, but she and Ilya have given me permission to tell you this now.'

'That is so,' Ilya said. 'Perhaps on this point I should update the meeting formally. As Kirsti says, we are aware of the recent ordeal suffered by our delegates, Valentina and Keir. I won't upset them by reiterating the details here, but one consequence is that Valentina will be called to give evidence at the forthcoming trial of the assailant known as Max. As things turned out, Keir was also at risk because he was believed mistakenly to be a high level operative in the UN investigation. He, too, will be called upon to give evidence.'

'Surely, that could expose them to more danger?' Lucien asked.

'That may be so,' Ilya said. 'A regrettable consequence of the democratic process. But the tightest security will be maintained up to and during the period of the trial.'

'And for the rest of our lives, we hope!' Keir said, with concern for Valentina as much as for himself.

'We'll do all we can for both of you, be assured of that,' Ilya said. 'Now, Kirsti. Will one more minute be sufficient?'

'I think so. I finish with a brief reference to the first point I made, about the actual contents of the meteorite fragments. The DNA material was implanted deliberately and was made to look convincing by clever manipulation of the physical and chemical constitution of the rock itself. About a quarter of the total effort was put into making these forgeries, providing them with plausible histories and arranging the so-called finds. This was a calculated and deliberate falsification of scientific evidence.' Kirsti's voice broke with emotion. 'It has put my field of study and that of my colleagues into disrepute. How can any *serious* investigation of organic materials in meteorites attract researchers now, let alone be funded?' Kirsti asked, close to tears.

'Thank you, Kirsti,' said Ilya. 'That was well done and so very brave of you. Technically, we've run out of time for questions, but I'll allow just one. The rest will have to be put on hold until after the meeting. Yes, Professor Burton?'

'Regarding the meteorite tampering allegations,' Burton said, 'Kirsti, I don't think you have anything to worry about. That's all they are, allegations. Nobody to my knowledge has found any physical evidence whatsoever for meteorite tampering. If they have, where is it taking place? Before we entertain that idea seriously, there has to be indisputable evidence based on experiment that can be replicated in the public domain. Or it's not science!' He looked around the table. 'With respect, judging by what has been said today, I can be forgiven for believing I'm the only scientist present.' As a gesture of finality, he brought his fist down on the papers before him.

'Thank you, Brian. I'm sure the next and final item is going to be extremely interesting for all of us,' Ilya announced, 'including those of an experimental disposition. Please proceed, Rollo.'

'Good afternoon, everybody!' Rollo said, his voice refreshingly jaunty. I'm Rollo Swift, employed as chief technician at a well known university department in Manchester. But at the end of this month I'll have served my notice, including some holiday days owing, I'm glad to say, which happen to tie in with my business in Scandinavia. The reason is, I no longer need that occupation as a cover. For eight years I've been working on another project which has had nothing to do with Project Electra, that is, until now. By the way, forgive my elation. I'm unashamedly happy because the news is through that my father has recovered totally from a brain tumour. It was cured with a little bit of help from genetic engineering and aliens working with the Pandora computer. Just thought I'd mention it.'

'*Formidable, mon ami*!' Lucien shouted, clapping his hands gleefully. Everyone, including Burton, joined in the applause.

'Thank you, thank you. Anyway, to proceed. The eight year old other job was, and still is, being Technical Co-ordinator for Project Icarus. We are involved, along with many other scientists and technicians around the world, addressing what has become known as "The Transport Problem". In a nutshell, if you look back at our methods of propulsion over the past hundred years or so, not much has changed. Even before then, the Chinese had invented rockets. This project isn't concerned specifically with rockets, but it is concerned with space travel, at least, implicitly. Our basic problem is still how to get from A to B with maximum speed and efficiency and minimum inconvenience and pollution.

'We already know about that! Why is this project so secret?' Burton asked.

'Really, Brian!' Ilya said. Please let Rollo continue.'

'It's OK,' Rollo said. 'I'll answer that. Because, well, put it this way: We've seen that during Project Electra, and the pre-Electra period, there were political and commercial problems. In the renewable energy field, too, we have met resistance. No doubt because there's still a lot of investment in the old technology. And I share the belief with others that some of its guardians are not very scrupulous. But to the main point. Project Icarus has been subsumed under Project Electra, and now enjoys United Nations benefits and protection. This upsurge of interest by the UN was prompted by a survey it carried out on all aspects of the work, including documentation of UFO reports world-wide, which until then were held by the governments of the various nations and, on the whole, were not taken very seriously.'

'What's the connection with the aliens, Rollo?' Keir asked. Ilya leaned back and splayed his arms.

Rollo continued: 'The connection is one of problem solving, pure and simple. We're all aware that the Type I aliens have been responsible for an unprecedented surge in computer power and the ability to solve problems through pattern recognition and analysis as well as brute numerical computation. In Project Icarus, the UN has helped by suggesting we feed the Pandora network with all the UFO reports they could find, including imagery. In response, Pandora, with help from the aliens, has come up with three stationary solutions to the formerly incomplete Guriev variation of Einstein's field equations!'

Rollo paused to allow those with backgrounds in theoretical physics and quantum electrodynamics to appreciate the import of what he'd said.

'What's the significance of that? Please spell it out, we're not all theoretical physicists, Rollo!' Keir said, adhering to his 2010 identity. He recalled that in his 2085 world Guriev's equations still remained incomplete.

'OK,' Rollo said, 'Some of us may have read a letter from a researcher at the Technical University in Prague to the journal

Nature, back in the 1990s, where she'd had a go at working out the three missing terms of Guriev's incomplete equations. She didn't succeed entirely, but got far enough to demonstrate that if this is ever achieved, there's a good prospect that gravity could actually be used to repel as well as attract objects. Then a Czech team gave us the real-world solutions using Pandora. That Czech team now works at Electra's Bystřice Base near Prague, which has, even today, about twenty seven aliens on-site. Anyway, their triumphal theoretical achievement spawned a lot of experimental research under the Project Icarus umbrella, spurred on by the idea that it's only a matter of time before a so-called anti-gravity ship could be built. It's because Projects Electra and Icarus are combined that I can tell you this.

'You're saying the aliens are involved in this process?' Keir asked.

'Yes.'

'Is this experimental work only happening in the Czech Republic?' asked Kirsti.

'Are the Oulu aliens involved?' asked Lucien.

At this point, Ilya stepped in. 'I think these questions will be resolved very shortly,' he said. 'Any minute now, in fact. Thank you, Rollo.'

Rollo stopped talking and glanced expectantly at his watch. At that very moment, a loudspeaker above the door sprang into life: *'Nyt rakennus kymmentä-viisi hyvin on.* Building 15 is now ready,' a crisp but pleasant female voice announced, repeating the message in Swedish, Russian, English, German and French.

*****

3:45pm.

'Right! Let's stretch our legs, my friends,' Ilya suggested, sweeping his papers into a well worn black briefcase. Apart from Valentina, he was the last to leave the log cabin. He turned to her wearily: 'I don't know whether they can take any more. Look at them!'

'I know, Ilya. And after R-15 there's still Mads' report! Has he finished it yet?' she asked.

'I left him writing it. I think he'd be too nervous giving a verbal delivery, so I'll scan it for them to read copies in the bar after the evening meal.'

'The bar?'

'Yes, it's quite secure, Ilya replied, 'Everyone on this site is triple-alpha vetted. The humans, that is.' Then he raised his voice for the benefit of the others as they approached the larger group assembled outside R-15, 'Are we all ready? Then follow me.'

They entered the building; an enormous cube, painted white with a horizontal row of rectangular windows about three metres above ground level on each side. Keir recalled the large hangar back at Andover where he had first encountered the Type I aliens. He wondered what had become of them, whether any had survived the riots. Certainly the two who'd rescued him and Valentina here in Finland from the now captive Max were indelibly impressed on his mind. He felt a comradeship, almost a kinship, with them.

'Keir,' Valentina said. She gripped his arm. 'Forgive me saying this, but the patch under your eye.'

'Oh! My small birthmark. I never really give it much thought.'

'Well, you ought to, I think.'

'Why?'

'It's almost disappeared.'

'Perhaps less sunlight?'

'Yes, perhaps.'

They were now at the end of a ramp and waiting for a green light above a side-door to signal their next move. Meanwhile, a steady drone of machinery thankfully prevented their whispered conversation being overheard.

'Keir?' Valentina continued.

'Yes.'

'You know this business of Harald and Mads?'

'Hmm?'

'Well, my navel, belly button, is starting to disappear as well.'

Keir froze. He knew about Mads, and about Harald, the chrysalis man from the beach. *The micro-surgery on her hand*, he thought. *They'd better not have done anything else to her*!

His expression must have alarmed Valentina. She stared into his face.

'Keir, your birthmark has returned! Before, it must have been the effect of the striplighting.'

'Or perhaps how I was thinking!'

'How do you mean?'

He slipped his hand into his shirt.

'OK, no problems. I was just checking out my own anatomy. Listen. It's just a hunch...'

The green light showed, and they moved forward through the steel door.

'Yes?' Valentina hung on his words.

'Try saying no. Like, "No! I don't want to be an alien, I want to stay human!" Keep at it and really mean it. See what happens. OK?'

She looked at him quizzically. 'You know, I hadn't realised it before, but I find that a very difficult thought to hold in my head!'

Keir felt a tightness in his throat. He sucked his breath through clenched teeth, hardly aware of the humming which grew louder as they shuffled along a further corridor.

He turned to her.

'Please, Valentina! This isn't just because we're companions in adversity. I really care about you, and I don't want you to become an alien! Don't let them do it!'

He hadn't intended to play such a high card and momentarily wavered. But to his overwhelming relief and satisfaction, she placed her hand in his and squeezed gently.

Looking up at him, she declared, 'I'll do as you say, Keir. I'll do it for you. And...'

'Yes?'

Her head brushed against his shoulder as they approached the brightly lit chamber ahead of them. She turned to look at him again.

'Thank you, Keir,' she said.

Suddenly, a familiar voice whispered as its owner's head came between them: 'Come on, you two love-birds,' Ilya said, grinning from ear to ear. 'Watch where you're going or you'll be tripping over the aluminium tread-plate step at the chamber entrance.'

On reaching a wide opening, the party stopped, awaiting further guidance from Ilya. Instead, there came an announcement from within the chamber itself. '*Would the visitors' party please move clockwise around the periphery and take up their seats in the north-west quadrant?*'

'That's us - follow me,' said Ilya.

The centre of the chamber glowed so brightly that the party could hardly see its contents. They sat, averting their eyes from the acid glare. A smell of ozone and metal, as if from electric welding rigs, filled the air. There followed a dull rumbling noise and as they looked upwards, the chamber roof began sliding back in two halves, in north-south directions. The slit of sky grew until it became a rectangle and then a square. It stopped at full aperture and the brightness of the interior competed with the sky. The white incandescent glow from the centre of the floor suddenly acquired radiating electric blue striations, for those who could bear to watch.

'The safety goggles!' Ilya shouted. 'They're tucked beneath the left side of your seats.'

'Now he tells us,' Burton said. 'We should have been told about these at the door.'

Another announcement: *'We apologise for the excessive corona discharge and the resulting light intensity. You will find anti-glare goggles...'*

'Under the left side of your seats!' several of the audience chorused, imitating the announcer amid some laughter. Even with the goggles on, the light dazzled. Suddenly the glow faded and the background hum diminished, then stopped. The central floor of the huge amphitheatre appeared flat, circular and metallic with a triangular groove inscribed in its surface.

At cinemas, Burton almost always left early before the credits. He listened for the closing announcement. Silence.

'That's it, then!' Burton muttered. 'The show's over.' He got up and neighbouring people stood to let him pass.

'Ten seconds to launch. Eight, seven ...' the countdown began.

'Prat!' someone behind him said.

Burton sat down again, visibly flushed.'

'Three, two, one, zero.'

Keir felt a gentle swish as the surrounding air mass rolled inwards to occupy the space left by the vacating craft, which fell silently upwards, slowly at first and then through the roof aperture, accelerating towards the distant cloud base until it became a triangular speck. Just below the clouds, it glowed momentarily and accelerated sideways. It moved in an easterly direction and quickly vanished out of sight, its remaining trajectory hidden from view by the hangar walls. The floor now appeared deeply hollowed out, as if by a missing smooth triangular slab. The spell-bound party felt jolted back to Earth by the loudspeakers:

'Kiitoksia paljon. Thank you very much for coming. We hope you have enjoyed watching the forty-fourth launch of anti-gravity craft Sirius-one. Please make your way to Apron B where you will be de-briefed. Hope to see you again. Näkemiin.'

*****

20 Katya

Oulu Base 3:06pm.

On Apron B, a concrete quadrangle situated between R-15 and a car-park area on the north side of the site, Keir and Valentina followed the others out into the daylight.

Keir noticed a second party arriving, among whom he recognised a familiar face.

'Alan!' he shouted, 'Hi! Great to see you. What's your business up here?'

'Well, hello again, Keir. And you, too, Valentina. The answer to your question, Keir, is *you*. I'm here in my capacity as your official UN-appointed guardian. I've taken over from Rowena. So, if you've a mind to, laddie, you can unwind and tell me what you've been through so far. I've read enough of the reports not to ask too many silly questions, but if there are particular things that I could help you with, let me know, anytime.'

'That's very good of you, Alan. I should really be getting my thesis submitted, I know. But there are some files I can't access because they're on memory sticks back at the university.'

'Aha! Don't worry, I've brought everything. You'd better check, but I think you'll find it all here. I'm glad to see you haven't mentioned anything biological rather than geological in your manuscript.' Alan pulled from his pocket a small flat package.

'Thanks. Are you joining us for the dinner?' Keir asked.

'You bet. I hope they've got some decent booze up here.'

'Not bad. I think we're about to be de-briefed, or something. Have you ever been in there?' Keir nodded in the direction of R-15.

'I've been staying in an apartment on the Linnanmaa Campus at Oulu University, and only arrived at this place an hour ago. I bumped into Mads, and they introduced me to Harald, the ex-sand-being or whatever. Interesting looking guy, isn't he? They've got him strapped up to a workstation and they're putting him through a hefty education programme, poor wee bastard!'

'He's not so wee, Alan. He's nearly seven feet tall!'

'Quite! But to answer your question, yes! Were *you* in there when I saw that triangle thing take off through the roof of that building?' Alan asked. 'Looks like it's all happening. Eh, Kier?'

'In Building fifteen. Yes.'

'I heard the startup. Dead quiet in flight, though. Am I mistaken, or was there no exhaust emission?'

'No exhaust, Alan. It was anti-gravity driven.'

'What next, I wonder? This promises to be an interesting visit.'

*****

Ilya stood apart from the group and began to address them for the de-briefing.

'Well, my friends. Ah, hello Alan! Glad you've joined us. That was a typical launch you all saw. One of the practical consequences of solving the Einstein-Guriev equations!'

'Even more entertaining,' interrupted Burton, 'if we'd all been blinded, roasted alive or blasted through the hangar walls! The standard of safety was abysmal!'

'You're quite right to be concerned about safety, Brian,' Ilya said. 'In fact, it's for safety reasons that the laboratory and launch sections in R-15 are usually closed to visitors. What you saw was not a test station, but a terminal. The Sirius-1 ship is no more dangerous than a light aircraft or a bus, except for the occasional electrical discharge, for which we do apologise. Most of the light emission we saw was from a luminescent phosphor coating on the hull, which glows brightly, like a strip light, when there is electrical activity. It serves as a warning to keep clear when the energy build-up occurs just before take-off. You will also have noticed the glow appear when the ship changed direction. The same thing happens when hovering and on landing.'

'Was the ship first developed here?' Keir asked.

'Not initially,' Ilya said, lighting a cigar, 'With the assistance of the aliens and Pandora, it took Renata Kordik's team near Prague two months from completing the first viable solutions of the field equations and going all out for a gravity ship design. The propulsion unit took three days, and nights. And another two days gave them the guidance system and hull structure. In the process, Pandora had acquired another ninety six new re-usable soft-architecture units in its resource library. Modelling and flight-simulating a fully fledged anti-grav ship took a further fourteen days.'

'What about prototype construction?' Keir asked.

'About eight months. Then two others were built. One in Australia and one in Karelia, the latter being delivered here three months ago.'

'Is the next ship being built?' Keir asked.

'Talk to Rollo!' Ilya suggested.

'The initial consignments of materials for the second ship arrived in Karelia a few weeks ago,' Rollo explained afterwards, while alone with Keir over a glass of beer in a secluded corner of the main bar. 'Construction is on schedule. Security is still triple alpha, of course. If word got out, the oil markets would take even more of a hammering than they have already.'

'Won't these craft be spotted flying around?' Keir asked.

'At the moment, it doesn't matter,' Rollo said, 'being so few in number they'd be "just another UFO", wouldn't they?'

'A bit optimistic! If they fly very high in small numbers, I suppose that's feasible. Can they change shape? Stealth geometry and all that stuff?'

'I think I'm allowed to say, that's one of the next projects,' Rollo said. 'And of course, the UN's taken over most of the UFO files and investigations.'

*****

_8:00pm._

Thirty five gathered for the dinner that evening, including the guest of honour, Professor Jukka Tanskanen. He delivered a lively and witty after-dinner speech, much to the amazement of Ilya's party. Afterwards, in the lounge, the guests sat in comfort with their coffee and mints. Keir pulled out his copy of Mads' report and started reading it through for the fourth time.

'Don't be too pre-occupied with it now, Keir.' Valentina chided gently.

'If you don't stop nagging me, I'll kiss you, in public.'

'Nag, nag, nag!' she said with a defiant grin.

'I'll let you off. Anyway, I must check this through again.' He resumed his reading.

'I'm most disappointed! You're stubborn. Just like Alex. I'm sorry, Keir. You didn't mind me saying that?'

'Alexandr? I'm honoured to be compared with someone of your choice. A little jealous, perhaps.'

'Thank you. You choose your words well, Keir. Anyway, I'd better let you finish your reading. I'll catch a cat-nap. I'm so tired.' Almost immediately, Valentina fell asleep in the chair.

Keir's copy of the report began with a short pre-amble which had probably been dictated by Ilya; the main content being put together in Mads' more amateurish fashion.

Report by Mads Erik Gade, assignee to Oulu Base.
Ref. OB-D060422-N13/MG 23/09/2010

My name is Mads Erik Gade, age 23 years. Lance Corporal in the Danish Army. Number 0100345823. I was assigned to OB by Major Borodin of the Russian Command, UN North European Deployment, with the sanction of the Finnish Command, represented by General Aho-Koivisto.

I took part in an excavation (detailed in 3X-06R-DK-1) at Skagen of a chrysalis later diagnosed as that of a 'sand-creature' alien (type I). Later, when I got double alpha clearance, Dr. Rowena Smythe told me that the creature would emerge as an alien Type 2. Those aliens can have a variety of possible forms, depending on gene switching. This one was a hominid. The hominid enclosed had no umbilicus. This surprised me because I have none either. My umbilicus first disappeared when I was 14 years old, soon after I had an encounter with a sand-creature at close range. I now remember that I was scratched on fence wire and the healing of my scratch was done by the alien. After this, I had strong feelings towards the aliens and my umbilicus disappeared as I said. Recently, my friend wrote a report for the Project Electra authorities.

Keir poured himself some of the remaining coffee.

The chrysalis we found at Skagen was so much like me that I got frightened, but I wanted to find out more, so I contacted an alien in the compound area at OB. This alien had returned from a mission with Keir Willson and Dr. Valentina Gazetny.

He smiled at his mis-spelled name, drained his cup and carried on.

This alien's name was Milyor. He talked with me for about half an hour yesterday (21 Sept) while I was on lunch break. He was the one who told me that the chrysalis stage was for easier transfer between body types and involved gene switching. But you may loose a lot of your memories, though not usually your other mental abilities, so you could be re-educated. The transfer to human form is an adaptation for human environment. And the sand-creatures are partly adapted already. This ability to transfer / transform through a chrysalis stage can be induced by what Dr. Smythe calls 'invoked trigger responses' mainly from body contact with aliens (Type 1 or 2). Humans can also be infected, even by accident, but more likely because some of the tiny finger extensions of Type I aliens are like fine hypodermic needles and can puncture our skin without us feeling it.

Keir recalled the invasive micro-surgery carried out first on Max and then on Valentina and possibly himself.

He warned me the first sign of infection is that any imperfect tissues, like scars, disappear. That includes the umbilicus, too, and I got round to telling him I had lost mine. He said it did not mean I would become an alien, only if I wanted to. They can enter their chrysalis stage by will, from either direction. Sometimes when they are depressed or not satisfied with life it comes on spontaneously and they need to be counselled or have their own special drug therapy to reverse the process. He said if humans return back again from chrysalis stages most of their imperfections will not return. It can be a good way of healing your body if you do not mind a long wait and being re-educated afterwards. He thought that was funny and laughed and said the main difficulty was, when you became an alien you may forget that your intention was to transfer back again, and also you may forget why you did it when you've transferred back, unless you left a note with somebody! That is also true when starting off as an alien as well.

As Keir scanned the rambling account, he wondered about the possibility of an antidote, which he'd follow up in the morning. As he read further, the text gripped him once again:

Mil-yor also said that he was encouraged by the joint progress being made with humans and their computers. He was worried about some things, though. First, there were too many aliens. When they had first formed colonies, the population was very low and limited to a few remote places, but adaptation to our environment caused sterility and they had to breed by proxy. They used human genetic information to enable transfer by chrysalis into human form. As humans, or humanoids, they reproduced, and then transferred their children at adolescence back to the original Type 1 alien form - Y'raav he calls it. This caused problems because it violated their principle of non-interference with native species and was stopped. The Y'raav then sent some of their humanoid versions among the human population of the technologically developing nations and they reported back. After many years of frustration they discovered the genetic experimental programme and made a thorough investigation. Their council decided, "If the indigenous Earth people are going to create life-forms for interaction with computers and to amplify their intelligence, then why not let them use our genetic material?" It seemed a convenient solution to their problem, and would hide the true origin of the Y'raav species. From then on it was easy. They planted their own genetic material in some of the laboratories and just waited. It worked, though most of the early Y'raav produced were throw-backs to their environmentally unadapted state. But this was soon overcome, with outside help from human agents and now you see the outcome. Too many of us, he said. It has caused chaos on your planet. He was very sorry and promised stricter rules.

Well, that's it. I tried to ask about a permanent cure for the effects of the aliens, but couldn't get anywhere.

'Tried to ask?' Keir said aloud. 'He doesn't say he *actually* asked.' He lowered his voice. 'I suspect he had a mental block. Well, I won't have one, I assure you, Mir'leor, my old friend! And why did the council refer to us as native species? What does that say about the aliens, Val?'

'Uh? *Mikä se on?* What's that?' Valentina stirred.

'Sorry! Just thinking aloud. I vote we pack it in and get some proper sleep.'

'S'fine,' she said drowsily. Keir pulled her to her feet and she rocked unsteadily, letting out a yawn which turned several heads. As if prompted, a few others got up to leave and followed them outside into the cool night.

*****

9:15am Monday 27 September.

After breakfast, Keir went alone to the alien enclosure. The area consisted of several low buildings containing suites of well appointed rooms. He pressed the main intercom button, waiting for a prompt.

'Keir Wilson for Mir'leor, please.'

'Proceed to avenue 3, block 2, number 14,' a quiet voice directed.

The alien hailed him from a short distance and made no attempt at physical contact. Mir'leor ushered Keir into a pleasantly furnished lounge with two comfortable armchairs and almost over-run with potted plants.

'Welcome! Please sit down, Keir. I'd offer you a drink, but the delivery is a bit late this morning. And as you know, we don't keep alcohol. There is water, of course.'

'No. Thanks anyway, Mir'leor. How are you being treated?'

'Very well, thank you. I wish the planet was in better shape, though. I spoke to your friend Mads the other day, and felt he wanted to ask a few more questions, but he had to return.'

'I believe there is some unfinished business, and that's what I've come about.'

'Yes?'

Keir felt a resistance building in his mind. He switched his thoughts to Valentina. She looked into his face. "*I love you.*" His heart leapt towards her and the resistance vanished.

'I've come to ask you for a permanent antidote to the infection. You know what I mean. Some of us have this thing in our blood which causes changes which pull us in the direction of your species. If we don't want the chrysalis option, how can we get rid of it, completely?'

'Your official Ilya has already asked this, and I'm surprised that you haven't gone to him about it, or that he hasn't announced it yet. I suppose like us you have your official protocols, approved medical trials and all that sort of thing. But as you've come directly, I'll be pleased to tell you.'

'Thank you, I'm listening.' Keir sat unflinching, still concentrating on Valentina's image in case his hearing became impaired by some unknown but reflex action.

'Yes, don't worry. The resistance you detect is not of my making. It is not what you call telepathic. It's a consequence of the genetic programming. It modifies your survival instincts to embrace the transformation process. But that can be changed by destroying the carrier. Now the carrier is a protein, rather like a retro-virus. It has some linkages which are vulnerable to attack by the right molecules. Your friend Rowena is coming to see me later today. She will enjoy hearing the details and relaying them to you.'

Keir's patience began to show signs of strain.

'Of course, I'm sorry!' Mir'leor continued. 'Back to business. Do you like what your people call "rhubarb"?'

'Eh? Er, rhubarb crumble's great. Please go on.'

'The protein is easily disabled by traces of oxalic acid. It is known as a very toxic substance to both humans and our species, but the inter-species conversion process can be eliminated totally by the very low levels of oxalic acid found in the stems of your rhubarb plant. But you must take your medication regularly for about two weeks.'

'Thanks. What's the dosage?'

'I would say that a single quarter kilogram canister of rhubarb per day for adult humans should be more than adequate.'

'One can a day for two weeks?'

'That's what I said. You may take it in any manner, including your crumble if you wish.'

'Thanks. We'll give it a try.'

'I owe you an apology. Ar'y-naa does anyway.'

'How is that?'

'While you were in the car, she investigated what you call your birthmark, mistakenly thinking it was a wound. There is a slight risk of infection with all micro-surgery we perform. But in the past, you see, our few human subjects have always known about the remedies.'

'In the past?'

'Yes. Has Mads not told you about our history on this planet?'

'Ah, yes. Not very detailed, though. He wrote a report for Ilya of his discussion with you. Why didn't you explain to him about the antidote?'

'He did not ask explicitly for a cure.'

'But you could have offered him the information.' Keir was beginning to feel like a high-wire artist. He could do without unpleasantness. It might put everyone in jeopardy.

'You really must understand, Keir. We have interfered enough with the dominant species on this planet. We can only act upon direct requests made by victims, like your request. Then you may freely pass the information to all members of your species. That is your responsibility, no longer ours.'

Keir didn't quite agree with the alien's logic but accepted the position.

'Thanks again, Mir'leor. There are many other things I'd like to ask, but I have time for only one, if that's OK with you.'

'Please ask.'

'It's a very basic question. Where do your people come from? I mean, what *are* your origins?'

'I am not authorised - if that is the word - to say. But I can tell you that you have sufficient clues already.'

'Yes, conflicting ones! And authorised by whom?'

'You said one question. You will eventually know all the answers. Meanwhile, let the rhubarb remedy suffice for now. It has been good to see you, Keir. I wish you and your mate well.'

*****

11:05am.

Valentina met Keir as he returned to the party's hostel accommodation.

'Hi! Been anywhere special?' she asked.

'Yes, Val. Are you any good at cooking?'

'Is that a proposal?'

Keir's thoughts were stopped in their tracks. He felt stunned, but he must not show it. For days, even weeks, his imagination had catalogued dozens of possible venues and opportunities when he might ask the key question. But could it be a signal from her, even a subconscious one? If he laughed it off, she may never take the matter seriously again. If he said "Yes" it might seem utterly banal and inappropriate. If he remained silent, it would simply be rudeness. *Is there a fourth way out?* He decided to concentrate on their immediate problems.

'Look! I was on my way to see you.' His hand grasped her elbow. 'This infection you have has to be got rid of. I couldn't bear it if anything happened to you!' He told her the truth and had her rapt attention.

'I'm still doing what you suggested, Keir,' she said.

'Well, I've been to Mir'leor to find a permanent cure.' He told her in detail about his visit, including his experienced resistance and its explanation; also the technicalities behind the rhubarb cure.

'Who would have thought that the remedy is so simple?' Valentina said, astonished. 'You're quite sure it's ordinary rhubarb? From the garden or shops?'

'Absolutely. And Valentina, will you marry me?'

'Keir?' Her voice wavered and rose again in an unusual cadence.

'A few moments ago, you said, "Is that a proposal?" Well, this is! I've been bottling it up for ages. I mean, when we get out of all this and I find a steady job.'

She put a finger to his lips. 'Don't make it sound so mundane, Keir!' she whispered. 'But listen, I am honoured that you have asked me. And please don't misunderstand me, but there is another factor.'

Keir felt a dark chasm of apprehension filling his mind and the blood drained from his face. Valentina looked at him. She could see how troubled he felt.

'Look,' she said decisively, 'we know we can speak to each other directly. Please listen, Keir. No, I will no longer just talk. Now is the time to *show* you!'

'What do you mean, Valentina?' he croaked. 'I just don't know what you mean. If there's someone else...'

'There *is* someone else, and that is the reason I need to show you. Look over there. See that building?'

Obediently, Keir looked. 'Building R-9?'

'That's the one.'

'It looks like a recreation centre.'

'It's that and more besides, Keir. I'd like you to *meet* someone.'

Keir decided that he would no longer battle with his emotions. He recalled a saying of his unarmed combat instructor during his first year as a student, which seemed like a geological age ago. His mentor had said, "Resist and you'll break; you must yield to survive," or some such words. With a sigh, he put himself into neutral and waited for what seemed the inevitable.

'Come on, now is a good time to visit R-9,' she said.

Like an automaton, he followed behind Valentina. It turned out to be a collection of low buildings linked by corridors and covered walk-ways, but he didn't take very much notice. She rang the bell at a side entrance and a neatly attired middle-aged woman answered. After a brief conversation in Finnish, the woman walked away down an interior corridor.

Valentina turned to him and said, 'I know it may be difficult, but try to look relaxed.'

She's in the driving seat now, he thought. He complied as well as he could, while they waited.

Another bell rang; loud and like those which signified break intervals at the site. Suddenly, the corridor filled with children, some scampering but almost all of them chattering ceaselessly, mainly in Finnish, but Keir occasionally heard Swedish, Russian and some English. Two girls broke formation from a group and approached Valentina. They were both about nine years old and used Finnish, at first. Then one of them spoke in Russian. Keir noticed that she only used Russian when addressing Valentina, who replied in the same tongue. Suddenly, Valentina said to the girl, in English:

'I want you to practise your English for me. Do you understand? Reply in English, please.'

The girl smiled. She ignored Keir. And just as well, as he very nearly fainted from shock. He'd considered the possibility, the moment of revelation being almost too much for him. *There is only one smile like that, she's Valentina's*! It seemed as if stinging waves of refreshing surf broke over him, washing away all his uncertainties. Confirmation came almost immediately:

'Certainly, mother,' the girl said. 'It's so nice of you to call.' Then she giggled.

Keir failed to suppress his laughter. The child noticed him and blushed with embarrassment.

'You speak English very well, young lady,' Keir reassured her, 'I understood all of what you said.' It worked. She turned to her mother with an obvious expression of triumph.

'Mr. Wilson is from England, so he knows *exactly* how English is spoken,' Valentina said; her tone serious and sincere. 'You have done very well indeed, Katya.'

Mother and daughter exchanged a few rapid words in Russian and Katya skipped away. Abruptly, she stopped and waved to Keir. He returned her wave and then she disappeared into the throng. The bell rang again as the break ended.

*****

11:25am, Outside R9

'Thanks, Valentina. She's lovely. That was really great!'

Keir moved to kiss her, when he and Valentina nearly bumped into Lucien on the path, as they left R9.

'*Bonjour, mes amis*! Pardon my intrusions. I am disturbing you both, yes?' Professor Fournier asked rhetorically.

I'm just glad it wasn't Burton, Keir thought. 'Hi Lucien! That's OK, please join us,' he said.

'Thank you. It was just to say that Ilya has found out something very interesting about your friends on the motorcycle.'

'Oh?' The matter seemed distant and unimportant to Keir, but he recognised the possibility of sounding churlish. 'Please tell us, Lucien,' he said.

'Yes indeed, Professor!' Valentina had switched modes in an instant. No longer the playful romantic, she resumed her position of security investigator.

'Well,' the professor continued, 'this you may have guessed already, my friends. He has shown me photographs of them both, including the one who is deceased. The other, Max, fits a description given to the police by my secretary, at the time of my accident. He wore a white raincoat and had a very slight limp. They had rented an apartment about two kilometres from the Paris Observatory at Meudon. Yesterday, during a search of that apartment, a UN security detachment found a back-up copy of the virtual reality SD card which Dr. Brodie showed us in Denmark.'

'Presumably your image of Max is without camouflage?' Keir asked, mindful of his first meeting with Viv.

'That's correct. Just a moment.' Lucien took a folder from his document case and showed Keir a printout.

'It's him!' Keir said, 'Has Rowena seen this?'

'Not yet, why?'

'He's one of her groupies at Oakingwell University,' Keir declared. 'He calls himself Viv Lemâitre.'

'I remember him from the conference.' Lucien said.' And I think we must ask him some more questions.'

'Yes,' said Valentina. 'Connections between these men, your accident and our recent problems are still far from clear.'

'That is true,' Lucien admitted. 'And it seems certain that there are others involved, too. I've not seen Mads this morning. Where is he?'

'Sorry! No idea,' Valentina said.

'Ah, well. Give my regards when you see him. *Bon jour - au revoir!*'

'Kier, was there something you wanted to say, just before we met Lucien?'

Keir felt nervous: 'I don't know if this is the right time to say it.'

'Go on,' urged Valentina, anxiously. 'Please don't tell me you're already married or something like that.'

'Nothing like that. It's just that where I came from, computer power has enabled us to do quite incredible things. I mean, way beyond the capabilities of Pandora - excepting anti-grav travel, perhaps. I just don't know how you're going to take this.'

'Try me.' Valentina looked thoughtful.

'What if I told you I was from the future?'

Valentina paused and took a step back. 'Are you? What date?"

'Third of July, 2085'.

'So Max was right.'

'Max?'

'In the forest he told me you and he were both from the future. I didn't believe him and said he was insane.'

'Unfortunately, he *is* from the future as well. He infiltrated the system we were setting up. It's a long story.

'Who's "we", Keir?

'I've only one colleague here from the future, Captain Bosworth.'

Valentina paused as a tear ran down her cheek. 'Oh Keir! I might have known this wouldn't last. When do you intend to return to the future?'

'I don't,' Keir said.

'What about your colleague, and the people you're leaving behind?'

'I'm an orphan, one reason why I risked choosing this project. But I must admit my PhD supervisor in 2085 was like a father to me. Other matters we can talk about in due course. All that I know is that I love you and I want to stay.'

'I love you, too, Keir.'

This time they kissed without interruption. Then Keir added:

'I came here with a mission - to find clues to where we went wrong. My former world was in chaos.'

'I don't think I can help you, there! Unless...'

'Go on...'

'Unless your problem was allowing artificial intelligence to make key decisions. Here, it's starting to compete with humans and we're becoming ever more reliant on it.'

Keir declined mention of the almost entirely self-evolved Galena system at Liverpool that was (or will be) responsible for his space-time shift. *Perhaps later...* 'Then you'll have to watch out,' he said.

'True. You mean "we", of course...'

'Yes, my love. There are no more skeletons in my cupboard, but if you'd like some more time to think about things, then OK.' Keir felt he had put himself and Valentina on a tight-rope.

*****

7:37pm.

Orville Bonar stowed his flying gear in a locker and walked away from the terminal hangar, exchanging banter and repartee with the other three crew members. He took one of them aside.

'OK, guys, see you in the bar in a few minutes,' he called to two of them. Then, turning to his remaining companion: 'Hey, Mads! You flew that ship as if you'd designed and built it!'

'I guess I'm not so bad with machinery, Commander,' Mads replied.

'Sure thing. Guess it's time for dinner - see you over there, Mads.'

'OK. I'll just collect something I left in Ilya's office...'

Mads turned a corner and headed towards the Genetics Block. Suddenly, he found his way barred by a tall figure in a loose tracksuit with the hood up. Mads recognised Harald.

'Is there somewhere where we can talk?' Harald asked.

'I'm in a hurry, but OK for a couple of minutes.'
'That's all I need,' said Harald.

*****

8:30pm.

'These are quite tasty,' Valentina said.

'Thanks, I'll try some.' Keir scooped a portion of sardine-like fish from a large bowl.

'Like a re-fill, Keir?' Orville Bonar reached across the table with a bottle in his hand.

'Just a little, thank you.' Keir resolved to keep his wits about him that evening. Orville replenished Valentina's glass before filling his own for the third time. Or perhaps the fourth? Keir pretended not to notice.

'Where's Mads, I wonder?' Orville looked along the length of their table and beyond, draining his glass as he did so.

'You're the second person to ask that,' Keir commented.

'Oh yeah? He was with me this afternoon,' Orville explained. 'We landed the ship about an hour ago.'

'Part of a test flight programme?' Keir asked.

'Yeah.' Orville rubbed a bloodshot eye and poured himself another drink. 'It's due up again at 11:30 hours tomorrow. This time with an alien crew.'

'Do the aliens fly them, too? I don't remember Mads and the aliens being part of the plan,' Valentina remarked.

Orville looked slightly uncomfortable. 'Er, I guess it's OK to tell you folks, but sure. The aliens have been in training for about three weeks. Now they're ready for a hop on their own.'

Out of the corner of his eye, Keir observed a slight pause in the conversation at the round table on the opposite side of the room. The aliens' methods of communication through flickering images and manual gestures were impossibly difficult for humans to follow, but a concerted change in the proceedings had coincided with the end of Orville's last statement.

'*He's let it slip!*' Keir thought. Each member of the group of eight aliens seated around Table Five would now be aware that he knew their secret. '*They have very good hearing or they can lip-read, possibly both,*' Keir surmised.

As the dessert was brought, Valentina declined. She excused herself from the table, casting a glance in Keir's direction. Keir guessed that she might be going to the powder room and finished his dessert before rising.

'Excuse me; I think I'll turn in. It's been quite a hectic day!' Keir crossed the dining area and made his way to the male rest room.

Apart from two persons unknown to him, he saw nobody else within. Anxious not to become involved in extraneous conversation, he made use of the facilities and left, but not hurriedly lest he should attract attention. He half expected to see Valentina in the corridor outside, but found her in an adjoining lounge.

She sat facing him as he entered, her expression urgent.

'Don't face the windows when you speak,' she said.

'Right.'

Keir sat in another chair and pulled it up beside hers, ostensibly sharing information from one of the newspapers on the glass-topped table. 'I know what you mean,' he added, 'The aliens are inherently well camouflaged and it's going dark outside. Well, it looks as if things have changed since Orville arrived here, doesn't it?' Keir put the newspaper back on the table.

'Orville has been in and out of this base for about three years,' Valentina replied.

'You mean, he's part of the Inner Echelon?'

'Yes. But in my view he is what you'd call a loose cannon. A maverick with his own way of doing things. This time I think he's gone beyond his brief.'

'Was it really his idea? The training of aliens to fly the gravity ship, I mean.'

Valentina paused thoughtfully. 'Since you mention it, I have my doubts, Keir. But it wasn't mine or Ilya's, either.'

'In that case, the aliens are up to something. I wonder why they made no attempt to suppress their reaction to Orville's give-away remark.'

'Their behaviour could have been spontaneous, I suppose. And anyway, they probably assumed that we'd be too pre-occupied or slow to see what was happening.' Valentina stretched herself in the armchair and sighed wearily. 'I think we both noticed it because of what's happened to us these past few days. I don't know about you, Keir, but I can still hardly sleep at night after what we've been through together. It's as if I'm on perpetual red alert.'

'Same here, Val.' Keir reached out to touch her hand, but retracted it at the sound of approaching footsteps.

Tanskanen! He stood framed in the doorway, his blond hair reflecting the light from the chandelier. With his head held back, he looked down at them impassively.

'Good evening. You both know about the alien training programme initiated by Bonar, yes?' Without waiting for an answer, he continued: 'Of course, that was a near-mistake. A significant indiscretion. You should tell nobody, of any rank. I'm sure that you appreciate the security aspects. I'll talk to you in the morning, Mrs. Gazetny. That's all, thank you. Goodnight.'

'Goodnight, Professor Tanskanen,' Valentina said quietly to the receding shadow in the corridor.

'There goes our attempt at security!' Keir sat staring at the carpet. 'Of course, he was facing the opposite window as he spoke. If he wanted to remind the aliens about us, he couldn't have done any better.'

'I'm doing my best not to be paranoid, Keir,' Valentina said, 'but I think it was significant that he mentioned my name in particular.'

'You think he's setting you up as a target?'

'Who can say? You know, Keir, I don't think I like it here any more.'

At that instant, the lights went out; the corridor outside also in darkness. Instinctively, they both looked up at the chandelier. The lights went on again for a second and then blinked out.

'Blast!' Keir hissed. 'Watch yourself, Val!' They each fought with their retinal afterglows of the chandelier, which irritatingly followed their line of vision as they looked around in desperation.

*****

21 Encounter at Kouvola

9:15pm Monday 27 September.

Their vision seemed to take an age to recover.

'The window!' Keir said, 'Look, over there!'

As his vision cleared, Keir discerned a fibrous wetness in the lower right corner of the frame, glistening as it caught the faint light of a distant sodium lamp. He sensed, rather than saw, the extended ribbon-like bundle of fibres which had already reached the floor. It began advancing towards them, partly hidden in the deep pile of the carpet. Valentina saw it and backed away. There followed a splintering crash as a vase behind her toppled on the glass-topped table, resulting in mutual destruction. She felt a shard touch her foot, but it did not penetrate and she bent to pick it up. Then, with lightning speed, Valentina moved towards the window, avoiding the faintly glistening excrescence on the carpet. She found it difficult to locate the exact entry point around the window frame, but using the shard as a knife, she slashed at the rope-like shadow which hung over the sill. It cut cleanly, the severed end dropping limply to the floor. They heard a sucking and flapping noise as the stump writhed and retracted from whence it had come. She saw that it in order to gain entry, the thing had spread itself out into a paper-thin sheet and slid through a narrow gap between the window frame and the casement.

'Good grief!' Keir exclaimed. They've installed a triple-glazed climatic window and left a clearance!'

'Yes, they don't build like they used to, do they? You haven't trodden in any of the stuff, have you?'

'Don't think so, Val. How about you?'

'We'll have to check when there's some more light, but I think I'm OK.'

'The rest of it has stopped moving, I think you've killed it.'

'Or rendered it dormant for the time being. Let's not stay to find out. I'll have this room sealed off and an investigation set up.'

'Who's going to carry out the investigation?'

'Not Tanskanen. I'll ask Ilya.'

'He might delegate it to you, Val. Frankly, I think we should get out of here while we can.'

'That's difficult, Keir. As you know, I share with Ilya the responsibility of security not just for this base, but for the Northern Europe operations under Project Electra. Remember, if *you* disappeared from here - and nothing personal, Keir - nobody except me would worry. But it would be quite different in my case.'

'Who's next in line?' he knew the answer before she replied.

'Tanskanen.'

'And I wonder how many others are working for the aliens?"

'We know that Bonar is somehow involved.'

'That means there are other gravity ship crews who are probably implicated in this, too,' Keir said.

They started in surprise at the sudden glare. This time the lights stayed on, suggesting a return to order. They looked down at the deep purple stain on the carpet. It still glistened, but without any movement.

Valentina used her link-set to organise her security team.

'Biohazard in Room E11. Eriksson to examine the deposit on the carpet,' she demanded. 'It may be biologically active, so use the necessary protection. When samples have been collected, have the remaining mess cleaned up, the carpet renewed, and carry out whatever sterilisation measures he considers necessary.'

The inspection party arrived within minutes. Rikku Eriksson, a burly man with fluid features and a broad smile, introduced himself to Keir. While his team began clearing up, he took statements and was about to wave a cheery good-bye when he paused: 'Just one thing, Mrs. Gazetny.'

'What's that, Rikku?'

'You *are* heading for R22 aren't you?'

'The Quarantine Lodge? Yes, we're both aware of that. Be seeing you.'

'Quarantine?' Keir asked.

'Yes!' Valentina said. 'There are strict regulations about proximity to unknown bio-hazards like this. We have to be checked out before we go anywhere else.'

'How long does that take?' Keir asked.

'Up to twenty four hours, routinely, depending on the results of tests. Anything serious is referred to the military hospital at Kouvola in southern Finland. We could be there for weeks.'

They were expected at R22 and were met by a young female nurse in protective clothing. She spoke to them through her helmet: 'Hello, Mrs. Gazetny. This will be Mr. Wilson? Sorry I can't shake hands. You know the rules, of course.'

'Of course, Tuula.' Valentina smiled.

The nurse led them into a brightly lit corridor and opened the first door on the left.

'I know it sounds silly,' Tuula said apologetically, 'but I'd like detailed statements from each of you. Use the microphone over there. When you are ready, enter those cubicles and change into gowns. Then wait for the signal for you each to be examined in turn by Dr. Oja. Announcements will appear on the panel above the door. Please press the green button when you are ready. Thank you both for your co-operation.'

After forty minutes, they received their verdicts in turn from Tuula, who assumed the roles of nurse, receptionist and counsellor.

'Three weeks?' Keir blurted.

Valentina took the news more calmly. 'It's Kouvola for us, then?'

'Yes, but don't worry,' Tuula said, 'All your duties will be covered for the duration of your absence. Your health is of prime importance. Here are your keys to rooms A19 and 20. You get up at 8 o'clock tomorrow morning and will be taken by special transport to the Kouvola Quarantine Lodge.'

'What about our things, our personal baggage?' Keir asked.

'Personal effects in your apartments are already in sealed containers.'

'But they shouldn't be affected,' Keir protested.

'Regulations. Decisions about your belongings will be made when they have been thoroughly checked and you will hear more when you complete the quarantine period. Otherwise, you will be provided with everything you need. Please fill in this form for any special requests.'

'You will need your link-set, Keir.' Valentina suggested. 'And I need to get a message to Katya.'

After a scenic journey by road to Kouvola the next day, Keir and Valentina were escorted to the military hospital recently set up eight kilometres north-east of the town.

*****

8:00am, Thursday 30 September, Kouvola Quarantine Lodge.
On the third day they ate their bland but wholesome breakfast in silence; a pattern for all the inmates, as they regarded themselves.

'Val, this breakfast reminds me of something.'

'Yes, go on, *rakastava!*' she said, stroking his hand.

'Have you heard the story about Winston Churchill?'

'Several stories - what's yours?'

'His recipe for happy marriage...'

'Well?'

'Don't have breakfast with your wife.'

'*Voi!* Charming, I must say.' Then she laughed and blew him a kiss.

Suddenly, Keir's attention switched elsewhere. He noticed that the person sitting alone at the next table was not eating and had a strangely vacant expression. He was about to ask if anything was the matter when two burly male nurses appeared and gently but firmly helped their patient to his feet. Twenty minutes later, a similar incident occurred in the far corner of the room. A woman, perhaps in her late forties, had fallen to the floor. This time, two female nurses took her away and she did not return. He looked across the table at Valentina.

'Listen,' she said, pushing her plate to one side. 'It's been three days and we still haven't seen anyone we know from Oulu.'

'Well, who do you think that is?' Keir nodded towards another corner of the room. She had her back to them, but they both couldn't mistake the golden hair and nonchalant way she held her glass.

'Rowena!' Valentia called, standing by her chair.

Rowena excused herself from her group and joined them at their table.

'I'll get some more bread rolls,' Valentina said.

While she'd gone, Rowena pulled Keir to one side. 'I must tell you about Kirsti. The news isn't good, I'm afraid.'

'You look terribly pale,' Keir commented.

'Kirsti was confronted by Harald while on her way to Tanskanen's quarters. Tanskanen heard raised voices. When he came out to investigate, she was unconscious, lying in a flower bed. They took her to sick bay, but she didn't survive.'

Keir stood, speechless. Then he said:

'Do you want to tell Valentina, or shall I?'

'You do it please, Keir.' Rowena looked as if her nerve would fail.

Keir nodded.

'Hei! Rowena. What's it all about? Let me in on it, please.' Valentina said. Rowena bit her lip and glanced at Keir.

'I'm sorry, Val,' Keir began, 'It's Kirsti. I'm afraid it's bad news. She's passed away.'

'Oh no!' Valentina sat down and sank her head in her hands. They let her grieve for about five minutes. Keir's put his arm around her shoulder and then poured her some black coffee.

'What happened, Rowena?' Valentina asked at length.

Rowena repeated the story for Valentina and, red eyed, got up from the table.

'I'm so sorry,' she said, putting a hand on Valentina's shoulder. 'Perhaps see you later.' Then she picked up her bag and left the dining hall.

'Let's go for a walk,' Keir suggested.

'We might as well,' Valentina said, 'The interior isn't very inspiring, is it?'

'Here,' Keir said. He took a tissue from the table, wiped her eyes and kissed her forehead.

From that morning onwards, after breakfast, a half-hour walk in the grounds became a regular part of their day, in all weathers. Also, they discovered an extensive library and a well equipped gymnasium.

*****

At breakfast on the twenty second day, Keir asked: 'They're taking their time chucking us out of here, aren't they? What do you think?'

Valentina replied, 'Afraid so. It should have been yesterday morning. I don't know what their game is at Oulu. But I don't like it!'

They were half way through their morning walk when Valentina paused by the lake.

'Remember Kolmisoppi?' she asked.

'Certainly do. I think that's where I really fell in love with you. When I pulled you up the bank after you'd found the piece of meteorite.'

She squeezed his hand and flashed him one of her alluring glances.

Over three weeks had passed since Keir's first try. He seized the moment, searching in his jacket pocket.

'Following on from a little while ago, there's something I'd like to give you,' he said, producing a small velvet covered maroon box.

He saw she knew what it contained.

'Go on, then, open it!' she said.

'Is that an order, Chief Security Executive?'

'It is!'

'Close your eyes, then.'

Keir handed her the ring in its box, the lid open.

Valentina gasped. 'It's beautiful!' she said.

'Not bad for a budding geologist, eh?'

'Is that all?' she asked in mock dismay.

Keir went down on one knee next to a park bench. 'Valentina, will you marry me?' he asked.

'That's better! Of course I will,' she said.

He put the ring on her finger, picked her up and seated her on the bench. They sat together and embraced.

After a few minutes, Valentia became pensive and said: 'Keir, I wonder what's happened to those people who've been taken away from here?'

'It's true,' said Keir, 'They seem to have vanished. Definitely not a suitable place for a honeymoon.'

'I think we should try to find out, for instance, whether any of them have started to undergo transformation.'

'You don't think they might have been denied rhubarb for research purposes?'

'You never know, Keir. On the other hand, there might be a minority for whom the rhubarb cure doesn't work.'

'Or a developing biological resistance to the rhubarb cure?'

'Hmm. I'm not a biologist, I'm afraid. And gaining access to medical records here would be difficult.'

'By the way, Val, do you think it's significant that neither of us has been told the results of any tests yet?'

'I'm not sure of the answer to that,' Valentina replied.

'If there was anything serious, they'd probably keep us apart.'

'Unless things were too serious for both of us!'

'Hmm.' Keir reflected.

'But there *are* other matters to think about!' Valentina put her arms around his neck and smiled her smile for him.

'You're right, of course, Dr. Gazetny,' he agreed, kissing her passionately.

*****

Suddenly, both of them froze as they caught sight of a third party standing on the grass verge, next to the bench. A Type I Alien! One of its arms pointed to its own abdomen, where the skin swam with patterns. As they watched, well defined shapes emerged. The luminous alphabetic characters came one at a time and were a mixture of upper and lower case. But they were unmistakable: 'I m M a d s,' the message read.

'You're Mads?' Keir asked, his face pallid.

'Y e s,' came the reply. Clearly, Mads could understand them but not speak. His sounds were incoherent gurgles. 'Can not t a l k Y e t,' he projected. 'B u t L oo k,' he urged, waving a free arm. An unsteady but quite sharp image of Keir appeared, with Valentina sitting next to him on the seat. Mads could handle scene images well. More pictures came, this time of a gravity ship, accompanied by three other similar craft, flying over a deck of clouds. Suddenly, the image changed to a plain background with more text characters. The message appeared slightly garbled at first, with some of the characters fading, to be replaced by others. It took a few seconds for three terse sentences to form: 'Not muCH time now. WatCH these piCtures. TheN you MUST find HARALD.'

Mads swayed, as if the effort of assembling the text had exhausted him. But whole scene images, projected from memory or imagination, were certainly less of a problem. After a brief pause, the gravity ships reappeared and the anatomical film show continued. A large, dark shape emerged below the four gravity ships.

'It's a stealth bomber!' Keir said.

The three triangular ships changed formation and veered toward it. A concerted battery of laser-like pulses came from the gravity ships and the stealth craft rocked unsteadily. It plunged downwards, disappearing through the mantle of clouds. There followed a diffuse flash of orange and the gravity ships continued on their way, apparently continuing to patrol the skies.

'What are you saying? Are aliens planning to attack us?'

Another pause, then a message: 'Not an att ack. But an inTent. It is Harald. He neeDs more Of us.' Mads took several seconds to recover, then resumed the animated narration. A group of five human shapes formed above a group of five aliens. The humans changed until the whole depiction contained ten aliens. This sequence repeated, but with a map positioned between the two groups.

'Look, Keir!' Valentina pointed at the map. It's this quarantine station, isn't it?'

'You're right,' Keir said.

The humans in the picture dissolved into the central map and then emerged beneath it as type-1 and type-2 aliens. The image changed abruptly. Now it was a map of Finland. The area near Oulu on the north-west coast labelled 'Infection'. Then Kouvola marked with the word 'Trigger'. The word grew larger until it filled the field of view, then changed into a round table with four place settings. Various kinds of food appeared. The picture zoomed in to a plate of smoked salmon. Next to it stood a glass half filled with orange juice.

'The trigger is in the food. Is that what you're telling us, Mads?'

'YES,' the complete word appeared in block capitals. Then he showed a picture of an arrow which pointed to a humanoid labelled Harald.

A fresh picture on Mads appeared; a door marked EXIT. Then another map of Finland. This time, the indicated place south west of Kouvola, near the coast. His text read 'Helsinki', the capital.

Mads' visual diction steadily improved. Three more words appeared above it, flashing urgently:

'Go there NOW'

'You mean immediately?' Keir rose from the bench.

'YES,' Mads projected.

'How do we get out of here, Mads?'

Mads pointed across the lake to the perimeter fence, beyond a group of spindly rowan trees. Keir surveyed the scene intently, but there seemed to be no way out.

'We'd better collect our things, Keir.' Valentina turned to start down the path towards the distant buildings. Another alien blocked her way. The gestures appeared familiar. She gazed at the scene unfolding on the abdomen of this second alien. A picture of Ilya!

'I am he,' the supporting text appeared as a caption. The words 'Keep back' appeared, surmounted by a red triangle, like a road warning sign. Within it, an image of Ilya's human face winked at her. Valentina recognised his sense of humour... Then she fainted.

Keir rushed to her side. The aliens kept their distance as another person knelt with him beside Valentina.

'Rowena!' he cried.

'Let's put her on the bench, Keir. You take her legs.'

Rowena placed her document case on the ground and helped to settle Valentina on the bench.

'She's out cold,' said Keir, 'from the shock of seeing Ilya, I think.'

'Yes. He's no longer a pretty sight,' Rowena whispered.

The two aliens had retired to stand-off distances of several metres and now they stood together, blocking the way back to the quarantine lodge. Keir placed his rolled up jacket under Valentina's head.

'Thanks for your help, Rowena. We need to get her back to her room.'

'I don't think that would be wise, Keir. Mads and Ilya are right. We should press on to Helsinki like they've suggested.'

'You know about that?' asked Keir.

'Yes. I had my encounter with them half an hour ago. I went looking for you and someone said that you were out here. Have you seen Burton?'

'Not here, as far as we know. Where are the others: Rollo, Alan and Lucien?'

'And Kirsti?' Valentina had come round while they were talking. 'I shall miss her!' she sobbed and then said, 'I'll be OK.'

*****

Gardens at Kouvola Quarantine Lodge.

After a pause, Valentina said, 'A great loss of a good friend.'
Ilya heard her and drooped like a withered plant. 'Sorry!' he flickered.

She put on a brave face and said, 'I know Ilya here will be all right. He's a survivor.'

Ilya moved towards them, holding a small rucksack. He placed it at their feet. It contained a selection of his belongings, along with some of Valentina's. In addition, there were several cans of rhubarb and an all important can opener.

'Your link-sets are in my bag,' Rowena told Kier. 'I've got some sandwiches as well. But it may be an idea to change them for what we can find on the outside. And in answer to your questions about the others; I just don't know.'

'Thanks, Rowena, and you, Ilya and Mads!' Keir said.

Ilya waved, then pointed to his abdomen. He projected a map of Finland with Helsinki as a reminder. Superimposed, he displayed an analogue-style clock face which showed three forty-five. The letters PM appeared in the centre.

'You mean, we are to be there by a quarter to four this afternoon?'

'PRECISELY,' Ilya replied in flashing upper case.

'Whereabouts in Helsinki?' asked Valentina.

'*ROUTATIEASEMA*,' Ilya replied. She felt that he smiled at her.

'The railway station,' Valentina translated. Again, the same message appeared in the dancing Cyrillic characters of Russian. 'And stop showing off! You haven't changed a bit,' she chided, wiping a tear from the corner of her eye.

'You must go now. Good-bye.' Ilya had less difficulty than Mads in creating passages of text, but they could tell that it took some effort.

'Will we see you again?' Rowena asked.

'Maybe. Bye,' Ilya projected. Mads held up an arm as if to wave, but he pointed across the lake.

Obediently, the three humans left and skirted the lake. When they reached the perimeter fence, a trench had been carved under it. They passed through one at a time and then paused together, looking back from the cover of the trees beyond. Ilya and Mads were at work already. Keir's group knew that within a short time all traces of the trench would be gone and hardly a blade of grass would be out of place.

It began to rain as the trio made their way to the nearest visible road.

'Look, a bus stop,' Keir called.

'Let's hope the bus will accept our travel cards,' Rowena said. 'When is the next one due, Keir?'

'If we want the town centre and railway station, fifteen minutes. But I don't think we should stand in the open waiting.'

'I agree,' Valentina said. 'We should get whatever bus comes next and get away from here before we're missed.'

*****

11:02am.

Two bus connections and half an hour later, they arrived in the main shopping centre of the town. Almost immediately, Valentina recognised a tall figure in the crowd and tugged Rowena's arm.

'Look out!' she whispered, 'Over there, by the marketplace. It's Tanskanen!'

As they ducked into the doorway of a department store, Tanskanen appeared to be talking into a mobile telephone or link-set.

'Do you think he's seen us?' Keir asked.

'Don't know,' Valentina said, 'But let's go through this store and see if there's a rear exit.'

They vanished among the shoppers and eventually emerged at a rear doorway.

'Look! There's a sign for the railway station, let's go.' Rowena led them cautiously across the street. They followed the signs and arrived panting at the ticket office. Rowena produced her UN travel card.'

'*Missä on raide Helsingin*?' Keir asked.

'Not bad, dear!' Valentina complimented him.

'*Raide yksi*,' the clerk replied.

'Platform one for Helsinki,' Keir whispered to Rowena.

'I know. And it's here in twelve minutes,' she added, looking up at a screen.

'We should arrive in plenty of time,' Valentina commented.

'Do you think we should go somewhere else and then double back?' Keir asked.

'No,' said Valentina, pecking him lightly on the cheek. 'See? We operate according to the KISS principle.'

'You mean, "Keep It Simple, Stupid"?' To Keir a familiar expression, even back in his 2085 world.

'Exactly.'

*****

3:27pm, Helsinki.

Rowena alighted from the train first. She turned to Keir and cried, 'Wow! Look who's rolled up. A friend of ours!'

Keir's stomach turned. From a concourse seat in the middle distance, a familiar face smirked at them.

'Well, well!' Burton said, no less condescending as they approached him. 'Presumably, you've all just arrived from Kouvola? Before you ask how I got here, I'll tell you. The overnight train from Oulu. A pleasant enough journey. I've spent the day touring the city. How about you?'

Rowena moved towards him: 'Why Helsinki?' she asked.

'Aren't you pleased to see me, Rowena?'

'Not particularly.'

Burton remained unmoved. 'I was told to be here, by three thirty. The order actually came from the UN High Command. At least you're on time.'

'I had no way of knowing who organised it,' Valentina admitted.

'As you and Ilya share responsibility for security, I find that hard to understand,' Burton commented.

'Strange, but true.' Valentina said. 'But this has Tanskanen's stamp all over it. I think he wants us all together for some reason.' She wondered if she should mention Ilya's transformation. However, Burton pre-empted her.

'I know about Ilya,' he said. 'I also know about the necessity for your quarantine. Yes, don't look surprised, I know you've escaped.' He produced an orange coloured plastic card and waved it nonchalantly. Valentina recognised it immediately.

'When were you issued with that?' she asked.

'Yesterday morning I was appointed as the new Head of Security for the North European Sector.'

'Why wasn't I told?' Valentina struggled to maintain her poise. 'And appointed by whom?'

'For one thing, you were otherwise pre-occupied. I was delegated in your absence and confirmed in post, as I said, yesterday. And if you mean which person confirmed my appointment, it was Tanskanen himself.'

'I didn't know he had that authority,' Valentina remarked.

'Well, you should and he has.' Burton returned the card to an inside pocket.

'Where are Lucien and the others?' Keir asked.

'I don't know, ' Burton said.

'Good Heavens, Brian!' said Rowena, unimpressed by Burton's new status. 'Your new job carries *some* degree of responsibility with it, surely? Or is that too much to expect?'

Again, Burton appeared unmoved. 'I can't be expected to know everything at this early stage of my appointment.'

'Come on!' Rowena interrupted, 'You don't have to be Head of Security to keep track of what's happening to your colleagues.'

'My former colleagues,' Burton said icily, showing signs of impatience.

'Have you relinquished your position at Oakingwell, too?' Rowena asked, keeping up the pressure.

'I will have, in a few days,' Burton admitted.

'Then until that time, you still have colleagues who are missing. You *must* do something to find them!'

Burton remained cool and unruffled. He leaned back on the seat and looked Rowena squarely in the eye: 'Be patient,' he said.

Valentina brought her face close to his and smiled at him, noting his almost imperceptible flicker of confusion. 'Brian,' she said, 'you may not know exactly where they are, but you have a fairly good idea, don't you?'

Burton said nothing.

'Are they safe?' Valentina asked.

'Yes.' Burton replied, 'But please be patient - all of you.' Burton held the orange card in his hand. He looked at it with an ironic smile. He folded the plastic until it cracked, then cast the useless card into a nearby trash bin.

'It's just expired. That means, as of now, my responsibilities within Electra no longer exist.'

'Professor Burton?' Valentina stood before him, her face impassive.

'Yes?'

'There's one more investigation I'd like you to help me with.'

'I'm catching the Airport shuttle from here and then flying back to the UK. I've just retired.'

'No you haven't. You've just *mislaid* your card.'

'All right, then. In that case, I'm back in charge. And the answer's no.'

'Neither you nor I have signed anything which alters our status from what it was before we left Oulu.'

'Jukka Tanskanen has hired me.'

'He has no jurisdiction!' Valentina said. 'And I have.'

'But you're disqualified. He told me you're in quarantine.'

'Quote me the statute that says a person in quarantine has to relinquish command. Come on, Professor. Have you ever been off work with influenza? Did that nullify your Professorship? And kindly stand up when I'm speaking to you!'

Burton grudgingly got to his feet.

Keir hadn't seen Valentina like this. Apart, perhaps, from that moment on the Oulu night train on the way to Vihanti when she'd faced down their assailant.

'What is it you want?' Burton asked.

'Professor, you've heard about what happened to Kirsti?'

Burton seemed genuinely puzzled. 'No, what did happen?' he asked.

Keir felt the effort would be too much for Valentina to say the words.

'Kirsti has been killed,' Keir told him.

'What?' Burton said, 'I'm so sorry, I didn't know. When?'

'Yesterday morning.' said Keir. 'We think Harald had something to do with it.'

'This is the fifteenth meteorite scientist to die under suspicious circumstances,' Valentina resumed. 'Something wrong is happening at Oulu, Brian. We need all the help we can find. We must do something about it.'

'OK,' Burton said, 'you can count me in. What do you propose we do, Valentina?'

*****

22 Harald

Helsinki Railway Station: restaurant:

They found a table near the restaurant entrance.

'What we do, now we're all together, Brian,' Valentina said, 'is have something to eat and then use the night train back to Oulu... Excuse me!' Valentina's link-set vibrator had interrupted her. 'Yes?'

'Mrs. Gazetny?'

'Yes, who is this?'

'It's Riita, the OB School Office.'

'Oh yes, hello Riita. Is everything all right?'

'You told us you were at Kouvola. Is Katya with you?'

Valentina swallowed hard. 'No, she's with you, isn't she?'

'I'm sorry, Mrs. Gazetny. She's not at school. We contacted her carer and she brought her to school this morning. Katya isn't with Anne, so maybe she's with someone else. Most unlike her, though!'

'How long has she been missing?'

'Since morning break. She didn't come in from the playground.'

'Have you reported this?'

'Professor Tanskanen isn't around and there's no answer from his internal phone!'

'That's because he's in Kouvola, somewhere. Please alert the site police and let me know when you've done it.'

'I'll do it now. Bye, Mrs Gazetny.'

'Bye, Riita.' Valentina sat down, head in hands. 'They've got Katya, I know it!' Valentina sobbed.

'C'mon, Val,' Keir said. 'Let's travel to Oulu by air from Helsinki Airport at Vantaa. I'll go to the kiosk and book the flights.'

*****

Vantaa Airport lounge, Helsinki.

Valentina desperately kept holding her link-set. As they moved to the boarding gate for their flight to Oulu, the set vibrated again.

'Riita? Did you get through?' Valentina asked.

'Hello Mummy!'

'Katya! Are you all right?' A moment of silence... 'Katya? Are you there?'

'Yes, Mummy. I'm, er, all right.' On the phone the sound of a train hooter - then the link-set went dead.

'Katya?' Valentina shouted. But to no avail.

*****

Near Oulu Railway station.

At Oulu, their airport taxi drew into the station forecourt. They went to the station café to review their strategy.

'I think we should start trying the hotels,' Keir said.

'I'll get us a notepad from the station kiosk,' said Burton.

'We could take notes on our link-sets,' suggested Rowena.

'We don't know what technologies they may use against us,' Burton argued.

'I think pencil and paper's a good idea,' Keir said. 'They could survive where electronics fail.'

Burton went off to the kiosk and came back with four notepads and pencils plus a street map and hotel directory.

'Very resourceful, Brian!' Rowena chirped.

'Naturally,' Burton said, placing the goods on the table.

Keir studied the street map and directory. 'There are dozens of hotels in this vicinity alone,' he said, 'Let's crack on and tick them off as we go.'

'We all keep together as agreed?' Valentina asked.

'Is everyone still happy with that?' Keir asked. 'I think we'll get more of a response if we're seen as a group.'

All nodded their assent.

'The train hooter on the phone sounded quite near,' Valentina said. 'Let's try the ones nearest the station first.'

'Yes, then the ones near where the rail tracks run through the city,' Rowena suggested.

'I think the purpose of the phone calls was to bring us here,' Keir said, 'They want us to find them and negotiate.'

'I tried phoning back, ' Valentina said, 'but all I got was the number-withheld message. And it isn't Katya's regular phone.'

'OK, let's find out what their game is,' Keir said. 'Shall we start here, next to the station, moving outwards?'

*****

Street outside Oulu station.

At a hotel near the railway station, Burton stopped.

'There's something moving,' he said, 'Across there on the second floor, second window from the right.'

'The property looks empty, which I suppose one might expect,' Rowena said. 'Yes. I see it, too. It's a picture!'

'It's Katya,' Valentina whispered, hardly daring to speak.'

'We didn't have to wait long,' Burton said. 'The venue was obviously chosen for its convenience. Possibly the captors thought Valentina would arrive by train.'

'It's as Rowena says, Val,' Keir said, placing his hand on her shoulder. 'A picture. About twice life size. There's writing on it as well.'

It resembled a Wild West style: 'WANTED: KATYA' along the top, and underneath: 'DEAD or ALIVE.'

'Looks like a poster he's made,' Rowena said.

'That's no poster,' said Keir. 'It's on a humanoid torso and it's flickering, like the images on Type I aliens.'

'Except this is a Type II alien,' Burton said.

'You're right,' Keir agreed, 'Look! There's no umbilicus.'

'It's Harald, all right!' Burton said.

'I'm going in to find out more,' said Keir.

'No!' Valentina grabbed Keir's arm, 'It's far too dangerous. Let's wait and see what happens.'

'Look! The image has changed!' Rowena said.

'Ha! See what it says?' Keir said.

The image had become a notice which read: 'I WANT WILSON.'

*****

At the hotel.

'I'm going in there, alone,' Keir said.

The main door of the hotel was unlocked. He opened it and went inside. A musty smell pervaded the place. He entered a lobby with damp walls and peeling green wallpaper. Two stairways on his right. One led downwards to a basement and the other connected with the upper floors.

Keir climbed the stairs and stood outside what he judged to be Harald's room. He hesitated then knocked at the door once.

It wasn't possible to knock twice because the door disintegrated before his gaze in a cloud of dust. Metal parts, including the lock and some screws clattered to the floor. The doorframe remained intact and Keir cautiously stepped inside.

The floor seemed firm and in the far corner Katya cowered. Then he sensed movement in the room. Keir wheeled round to face the source of a creaking sound;

Harald had moved backwards towards the wall to Keir's left.

'I've been monitoring you for a considerable time, Keir Wilson. You seem to me like a reasonable person,' Harald said. 'You must tell Doctor Gazetny,' he continued, 'that my terms are Katya for the release and continuity of my people. Now go.'

'What do you mean by continuity, Harald?'

'In the world at large, our numbers have been significantly reduced. Victims of the war against us by your primitive race! These numbers must be restored. We have plans for the human species. You and your Oulu Base colleagues can make an exemplary start, now. As I said, go!'

An extension of Harald's arm flicked out like a whiplash before Keir's face. Keir ducked and went to pick up a chair. The chair, like the door, crumbled to dust. This time, before he reached it. The metal parts again clattering to the floorboards.

'Go!' Harald repeated.

*****

Outside the hotel.

Keir tried to hide his dejection as he backed off and descended the stairs to join the others in the street.

'He wants freedom and expansion of his people,' Keir explained, 'starting immediately. In exchange for Katya.'

'He must know that's not practicable within a reasonable timescale,' Rowena said.

'Remember the images we saw on Mads at Kouvola?' said Keir. 'He really wants more anti-gravity ships and trained crews for them. He's a usurper who wants more aliens, ultimately for his control of the planet. A megalomaniac!'

'Is there any way we could rush him?' asked Burton.

'Don't even think about it!' said Keir, 'He appears to have a strange weapon that disintegrated the door of his apartment and a chair that I tried to pick up.'

'Were they made of wood?' asked Rowena.

'Yes. And now you mention it, the metal bits were unaffected.'

'Right. I think I know what's happening,' Rowena continued, 'His kind, the Type II aliens, have a web-like secretion they deploy at will. It can disrupt the structure of many organic materials. But it takes time.'

'This was instantaneous!' Keir remarked.

Rowena looked pensive.'Maybe he could do that,' she said, 'by setting things up in advance for your benefit and then triggering each destructive event through some kind of energetic impulse. But don't ask me how!'

'Interesting,' Burton commented.

'Never mind interesting, Brian!' Valentina pleaded, 'How do we get my baby out of there?'

'If only we can get hold of some, we could try oxalic acid,' Rowena suggested.

'We do have some, but not enough, and it takes time to act.' Keir said, 'We have to think of something else. It should be possible. After all, there's four of us and only one of him.'

'Don't count on it,' Burton remarked, nodding in the direction of the station.

They saw six humanoid figures with a strange walk and unblinking eyes approaching. They ignored Keir's group, walking past them, and entered the building.

Elsewhere, life in the street remained quiet, but otherwise went on as normal. Valentina covered her face in horror. 'When will this nightmare end?' she cried.

Keir held Valentina's arm as he addressed his colleagues:

'I think the only hope is for me to go inside again and resume the dialogue. But I need to offer more freedom than we're giving them at present. What should I tell them?'

'Tell them, 'Valentina said, 'that if they let Katya free, we'll discuss how their wishes can be met.'

Keir moved towards the building.

*****

At the hotel.

Keir glanced up at the hotel window as he approached. He saw another poster message with the invitation:

'Keir, we would like you to come up and join us.'

'What does *join* mean, I wonder,' said Rowena.

'Burton looked worried. 'You're the expert, Rowena. What do you think?' he asked.

'I can hear what you're saying,' Keir called back to them, 'but I'm going in.'

He opened the front door and expected to face a crowd of them, but the lobby seemed empty. He climbed the stairs again. Only Harald and Katya were in the room.

'Come,' said Harald.

As Keir stepped through the yawning doorway and its pile of debris, he heard a splintering crash behind him. The stairway had collapsed amid more dust and broken timbers. Keir found himself cut off.

From outside, Valentina called, 'Keir, are you all right?'

*****

In the street.

Rowena grabbed Valentina. As she pulled her back, Rowena thrust her link-set into Valentina's hand.

'While Keir was in there, I texted Ilya. Now you must text him!'

'What?' Valentina cried in disbelief, 'Isn't he at Kouvola?'

'Just do it!' Rowena said.

A voice menu, after a list of irrelevancies, said: 'For recorded text messages, press 5.'

Valentina, hands shaking, pressed the key.

The text message read: 'Hi Valya. DO NOT USE. THEY CAN READ RADIO SIGNALS. Ilya.'

'Read radio signals?' Valentina asked.

'Yes, even very weak ones,' Rowena said, 'Their sensory perception includes the radio spectrum.'

'Can they detect frequency-hopping secure channels?' Burton asked.

At that instant, the word 'YES' appeared on the torso at the upper window.

'Not to mention lip-reading', said Rowena.

Valentina turned off the set and put it in her own pocket. 'I have a plan,' she whispered in Rowena's ear. She then walked towards the building.

*****

Interior. Ground floor of hotel.

Valentina stood apprehensively at the entrance looking at the wrecked staircase.

'Keir!' she called.

'Ah! The more the merrier, I think the phrase is,' said Harald. 'You'd better see what she wants.'

From where he stood on the landing, Keir saw Valentina framed in the front doorway.

'Is anyone else coming?' Harald asked. As if in answer to his question, the sounds of a loud dispute erupted from the street below. Harald's curiousity aroused, he went back to the window and lifted the catch to open it as Rowena and Brian shouted at each other. A smile crossed Harald's face as he watched with interest. 'Strange habits you humans have!' he said to Katya, who sat in the corner watching him fearfully.

Below in the lobby, Valentina saw a movement in the shadows as she turned the link-set up to full power.

'Catch!' she shouted to Keir.

A shadowy alien figure in the hall and his companions cowered back as what they perceived as a ball of fire hurtled upwards.

Keir caught the shiny black instrument and read Valentina's throwing gesture before she spun around and left. He felt slight warmth from the small antenna and realised in an instant what he should do.

Meanwhile, Harald had seen Valentina through the window as she returned to her colleagues. He scowled and a dribble of saliva drooled down his chin. Hissing, he turned to face Keir.

*****

23 Farewell

Harald saw Keir about to hurl the link-set and sent out a whip-like tendril to seize his arm. But too late! The radio brightness dazzled him and spoiled his aim. The prehensile tendril struck a glancing blow on the link-set casing, sending the device spinning to the floor. It skidded across the floorboards out of Keir's reach.

Katya, her hands and feet tied, couldn't reach it. So she swivelled her legs and tried to kick it back to Keir. But she only managed to move it a metre. Just sufficient!

The instrument skidded towards Harald. He saw the fireball approach his own glistening flesh. The antenna touched his bare foot, causing him unbearable pain. Harald stumbled backwards, his outstretched hand pressing against the glass. The window catch already open, resistance was negligible. The window yielded quickly and silently, dispatching Harald to the street below.

*****

Outside the hotel.

Harald lay sprawled on the sidewalk, the remains of his head hanging in the gutter. The body convulsed several times and then lay still.

'It's a sad sight, isn't it Rowena?' Burton said.

'Can you see Keir anywhere? There are six others to deal with, yet!' Rowena reminded him.

'Look, they're coming!' Valentina shouted. 'Katya, Keir, are you there?'

Her heart jumped as she saw Katya's face at the window. Keir pulled her back inside as he waved and shouted:

'Keep back! As far as you can!'

Spectators were beginning to appear.

'I'm a doctor!' said one. 'I can see he's sustained serious injuries. Let me call an ambulance.'

'Could you please keep the crowd back?' Valentina called to the doctor.'

'Of course,' the doctor replied.

Suddenly, five of the six other hominid aliens advanced towards their fallen colleague. They formed an outward facing cordon around the body.

To Valentina's group it seemed as if the hominids were changing colour. Perhaps only their clothing? If it *was* clothing. As a result, they appeared to have acquired official looking uniforms. Then two of the aliens were deployed at each end of the street and one at the railway station entrance.

'What? They've all got hats. I hadn't noticed before.' Burton said. The hats were dark blue ski caps that looked from a distance like those worn by the Finnish police. And sure enough, appearing on the backs of their uniforms the word 'POLIISI' stood out in white block capitals.

'What are you doing?' one of them asked the doctor.

'Calling an ambulance for this casualty,' he said.

'Leave it to us! We will deal with this,' said the hominid.

'But I'm a medic.'

'Go! This is a government operation! There's a risk of radioactive contamination. Everybody, please leave.'

At the mention of radioactivity, the street emptied within 30 seconds. Word got around elsewhere and people hurriedly left buildings in the vicinity.

Rowena and Burton backed off nervously. They watched in astonishment at the two aliens left guarding the body.

'Look,' whispered Rowena. 'They're merging with Harald!'

'Now the streets are clear,' Burton said, 'I wonder if the others will come back and merge as well?'

I don't know,' Rowena said. 'But already, Harald and his two sidekicks seem to have formed one composite being.'

'It looks hideous!' Valentina said.

*****

Inside the hotel.

'It's all right, Katya,' Keir said. 'Keep perfectly still while I finish untieing you.'

Within a minute, Katya had shaken her feet free from her bonds.

'There, Katya. Your mother's outside. She's quite safe, with her friends. Now we must get you out of here, but don't follow me until I say so.'

'Thank you, Mr. Wilson,' she said, putting her arms around his neck and hugging him.'

'You're very welcome!' Keir said.

Katya looked at the street scene through the window. But her mother's attention, along with that of her colleagues, became riveted to the scene on the kerbside below.

'*Mikä se on?* What is that, Mr. Wilson? Outside?'

Keir carefully picked Rowena's link-set off the floor, wiped it and put it in his pocket. He went to the window and checked the events unfolding outside. Then he turned to Katya.

'Katya, your English is much better than my Finnish. Don't move until I tell you, OK?'

'OK, Mr. Wilson,' she said.

'Please call me Keir, Katya.'

'Yes, Mr. Keir.'

'Just Keir is fine, Katya.'

He crossed to the opening where the door had been. The veranda remained intact, but for all practical purposes the stairway was useless.

Directly below, however, things looked more hopeful. The lobby seating included a sofa next to a glass-topped table with some magazines.

'Katya,' he called.

She stepped through the doorway, trying her best to avoid the pile of dust.

'Are we going to jump? It's very high up, Keir.'

'Hold on to my hand and take a careful look below. What do you see down there, Katya?'

'A very long *sohva*.'

'Very good. We're going to try landing on it, one at a time.'

He looked around, but he could find no convenient length of rope.

'Hold my hands very tight,' Keir said. At the same time, he gripped her wrists with his hands.

'Right. Now while I get down on the floor on my tummy, you do the same. Face me and stretch your legs out behind. Keep tight hold of me all the time, right?'

Keir lowered himself to his knees while gripping her wrists, the edge of the veranda floor being a metre away. But already, Katya's feet were just over the edge.'

'OK, Katya, now keep looking at me and move backwards while I follow you. Keep tight hold.'

Katya's waist now level with the edge, her feet dangled in the abyss.

'That's very good. I want you to keep going all the time until you're hanging by your arms. If there's a problem, tell me.'

A piece of ceiling plaster on the floor slipped and fell to the sofa below, then bounced onto the glass table. But by now, Katya hung in space above the centre of the sofa. The tips of her shoes were only two metres above it.'

'Have you done any jumping in your school sports?' Keir asked.

'Yes,' she replied.

'Well this is your championship jump. I'm going to turn you now.' Keir twisted his arms slightly to align Katya with the target.

'Are you ready?'

'Yes, Keir.'

'Now!' he cried.

Katya made the drop. Her hands clawed the back of the sofa and her legs were folded beneath her. But she rebounded and rolled off between the sofa and the glass table.

'Katya, are you OK?'

'Yes, Mr. Keir,' she said.

'Right, It's my turn! Keep back, Katya.'

Just as he jumped, a remaining alien came up the basement stairwell. Keir landed without difficulty and grabbed Rowena's link-set.

'*Voi!*' Katya screamed, as an uncoiling tendril whisked past her head.

Keir hit the high power key and threw it with all his strength at the hominid's face. Blinded and confused, the alien crashed forward, just missing Keir. They heard an explosion of glass shards as the alien fell onto the table. He didn't get up.

'Keir!'

Keir's stomach churned as he saw blood streaming down Katya's face.'

'Stay still!' he raced to her side and noticed above her hairline a shard of glass. Carefully he inspected and removed it.'

'You'll be all right,' he said, 'Let it bleed for a little while to clean the wound and we'll check it again soon. Let's get out of here.'

They made for the main entrance and ran across the street to join the others.

*****

Outside the hotel.

Keir and Katya had to give the writhing composite being, still thrashing its tentacle-like arms, a wide berth.

Katya ran into her mother's arms with shouts of joy. They both dissolved in tears.

'Thank you so much, Keir!' Valentina cried.

'Yes, thank you, Mr. Keir!' Katya shouted, 'Mummy, I want him to be my Daddy.'

Valentina bit her lip and then hugged her daughter: 'We'll have to see, won't we?' She looked at Keir.

Keir glanced at the pair of them together. A camera shutter in his mind recorded an image he'd keep for all his life. 'Sorry about your battle scars, Katya! Does anyone here have a first aid pack?'

'Yes,' said Rowena. 'Some of us have to come prepared. Don't worry. I'll attend to Katya. And then it'll be your turn,'

'What, me?' asked Keir.

'Huh! Have you seen the state of your trousers?'

Keir saw a blood red stain had enveloped his lower right leg.

'Must have caught another piece of glass!' he commented. His right shoe squelched ominously.

'Like I said, I'll sort you out in a couple of minutes.' Rowena unpacked her kit and turned her attention to Katya.

*****

'How long ago did you put my link-set on full power?' Rowena asked Keir, tightening the makeshift tourniquet.

'Ow! About six or seven minutes.'

'It'll have timed out by now and be in receive mode. Want to destroy it?'

'I didn't rescue it because of infection risk from the alien.'

'OK,' Rowena acknowledged. 'Brian! Give my link-set a call would you? And destroy it. Come on, can't you see I've got my hands full? Talk about Brian the Snail!'

Brian Burton winked at her and smiled, which never failed to annoy her, and fired up his link-set to perform the necessary operation. A dull thump came from the hotel entrance, followed by a cloud of grey smoke.

The lashing of tentacles became more agitated.

*****

'Look!' Valentina called.

For the second time, visitors from the station moved towards them. The alien sentry on police duty let them through, recognising them as his own kind, albeit Type I aliens rather than the Type II hominids.

The group moved back as the composite alien mass began moving towards them.

'We have activity on two fronts!' Keir called out.

'It's Mads and Ilya,' Valentina said, in Rowena's ear.

'Look! They're carrying type T140 sets!' Keir whispered to Burton, recognising the portable high power military transmitters tucked under their multiple arms.

Mads and Ilya halted and curled up on the ground, their transmitters now completely hidden. They rolled onward towards the seething mass.

'No!' cried Burton, 'Don't do it.'

'It's accepting them!' Valentina cried. 'See? They've disappeared into the big blob!'

'As if it had acquired new strength, the arm-like tentacles coiled and uncoiled, some in the air and some on the ground Two came dangerously near to striking Rowena as she stood her ground to study the phenomenon.

*****

Valentina and Rowena hugged each other in their shared distress at the assimilation of Ilya and Mads. Katya was crying, too.

'The tentacles seem less coordinated,' said Burton, 'and my link-set's alarm tells me its receiver is being jammed!'

'That's because Ilya and Mads have managed to turn on their transmitters!' said Keir.

The composite alien writhed in agony as its interior became ravaged by the radio emissions. Humanoid faces were imaged and protruded sporadically from the heaving form. After several minutes, the energy of the menace dissipated and a residual slime began to flow into the gutter and the street drains.

*****

Burton and Keir moved forward to cautiously inspect the scene. Two flat, shield-like bodies remained, presumably of Mads and Ilya.

'I think they're alive,' said Keir. 'They're glimmering.'

'Yes, just about.' Burton said. 'My link-set battery is nearly flat, but I'd better call up Dr. Born in Denmark.'

'Hello, Professor Burton! How's it going with you?'

'Hi Christian! Sorry, but this is an emergency. We're trying to revive a pair of injured aliens, Type I. Can you get onto any colleagues you have with the necessary expertise over here at Oulu Base?'

'I'll contact Dr. Meeri Kekkonen. We'll get a helicopter ambulance with the right kit on board. Type I aliens, you say?'

'Affirmative.'

'Injuries?'

'Rowena? Dr. Born wants information about their injuries,' called Burton. 'Here, take it.' He passed her the link-set.

'Severe burns and possible internal haemorrhage at the very least,' Rowena reported.

'Where are you?' Dr. Born asked.

'Valentina, where are we?' Rowena asked in turn.

'*Rautatienkatu*. Railway Street,' Valentina said.

'Did you hear that?' Rowena asked Dr. Born.

'Railway Street, Oulu.'

'Fine. Thank you. Over and out.'

*****

Oulu Base.

'Hello, Born speaking.'

'Hello, Dr. Born. Meeri here. We have two injured aliens in our sick bay. Unfortunately there's little we can do here. They're both on life support. Can we get them across to you at Aalborg?'

'Too far, Meeri! They may not make the journey, even by equipped military transport.'

'They might if we use our, er, express air service.'

'Military jets? OK for pilots, not so OK for patients, especially aliens.'

'They're being loaded now, aboard a grav-ship.'

'A what?'

'This transport is triple alpha. Do you understand, Dr. Born?'

'Understood. When do you arrive?'

'From Oulu? Twelve minutes at your main heli-pad. Look out for a triangular craft. Like a UFO.'

'I hope you're not joking.'

'I'm deadly serious. Have to go now. Is that all right?'

'Catch you when you land, Meeri.'

*****

Interior: Aalborg Hospital.

Keir and Valentina, with Katya, stepped out of their craft, parked on the roof, followed by Brian. They watched and followed as Rowena and Dr. Born escorted the two stretcher trolleys to Dr. Born's secure ward. The others were taken to his reception room.

Two and a half hours passed. They were about to go for lunch when some news came through.

'Mads didn't' make it, I'm afraid,' Dr. Born said. 'But come with me, Rowena.'

She was shown an intensive care bed, surrounded by instruments and covered by a green sheet. Gently, Born lifted it clear. Faintly visible on the alien-like patient's abdomen they saw an image that one could barely call a face. It forced a smile and Rowena just about recognised Ilya.

Dr. Born took her to one side.

'I know it doesn't look too good at present, Dr. Smythe, but we believe he'll recover. You'll be kept informed and I think recovery will take about six weeks.'

*****

Aalborg Hospital, after lunch.

'That was a well deserved lunch, I think,' said Valentina.

'It certainly was,' Brian agreed. At the table, he attempted to clasp Rowena's hand. She adroitly moved it out of his reach.

'Well, time to go, I think,' Brian said. 'We should be back before teatime.'

After goodbyes with Dr. Born and his staff, the group made its way to the roof heli-pad.

The craft went as quickly as it came. They'd barely had time to collect their thoughts when it touched down at the hangar, Building R15 at Oulu Base.

At a door near one of the corners of the grav-ship, the pilot shook hands with his grateful passengers.'

'Thank you, Mr. Bonar,' Katya said, all smiles again.

'You're welcome, honey!' Orville said.

'Great flight, Orville. And thanks!' said Keir, as he and Valentina shook Bonar's hand in turn.

'*Bon voyage* back to the UK,' Orville said to Keir. 'While you're flying in that old crate, think of this beauty.'

'I will!' Keir said, mindful of unfinished business to be addressed before his departure.

*****

They left the building and walked back to the main hall. Tanskanen met them on the way.

'Welcome back!' he shook hands all round. 'There's a meeting in half an hour. Usual place. Go and get yourselves a coffee before it starts!' Then he left them, in his usual hurry.

'Not another meeting!' Burton growled.

'I'll join you there, Keir,' Valentina said. She left to take Katya to the school block.

'See you again, Mr. Keir!' Katya shouted.

*****

Jukka Tanskanen called the meeting to order.

'Thank you, everybody, this should only take a few minutes,' he shouted above the din.

He achieved control with some delay, as the party from Aalborg had only just been welcomed back by Lucien, Doug, Rollo and Alan. When the reunion had subsided, they sat around the table. Tanskanen had arranged an empty chair to be left in honour of Kirsti.

'Don't worry, this isn't a discussion paper,' he announced: 'It's a UN bulletin, updating the situation regarding our aliens.

Here are the copies. In a moment, I'll play back an audio transcription...'

"From the Office of the UN Secretary General.   Oct 04 2010.
Bulletin PEC 199-863 ZM/rw   To All Project Electra Centres.
Security: 3A

Senior representatives of the Type I alien life form have expressed the wish for their kind to migrate back to their place of origin, the sea.
In some quarters, this comes as little surprise, given that oceans and their connected water bodies occupy 70 percent of the Earth's surface and volumetrically, for example, the Atlantic Ocean alone contains over a third of a trillion cubic kilometres of water, largely unexplored. Admittedly, they return there in a considerably evolved and enhanced state compared with what they were like beforehand. The so-called aliens were tempted to interact with humans mainly because of our technology, but will not appear again until bidden and when the time is ripe. All Type II aliens have agreed to enter chrysalis stage and revert to Type I. They regard their attempted coexistence with the human species to be premature, if not a failure, for which they apologise. Yesterday morning, I signed the treaty on behalf of humankind to grant their wishes.
They have bequeathed us anti-gravity travel, new directions in computation and certain biological and medical advances. In spite of pleas from some of our governments, ranging from the welcoming to the remorseful, they will not return. The aliens will disperse into the waters of the ocean, taking with them many secrets that would have benefited humans.
However, they wish us well and hope that we will use our inherited benefits wisely. They apologise for the aberrant behaviour of Harald and a few other Type II aliens whose gene switching did not go according to plan. This is a subject for further investigation. Likewise, we thank them for their tolerance and goodwill.
After the last alien has left, an announcement will be made from this office to close down Project Electra. Until then, the debriefing and security infrastructures remain in force.

Finally, a judicial inquiry will be instituted concerning reports of alleged disruptive and irresponsible actions by certain humans. Be assured that the unfortunate behaviour of a bigoted and aggressive minority of humans will be penalised according to laws of the countries concerned. We also note that it was only when the Type I aliens attempted to become human that undesirable consequences arose. I think there are lessons to be learnt.

Thank you all for your participation.
Signed: Zainad Masoud."

'So there was an organisation?' asked Lucien.

'It looks like it,' said Tanskanen, 'and the United Nations investigation will last for as long as it takes.'

'When are the inquiries?' Burton asked, 'I'd like to know!'

'It's now unlikely any of you will be called to the formal hearings,' Tanskanen said, 'I'm your representative for all at Oulu Base in this matter. But some of you may be asked to provide me with written witness statements in advance. I'll inform you if that's the case. In the meantime, there must be no disclosure to the media or anyone else outside this group. Is that understood?'

'Yes,' they agreed in unison.

'Good! Any further questions?'

'I hope you don't mind my question,' said Keir.

'Go ahead,' said Professor Tanskanen.

'Can you please explain what you were doing in Kouvala when Valentina and I were there?'

'At the quarantine lodge,' said Tanskanen, 'I was called to investigate the assimilation of humans into a clique of Type II aliens which was hatching, if you forgive the pun, a plan to take over those bases which survived the riots. We had a counter-plan. That's how you and Valentina came to be quarantined. Ilya volunteered to become a Type I alien. Mads had already become one under Harald's influence. But the two of them managed to find out important information exposing what can only be called the Type II alien factory down at Kouvola. I then drove them from Kouvola to Oulu railway station car park, having kitted them out with the powerful radio transmitters. We were only just in time to liquidate Harald, who had become a lethal threat. There were a lot of unknowns and the task wasn't easy. And I apologise to Katya and Valentina in particular.'

'What about the incident in the lounge at Oulu?' asked Valentina.

Tanskanen looked anxious.

'That was my worst moment. I had to allow the aliens, including the conspirators, to lip-read me so that I could set up what turned out to be a high risk strategy to get you to Kouvola. Because of your loyalty and preoccupation with your job at Oulu, and Katya, I thought it unlikely that I could persuade you to go voluntarily. If I'm wrong, then I'm sorry. Anyway, once you went, it was easier to persuade and arrange for the others to join you, out of the way, as I thought then, should anything go wrong at this end.'

'You were pushing your luck, though!' said Keir.

'Yes, there were risks. But your team pulled it off. And you weren't aware, but I was on hand, with Mir'leor and two of his colleagues, if needed. By the way, I'm pleased to announce Ilya's complete recovery - as a human! He's off on a holiday with Tonya, I understand.'

When the jubilation subsided, there were no more questions; except one, again from Keir: 'The aliens have left us with a mystery. During that official tour in their enclosure, their atmospheric oxygen was way down at sixteen percent. Was this true of other alien enclosures worldwide?'

'More or less, yes,' Tanskanen said.

'That's the same as in the earlier French experiment, where they first calculated the "best conditions" for a land environment to suit these amphibians - before they adapted themselves to our atmosphere, that is.'

'Correct. Why do you ask?'

'Some recent research suggests the last time planet Earth had such a low atmospheric oxygen percentage was at the time of the early dinosaurs. Just a thought.'

'Hmm... No other questions? Then I declare this meeting closed. Thank you. Oh, and by the way, Valentina and Keir - allow me to congratulate you on your engagement. At least something good has come out of your stay at the so-called quarantine station!'

As Keir and Valentina chorused their thanks, Tanskanen, in characteristic style, whisked his papers off the table, transferred them to his briefcase and disappeared though the doorway.

*****

Once outside, Keir went with Valentina to her apartment to help pack her cases.

In the hallway they embraced; then again inside the apartment.

'You can see, they've cleared the rooms already,' said Valentina, pushing Keir gently away. He got the message. She continued: 'I've packed Katya's case and mine shouldn't take long. Do you have anything to go?'

'Just one holdall,' Keir said. 'I'd better check it out. Where shall we meet?'

'I think the plan is to have a light meal in about an hour, say our goodbyes and then make our way to the gatehouse for transport into Oulu city.'

Just then her link-set vibrated.

'Hello, Valentina! Tanskanen here. Look, we're decommissioning some property at Oulainen. There's a house near the station.' The phone screen showed a selection of images, some familiar. 'Would you like it?'

'I know where you mean. But is there a school nearby?'

'A town that size, I'd say there must be several. But you need to make your mind up, sharp. Others could jump at it. What do you say?'

'Bear with me, Jukka. I'll use my phone to see if there is a nearby school for Katya.'

'I've already checked. And yes, there are two, one of them about three blocks away!'

'Is the house still furnished?'

'Yes. Just as you left it. And everything works. Cleaned again this morning.' More pictures were displayed.

'Then yes, please!' Valentina said, 'We'll have it! And many, many thanks!'

'Good! Catch you at dinner, then.'

'Bye.'

'That's the fastest property deal I've witnessed!' Keir said.

'Not bad, eh? I hope you can join us.'

'Fantastic! I fly tomorrow lunchtime. I need to tie up some loose ends, but I could be back whenever you like.'

'On the subject of loose ends, now that the Electra project has finished, there's something I can tell you.'

'Surprise me,' said Keir.

'The aliens *are* extraterrestrial.'

'But they're in the sea! Who told you?'

'Mir'leor. Not to be divulged until now. And this is for our ears only. You were on the right track when you mentioned the dinosaurs. The aliens arrived here 153 million years ago. They were brought by another race which seeded the planet.'

'You've succeeded, sweetheart - I'm dumbstruck! But how does this square with the French claim about incubating an intelligent life-form?'

'It's true, but Kirsti wasn't fully informed. And you've read Mads' report. There had been covert contact with aliens even that early stage, and not just in France.'

'OK. But Val - if their species is 153 million years old, they should be light-years ahead of us! And where is their home grown technology?'

'According to Mir'leor, several million years ago they asked the question, "Which were the most beneficial times for us?" The aliens selected three periods, blended them and went retro. They still kept records of all their scientific achievements, most of which outstrip ours.'

'So that's how they took so well to our computing and genetic engineering!'

'Yes, Keir.'

'I wonder if we'll meet them again. Glad I met you, anyway!' Keir kissed her.

'You can stay with us tonight, if you like. It'll give you a chance to look our new place over. Just one thing, though '

'Yes?'

'After Katya's ordeal, Keir, I'm sleeping with her tonight.'

'Fair enough, no problem.'

'Then we can discuss our wedding arrangements. There's no hurry for you tomorrow. You can fly out from here.'

'You mean in that anti-grav machine?'

'It may be possible. Remind me to talk with Orville this evening. Meanwhile, I think you should open this envelope.'

Keir stood spellbound on reading the contents. 'I can't believe it - where did you get this?'

'Guess.'

'Tanskanen?'

'Correct. Read me the top line of the second paragraph.'

'It says, "This is to certify that Keir Wilson is awarded the Staaten Peace Prize for his part in the successful endeavour to save Planet Earth..." - Val, that's incredible!'

'Don't you have a Staaten Prize in your future world?'

'We call it the Nobel Peace Prize. I believe it's awarded to groups or institutions - and held in Oslo, Norway.'

'This one's shared, too. Here's my envelope,' Valentina said, placing it on the table. 'It looks like we'll be spending our honeymoon in the Netherlands - yes?'

'You bet! What about Ilya - and Mads?'

'Ilya's coming with Tonya! Mads gets a posthumous medal.'

*****

Car Park, RIPE, Chadwick Building, Liverpool University, Monday December 3 2085.

Professor Bryant Litchfield peered out of his office window at the flashing lights on the air-ambulance parked in the grounds below. The police had emerged from their three marked hover-cars and were busy cordoning off the area.

The professor placed a consoling arm around Rosalind, as they went down the stairway to give their statements.

Outside, the ambulance doors were closed. The flashing stopped and the vehicle flew away empty.

'None of us can understand it, Ros. Rory was there one minute and gone the next. The cameras caught his headset falling onto the floor. His clothes are still in the chair...'

'Can I see this for myself?'

Bryant raised an eyebrow. 'Well, I suppose so, if it won't upset you. Do you want me to go with you?'

'No, I'll be OK,' Ros said. She entered the laboratory.

'Hello, Neville!'

'Hi, Rosalind. You're sure about this?' Neville Ford asked.

'Yes,' said Ros. Her companion Leo nodded assent. 'But if you could just give me a minute,' she added, 'I've some prepared emails to send from my mobile.'

'No problem. Everything's ready. Take your time, the pair of you...' said Neville.

*****

24 Epilogue: Forming of the Five

Research Staff Common Room, Department of Physics, University of Liverpool. February 9, 2086.

Stella, a lecturer, entered the TV lounge.

'Could you please turn on the news?' asked one of her colleagues. She obliged by mental focus on the barcode in her implant. The wall panel TV leapt into vibrant life:

'First, some breaking news about progress in the case of Rosalind Tyler's disappearance.'

The screen showed a picture of Ros, whom most in the common room recognised. After a few seconds, the picture changed to that of a police officer.

'The last known CCTV sequence shows her entering the Chadwick building at the University of Liverpool and calling at one of the laboratories.'

A video clip followed, with a close-up still of Ros near the university entrance.

'The editor of the well known New Virtual Reality Magazine has come forward with a printout of a letter sent to them from Miss Tyler on that day.'

A still of the magazine cover appeared followed by a portrait shot of the editor.

'Consequently, we're particularly anxious to interview a man known as Captain Leo Bosworth...'

The TV now showed Bosworth in his military uniform and zoomed to a close-up of his face.

'...so that we can possibly eliminate him from our enquiries. He also was last seen at Liverpool University on the same day. He was contracted there as a consultant up to the end of December, 2085. Could he please contact us? Anyone with knowledge of his whereabouts should not approach him, but contact any police station or the number on your screen. Such calls will be dealt with in strictest confidence.'

Stella mentally activated the red button to read Ros's letter.

Contents of the letter:

FAO The Editor, New Virtual World Magazine, December 3, 2085.

Dear Mr. Hanson,

This is in response to your recently advertised request for information on the Skagen Mystery, following your excellent editorial summary last November entitled, 'Voices from the Past'.

My name is Rosalind Tyler, former personal assistant to Professor Bryant Litchfeld at the University of Liverpool and now an investigative reporter for the English Broadcasting Corporation. These organisations have kindly granted permission for me to submit the following supplementary information. I hope it will be of interest to you and your readership.

The following excerpts are verbatim from Professor Litchfield's records (by his kind permission) obtained via the monitoring team who worked on RIPE's final project.

Excerpts: 2085.

Leo Bosworth, November 2, 2085 (report for RIPE).
"When the VR character Rowena took over Keir's guardianship, I almost lost control of what he was doing. Now Rory, as Keir, has 'gone native' and it looks like we've lost him from this world. Nevertheless, I accept full responsibility for this and I hope Professor Litchfield will forgive me. I intend to update the Professor if that becomes possible at sometime in the future."

Professor Bryant Litchfield, December 12, 2085 (diary).
"Rory MacIntyre was one of my best research students and the first to 'abscond' to the alternative world of a postdoctoral research project. Sadly, our sponsors are to withdraw their funding. This will bring about the demise of our research. RIPE will be disbanded by April, after which there'll no longer be the

capability to re-visit Rory's (now Keir's) new scenario and persuade him to return. So far, the only glimpses we've had beyond the December 2010 horizon for his project are the fallout items from records concerning the persons Lucien, Max and Ilya. Despite what's happened, I'm surprised and flattered to hear that in that world, the wedded pair Keir and Valentina named their son Bryant!

My only other problem was Max Lloyd, who was fortunately stopped by Keir and his alien friends from implementing a failed project and exploiting the Galena system for his own ends. Now that I am retired, I can state that I believe they *were* real aliens - and that Keir had, or has, a real family and friends. I wish him well in his new life."

Excerpts: 2011-15 (filed on VR/NHR computer Galena, U. of Liverpool).

Lucien Fournier, February 5, 2011 (VR press conference).
"Keir Wilson and I had many deep and useful discussions, but in the end, after the aliens had effectively given up on humanity, the UN wrapped up Project Electra. This didn't prevent much being learnt, particularly in biology, computer science and energy efficient transportation. Neither did it prevent prosecution of the parties responsible for the demise of many of my research colleagues and the convictions that are following. Unfortunately, that will bring none of them back."

Max Lloyd, alias Vivien Lemaître, April 2011 (VR prison interview transcript).
"For the part I played in opposing Project Electra I've been sentenced to a total of nineteen years incarceration, largely on the evidence of aliens who'd gone by the time of the trial! On the other hand, I'm grateful to my company lawyer for the compensation award after sustaining neurological damage to my sight by aliens released under the Project Electra programme."

Ilya Karpov, 2 October 2022; diary entry. (VR post-project scan before decommissioning, April 2086).
"Now that I'm recovered, well, more or less, I always enjoy my occasional visits to Keir and Valentina. Katya hopes to read English at Oxford. And their (so far) one addition, Bryant, is a

bright, energetic child. He's really keen on electronics and computers, not just games, but the real thing. He never stops discussing the works of luminaries like Einstein and Feynman. Also Alister McGrath and John Polkinghorne (mother's influence). He'll go far, I'm sure."

The following additional information is unofficial and cannot be published because I'm told it must be kept secret from Professor Litchfield. After the stresses of recent events he deserves a peaceful retirement.

However, I do feel it's important to science and in the public interest in spite of its sensitivity. But only if he finds out for himself, or perhaps after he's passed on, should permission be granted for its release.

My sources told me a great deal about the virtual world scenario. I admit they didn't know I'd become a reporter. Last week I gained access to the register of marriages in Oulainen, Finland, for year 2011.

There was an entry for Saturday 29 January: Keir Wilson and widow Valentina Laitonen (her maiden name). Evidently, in VR, she had an alias, 'Olga'; but I understand that Keir also used the name Keir Litchfield for a time afterwards - possibly in honour of his Professor at Liverpool, or perhaps for security reasons. As far as I know, Professor Litchfield is unaware of young Bryant's surname.

There are other items I would have been happy to discuss with you, including Professor Litchfield's theory that the 'VR persons' are real and now locked into an alternative universe. But time is short and I am due for a period of extended leave. Please feel free to contact the Professor for any further information, bearing in mind the caveat mentioned above.

Thank you for reading this.

Yours sincerely,
Rosalind V. Tyler.

*****

Oulu Base, Monday October 15, 2010.

On the wet tarmac of an empty car park, two figures walked hand in hand in the light rain.

'Will they know about us now?' Ros asked.

'Yes, Ros,' said Captain Bosworth. 'I sent our messages that we're all safe last night. You realise that was the final CMI? No more RIPE communications are possible after today. They're already limiting the use of the Galena node at Liverpool, pending an investigation.'

Ros squeezed his hand, tears in her eyes.

'I'll be all right,' she said, 'Now we're together.'

Leo kissed her on the forehead.

'I know it's a wrench,' he said, 'but so long as you're happy, I wouldn't have it any other way.'

'Who's that over there, Leo? He's looking strangely at us.'

'Oh, he's OK.'

Professor Tanskanen walked briskly towards them, crossing the apron at the gatehouse of an almost deserted Oulu Base.

'Well, Captain Leo Bosworth,' he said. 'It's hello and goodbye then, I suppose.'

'Yes, Jukka. It's been quite an adventure for me here in Finland.' They shook hands as Leo continued: 'I've enjoyed your hospitality and looking after Keir during the earlier stages of his project. By the way, may I introduce Ros, my partner?'

'But of course!' Tanskanen bowed stiffly as he shook her hand. 'I'm Jukka Tanskanen. A pleasure to meet you!' Then, turning to Bosworth, he said: 'I admire what you did for Keir. It was an invaluable contribution.'

'Thank you.'

'You've heard about Burton, I suppose?'

'No, what news have you?'

'He was arrested at six o'clock this morning near Oakingwell, as was Mike Savage a little later in Edinburgh. Pity. Mike was a brilliant worker and I feel quite shocked.'

'Good heavens!'

'Yes, I understand they caught up with Burton in his clandestine laboratory on the Oakingwell campus. And Alan Menzies had a narrow escape.'

'Wow! The long arm of the UN, eh?'

'Quite! But I suspect Burton will get off with a warning. It seems he was duped. Apparently, one of the real culprits is Savage.'

'Oh? And how did Max and Brad fit into all this, Jukka?'

'They joined up as part of a cell about three months ago. We think there were at least 22 anti-alien cells, world wide. We know what happened to Brad, of course. And then the police found a match between Max's gun and the bullet in Keir's crashed Mercedes. So Max Lloyd ended up with three counts of attempted murder. He tried to get off by pleading insanity - insisting he was from the *future!* Have you ever heard such ridiculous nonsense?'

'Really?'

'Yes! There is more. When the arrests were made, it was revealed that Harald was quick to contact the opposition cells. He and his followers in fifteen of them wanted nothing less than to start World War 3 and then pick up the pieces - and impose their form of world domination.'

'Then it looks like Keir and his team saved the planet!'

'No doubt! We can expect to get access to the full outcomes of the enquiry in due course. Anyway, what are your plans now, Leo?'

Bosworth and Ros cast each other glances and smiled in unison.

'Ah! But I intrude,' Tanskanen said, 'Forgive me. I just wondered if you were possibly thinking of deploying your training skills elsewhere. Truly exceptional skills, I might add.'

'I've no immediate plans, Professor. Except perhaps for leaving the army and doing a spot of farming.'

'Indeed? Would you consider part time training supervision? You see, now the aliens have left us, all these facilities are being reconfigured by the military, for Finnish national service personnel. You know, assault courses and other fitness training. You could be involved in a civilian consultancy role, if you wish.'

'Well, I'd have to think about it, Professor.'

'And of course, we'd be only too pleased to help with the matter of your accommodation, for both of you, that is. We've been disposing of a number of outlying properties in the area and there's a farmhouse coming vacant just outside Yli-Ii, about ten kilometres from here. We'd particularly like it to go to someone we can trust.'

Bosworth brightened at the thought.

'How about it Ros?'

'Wonderful! When could we see it?" she asked,

'This afternoon, if you like,' said Tanskanen. 'I'll get the keys from Major Selkäinaho.'

*****

Former safe-house in Oulainen, November 2023 (post-project).

The four sat around the table as refreshments were brought in.

'Thanks, Valentina, or Olga.' Leo said.

'You know my preferences: Valentina, Val, Valya or Tiina, in that order!' she said. 'Even so, it's long been a family joke here, using our old aliases.'

'Sometimes I'm confused too, Leo,' Keir said, spreading his arms, 'which is why I call her Kukka.'

'Very appropriate! She certainly makes splendid cakes and fine coffee,' laughed Ilya. 'I'm only joking... No I'm not, the food is great! And I do know the word is 'flower' in Finnish.'

'Just behave yourself, Ilya!' Valentina chided. She turned to the others. 'Now if you don't mind, Ros and I will carry on with our music practice while you lot deliberate the anatomy of computers. I'll be back with more of anything if you just give me a shout.'

'*Kiitos, miellitietty.* Thanks, sweetheart,' Keir said. 'Will Bryant be long?'

'A couple of minutes,' Valentina replied. 'Head in books again.' She left the door ajar.

'What instrument does Ros play?' Ilya asked.

'The kantele,' Keir explained. 'Valentina's teaching her. As you know, Val's really good. Working on a concerto, including the orchestral arrangements.'

'Wow! Ros is in good hands, then!' Leo said.

'And after that, I'll teach them both the balalaika,' Ilya said.

The door creaked as Bryant padded in.

'Sorry,' he said, clutching a journal paper.

'No problem, young professor!' said Ilya. 'Do join us.' He passed Bryant a plate of fare.

'Cool! Thanks, Ilya.' Bryant grabbed a rum truffle and sank his teeth into it.

'A bit more decorum please, lad!' said Keir.

'Sorry, Dad. But Mum's pretty good at making them, isn't she?'

'Good reason to have another, I think.' Keir followed suit, unashamedly.

'When you two have stopped guzzling, hadn't we better get on with the job?' Ilya said.

'Well, I'm ready,' Said Leo.

'Me, too,' said Bryant, wiping his hands on a tissue.

'We could do with Mum here,' said Keir. 'But I'll update her afterwards.'

'OK, where should we start?' asked Leo.

'Firstly, let's ratify this first formal assembly of the Five,' said Keir, 'even though Valentina's away in the music room.' He turned to Leo. 'Are you quite sure Ros won't be joining us for these meetings?'

'Definitely not,' said Leo. 'Don't get her wrong. You know Ros. She enjoys the company but she's had it up to here with computers and quite happy to read or write articles, have music lessons and leave us to our nattering, as she puts it. She's quite interested in Bryant's hobby of amateur radio, though.'

'Didn't realise you were a ham, Bryant,' said Leo.

'Yeah. I've just got my full Oscar Hotel ticket.'

'You mean you're fully fledged?' asked Ilya. 'Well done!'

'Well, yes,' said Keir, 'you should see the state of his bedroom. And he thinks a Christmas tree is an all-band eight element rotatable beam on a 10 metre mast.'

'Oh, dear! Are you putting one of those up?' Ilya asked.

'No way!' said Bryant. 'I'm more interested in stealth radio with low power and invisible antennas. Data transmission like CW and PSK.'

'Morse code and phase shift keying? Interesting!' Ilya said.

The twelve year old became more earnest, as if about to sally forth into further detail.

'Way-oh!' cried Keir. 'Better put it on ice, Bryant. Let's get down to business, shall we? We've established our Group of Five as Ilya, Leo, myself, Valentina and Bryant. Do we call ourselves anything? Like, "The Watchers", "Monitors" or, dare we say it, "Controllers"?'

'Not wise, I think, 'said Leo. 'And we don't write any of this down, certainly not as a formal agenda.'

'OK,' Keir nodded in assent. 'Neither do we record anything explicit. Are we all happy with that?'

'I understand, and real cool of you to let me in on it,' said Bryant.

'Glad to have you on board, Bryant,' his father said. Leaning back in his chair, he added: 'Right, then. Let's bring ourselves up to date. What seems to be going on. Leo?'

'Well, we all realise that our colleague Tanskanen's explanation was incomplete,' said Leo, 'as was the UN General Secretary's summing up. The powerful upsurge in computing capabilities triggered by interaction with the aliens was largely taken for granted. Up to now, as far as we know, there are three systems actually at war with each other, a situation that potentially poses risks to the human species because nobody knows how to control them. These systems are Pandora, Arrow and a new one called Galena.'

'I propose,' said Ilya, 'that we use code words for computers we're concerned about. You never know when or where we might be overheard. We're also vulnerable to lip-reading, as some of us know from experience.'

'All right,' said Leo. 'Any suggestions, Ilya?'

Ilya clasped his bear-like hands together and leaned across the table. 'What do you reckon, Bryant?' he said.

Bryant thought and then replied: 'To begin with, let's not make things too complicated. How about a simple code like One for Arrow, Seven for Galena and Sixteen for Pandora?'

'Thanks Bryant,' Keir said. 'Sounds OK to me. Eh, Leo?'

'Sure,' Leo agreed. 'Quite apt, really, as One has actually become number one, having taken over Seven and Sixteen. I don't like what's happening, though. I'd prefer Seven, in spite of its foibles.'

'A cyber war,' Ilya reflected, 'between computer network systems, rather than nations, organisations or hackers. I must admit, in my day, things seemed much more controllable and less complex to monitor.'

'Careful, Ilya!' Keir said. 'You're sounding like a great grandfather.'

'But you're right, Ilya', Bryant said. 'And you'd make a cool great uncle!'

They all laughed, but nervously. Their task would not be trivial.

THE END

Printed in Great Britain
by Amazon